CARLYLE
CAMPBELL
LIBRARY

HI-TIRED

Meredith College
Raleigh, NC 27607-5298

"An Anarchy
in the Mind
and in the Heart"

"An Anarchy
in the Mind
and in the Heart"

Narrating Anglo-Ireland

Ellen M. Wolff

Lewisburg
Bucknell University Press

CARLYLE CAMPBELL LIBRARY
MEREDITH COLLEGE

©2006 by Rosemont Publishing & Printing Corp.

All rights reserved. Authorization to photocopy items for internal or personal use, or the internal or personal use of specific clients, is granted by the copyright owner, provided that a base fee of $10.00, plus eight cents per page, per copy is paid directly to the Copyright Clearance Center, 222 Rosewood Drive, Danvers, Massachusetts 01923. [0-8387-5556-9/06 $10.00 + 8¢ pp, pc.]

Associated University Presses
2010 Eastpark Boulevard
Cranbury, NJ 08512

The paper used in this publication meets the requirements of the American National Standard for Permanence of Paper for Printed Library Materials Z39.48–1984.

Library of Congress Cataloging-in-Publication Data

Wolff, Ellen M., 1958-
    An anarchy in the mind and in the heart : narrating Anglo-Ireland / Ellen M. Wolff.
        p. cm.
    Includes bibliographical references (p.   ) and index.
    ISBN 0-8387-5556-9 (alk. paper)
    1. English fiction—Irish authors—History and criticism. 2. British—Ireland—History—20th century—Historiography. 3. English fiction—20th century—History and criticism. 4. National characteristics, Irish in literature. 5. Ireland—Intellectual life—20th century. 6. Ireland—In literature. 7. Narration (Rhetoric) I. Title.

    PR8803.W65 2006
    823'.91099417—dc22

                                                    2005009635

PRINTED IN THE UNITED STATES OF AMERICA

to Kevin and Aidan

Every cultural narrative . . . is in some sense a reinterpretation
of its own history; an attempt to retell the story of the past
as it relates to the present. . . Narrative, in short, is where
the text of imagination interweaves with the context of history.
It is a point of transit between past and future.
　　　　　　　　　　　　—Richard Kearney, *Transitions*

The past is only just over the frontier of living memory;
it is the epoch of our immediate forbears.
It is the youth of our parents,
the prime of our grand-parents and great-grand-parents,
which most subtly seem to have stolen our hearts away.
　　　　　　　　—Elizabeth Bowen, "The Mulberry Tree"

The real consciousness is the chaos, a grey commotion of mind, with no
premises or conclusions or problems or solutions or cases or judgments.
　　　　　—Samuel Beckett, letter to Thomas MacGreevy

Novels arise out of the shortcomings of history.
　　　　—Novalis, *Fragmente und Studien, 1799–1800*

Contents

Acknowledgments

MANY HAVE CONTRIBUTED TO THE MAKING OF THIS BOOK. GENE Goodheart and John Burt generously read and re-read early drafts; I thank them for their discerning guidance and their steady belief in the project. I thank the late, the incomparable Adele Dalsimer for her perceptive input and animated encouragement, and Jonathan Allison for his generous responses to an early draft. I am thankful for the suggestions of anonymous readers whose careful work helped this evolve into a much stronger book than it would have been without their expertise and intelligence. All faults are mine.

Weldon Thornton provided formative scholarly company early on, and many forms of support and encouragement since. Karen Klein, Helena Michie, and Margaret Maurer opened new ways of thinking about literature; they have helped shape the deep structures of this book. The many colleagues in Irish Studies with whom I've conversed and whose writing I've read over the years have been consistently good company, in person and in print. I'm grateful, also, to John McGahern who (without his knowing it) started me along this road.

Phillips Exeter Academy has furnished various forms of support. Elizabeth Garrity, Karen Hilton, and Jacqueline Thomas, of the Class of 1945 Library, provided invaluable assistance, particularly during the last wave of research; Elizabeth also helped with mutinous technology. Jessica McClain helped get the manuscript to press. The English Department and the Dean of the Faculty's office supported travel to conferences near and far, which made substantial contributions to my thinking. My students continue to help keep literature, Irish and otherwise, a living thing.

I thank Priscilla and Ken Carrington and Lucy and Reynolds Sachs for their gracious gifts of ideal summertime spaces in which to work.

An earlier version of my chapter on Beckett appeared in the *Journal of Beckett Studies*. I thank the editor for permission to use this material. Thanks, too, to the organizers of the University of Louisville Twentieth-Century Literature Conference and to the Beckett Society for opportunities to air my ideas early on.

Finally, I owe lasting thanks to Barbara Jean O'Brien, Elizabeth Dowey, and Jean-Philippe Brunet for their spirited support—and, emphatically, to Kevin King.

∼   ∼   ∼

For permission to quote from the following copyright works, the author gratefully acknowledges:

J.C. Beckett, *The Anglo-Irish Tradition*, Cornell University Press; Samuel Beckett, *Watt*, Grove/Atlantic, Inc.; Terry Eagleton, *Ideology: An Introduction*, Verso; Molly Keane, *Time After Time*, Virago; James Knowlson, *Damned to Fame: The Life of Samuel Beckett*, Grove/Atlantic, Inc. and Bloomsbury Publishing; F.S.L. Lyons, *Culture and Anarchy in Ireland, 1890–1939*, Oxford University Press; Susan Meyer, *Imperialism at Home: Race and Victorian Women's Fiction*, Cornell University Press; Ann Owens Weekes, *Irish Women Writers*, University Press of Kentucky. An earlier version of my chapter on Beckett's *Watt* appeared in *The Journal of Beckett Studies*.

"An Anarchy
in the Mind
and in the Heart"

1

Some Contexts for Reading
Twentieth-Century Anglo-Irish Fiction:
An Introduction

ANGLO-IRISH FICTION AND
POSTCOLONIAL IRISH STUDIES

SINCE THE MID-1970S, THE STILL BURGEONING FIELD OF IRISH
Studies has been driven, in the main, by what Irish social historian
Terence Brown has labeled "a steadily increasing urge toward an informed Irish self-understanding" (Brown 1985, 247). As Irish historian F. S. L. Lyons announced in the first of his Ford Lectures, delivered at Oxford in 1978: "the roots of difference within Irish society
are being explored with much greater sensitivity and thoroughness
than ever before" (Lyons 1979, 2).

This attention to the diversity of Ireland's cultural and religious
traditions marked an important transition in Irish cultural studies,
mirroring an urge to rescue the representation of Irish identity from
the essentialism which, as Clifford Geertz has argued, characterizes
the first phases of all new states (Geertz 1973, 234–35). This trend is
also, its practitioners have made clear, a response to the 1969 out-
break of violence in Northern Ireland and to the violence that has
continued to plague the politics of the North. The aim, in Brown's
words, has been to answer sectarian violence by studying "acts and ar-
tifacts of human beings in their Irish setting," in order to show that
Irish "identity" is not constituted by some Catholic and Gaelic
essence, as certain nationalistic representations would have it, but
entails "a complicated mosaic of cultures and social forces" (Brown
1985, 248).

Lyons clarifies the projected political implications of such revisionist readings of "Irishness": "[T]he essence of the Irish situation . . . is the collision of a variety of cultures within an island whose very smallness makes their juxtaposition potentially, and often actually, lethal" (Lyons 1979, 1–2). "To seek to lay bare the historical roots of difference will not necessarily lead us to a solution" to political violence, he admits. "But the recognition of difference . . . is a prerequisite for peaceful coexistence. Such recognition . . . might at least bring us one stage further towards that sympathetic insight which is what the problem has always demanded but too seldom received" (145).

The field of Irish literary studies has played a central role in this project of revising essentialist representations of Irish identity. The preface to a collection of pamphlets published by Ireland's Field Day Theatre Company (which, with the discontinued Dublin journal, *The Crane Bag*, formed the vanguard of the literary branch of this interdisciplinary effort) echoes Lyons and Brown, defining the project as an attempt to redress "the present crisis by producing analyses of the established opinions, myths and stereotypes which have become both a symptom and a cause of the current situation." Seamus Deane elaborates: "The communities have become stereotyped into their roles of oppressor and victim to such an extent that the notion of a Protestant or a Catholic sensibility is now assumed to be a fact of nature rather than a product of these very special and ferocious conditions. . . . It is about time we put aside the idea of essence—the hungry Hegelian ghost looking for a stereotype to live in. As Irishness or as Northernness he stimulates the provincial unhappiness we create and fly from. . . . Everything, including our politics and our literature, has to be rewritten—i.e., re-read. That will enable new writing, new politics" (S. Deane 1986, 57).

This book re-reads literature by writers with complicated relations to modern Ireland: fiction written in the era of the Irish Republic by men and women with ties, literary and familial, to what was called "Anglo-Ireland."

I use the terms "Anglo-Ireland," "Ascendancy Ireland," and "Protestant Ireland"—each problematic in its own way—broadly to designate that social group, culturally distinct from the native, Catholic, Gaelic population, and from the Presbyterian majority in the North, which found material prosperity in what is now the Irish Republic. Descendants of several waves of settlers or conquerors (depending on who is doing the naming), mostly English and eventually members of the Church of Ireland, the Anglo-Irish comprised that group which enjoyed access to privilege and prosperity by virtue of its religious affiliation, and which, in the twentieth century, lost all remnants of its former political power.[1]

Readings of modern Anglo-Irish fiction have sometimes been distorted by the tendency to import interpretive assumptions from the English tradition of country house literature, both poetry and prose.[2] But they have been distorted, more seriously, by the tendency to read in terms of an identity politics dominated by the ghost of Yeats—less Yeats the poet (whose poems often challenge their own nostalgic apologies for Anglo-Ireland) than Yeats the polemicist, the author of the 1925 speech protesting the prohibition of divorce, in which he railed: "We against whom you have done this thing are no petty people. We are the people of Burke; we are the people of Grattan; we are the people of Swift, the people of Emmet, the people of Parnell. We have created the most of the modern literature of this country. We have created the best of its political intelligence" (Yeats 1925, 99).[3]

An influential early essay by Seamus Deane exemplifies this type of distortion. Contrary to Deane's exhortation against essentialism quoted above, "The Literary Myths of the Revival" misreads Anglo-Irish novels as endorsing if not advocating a Yeatsian myth of an heroic and aristocratic Ascendancy:

> The Big House surrounded by the unruly tenantry, Culture besieged by barbarity, a refined aristocracy beset by a vulgar middle class—all of these are recurring images in twentieth-century Irish fiction which draws heavily on Yeats's poetry for them. Since Elizabeth Bowen's *The Last September* (1929), to more recent novels such as Aidan Higgins's *Langrishe, Go Down* (1966), Thomas Kilroy's *The Big Chapel* (1971), John Banville's *Birchwood* (1973), and Jennifer Johnston's *How Many Miles to Babylon?* (1976), the image and its accompanying themes have been repeated in a variety of forms. (S. Deane 1985, 31–32)

"The survival of the Big House novel, with all its implicit assumptions," Deane concludes, "is a tribute to Yeats and a criticism of the poverty of the Irish novelistic tradition" (31–32).[4]

In contrast to arguments such as Deane's, which read modern Anglo-Irish fiction as a predictably colonialist literature that nostalgically champions a ruling-class culture, I will argue that these novels are in fact richly textured narratives that sustain continuous debates with their own visions and revisions of history and culture. How shall I assess my home culture's systems of value and belief? How shall I account for its appropriation of Irish land? How shall I portray the historically flawed relation of Anglo-Ireland to Ireland "proper"? How shall I represent "Irishness"? "Anglo-Irishness"? Wrestling with charged questions such as these, Anglo-Irish writers generate agitated, self-divided texts. Their novels bear out Walter Benjamin's claim (offered as a rejoinder to Adorno's dictum that "there is no document of civilization which is not at the same time a document of barbarism"): "works of literature are also acts of resistance, conditioned but never wholly determined by what is resisted" (Arendt 1968, 258). Exceptionally turbulent and unsettled, the texts considered here at once assent to and resist their conditioning, embodying "an anarchy in the mind and in the heart" of twentieth-century Anglo-Irish women and men.[5]

Two other book-length studies of Anglo-Irish fiction precede mine: Julian Moynahan's *Anglo-Irish: The Literary Imagination of a Hyphenated Culture* (1995) and Vera Kreilkamp's *The Anglo-Irish Novel and the Big House* (1998). Kreilkamp's study and mine share significant common ground. Her work, like mine (in her words) "participates in the undermining of a nationalist criticism that has minimized the importance of Big House novels in the canon of Irish writing" (Kreilkamp 1998, 10). Kreilkamp provides a kind of history of Anglo-Irish fiction, stretching from Maria Edgeworth's *Castle Rackrent* to John Banville's *Birchwood*. Taking the panoramic point of view, she "defines the form" of Anglo-Irish novels, describing "the continuing thematic relationships between major novels in this tradition" (9). I am concerned less with the broad defining view than with the analysis of minute particulars of individual twentieth-century texts. And I am also interested in exploring its implications for critical debates beyond Irish Studies.

Moreover, though our work addresses kindred themes from kindred points of view, our emphases ultimately differ. Early in her book, Kreilkamp asserts that Anglo-Irish fiction is "a complex and ambivalent form that is, generally, neither elegiac nor nostalgic" (Kreilkamp 1998, 2). In her subsequent readings of individual texts, however, her emphasis tends to fall on writers' critical distance from, rather than vexed engagement with, Anglo-Ireland. Thus, she concludes, "most Big House novels relentlessly undermine Yeats's deification of the Anglo-Irish tradition"; most cast a "subversive gaze on the gentry estate" (267). In rescuing Anglo-Irish novels from the nationalists, Kreilkamp at times risks overstating the extent to which they constitute decided "acts of resistance." As I read them, these novels ask us to relinquish altogether the clarity of either/or opposites such as resist/assent, subvert/affirm. They require us to embrace the shifting, various realm of both (or more)/and.[6]

Like Kreilkamp's, Moynahan's study aims to demarcate the limits of the Anglo-Irish literary tradition, to show that it is in fact a tradition with a "beginning, a middle and an end" (Moynahan 1995, 253). His book provides important background to the work of the authors it addresses, and contains a particularly fine chapter on the work of Sheridan Le Fanu. Our views diverge dramatically, however, given his guiding assumption that "the issue of colonialism doesn't apply [to the study of Anglo-Irish literature]. Most of the writers . . . were offspring from a colony that was canceled and canceled itself through the Act of Union in 1800" (xiii). Moynahan also assumes that the Anglo-Irish literary tradition "is about making amends and reconciling, not about attempts to hold or grab power" (256). As I will argue, it is precisely these novels' oscillations between such extremes that make them the compelling human documents, and the potent challenges to prevailing theories of ideology's relation to literature, that they are.

Insofar as my argument coincides with poststructuralist theories of language, narrative, and knowledge, it shares some common ground with the work of Homi Bhabha and like-minded writers on "nation as narration" (Bhabha 1990a, 4), and the work of Henry Louis Gates on race (Gates 1985). Bhabha affirms the "conceptual indeterminacy" of "the ambivalent figure of the nation": "To encounter the nation *as it is written* displays a temporality of culture and social consciousness more in tune with the partial, overdetermined process by which textual meaning is produced through the articulation of difference in language; more in keeping with the problem of closure which plays enigmatically in the discourse of the sign. Such an approach contests the traditional authority of . . . national objects of knowledge—Tradition, People, the Reason of State, High Culture, for instance" (2–3, italics Bhabha's). Bhabha's practice, it follows, is to investigate "the nation-space in the *process* of the articulation of elements: where meanings may be partial because they are *in medias res*; and history may be half-made because it is in the process of being made; and the image of cultural authority may be ambivalent because it is caught uncertainly, in the act of 'composing' its powerful image" (3, italics Bhabha's). He focuses on "the performativity of language in narratives of the nation," which requires what Edward Said terms "a kind of 'analytic pluralism' as the *form* of critical attention to the cultural effects of the nation" (3, italics Bhabha's). Bhabha's nation, like the Anglo-Ireland I will posit here, "is neither unified nor unitary in relation to itself, nor must it be seen simply as 'other' in relation to what is outside or beyond it" (4). Both are characterized by an "interruptive interiority" (5).[7]

Or both, Gates might say, are tropes. Race, Gates maintains, "pretends to be an objective term of classification, when in fact it is a dangerous trope": "Race has become a trope of ultimate, irreducible difference between cultures, linguistic groups, or adherents of specific belief systems which—more often than not—also have fundamentally opposed economic interests. Race is the ultimate trope of difference. . . . [W]e carelessly use language in such a way as to *will* this sense of *natural* difference into our formulations. To do so is to engage in a pernicious act of language, one which exacerbates the complex problem of cultural or ethnic difference rather than to assuage or redress it" (Gates 1985, 5, italics Gates's). The term "Anglo-Ireland" has its roots in just this dynamic, as we shall see.

I assert above that the novels I consider here express "an anarchy in the mind and in the heart" of their writers. The phrase is, of course, F. S. L. Lyons's (Lyons 1979). Lyons uses it to describe the cultural instability that plagued all Ireland from 1890 to 1939, the period beginning with the fall of Parnell and ending with the death of Yeats. "It was not primarily an anarchy of violence in the streets," Lyons argues. "It was rather an anarchy in the mind and in the heart, an anarchy which forbade not just unity of territories but 'unity of being'" (177). Distinguishing his *Culture and Anarchy* from Arnold's, Lyons explains: "where Arnold saw culture as a unifying force in a fragmented society and as a barrier against anarchy, my thesis is that in Ireland culture—or, rather, the diversity of cultures—has been a force which has worked against the evolution of a homogeneous society and . . . has made it difficult, if not impossible, for Irishmen to have a coherent view of themselves in relation to each other and to the outside world" (2).

I invoke Lyons's phrase and convey it to an Anglo-Irish context because it so aptly describes the state of mind and heart that fuels this fiction. Seeking to solve the twin problems of Anglo-Ireland's place in Irish history and the writers' place in Anglo-Irish culture, these continuously self-questioning texts stand, finally, as thwarted journeys toward a coherent view of self and culture, unfinished quests for a discursive home.

I invoke Lyons's phrase to imply another point. As Seamus Deane's argument with essentialism suggests, relations between Ireland's different traditions have historically been figured in the hierarchical terms of binary opposition. I would advance the revision of received notions of self-evidently oppositional relations, by suggesting that a phenomenon that helps shape Ireland—an anarchy in the mind and in the heart forbidding homogeneity, internal coherence, "unity of being"—also shapes that social formation ostensibly essentially different from Ireland "proper." Anglo-Ireland and Ireland, like Anglo-Ireland and England, that other Other against which Anglo-Ireland has needed to defend and define itself, engage in shifting relations of sameness and difference.

Christopher Wheatley poses this not entirely rhetorical question in his study of what he calls "Irish Protestant drama" of the Restoration and eighteenth century: "why bother to examine these historical losers?" (Wheatley 1999, 13). Kreilkamp comes closer to naming the crux of the issue: "To some extent, of course, Anglo-Irish country house novels inevitably create a discomfort that emerges largely from extratextual sources"—from Anglo-Ireland's storied role in Irish history (Kreilkamp 1998, 12).

Such "discomfort" constitutes paradoxical evidence of these novels' continuing relevance, pointing as it does to the durability of certain stereotypes in Irish cultural discourse. Not only do these novels attenuate boundaries between social groups, suggesting "that Irish culture is a complex tapestry, not merely a series of oppositional units" (Wheatley 1999, 14). They posit an anti-essentialist re-definition of (one) Protestant Irish identity as an inconclusive attempt to narrate itself, a dynamic, internally diverse, ongoing process of responding to irremediable cultural predicament.[8] Benedict Anderson writes, "Communities are to be distinguished not by their falsity/genuineness, but by the style in which they are imagined" (B. Anderson 1991, 15). As we shall see, the style in which these writers imagine home culture undermines persistent stereotypes of Anglo-Irishness, supplementing images both green and orange that are still conjured by the terms "Protestant" and "Anglo-Ireland": images, as a

cultural nationalist like Daniel Corkery would have it, of a fundamentally alien ruling class, as well as Yeatsian images of an unjustly
spurned guardian of "traditional sanctity and loveliness."

Moreover, as compelling attempts to account for Anglo-Ireland's
deeply flawed social and political situation, these novels generate, in
some readers, that "sympathetic insight" which Lyons argues might
provide a basis for political harmony. Any sympathy that these texts
generate, I would emphasize, is not based in apologetic portraits of
their culture of origin. On the contrary, like many of their "Irish-
Irish" counterparts, Joyce best known among them, these writers express wrenching ambivalences toward their heritage, a play of attraction and repulsion that elicits from readers a similarly shifting and at
least double response. If they call out intermittent sympathy for the
Anglo-Irelands they portray, these novels may generate more sustained sympathy for their authors' attempts to narrate culture. The
moral, intellectual, and ontological anguish that these novels embody, the anarchy in the mind and in the heart to which they attest,
corroborate the story that Irish history tells us: that despite the substantial and long-standing rewards Anglo-Ireland reaped from its status as Empire's accomplice, in the end, it can be numbered among
Empire's casualties, if not the most severely wounded.

Of course, Anglo-Ireland *per se* is, practically speaking, irrelevant
to contemporary Irish politics. By 1980, Protestants comprised only
four percent of the Republic's population and wielded no significant
political power. But Anglo-Irish fiction retains relevance. Challenging those incendiary stereotypes of which Deane complains and
which his own early reading of these novels helped fuel, these texts
help "*detribalise* those myths which have divided our national communities" (Kearney 1984, 65, italics Kearney's), and which have
proven both symptom and cause of Irish troubles North and South,
past and present.

ANGLO-IRISH FICTION
AND LITERARY MODERNISM

Not despite but indeed because of its roots in provincial culture,
twentieth-century Anglo-Irish fiction proves germane to debates beyond Irish and postcolonial studies. I am particularly interested in its
relevance to two critical conversations: to ongoing efforts to revise
inherited notions of literary modernism, and to ongoing debates re-

garding the relation of ideology and literature and the practice of ideology critique. I will set the stage, here at the outset, for a chapter-by-chapter consideration of this fiction's implications for both of these discussions, beginning with modernism.

As Sandra Gilbert and Susan Gubar maintain in their own reconsideration of literary modernism, *No Man's Land*: "historians and literary critics have traditionally associated the problems of so-called 'modernity' with 'the long withdrawing roar' of 'the Sea of Faith,' with Darwinian visions of 'Nature, red in tooth and claw,' with the discontents fostered by an industrial civilization, with the enemies within the self that were defined by Freud and ultimately with the no man's land of the Great War" (Gilbert and Gubar 1988, 21). Gilbert and Gubar seek to refine long-standing associations of modernism with the rise of industrialization, the dilution of faith and the decline of Empire, by arguing that modernism in fact reflects writers' attempts "to come to terms with, and find terms for, an ongoing battle of the sexes that was set in motion by the late nineteenth-century rise of feminism and the fall of Victorian concepts of femininity" (xii). Perry Meisel's etiology of modernism also reframes the influence of such events as World War I, the democratization of learning, and the horrors of modern war. He argues: "any claim that literature's self-announced crisis of the modern is rooted directly in the events of the [twentieth] century is based on a variety of dubious premises" (Meisel 1987, 3). Perhaps the most radical changes to received ideas of modernism have emerged from modernism's encounter with cultural studies; culture critics have countered modernism's associations with apolitical elitism by broadening the modernist canon, analyzing the market forces that shaped it, and expanding the field of inquiry to include the study of modernity.[9]

Though my project demonstrates the political relevance of certain texts and perhaps identifies new candidates for canonization, its implications for inherited conceptions of modernism are, I think, more like Gilbert's and Gubar's and Meisel's. Like theirs, my book attempts to reframe our understanding of literary modernism's historicity. Gilbert and Gubar add the rise of feminism to the historical picture; Meisel extends the relevant historical time frame, calling modernism "no less than the third and most overt eruption of a drive—a will to modernity—endemic to modern, that is to say, postmedieval English literature as a whole," a response to the literary historical condition "of coming too late in a tradition" (Meisel

1987, 4, 8). My project affirms the significance of local history and provincial culture to trends that have been homogenized under the labels "modernism" and "postmodernism."

Of course, one may read "modernism" and "postmodernism" as disparate literary phenomena. But I am interested here less in distinguishing between them than in showing how elements they share may be seen, in the novels under consideration, as traces of Anglo-Irish culture.[10] A heightened concern with the dissipation of value and meaning; a sense of the insufficiency of the sign; an increasingly self-conscious enactment of those concerns in linguistic disruption and textual breakdown; the theory and practice of narrative as a series of incoherences and disjunctions—novels such as Elizabeth Bowen's *The Last September* and Iris Murdoch's *The Red and the Green* (1965) hint at such standard modernist and postmodernist fare, which is writ large in the novels of Beckett and his apparently deracinated heirs: in Aidan Higgins's *Langrishe, Go Down*, for example, and John Banville's *Birchwood*.[11] Such effects, both incipient and full-blown, may be traced to Anglo-Irish determinants, among others.

Both our received wisdom and reconfigurations such as Gilbert's and Gubar's and Meisel's tend to cast "the modern" and "the postmodern" as relatively generic, cross-cultural reverberations of broad trends. Such an understanding, however, occludes the impact of particular cultural predicaments. Like the American literature gathered under the rubric of "the Southern Renascence" and the literatures termed "postcolonial," twentieth-century Anglo-Irish literature suggests the extent to which literary modernism and postmodernism have been fueled by local cultural crises.

Houston Baker's *Modernism and the Harlem Renaissance* advances a kindred argument. Distinguishing what he calls Afro-American discursive modernism from Anglo-American modernism, he argues: "Our modernism consists . . . not in tumbling towers or bursts in the violet air, but in a sounding renaissancism where a blues reason may yet prevail" (Baker 1987, 106). Baker, however, claims for African American modernism a degree of distinctiveness that I would not claim for Anglo-Irish fiction, which is more closely affiliated with the work of novelists considered paradigmatically modern and postmodern. Bowen's *The Last September*, Murdoch's *The Red and the Green*, Beckett's *Watt* (1953), Higgins's *Langrishe, Go Down*, Banville's *Birchwood*, Keane's *Time After Time* (1983), Jennifer Johnston's *How Many Miles to Babylon?*—these novels tell familiar tales: of the dissolution of old certainties and the onset of radical uncertainty; of the collapse of sure value and meaning; of belief systems' relativity, social structures' provisionality, and the beginning of the end of the novel. But if they bear these family resemblances to the novels of Conrad, Lawrence, Joyce, and Woolf, they also bear marks that link them specifically to Anglo-Ireland, as we shall see. Their avant-garde thematics are locally inflected, expressions of their authors' attempts to reckon with their particular cultural situation, and their culture's apparently definitive demise.

The same may be said of their aesthetics. These tales unfold by way of increasingly self-reflexive narrative structures that register varying degrees of skepticism as to their own viability, as writers gradually acknowledge their inability to attain traditional narrative virtues such as clarity, coherence, conclusion, order. Like their kindred thematics, these modernist and postmodernist aesthetics are in part provincially based, deriving from these writers' attempts to address in narrative the dilemmas which constitute the problem of being Anglo-Irish, and an Anglo-Irish writer, in the era of the Irish Republic.

More specifically, these hallmarks of what might be called Anglo-Irish literary modernism reflect the combined impact of a series of intense and interrelated pressures which history and culture exert upon these writers. These pressures include: the network of hot topics that compel Anglo-Irish writers, the charged cultural context in which they engage them, the hybrid identity of their implied audience, and the vexed relation to authority that is part and parcel of their cultural inheritance.

These novels record the compulsion to give literary form to a set of topics that stand at the center of Irish history and culture. This fiction returns again and again to a matrix of issues—including land, property, work, servitude, "Irishness," "Anglo-Irishness," interclass relations, hierarchy, authority—which together constitute what might be called the Anglo-Irish problematic.[12]

I have deep differences with Terry Eagleton's theories of literature, as will become clear, but his *Criticism and Ideology* describes literary texts in terms that illuminate the anarchic fashion in which Anglo-Irish novels register their topics' powerful charge. Eagleton calls the text a "problem-solving process": "The text is thus never at one with itself," Eagleton argues, "for if it were it would have nothing to say. It is, rather, a process of becoming at one with itself—an attempt to overcome the problem of itself" (Eagleton 1976a, 88–89). Anglo-Irish novels embody just this sort of problem-solving process. They wrestle inconclusively with their recurring concerns, offering shifting representations of their customary topics.

This narrative dynamic recurs in part because history, along with Anglo-Ireland's historically uncertain geopolitical identity, catches these writers up in double and even triple binds. J. C. Beckett's account of the politics of that famous eighteenth-century Anglo-Irishman, Henry Grattan, provides a paradigm of the kind of intellectual, moral, and finally ontological conflicts facing the Anglo-Irish writer. Beckett observes: "Grattan could not escape the inner contradiction that seemed inseparable from the Anglo-Irish position. On the one hand, he pressed the political claims of the Roman Catholic majority; on the other, he committed himself to maintaining the Protestant constitution of the kingdom." In Beckett's view, Grattan "was ready to accept contradictory positions without realizing that a contradiction existed. By ancestry and by conviction he was an upholder of the Anglo-Irish in their claim to be the natural rulers of Ireland; a sense of justice made him champion the rights of the Roman Catholics; but, in his own mind, there was no conflict between the two causes" (J. C. Beckett 1976, 55). Of course, as Beckett observes, given the distribution of power and property in Ireland in Grattan's time, Catholics "could present no threat either to the church or to property," effectively neutralizing Grattan's just promotion of the Catholic cause (55). And Beckett's account does not acknowledge that the Anglo-Irish position frequently involved not just this mix of Irish and Anglo-Irish leanings, but the additional complication of pro-English sympathies with which Grattan apparently did not struggle.

Still, Beckett's account of Grattan's situation points up a structure of thought that helps precipitate the instabilities that come to plague, or grace, Anglo-Irish fiction. Mutually exclusive sympathies and divided loyalties compete for dominance, engendering intellectual and textual conflict. Opposing claims—contradictory intellectual and moral systems for understanding Ireland and the world—vie for textual prominence.

For twentieth-century writers, this competition would have been less cleanly bipolar, less a matter of unconscious contradiction, and less an abstract public policy issue, than it may have been for Grattan. For these writers knew, deep in their bones, that their colonizing ancestors did wrong. Yet they were those ancestors' descendants;

their blood ran in their veins; they grew up surrounded by their portraits; they enjoyed comforts secured by their residual wealth, often
accumulated over centuries in Ireland. They may have experienced
a comparably contradictory set of attitudes toward native Irish men
and women: compassion and compunction at Irish dispossession, resentment at increasingly successful nationalist challenges to Anglo-
Irish power, discouragement at Anglo-Ireland's long-standing lack of
a sense of legitimate Irish identity, envy of "Irish-Ireland's" contrasting legitimacy, residual fear of and even repulsion toward the social
group that their ancestors needed to imagine as repulsive in order
to rationalize its subordination. Such complexly constructed attrac-
tions and repulsions helped generate vexed narratives, narratives in
the process of attempting to align themselves with parties that generated mutually exclusive, contradictory representations of the
charged topics comprising the Anglo-Irish problematic.

The attempt to narrate Anglo-Ireland was unsettled, too, by these
writers' implied audience. They confront their charged topics knowing that the confrontation was witnessed by readers from just those
social groups to whom the Anglo-Irish had competing loyalties. Particularly in the twentieth-century, Anglo-Irish writers wrote aware of
English, Anglo-Irish, *and* Irish readers. But one can't please all these
parties all the time. Representing an explosive issue—such as servitude, or the Anglo-Irish person's relation to his or her land, or interclass relations—in one way may help the novelist escape one bind,
but it inevitably lands him or her in another. So these novels answer
pressing questions one way and then another, in an ongoing search
for narrative closure. Add to this dilemma the fact that, given their
cultural ambivalences, Anglo-Irish writers might just as easily have
wanted to offend each component of their factionalized audience as
placate it, and it begins to seem, as I will argue, that this literature is
grounded in contradictory cultural determinants too numerous and
entangled to reduce to the monolithic motives of self-interest or
guilt.

In sum, under the pressure of the unsettling topics that they confront, the fraught cultural context in which they confront them, and
the divided readership before whom they do, these writers produce
a distinctly self-divided fiction. Which is not to say that these texts de-
volve into meaninglessness, for they do not, but that they align
Anglo-Irishness with narrative frustration and self-division, so inex-
orably as to suggest that these are, perhaps, Anglo-Ireland's defining

features. Certainly the fiction's form mirrors the culture's plight, a process of disintegration and a refusal to disintegrate utterly, Beckett's "I can't go on, I'll go on."

Further exacerbating their fiction's disjunctions, these writers seek narrative form for Anglo-Ireland's compulsory topics knowing that to utter the final word, indeed to author any words at all, will implicate them in an association that might prove at least double-edged. Authority, literary authority, is of course what they need to write. And authority—not in the sense of political mastery, but in the sense of prestige, or at least ontological legitimacy—is what they may long to restore, or grant, to their beleaguered culture of origin, so depleted of power in twentieth-century Ireland. But these writers are, their novels show, haunted by the history of Anglo-Irish authority, such that literary authority might feel like salt in the wound of guilt by ancestral association. Thus, in addition to addressing issues about which it proves all but impossible to conclude, given the issues' own complexities and the binding cultural and literary contexts in which these writers entertain them, these writers bear an unstable relation to literary authority that might well sanction their production of self-contradictory and open-ended texts, texts that authoritatively reverse what they affirm, simultaneously grasping and undermining their own authority.

A striking short story by a nineteenth-century Anglo-Irishman, Joseph Sheridan Le Fanu, expresses the pressures that motivate and bind the Anglo-Irish writer, and crystallizes their literary outcome in the anarchic Anglo-Irish novel.[13] "Green Tea" centers on the relations of a tormented Anglican churchman, Reverend Jennings, with his ill-chosen confidante and protector, Dr. Hesselius, on the one hand, and with an enraged and malignant monkey, on the other. Having spent too many late nights studying "the religious metaphysics of the ancients" while drinking green tea, Jennings begins to have visions of a "jaded and sulky" monkey (Le Fanu 1869, 92, 95). Jennings turns to Hesselius in search of relief from the monkey's increasingly tormenting visitations.

The Hesselius-Jennings-monkey triangle on which Le Fanu's story turns mirrors the triangular relations by which Anglo-Ireland is defined, as well as the at least tripartite audience in view of which the Anglo-Irish author writes. Apparently solicitous and powerful, ultimately exploitative and treacherous, Dr. Hesselius accrues associations of Englishness as the tale unfolds. The monkey emerges as a nightmarish figure of imperial representations of the oppressed Irish Other, as well as an embodiment of the ruling class's guilt regarding its oppressive rule. Caught between these two forces, victimized by both, Jennings declines and finally dies, an apparent suicide. Jennings's death stems in part from Hesselius's culpable failure to defend him from the monkey's increasingly ominous threats, as he promised he would. But Jennings's death is also, more hauntingly, a function of the monkey's invasion of and tyrannical control over Jennings's mind, an Anglo-Irishman's nightmare of a radical Irish repossession. "Green Tea" thus expresses Le Fanu's nineteenth-century awareness of Anglo-Ireland's encroaching demise, and predicts the survival of the empire and colony between which Anglo-Ireland was trapped.

It is in a note from Jennings to Hesselius regarding the monkey that "Green Tea" so strikingly captures the manner of Anglo-Irish narrative. Jennings writes: "Dear Dr Hesselius.—It is here. You had not been an hour gone when it returned. It is speaking. It knows all that has happened. It knows everything—it knows you, and is frantic and atrocious. It reviles. I send you this. It knows every word I have written—I write. This I promised, and I therefore write, but I fear very confused, very incoherently. I am so interrupted, disturbed. Ever yours, sincerely yours, Robert Lynder Jennings" (Le Fanu 1869, 103). Jennings's note concludes in what appears an integrated, authoritative signature, giving it a look of wholeness and completion. Internally, however, the text staggers and breaks. Jennings is compelled to write to Hesselius, out of a sense of obligation comparable to Anglo-Ireland's historical sense of debt owed England, and out of longing for affiliation with Hesselius's apparently indestructible health, wisdom, and power. Yet he cannot write freely to or align himself completely with that party, given that the historically wronged Irish Other, to whom he also bears an ambivalent attachment, overhears and scrutinizes his discourse for authenticity, all the while reviling his guilt. The impact of such pressures on this Anglo-Irish text, as on twentieth-century Anglo-Irish novels, is self-conscious agitation, confusion, incoherence, interruption, disturbance—self-reflexive textual breakdown of profoundly disturbing expressive power.

As "Green Tea" suggests, this narrative dynamic surfaces in Anglo-Irish fiction of the nineteenth century. It emerges even in fiction on the cusp of the eighteenth. As W. J. McCormack has shown, Maria

Edgeworth's *Castle Rackrent*, which most constructions of the Anglo-Irish literary tradition take as its foundational text, is also self-divided, and full of the kind of wavering representations that I have ascribed to Anglo-Irish fiction of the twentieth century (McCormack 1985, 97–168).[14] I would not contend that novels of the post-Treaty twentieth century form a clear and distinct unit that we may definitively set against novels preceding them in time. I would, however, deepen our understanding not just of Anglo-Irish fiction but of modernism and postmodernism as well, by emphasizing—in contemporaneous texts that (Beckett's aside) have been cast as primarily regional and topical—how intimately the local and the avant-garde are intertwined.

In this body of literature, then, the modern and even the post-modern can be seen to echo local history and provincial culture. Anglo-Irish fiction requires that we supplement our conceptions of these cross-cultural trends with an acknowledgment of their heterogeneous local sources. Deeply implicated in the history and culture of the "backwater," these novels teach us that the ostensibly cosmopolitan is also the fiercely provincial; the modern and the postmodern announce the absent presence of a traditional locality.

Anglo-Irish Fiction and Ideology Critique

The discourse of literary studies has taken the term "ideology" to refer to what Terry Eagleton, among others, has described as discourse interested in the outcome of power struggles central to a particular form of social life (Eagleton 1991, 8). "Ideology," in this view, entails "the way signs, meanings and values help to reproduce social power" (221). "Ideology critique," in turn, is "a matter of explaining the forces at work of which" the text itself is "a necessary effect," revealing "the concealed power interests by which [a text's] meanings are internally moulded" (133, 134).

I have described the ways in which Anglo-Irish fiction differs from Seamus Deane's early assessment of it. Rather than a predictably colonialist literature memorializing a waning culture, these novels constitute provocatively self-questioning, self-divided texts: uncertain, unsettled, even anarchic narratives generating competing visions and revisions of history and home. I have described some of the countervailing pressures that help shape these novels, spawning agitation, incoherence, self-reflexive textual breakdown. I have described, in this connection, how embedded these texts are in aesthetics and thematics commonly considered modernist and post-modernist—or how integral these aesthetics and thematics are to these texts.

I suspect these descriptions begin to suggest why and how, from my perspective, Anglo-Irish fiction and ideology theory have not mixed—a theme that spans this book. Novels by Molly Keane, Elizabeth Bowen, Samuel Beckett, and others have not accommodated the practice of ideology critique as defined above. Indeed, as I found at the start of my work on this project (which I describe fully in my closing chapter), these novels in fact posed formidable obstacles to it. For these novels proliferate indeterminate meanings, inscribing the realm of the multiple, the contradictory, the interpretable. These novels chart intricacies of attitude—variations on and combinations of acceptance and rejection of "ideological perspectives"— which the binary logic of ideology critique precludes. Whereas ideology theory assumes that at the root of human consciousness and its literary productions a culpable self-interest reigns, Anglo-Irish fiction dramatizes consciousness's rootlessness, its dynamic, interruptive, inconclusive processes as they are constituted and reconstituted by partial, provisional language. These novels enable a range of reader responses, a range that ideology theory restricts and proscribes. In short, as I will show in the ensuing chapters, the practice of ideology critique described above prohibits the "analytic pluralism" these disrupted narratives require.

2

"The Paradox of these Big Houses": A Reading of Anglo-Ireland

"[O]ur side . . . is no side—rather scared, rather isolated,
not expressing anything except tenacity to something
that isn't there—that never was there."
—Elizabeth Bowen, *The Last September*

I

WHO ARE THE "ANGLO-IRISH"? WHAT, OR WHERE, IS "ANGLO-Ireland"? It is essential, before considering the fiction, to explore more fully the difficulties such questions spawn. Drawing an accurate portrait of the social formation so ambiguously and evocatively named requires a very fine brush. Some of the most incisive scholars of Irish history and culture find themselves making and retracting generalizations about this social group, only to re-invoke and revise them again.[1] As I have suggested, Anglo-Ireland might be broadly construed as that social group, culturally distinct from the native, Catholic population and from the Presbyterian majority in the North, that traced its ancestry to Ireland's Elizabethan conquerors and found material prosperity in what is now the Republic of Ireland.

But "Anglo-Irishness" is structured by paradoxes that such a description fails to evoke. Sir Samuel Ferguson, an Anglican born in Belfast in 1810, offers this rich definition of what he knew as "Anglo-Ireland":

Deserted by the Tories, insulted by the Whigs, threatened by the Radicals, hated by the Papists, and envied by the Dissenters, plundered in

our country-seats, robbed in our town houses, driven abroad by violence, called back by humanity, and, after all, told that we are neither
English nor Irish, fish nor flesh, but a peddling colony, a forlorn advanced guard that must conform to every mutinous movement of the
pretorian (*sic*) rabble—all this, too, while we are the acknowledged
possessors of nine-tenths of the property of a great country, and
wielders of the preponderating influence between two parties; on
whose relative position depend the greatest interests in the empire.
(Lyons 1979, 29)

This passage evokes some of the problematics of "Anglo-Irishness"
that Anglo-Irish fiction writes out, unveiling complexities that remain masked by images of a categorically powerful and merely culpable regime. First, Ferguson identifies Anglo-Ireland by enumerat-
ing violations done to its property, that most tangible symbol of its
authority and identity, as we shall see. Ferguson's Anglo-Ireland is,
moreover, an entity that is defined by others—told what it is or,
rather, what it is not: that it is some odd nonentity, an unnameable,
species-less grotesque with no ontological home. Ferguson goes on
to identify Anglo-Ireland by listing its enemies, those who would destroy it, or at least do it serious harm. Central to Ferguson's account
is his conception of Anglo-Ireland as a beleaguered center of tenuous power. Ferguson's own Anglo-Irish voice corroborates this image
of an absence insisting on its presence, a presence protesting it
should be acknowledged as such; he writes a rhetorically powerful
sentence fragment, an insistent list of attributes which, in the end,
seems still not to capture its intended referent. And this fragment's
tone reveals both a mournful consciousness of the provisionality of
Protestant authority, and a self-confident disbelief in that provisionality, an insistence on Anglo-Ireland's rightful power.[2]

Like Ferguson's chaotic description, the ubiquitous label "Anglo-
Ireland" has a certain telling rightness to it, as many commentators
have noted. Anglo-Ireland is defined again and again, by others and
by its own, in terms of the cultural duality and ontological ambiguity
that its tensed, bipolar name announces. Some commentators emphasize a "both/and" reading of Anglo-Irish identity, focusing on
the extent to which Anglo-Irishness constitutes a state of gravitating
toward two competing identities. Elizabeth Bowen writes: "Inherited
loyalty (or at least, adherence) to Britain—where their sons were
schooled, in whose wars their sons had for generations fought, and
to which they owed their Ascendancy lands and power—pulled them

one way; their own temperamental Irishness the other" (Bowen 1952a, 125). A. Norman Jeffares makes Swift a case in point, claiming that "between the extremes of Ireland and England the Anglo-Irish had constantly been pulled, seeking a true awareness of their own middle state, making their own individual seismic readings of the shock waves one culture brings upon the other" (Jeffares 1986, 8–9). Lyons argues that the term "Anglo-Ireland" "expresses very precisely the schizophrenia which was their natural condition":

> They had habitually called themselves simply "Irish" and in their eighteenth-century heyday had even monopolized the term, to the exclusion of the native and Catholic Irish whose legal existence the penal laws had then scarcely acknowledged. On the other hand, conscious that they were a privileged minority, separated by race and religion from those whose land their ancestors had seized, they still looked to England as their ultimate protector and regarded themselves as members of an empire which they were proud to serve. This divided loyalty led them eventually into the characteristic dilemma of a colonial governing class, torn between their country of origin and their country of settlement. (Lyons 1979, 18–19)

Other commentators highlight the "neither/nor" dimensions of Anglo-Irishness, what Desmond Bell calls a "*no nation* view of Protestant identity and difference" (Bell 1985, 92, italics Bell's). According to the Anglo-Irish critic, Vivian Mercier: "The typical Anglo-Irish boy . . . learns that he is not quite Irish almost before he can talk; later he learns that he is far from being English either. The pressure on him to become either wholly English or wholly Irish can erase segments of his individuality for good and all. 'Who am I?' is the question that every Anglo-Irishman must answer, even if it takes him a lifetime, as it did Yeats" (Mercier 1955, 133). Lennox Robinson expands: "It was characteristic of them and their class that though they were of Ireland—their families having been in Ireland for very many generations—they were slightly *déraciné*, they didn't quite 'belong,' yet they belonged to no other country in the world, certainly not to England though they were firm loyalists" (Murray 1992, 109). Although these men and women "thought of themselves as Irish, they were doomed never to penetrate the Catholic and Gaelic recesses of Irishness, and could not afford to sever their ties with Englishness. . . . Their tragedy was that, hesitating as they did between two worlds, they could never be fully accepted by either" (Lyons 1979, 22).

Anglo-Ireland's name rings true also in that it alludes to the two geopolitical entities in relation to which Anglo-Ireland has historically been defined. Andrew Parker et al. write:

> nationality is a relational term whose identity derives from its inherence in a system of differences. . . . [N]ational identity is determined not on the basis of its own intrinsic properties but as a function of what it (presumably) is not. Implying "some element of alterity for its definition," a nation is ineluctably "shaped by what it opposes." But the very fact that such identities depend constitutively on difference means that nations are forever haunted by their various definitional others. Hence, on the one hand, the nation's insatiable need to administer difference . . . And hence, on the other, the nation's insatiable need for representational labor to supplement its founding ambivalence, the lack of self-presence at its origin or in its essence. (A. Parker et al. 1992a, 5)[3]

The "identity" of social formations such as Anglo-Ireland, like that of nations, is fundamentally relational, deriving in this case from its relations to the entities announced in its hyphenated name.

Despite this name's demonstrable propriety, it might also be seen to misrepresent its referent. For one thing, "Anglo-Ireland" was not originally Anglo-Ireland's name. In fact, this label was not common until late in the nineteenth century, well after Anglo-Ireland's birth and rise to power, and well into the first stages of its decline. The term gained currency at that point in the nineteenth century when the nationalistic "Irish Ireland" movement had garnered the power to set the terms of Irish cultural debate. W. J. McCormack might call it—like "Protestant Ascendancy" and "Big House"—"primarily a term or form of retrospect" (McCormack 1992, 56).[4] In J. C. Beckett's view, the "essential purpose" of the term "is to pick out one section of the population as less truly 'Irish' than the rest" (J. C. Beckett 1976, 11). It is in this connection that Henry Louis Gates's notion of the performative trope most vividly applies; the term "Anglo-Irish" functions as "a trope of ultimate, irreducible difference between cultures" and serves "to *will* this sense of *natural* difference" into the cultural discourse (Gates 1985, 5, italics Gates's).[5]

Moreover, as we have seen, the "Anglo-Irish" did not typically think of themselves as such. Members of this social group "never doubted that they were Irishmen, without any qualification. Though they were, for the most part, of English descent and loyal to the English crown, it did not occur to them to suppose that they could, on that account, be regarded as less than Irish, or that their claim to represent the Irish nation could be denied" (J. C. Beckett 1976, 10).[6]

"Anglo-Ireland" misrepresents its referent most fundamentally, perhaps, in that, neither English nor Irish, nor a mix of the two, Anglo-Ireland entails something else altogether, for which there seems no proper name. But then, this impropriety is in its way appropriate, recalling as it does those paradoxes on which, as in Ferguson's definition, Anglo-Ireland's "identity" rests.

The history of Anglo-Ireland's name is as revealing as the name itself. Its history makes clear that the name alludes to those contradictory experiences that define this social group: its double experience of power and its loss, or, one might say, its fluctuating experience of an always provisional power. Authored by "Irish-Irish" descendants of those whom the first Anglo-Irish settlers dispossessed, its name identifies Anglo-Ireland as a resented ruling class that enjoyed an impermanent power and, lacking the power to name itself, is now known by a name announcing opposition to its historical authority, a name that it neither invented nor approved. Moreover, its name identifies Anglo-Ireland as an entity whose identity shifts over time, a provisional social formation around which swirl debates as to how it should be objectified, debates which, the name announces, it loses. "Anglo-Ireland," like Samuel Ferguson's description, announces the paradox of absent presence.

A word of clarification is in order. In emphasizing the paradoxes that structure Anglo-Irish identity and authority, I do not mean to understate the real power wielded by Protestants in Ireland, or the real injustices suffered by Irish men and women. Elizabeth Bowen asserts: "In the Anglo-Irish, those invaders and settlers who came to conquer, stayed to possess and love, national responsibility did come to be born, but social responsibility, alas, not" (Bowen 1952b, 176). Without minimizing Anglo-Ireland's abuses of power—some of which, *pace* Bowen, were in fact committed in the name of "the Irish nation"—I want to supplement received ideas of "Anglo-Irishness," toward a more nuanced representation, a representation to which Anglo-Irish fiction itself gives voice.

II

Another way of probing our opening questions about Anglo-Irish identity is to take a closer look at Anglo-Ireland's roles in Irish history.[7] Originally paradoxical, by definition unlocatable, Anglo-Ireland has always—not just in the twentieth century—had a story that is difficult to tell.

The story of Anglo-Ireland is a story of incompletely realized quests for authority, legitimacy, and place: a story of withstanding ongoing and increasingly potent challenges to an always unstable identity. This story culminates in a virtually complete cancellation of Protestant power in the twentieth-century Republic, although not, of course, in the North. Divorcing Anglo-Ireland from those traditional sources of what authority it did possess and what identity it could construct—from Irish land and English Empire—twentieth-century history set Anglo-Ireland radically adrift. Like "the Western mind" generally in the twentieth century, Anglo-Irish men and women found themselves disabused of their most comforting illusions, deprived of their belief in stable values and meanings. Twentieth-century Anglo-Irish fiction registers this cataclysm.

The twelfth-century appearance of an English presence on Irish soil comprised something of a false start: an emblem, it might be said, of Anglo-Ireland's longer tenure in Ireland. English soldiers first arrived in Ireland in 1170, when Dermot MacMurrough promised fealty to Henry II in return for his aid in fighting rival Irish kings. Though these Englishmen pushed deep into Ireland, the only territory that remained even nominally under their control, as centuries passed, was that area within a thirty-mile radius around Dublin that came to be known as the "English Pale." "Even within the Pale," R. F. Foster argues, "the Anglicized ethos maintained only a precarious position"—evidence of the "incompleteness" and "uncertainty of conquest" (Foster 1989, 8, 3–14).

Like the Viking invaders before them, the "Old English" (as this first wave of conquerors is often called) intermarried with the indigenous population, adopting its customs and language. When England's decisive seventeenth-century conquest of Ireland took hold, the Old English tended to ally themselves with the native Irish, determined to retain both their unreformed religion and their long-held land. Though they had some political power early in the seventeenth century, this power gradually waned. In 1641 they joined in the Irish rebellion. Beckett explains: "the decision they took in 1641 marked, for them, the beginning of the end. It was to lead to confiscation of their estates, destruction of their political influence and, eventually, to their disappearance as a distinct group in the population of Ireland" (J. C. Beckett 1976, 30).

We may trace the beginning of what has come to be called "Anglo-Ireland" to the seventeenth century, when a second wave of invaders spearheaded England's more decisive conquest. Elizabeth fought four Irish wars in her effort to consolidate her power in Ireland, and initiated the infamous policy of "settlements" and "plantations," the most systematic of which was the 1609 plantation of Ulster, settled largely by Scottish Presbyterians. The south of Ireland felt Elizabeth's policies most harshly after 1649, with Cromwell's campaign to dispossess rebellious Irish men and women and settle English investors and soldiers on their confiscated land. Cromwell sought what Conor Cruise O'Brien calls "a lasting solution," in the form of a wholesale transplantation of the Irish population (C. O'Brien 1972, 69). In the end, however, given the demand for Irish labor in the east, what resulted was less a relocation of population than a radical change in structures of ownership and political power. "What had been established over most of the island," O'Brien summarizes, "was in fact a landed ruling class, mainly of English and Scottish origin, professing some form of Protestantism and dominating a native Roman Catholic and still Gaelic-speaking peasantry. This was the Protestant Ascendancy" (69).

With conquest, religion and politics became closely identified. As J. C. Beckett emphasizes:

> [W]e shall misunderstand the situation completely unless we remember that for Irishmen religion was more than the expression of theological belief. Protestant and Roman Catholic were separated by a gulf deeper than that between the Thirty-nine Articles and the Creed of Pope Pius IV. They formed, in fact, two communities, to some extent intermingled and interdependent, but consciously different; and between them lay the memory of conquest and confiscation, massacre and pillage, conspiracy and persecution. In this long struggle religion had determined the side on which a man stood; but the struggle had been one for land and power, and religion had been a badge of difference rather than the main issue in dispute. (J. C. Beckett 1976, 45)

One's religion marked one's tribe.

By 1703, Protestants owned about 86 percent of Irish land and, by mid-century, approximately 95 percent (Foster 1989, 155). Protestant prosperity financed the building of Georgian Dublin, and of those "Big Houses" that stand at the center of much Anglo-Irish fiction. But to invoke such facts of eighteenth-century Protestant power threatens to diminish the complexity of developing Ascendancy culture. Anglo-Ireland's eighteenth-century sociological profile does not jibe with that of English landed classes, nor with the myth of a landed aristocratic Ascendancy. For one thing, confiscated Irish properties were allocated to a motley assortment of beneficiaries: to investors who had underwritten the war, to soldiers and contractors who remained unpaid, and to government officials (J. C. Beckett 1976, 34). Irish peerages were used extensively as a form of political patronage, so that Irish peers bore "relations to society [that were] as a whole quite distinct from those which had given the English aristocracy its lustre" (McCormack 1985, 56). Anglo-Ireland had a "gamy flavour—an echo of colonial Virginia, or even the Kenya highlands in the 1920s" (Foster, 1989, 170). The "luster" of this "aristocracy of self-made men" was further attenuated by the presence, in the wings, of Ireland's native Catholic aristocracy, living both on the Continent and still at home (170).

Moreover, not all Protestants were landlords. The Anglo-Ireland of the day in fact encompassed sizable middle and lower classes—a heterogeneity that Foster finds "exemplified by that quintessential Ascendancy institution, Trinity College: defined by Anglicanism but containing sons of peers, of shoemakers, of distillers, of butchers, of surgeons, and of builders" (Foster 1989, 173). And not all the "Anglo-Irish" were, strictly speaking, "Anglo." Early in *Bowen's Court*, Bowen's historical account of her family's Cork home, we learn that "Bowen" derives from the Welsh "ab Owen" or "ap Owen" (Bowen 1942a, 33). Other Anglo-Irish men and women traced their ancestry to the Old English and to Catholics who converted to Protestantism in order to reap the accompanying social, political and material rewards. Violet Martin (better known as Martin Ross) descended from the Old English Martins of Ross, who had owned land in Galway and had converted to Protestantism in the eighteenth century (McMahon 1968, 123). As Thomas Flanagan concludes, "there were many ways of being Anglo-Irish" (Flanagan 1966, 59).

So what, then, defined Anglo-Irishness? In Foster's view, it was Anglicanism. Anglicanism "defined a social elite, professional as well as landed, whose descent could be Norman, Old English, Cromwellian or even (in a very few cases) ancient Gaelic. Anglicanism conferred exclusivity, in Ireland as in contemporary England; and exclusivity defined the Ascendancy, not ethnic origin" (Foster 1989, 170). What

Anglicanism excluded, of course, was Roman Catholicism. No matter how much wealth a Catholic might amass in business or a profession, he could never gain access to political power. In Beckett's words: "'Protestant ascendancy' . . . was the supremacy of the Protestants, as a body, over the Roman Catholic majority" (J. C. Beckett 1976, 44–45). Anglo-Irishness was defined by what it was not.

The much-celebrated building of Georgian Dublin was an equivocal gesture. While Ascendancy society was not particularly refined, Ascendancy architecture was monumental, a trace of Anglo-Ireland's "extraordinary determination to embellish Dublin with public buildings that would be not only equal to but *greater than* those of London" (Foster 1989, 174, italics Foster's). The Parliament House, the Four Courts, the Customs House—these structures "indicated [Anglo-Ireland's] realization that their status was not international but colonial, and a determination to compensate for it" (174). And so "Contemporaries, especially Londoners, were amazed by the inappropriate grandeur of what they expected to be a provincial town" (186).

If Georgian Dublin functioned as a symbol, announcing less who the Anglo-Irish were than who they wanted to be, so too did the "Big House." These houses began to appear in the first quarter of the eighteenth century and by mid-century, the Anglo-Irish were "building obsessively" (Foster 1989, 191, 190). Like Georgian Dublin, the houses were performative gestures, built to help their owners "convince themselves not only that they had arrived, but that they would remain" (194). Bowen explains: "For these people—my family and their associates—the idea of power was mostly vested in property (property having been acquired by use or misuse of power in the first place)" (Bowen 1942a). Not surprisingly, though in the end fruitlessly, "loyalty to their property was a loyalty from which they would never swerve" (J. C. Beckett 1976, 35).

Protestant law attempted to protect the power for which the Big House tried to stand. The infamous penal code, enforced most severely in the first quarter of the eighteenth century, shored up Protestants' property-based power and attested implicitly to that power's weak base. The penal code denied Catholics the most basic of civil rights, prohibiting them from voting, from sitting in Parliament, from owning arms, from establishing schools, from sending their children abroad to school, and from attending university. Under the code, Catholics who converted to Protestantism stood to win their family's land. As Foster reminds us, such prohibitions were not unique to Ireland, and must be seen in the context of contemporaneous anti-Jacobite fears; the legal status of Irish Catholics was no worse—indeed was sometimes better—than that of English Catholics (Foster 1989, 121). But whenever the English proposed to ameliorate Irish Catholics' position, the Ascendancy parliament insisted that the law stand (206). "Out of all proportion to their actual effect," Foster concludes, "the Penal Laws reflected Protestant fears" (207).

Though the penal code did help protect the seventeenth-century land settlements, the eighteenth-century power structure did not go unchallenged. England made Anglo-Ireland's subordinate position clear. The Declaratory Act of 1720 established Ireland as a dependent kingdom, in effect revoking those rights to which colonial nationalists referred when asserting their "Irish" independence (Foster 1989, 162). And there was significant agrarian agitation at home—a vivid expression of the precariousness of Anglo-Ireland's place on Irish soil. The century of the "Protestant Irish nation" culminated in the unsuccessful rebellion led by Theobold Wolfe Tone who, inspired by the principles of the French Revolution, sought to establish an Irish republic after the French model. Like Charles Stewart Parnell, Wolfe Tone was Protestant.

III

If the eighteenth century has been termed Anglo-Ireland's heyday, the nineteenth has been said to mark the tangible beginning of its end, as manifested by the 1800 Act of Union, and the onset and gradual ascendance of a potent Catholic nationalism.

As I have suggested, Anglo-Ireland's relation to English Empire had granted it an uncertain political identity from the start. David Miller describes this uncertainty this way:

[Anglo-Ireland] conceived of its relationship with the British metropolitan power in terms of a contractarian rather than a nationalist ideology. . . . [T]heir historical experience as a planted population in a hostile land led them to conceive of themselves as representatives of a British Imperial power and Protestant interest (rather than as members of a British nation). . . . The allegiance is conditional, that is, conditional on Britain safeguarding Protestant interests and privileges. These in turn are seen as entitlements from

> Protestant historic loyalty to sovereign and Empire, . . . *exclusive enti-tlements* bequested to Protestants qua Protestants rather than as *inclusive rights* afforded to every member of a country. (Bell 1985, 93, italics Miller's)

The Act of Union establishing the United Kingdom of Great Britain and Ireland would have taken a significant swipe at such a contractual conception of identity. In instituting the Union of England and Ireland, the Act abolished Ireland's independent parliament in Dublin—Ireland's Protestant governing body. Thereafter, Irish representatives sat at Westminster. If, as Beckett writes, the Anglo-Irish "had lost their exclusive position in the government of a kingdom, they had gained a share in the government of an empire" (J. C. Beckett 1976, 85). But with Union, Anglo-Ireland generally and Anglo-Irish Dublin particularly were transformed from political and cultural centers in their own right into outposts of Empire, while Protestant representatives were transformed from ultimate Irish authorities into alien minority members of an English governing body. Anglo-Ireland lost what hold it had on "the Protestant Irish nation." And it became directly dependent on the good will of an Empire which, it became increasingly clear, would not always play the part of Anglo-Ireland's protector.

But it was the rise and consolidation of Catholic nationalism that most vividly announced the onset of Anglo-Ireland's decline. Though Wolfe Tone's revolution had failed, his revolutionary ideas had taken hold, encouraging increasing antagonism toward Anglo-Ireland, which came increasingly to be seen as England's Irish garrison. This burgeoning nationalism was galvanized by Daniel O'Connell, who won Catholic emancipation in 1829, opening parliament to Catholics. "Symbolically," Conor Cruise O'Brien explains, emancipation "marked the end of the penal system, the return to existence of people whom the law had presumed not to exist" (O'Brien, C. 1972, 100). Literally, it constituted the end of the Protestant monopoly on power.

Not surprisingly, electoral reforms ensued, transferring power from those with property to those with numerical superiority, so that "By the middle of the nineteenth century, the Protestants of the south and west . . . found that neither their support nor their opposition could alter the balance of political power and that no government was likely to be influenced by any opinion they might express" (J. C. Beckett 1976, 90). Anglo-Ireland's word was no longer law.

Land reform followed. Fast on the heels of the disestablishment of the Church of Ireland (in 1868) came the Irish Land Act of 1870, in which "for the first time the imperial parliament had intervened on the side of the tenant against the landlord. . . . The ownership of the land was passing . . . to those who cultivated it" (Lyons 1979, 10). The Land Act of 1881 required fair rents and prohibited arbitrary evictions, further undermining the economic and psychological foundations of Anglo-Irish authority: "once the landlord's authority became conditional and open to question it was only a matter of time, as both landlords and tenants saw, before it would cease to exist" (C. O'Brien 1972, 113–14). With the Wyndham Act of 1903 (which allowed tenants to buy their holdings) "the grip of the ascendancy on the land was at last decisively loosened." This was, in Lyons's view, the culminating stroke in the steady separation of the landed class from the source of their traditional authority. Not surprisingly," he observes, "it left them confused and vulnerable" (Lyons 1979, 71–72).

Nineteenth-century Anglo-Ireland, then, was a social formation that had increasingly to be described in terms qualified by quotation marks: "garrison," "gentry," "ascendancy," "ruling class." J. C. Beckett evokes that provisionalizing punctuation in the following description of a "garrison" that was significantly more beleaguered than Sir Samuel Ferguson's of 1810:

> if the Irish Protestants were in truth a garrison, they were a garrison in peculiar and difficult circumstances. Though almost perpetually under siege, they had neither means nor authority to organize their own defence. They must work always under orders from a remote headquarters, where strategy and tactics were liable to frequent fluctuation. . . . They had no power to come to terms on their own behalf; but they lived in constant fear that terms would be arranged behind their backs; that . . . sooner or later, the whole fortress would be abandoned and they themselves left to their fate. (J. C. Beckett 1976, 88)

The land-owning Anglo-Irish were clearly, by this time, a kind of counterfeit gentry. As Lyons describes them:

> they gave a passable imitation of a governing class on the English model. They acted as deputy lieutenants of their counties, as high sheriffs or as justices of the peace, and they were prominent in local government until the end of the nineteenth century. Apart from visits to the Dublin Horse Show and to the winter season at the Vicere-

gal Court, many of them resided all the year round in their Georgian houses—sometimes beautiful, sometimes ugly, but often dilapidated and generally uncomfortable. . . . Shooting, fishing, and hunting, interspersed with hospitality frequently more lavish than they could afford—this was the framework of their lives. Worship of the horse was universal. . . . Books, unless they had to do with angling or turf, were not widely read in their households, though some had splendid libraries dating mainly from the eighteenth century. (Lyons 1979, 21)

This Anglo-Ireland may have been defined less by class, *per se*, than by its members' access, or ability to *imagine* access, to authority: "even the poorest Protestants commonly felt a greater degree of solidarity with the upper ranks of the Protestant community than with Roman Catholics of their own class. Nor was this attitude simply the product of sectarian bigotry: there was a regular gradation in Protestant society, from top to bottom, so that a poor Protestant might, by industry, ability or luck, make his way up not only to wealth but to political power" (J. C. Beckett 1976, 44–45).

The most damning images of Anglo-Irish power took root during this century of Anglo-Irish decline. Perhaps the most familiar is the stereotype of the hard-hearted absentee landlord. Though the stereotype "may be morally deserved," Foster argues, it "derives in many cases from a highly questionable historiographical tradition" (Foster 1989, 185). Lyons explains the stereotype this way: "Caught between unsympathetic [English] governments and resentful tenants [the Anglo-Irish] provided a convenient scapegoat for most of the ills of nineteenth-century Ireland" (Lyons 1979, 22). Insofar as the image is the product of an increasingly authoritative nationalism that was able, in the nineteenth century, to focus an incriminating spotlight on landlords as alien usurpers, the image, like the term "Anglo-Ireland," announces Anglo-Ireland's waning power.

Likewise the image of the totemic "Big House" which, as we have seen, served an important function for Anglo-Ireland from the start: as a talisman, a literal and metaphorical bulwark against minority status and the neither-norness of Anglo-Irish identity. W. J. McCormack provides this convincing reading of the image. In his view, the nineteenth-century Big House was a prop in a charade of Ascendancy self-legitimization. The Ascendancy was, he argues, a bourgeois social formation disseminating a "false sociology," strategically associating itself with the "provenance of landed estate" so as to counter the reality of "the gradual erosion of landed estate as a political reality during the nineteenth century in Ireland" (McCormack 1985, 88). He elaborates: "A Protestant elite, administering a largely rural society, assumes the identity of the Ascendancy, thereby gradually arrogating to itself the status of a raffish aristocracy and the security of a restricted bourgeoisie from which Catholics will be rebuffed by a flamboyant sectarianism devoid of Christianity" (92). The "Big House," then, is "a constructed concept rather than an historical fact"—not an "historically unproblematic socio-architectural entity" but a speech-act, "a cultural formation [that] is a product not of the building boom (in the 1770s or whenever) but of the assault upon the house's economy" (McCormack 1992, 38, 41). The Big House is "a signifier without a signified" (42).

The frequency of the Big House's recurrence in Anglo-Irish literature suggests the intensity of Anglo-Ireland's need for it. It appears again and again in the literature, a symbolic clearing house for writers' variable attitudes toward home culture. Writing from deep within Ascendancy myth, Edith Somerville constructs her Big House according to a blueprint much like the one McCormack describes. Her "gentry-houses" were once "disseminators of light, of the humanities; centers of civilization; places to which the poor people rushed, in any trouble, as to Cities of Refuge" (Flanagan 1966, 69). Martin Ross invokes the paternalistic myth of family in envisioning her ancestral estate: "The quietness of untroubled centuries lay like a spell on Connemara, the old ways of life were unquestioned at Ross, and my father went and came among his people in an intimacy as native as the soft air they breathed. . . . All were known to the Master, and he was known and understood by them." "[A]s a system it was probably quite uneconomic," Ross grants, "but the hand of affection held it together, and the tradition of centuries was at its back" (Somerville and Ross 1917, 4).

Bowen's symbology, like her fiction, is more equivocal. "The paradox of these big houses," she writes in her 1940 essay, "The Big House," "is that often they are not big at all. . . . [T]he houses that I know best, and write of, would only be called 'big' in Ireland—in England they would be 'country houses,' no more. . . . Is it height," she wonders, "in this country of otherwise low buildings—that got these Anglo-Irish houses their 'big' name? Or have they been called 'big' with a slight inflection—that of hostility, irony? One may call a man 'big' with just that inflection because he seems to think the hell of himself" (Bowen 1940, 26). If "Anglo-Ireland" was misnamed by antagonistic voices, Bowen suggests, Anglo-Irish dwellings may have been, too.

Bowen tries to cast the Big House as a symbol of "the European idea":

> After an era of greed, roughness and panic, after an era of camping in charred or desolate ruins (as my Cromwellian ancestors did certainly) these new settlers who had been imposed on Ireland began to wish to add something to life. The security that they had, by the eighteenth century, however ignobly gained, they did not use quite ignobly. They began to feel, and exert, the European idea—to seek what was humanistic, classic and disciplined." (Bowen 1940, 27)

The house "raised life above the exigencies of mere living to the plane of art, or at least style" (Bowen 1940, 27). "It is something," she concludes, "to subscribe to an idea, even if one cannot live up to it" (27).

IV

Twentieth-century history overruled the symbolic value Anglo-Ireland tried to assign its Big House. "[F]or most landlords," Lyons argues, "life in the first decade of the new century was a strange chiaroscuro. The dark shadow of ultimate expropriation indeed hung over them, but it could be relegated to the borders of consciousness" (Lyons 1979, 72). O'Brien calls the period from 1890 to 1910 "a kind of Indian summer for the old Ascendancy" (C. O'Brien 1972, 128). Bowen's *The Last September* is suffused with this mood of imminent loss.

Indian summer effectively ended with the 1916 Easter Rising or, more precisely, with the English bungling of its aftermath. The subsequent radicalization of Irish politics left the Anglo-Irish feeling increasingly alienated and alone. Lyons reads this chapter of their story this way: "the essence of their tragedy was that the Empire was now about to repudiate them at the very moment when they had spent their blood so prodigally on its behalf" in the First World War (Lyons 1979, 102). The 1919–1921 war of independence and the civil war of 1922–1923 demonstrated, with a conclusiveness that must have been chilling, Empire's disinclination to contain Irish republicanism. Edith Somerville's 1921 novel, *An Enthusiast,* ends tellingly: Dan Palliser, a dispossessed Anglo-Irish landlord, is killed in the crossfire during a battle between I.R.A. and British troops. One hundred and ninety-two Big Houses were burned down between December 1921 and March 1923 (Brown 1985, 86). The 1921 partition, which divided the island into the twenty-six-county Irish Free State and the six counties of the North, revoked southern Protestants' membership in Empire. And it stripped them of their membership in a Protestant minority that had comprised one-fourth of the island's population; with partition, they became members of a much smaller minority, one that accounted for only 7.4 percent of the Free State's population in 1926 (84).

The Free State government was careful to recognize Anglo-Irish property and civil rights. Kevin O'Higgins argued in Parliament: "We being the majority and strength of the country . . . it comes well from us to make a generous adjustment to show that these people are regarded, not as alien enemies, not as planters, but . . . as part and parcel of this nation" (Lyons 1979, 112). But as O'Higgins's vaguely triumphalist tone implies, the Anglo-Irish had reason to feel uneasy in the emerging Ireland. Terence Brown elaborates:

> It is true that about seventeen former Southern Unionists were to be granted seats as nonelected members of the Upper House of the Oireachtas, the Senate, but the actual political insecurity experienced by the Protestant community in Ireland at independence can be adjudged the more certainly by the remarkable spectacle of a delegation dispatched by the general synod of the Church of Ireland on 12 May 1922. . . . to inquire in what may strike one now as plaintive terms indeed, 'if they were permitted to live in Ireland or if it was desired that they should leave the country.' (Brown 1985, 85)

After independence Anglo-Ireland's predicament worsened, under pressure from a prescriptive definition of Irish identity as essentially rural, Catholic, and Gaelic. The views of polemicist D. P. Moran typify the era's exclusive nationalism: "The foundation of Ireland is the Gael, and the Gael must be the element which absorbs" (Moran 1905, 37). Free State legislation reflected the new social order. The constitution of 1937 was grounded in Catholic doctrine regarding marriage, family, education, and property, and acknowledged the "special position" of the Catholic Church (Lyons 1979, 151–52).

Such cultural dynamics are, of course, not unique to Ireland. As Ernest Gellner explains: "Nationalism usually conquers in the name of a putative folk culture. Its symbolism is drawn from the healthy, pristine, vigorous life of the peasants, of the *Volk*, the *narod*. . . . If the nationalism prospers it eliminates the alien high culture, but it does not then replace it by the old local low culture; it revives, or invents, a local high (literate, specialist-transmitted) culture of its own, though admittedly one which will have some links with the earlier folk styles and dialects" (Gellner 1983, 57). If Anglo-Irish institutions had barred Catholics from their ranks, "Irish Irelanders," striving to reverse dispossessions suffered under Empire, in turn effectively excluded Protestants from theirs. The emerging nationalist culture (in Brown's words): "denied full spiritual communion with the Irish nation to the colonizing, landed Anglo-Irishman with his apparently English accent, manner, and loyalties and his Protestant faith . . . Even those of them who had sought to sympathize with Irish needs and aspirations had found themselves denied a secure hold on their own Irish identity in these years. . . . [T]hey had found themselves swiftly becoming treated in the newspapers, in political speeches, and in polemical pamphlets as strangers in their own land" (Brown 1985, 83).

Moreover, Brown argues, the upheavals of the home rule conflict, the World War, and the Irish wars "had not allowed many Protestant Irishmen and women sufficient leisure and sense of security to devise an intellectual counter to the assaults of Irish Ireland," leaving them "without ideological resource, concerned only with economic and actual survival" (Brown 1985, 84). Its former identity structures dismantled, its ancestral value systems undermined, disabled from imagining new narratives to take the obsolete ones' place, post-independence Anglo-Ireland occupied, or perhaps constituted, an ideological and ontological void (84). And in addition to suffering beleaguerment from without, it grew more visibly fractured from within. Fault lines dividing landowners, Ulster farmers, and professionals grew increasingly evident once the galvanizing cause of unionism expired (85). The social formation that had been cast (by false sociologies and polemical mythologies) as a coherent, gracious "unity of culture" was, undeniably now, a hodgepodge of subgroups defined by different and even competing economic interests—further proof that Anglo-Ireland's center could not hold.

Where is Anglo-Ireland now? In Lyons's view, the battle between civilizations abated between 1928 and 1937, "not because the issue had been resolved to anyone's satisfaction, but because the proponents of one side of the argument had begun to droop and die" (Lyons 1979, 168). He provides this catalog of Anglo-Irish decline:

> In 1928 Yeats ceased to be a senator and in effect left public life. In 1929 the Censorship of Publications Act was passed over the bitter opposition of the Anglo-Irish and some others. In 1930 [AE's] *Irish Statesman* ceased publication. In 1931 the Cork writer, Daniel Corkery, published *Synge and Anglo-Irish Literature*, perhaps the most sustained attack on the whole concept of Anglo-Irish culture ever written. . . . In 1932 there came to power Mr de Valera and his party, pledged to greater self-sufficiency and to the ideal of a Gaelic Ireland. In that same year also Lady Gregory died, and in Dublin the Eucharistic Congress exhibited to the world an Ireland which appeared to be wholly and devotedly Catholic. In 1933 imported newspapers were taxed. In 1935 the sale and importation of contraceptives were forbidden by law and the dance halls at last regulated to the satisfaction of the Roman Catholic hierarchy. . . . Of the great figures of the renaissance the only one left to confront the flowing tide was Yeats, and Yeats in these last years, though reaching new heights as a poet, in public matters blew with an uncertain trumpet. More and more he seemed to be retreating . . . into an Anglo-Irish eighteenth century of his own fabrication—a creation which had little to do with history, but a great deal to do with his hungry quest for authority in the modern world. (Lyons 1979, 168–69)

Yeats's death in 1939 marks for Lyons the effective end of Anglo-Ireland.[8]

Rather than attempt to locate its end, it may be more fitting to explore the possibility that Anglo-Ireland's story winds down as it begins—in the kindred realms of absent presence and paradox. Since the middle of the twentieth century, the combined pressures of Anglo-American consumer culture, economic prosperity, and a deepening commitment to the European Community have dramatically weakened the Irish-Irelanders' hold on Irish culture. But at this perhaps more receptive moment in Irish history, Anglo-Ireland has all but vanished, primarily by way of emigration to England. Indeed, as a viable political entity, as an identifiable social group of any numerical consequence, Anglo-Ireland could be said to have given up the ghost long ago. Thomas Kilroy asserts: "The Anglo-Irish belong to history, to the past" (Kilroy 1997–98, 8). Yet J. C. Beckett claimed, as late as 1976: "The Anglo-Irish tradition *is now* more than eight hundred years old" (J. C. Beckett 1976, 148, my italics). And Molly

Keane, raised deep within Anglo-Ireland, lived and wrote from within those depths until her death in 1996. Yet her late novels—*Good Behaviour, Time After Time, Queen Lear*—can seem anachronistic books, written as if from the grave.

The current status of the Big House is illuminating in this regard. Though many houses were burned down in the 1920s, some were converted into convents, monasteries, hotels, and schools. Many were sold. Bowen sold hers in 1959—the upkeep was just too expensive—and by the following year, it was razed. The Irish tourism industry now banks on the Big Houses, reclaiming both the properties and their mythological semiotics as cornerstones of the tourist economy. The Big House "is, as it were, a 'national asset' of considerable financial significance" (Rauchbauer 1992b, 11). Vera Kreilkamp complains of the "misleadingly ahistorical presentation of gentry residences by preservationists"; the Big Houses "are valued and interpreted as aesthetic masterworks . . . [while t]heir economic and social roles in the colonial system are left unexplored" (Kreilkamp 1998, 262). I would argue that their position in the colonial system is at the same time revealed. For these preserved houses highlight the extent to which the historical Anglo-Ireland is and was *itself* an artifact. The remaining houses seek to evoke an elegant and illusory grandeur. But they also denote—indeed, embody—the process of constructing (a now saleable) Anglo-Irish myth. They are thus at once monuments to and performances of "Anglo-Ireland," highlighting not just Anglo-Irish style, but Anglo-Irishness *as* style.

V

So "Anglo-Ireland" refers to a social formation (and a construction of a social formation) which, from its inception on, derived identity and authority from two profoundly uncertain sources: its tenuous plantation on conquered Irish land and its tenuous bond to an Empire, based across the Irish Sea, with interests extending beyond and often operating against Anglo-Ireland's own. Its "schizophrenic" name refers to its relational identity: its definition by way of its situation between two other cultural identities. Having a liminal geopolitical identity that is by definition open to question, Anglo-Ireland is born, as Samuel Ferguson complained, neither fish nor flesh. Consigned to this "middle state," constituted by the need to ask "Who am I?", Anglo-Ireland is historically constructed so as to be unable to compose a coherent answer to that question—unable, even, to speak its own name.

If Anglo-Ireland originates as that which lacks name and home, over time it endures repeated threats to its uncertain place and power. History deepens Anglo-Ireland's birthmarks, and in the process all but obliterates it. Or one might say history brings Anglo-Ireland more fully into its own: perfecting its identity as that which unsuccessfully combats threats to its imperfect integrity, forcing it to play out to the limit what may be its defining gesture: the struggle to say its name and make it stick.

As I have argued, novels by Anglo-Irish writers in the twentieth century allude to a web of cultural predicaments in which the project of narrating Anglo-Ireland invariably catches them up. These unstable, inconclusive, self-divided texts carry traces of their authors' encounters with apparently insoluble problems in a highly charged historical context, in view of a starkly divided audience, from within an ambivalent relation to authorship. But these texts also inscribe the paradoxes and contradictions that have structured Anglo-Ireland from the start. They bear witness to the fact that these writers narrate that which has *never* had an answer to the question of itself, which has long struggled to generate viable self-definitions. As topic and source, subject and object, Anglo-Ireland spawns, then and now, dynamic narratives in an interrogatory mode.

But for all they share with their forebears, Bowen, Beckett, Keane, and their contemporaries wrote under different circumstances than those surrounding earlier Anglo-Irish writers.[9] Anglo-Ireland's twentieth-century displacements rendered its constitutive problems at once increasingly urgent and increasingly insoluble. The physical, political, and intellectual structures by which the Anglo-Irish tended to figure themselves and their place in the world collapsed; their provisional self-concepts, to which they perhaps clung the more fiercely because they were palpably provisional, were blasted at the root. Their master narratives and tribal myths revoked, twentieth-century writers might well have grown increasingly anxious to authenticate their culture of origin, to repair its relation to legitimacy and authority, and to continue the struggle to write it into history with a name of its own choosing that counters pejorative nationalistic terms.

But twentieth-century writers had less certain ground on which to stand than their forebears did, less raw material from which to cull a competing narrative. Having lost land, Big Houses, parliamentary power, and colonial status, they might have been less able than their ancestors were to *imagine* authority. And if these writers were driven to authenticate their beleaguered culture of origin, so depleted of power and place in the twentieth century, events might well have compelled them in radically different directions too. For as twentieth-century history revoked Anglo-Ireland's myths, it shook writers loose from their heritage with a violence their ancestors never suffered. Revealing incontrovertible cracks in their culture's founding and sustaining structures, history rubbed their noses in Anglo-Ireland's contingencies, requiring that they plumb them more deeply than their forebears—who could retreat to their houses, some money, social status—ever could. Such tensions and pressures, such dire need combined with such impossible odds—different less in kind, perhaps, than in degree from those that compelled earlier Anglo-Irish writers—helped push twentieth-century novelists to pose Anglo-Ireland's perennial "Who am I?" in a fashion that is exceptionally disrupted. This is fiction *in extremis*, a product of great cultural duress.

Ultimately, in this body of fiction, Anglo-Ireland proves not just a fraught social formation, both sinned against and sinning in the real world of imperial politics, but a vivid trope for the condition of ongoing debate, irremediable predicament, insoluble social, ontological, and perhaps finally existential paradox. Anglo-Ireland emerges from these narratives as a metaphor for the state of needing to ask but not being able to answer defining questions, the state of longing for but not being able to assert self-assured claims to identity, place, and value. Caught up in and helping to create a history that rejects its belief systems and its definitions of self and Other, Anglo-Ireland emerges, finally, as a figure resembling what we might call modernist consciousness: the state of becoming increasingly aware that culture and self are constructed in relation to competing constructions; the state of enduring a nagging sense of the temporality and circumstantiality of one's systems of value and belief; the state of feeling prodded to acknowledge that they are, as Roland Barthes would have it, not nature but myth (Barthes, 1972). Read this way, these narratives reach well beyond Anglo-Ireland, representing not just what happens in Anglo-Irish consciousness, or in political consciousness generally, as it reckons with its implication in a deeply flawed history. This fiction narrates the confrontation of consciousness with the paradoxes that construct human life in time: seeking sense in an enigmatic existence, seeking closure in relations personal, political, and intellectual, suffering and denying loss, craving stable identity in all these self-fracturing transactions.

3

To Tell and Not to Tell:
Molly Keane's *Time After Time*

A truth in art is that whose contradictory is also true.
—Oscar Wilde, "The Truth of Masks"

They make a story that seems to have no moral,
and that one cannot believe will ever have an end.
—Elizabeth Bowen, *Bowen's Court*

MOLLY KEANE (1904–1996) WROTE PROLIFICALLY ABOUT THE ANGLO-Ireland in which she was reared and which over the years she watched fade. The author of thirteen novels and five plays, Keane wrote her first novel, *The Knight of the Cheerful Countenance*, at seventeen. The long list that starts there ends with *Queen Lear* (1989), a vivid monument to the staying power, in imagination if not in fact, of the social formation in which Keane's novels are set. Anglo-Ireland was not Molly Keane's topic; it was her compulsion. Or as she put it, with characteristic self-denigration: "The awful thing is, I really haven't got much else to write about" (Kierstead 1986, 98).[1]

Keane's biography evokes some of the complexities of Anglo-Irishness that I trace in the preceding chapter. Born Mary Nesta Skrine in County Kildare, Keane was the third of five children. Her father, Walter Clarmont Skrine, was English. The twelfth child of a Somerset landowner, he lived for two decades on an Alberta cattle ranch bought for him by his family. In a 1986 interview with *The New Yorker*, Keane described her father in the equivocal language so common to discourse about Anglo-Ireland: "My father didn't know Ireland at all—he was thoroughly English—and no man ever got on better than he did in Ireland." "I suppose it was because he was so great about horses," she explained (Kierstead 1986, 99–100). Keane's mother, Agnes Shakespeare Higginson, was from County Antrim. "She belonged to the time of Yeats and those Gore-Booth Ladies," Keane recalled in 1982. "She was quite a good poet, really; . . . But she quit writing. She wrote her poetry when she was very young. After she married my father she wrote only critiques" (*Contemporary Authors,* 1985:265).

Keane's parents lived in Canada until the birth of their first child Susan in 1900. Then they moved to Ireland, to a County Wexford house named Ballyrankin, which they purchased from a Major Devereux. "Ballyrankin stood on the banks of the River Slaney," Keane recalled. "It was really awfully pretty. You reached it through a very long avenue, with a gate lodge at each end. And there were large, sort of parklike fields around us, with beautiful trees in them—really good trees—and a lovely stable yard, in that way people had then, built in a big oval adjoining the vast kitchen premises of the house" (Kierstead 1986, 99). In the kind of disorienting reversal we see again and again in *Time After Time* as in other Anglo-Irish fiction, Keane revealed, in the same interview: "It was a frightfully uncomfortable house. Terribly cold—the schoolroom was really awful. Chilblains. I had to share a bed with Susan. It was quite a big bedroom, and it was full of birdcages, and the mice were simply running around—they loved the birdseed. I'm sure it was rather unhealthy" (100).

Keane gives this archetypal account of Ballyrankin's torching: "I was just sixteen, so it must have been 1920. I wasn't there. None of us children were there. They came on a summer's night and banged on the big door, and burst their way in. They took my mother and father out of the house to a field, and put them there against a haystack so they could watch the burning. And they torched the house, and my father and mother sat there in their nightclothes watching it burn up with everything in it. It must have been pretty shocking" (Kierstead 1986, 99). After spending two years in the north thereafter, the Skrines returned to Wexford, where Keane's father bought "a rather smaller house" adjacent to where Ballyrankin had stood (99).

Like her mother, Keane "never had any education." "Only a frightfully clever girl went to Oxford; otherwise you learned from governesses, and one knew less than the last" (*Contemporary Authors,*

1985:265). But she was a talented horsewoman. As Alison Rimmer suggests: "In the field the women found all they otherwise lacked in their lives: the thrill of the hunt, the danger, achievement, exaltation" (Rimmer 1989, 379). Keane herself explained: "Excellence in the hunting field made a strong link in the chain of flirtation, courtship, and, hopefully, marriage, while a good swinging underhand service on the grass tennis courts considerably advanced a girl's prospects" (Keane 1991b, 140).

The genesis of Keane's first novel, *The Knight of the Cheerful Countenance*, has become legendary. She told one interviewer: "I suppose I was seventeen. And I was in bed [with an apparent case of tuberculosis], and I thought, oh well, I'll write a book, and I sort of wrote it under the bedclothes because, you know, writing books wasn't terribly well thought of for most purposes back then . . ." (Keane 1991a, 23). She went on to publish ten novels and five plays between 1928 and 1961. The plays, some of them written with her friend John Perry, were produced in London, directed by John Gielgud.[2]

Keane wrote her early novels, all of which have been reissued by Virago, under the name M. J. Farrell. When asked why she used a pen name Keane explained: "[I]t seems absolutely incomprehensible now, but in those days, in the kind of hunting and fishing and shooting background that I grew up in, anybody who had anything to do with the intelligentsia was out on a limb. People would have really avoided you. And when you're about twenty, the great thing is to have success with the fellows, isn't it? I used a pseudonym so that no one would know that I was writing" (*Contemporary Authors*, 1985:265). Even her family didn't know she was writing, and this even after several books; in fact, Keane recalled, "they were the last ones who knew" (Keane 1991a, 24). Asked how she chose "M. J. Farrell" she related: "I just went the furthest away from my name as I could. Terribly Irish name, terribly Irish, you know" (25).

After she and her husband met (at a Tipperary hunt ball) and married (in 1938), he ran his family's bacon business, while she cared for their two daughters at Belleville, his Waterford home. After his sudden death in 1946, Keane began what she called her "years on the breadline." She wrote two more novels and two plays, and then stopped writing. Twenty years later, when she was in her late seventies, Keane burst back on the scene with *Good Behaviour* (1981).[3] This widely acclaimed novel became a literary sensation, garnering admiring reviews, earning Keane membership in *Aosdàna*, and landing on the short list for the Booker Prize.[4] Two more novels followed: *Time After Time* (1983) and *Loving and Giving* (1988), which appeared in the United States as *Queen Lear* (1989).

As this biographical sketch suggests, Keane's work constitutes a rich site for exploring the ways in which gender fractures the mythical unity of Ascendancy culture—a topic that I will make focal in my discussion of Elizabeth Bowen's 1929 novel, *The Last September*.[5] My more central interest in Keane, and in *Time After Time* in particular, lies in this novel's exemplary status in the Anglo-Irish tradition of fiction. Though *Time After Time* is in some ways unrepresentative of novels in its tradition—written very late, from long retrospect, about long decline—it is a paradigmatic instance of the narrative tendencies that characterize Anglo-Irish fiction. Multivocal and multivalent, this novel constitutes a dynamic and indeterminant attempt to represent topics at the core of the Anglo-Irish problematic: land, property, interclass relations, authority, hierarchy, Irishness, Anglo-Irishness, and others. How shall I assess my home culture's systems of value and belief? How shall I account for the appropriation of Irish land? How shall I portray the relation of Anglo-Ireland to Ireland "proper"? In its agitated reckonings with such questions, *Time After Time* deserves sustained attention, providing as it does such a revealing frame for reading Anglo-Irish fiction.[6]

Keane's readers have tended to emphasize her novels' critical distance from Anglo-Ireland. Working from feminist theories of women's humor, Rachel Jane Lynch claims that Keane "displays and ridicules" Anglo-Ireland by way of "merciless" satire; "Laughter wins, because the world of Keane's fiction does not deserve to survive; we sense that Keane herself is bringing down her house, killing and burying a decaying microcosm with an overwhelming sense of relief" (Lynch 1996, 74, 77). Vera Kreilkamp opens her most recent discussion of Keane's fiction with this strong claim: "Molly Keane's great achievement as a novelist was to reject the nostalgia that is a major cultural production of a declining imperial state" (Kreilkamp 1992, 174). In Kreilkamp's view, Keane's last three novels "insistently reject the formulations of a lost organic cultural tradition," casting nostalgia as "the disease of victims who are trapped by delusions about the past" (174). Unlike Lynch, Kreilkamp does discern tonal instability, claiming, for instance, that "On occasion, Keane seems to replace one kind of nostalgia—for a coherently hierarchical society—with another, through her celebration of the sensuous texture of the gardens, architecture, and especially the food of the Big House" (175). But, Kreilkamp concludes, the late novels constitute a "devastating critique of Anglo-Irish culture" (187), a "fiercely corrosive dissection . . . With age, Keane achieved a chilling distance from her Anglo-Irish heritage" (182).[7]

One of *Time After Time*'s focal characters enacts in microcosm the indeterminate disposition toward home culture that I argue propels Anglo-Irish fiction and determines its dominant narrative mode. May Swift, as we shall see, is a chronic kleptomaniac. She lifts small objects from Harrod's, from supermarkets, even from the houses of friends. Undecided as to whether she should confess her "secret vagrancies" (Keane 1983, 132) to her visiting cousin Leda, May generates a brief text that at once reveals and conceals what she wishes and dreads to say. She tells Leda, "'I suppose I have a fairly good eye for porcelain, I've picked up some rather nice little pieces in my time.'" Keane's narrator comments shrewdly, "It was exciting to tell and not to tell" (134).

The narrator's formulation calls to mind the command, provided by the evocatively named Shreve, which provokes Quentin Compson to contemplate "the long unamaze" and generate his own agitated narrative of his own flawed culture in Faulkner's *Absalom, Absalom!* "*Tell about the South*," Shreve demands. "*What's it like there. What do they do there. Why do they live there. Why do they live at all*" (Faulkner 1936, 8, 174). Throughout *Time After Time*, Keane—like Quentin, like May—straddles a fence. Wondering "Shall I announce my flawed culture's 'vagrancies'? Shall I hold its secrets close?", she scrutinizes Anglo-Ireland critically and represents it sympathetically, chastizing its habits of mind while reproducing them herself. Alternately inscribing and retracting what she wishes and dreads to say, Keane vindicates and incriminates Anglo-Ireland, and evokes a broad swath of attitudes in between those extremes.

I

Time After Time is replete with many of the conventional Anglo-Irish literary motifs. It centers on a decaying estate and its eccentric, insular occupants: April, May, June and Jasper (Julius) Swift. The estate is the ramshackle Durraghglass, "built at the date when one of the marks of a gentleman's ownership, dividing his property from the vulgar public, was a long quietness of avenue" (Keane 1983, 19).

The Swift siblings, ranging in age from 64 to 74, face financial ruin, a nagging sense of purposelessness, and the weight of a painful past. The novel's dramatic tension is generated by the arrival of the Swifts' half-Austrian, half-Jewish cousin Leda, who comes to Durraghglass hoping to simulate, with old Jasper, the illicit childhood affair she had with the Swifts' father, her Uncle Valentine, many years ago. Leda wreaks havoc. Her machinations in pursuit of her anachronistic goal prove brutal. But she also proves a somewhat vitalizing force, churning up for the Swifts a modicum of desire and change. Each of the Swifts' static, well-ordered lives takes on a new shape by the novel's end. But none has been changed utterly.

Time After Time sometimes tells Anglo-Ireland's "vagrancies" with zeal, displaying a range of its values, beliefs, and practices for our critical scrutiny. Many fall under the umbrella of what Elizabeth Bowen called the habit "of not knowing" (Bowen 1929a, 57)—what V. S. Pritchett (reviewing Good Behaviour and Time After Time) labeled "the habit of euphemism and evasion," "the game of manners" (Pritchett 1984, 7). Keane herself described the constricting politeness and unthinking equanimity of her beleaguered bourgeois culture this way: "Things go on; things are not talked about" (Contemporary Authors, 1985:265). Whether the "habit of not knowing" is, as some students of Anglo-Ireland have argued, an extension of Anglo-Ireland's insulation from the Catholic majority, or a function of Anglo-Ireland's characteristic inability to face alarming political realities, Keane does not speculate. In fact, unlike Bowen, Keane does not explicitly associate the habit of mind with Anglo-Irishness. Time After Time casts it, like other Anglo-Irish proclivities, as a private family affair or, as May calls her kleptomania, a "small private guilt." It's just the way the Swifts are. Although Time After Time is in many ways more severe and in all respects less polite than The Last September, Keane is less explicit than Bowen in her condemnations of Anglo-Ireland per se. Keane narrates Anglo-Ireland more metaphorically.[8]

The habit of not knowing spawns, in the Swifts, behavior ranging from the comical, to the irritating, to the destructive, to the inhumane. The deceased matriarch, Violet Swift, was the habit's consummate practitioner. Like many characters in Anglo-Irish fiction, she refused to heed matters of vulgar money. Her children "must have only the best, and the best cost money," though "[i]n spending money and selling off land when the banks got nasty, she was regardless of future years" (Keane 1983, 46). Jasper recalls "the place as it used to be, fully staffed in house and gardens and farm, losing money year upon year while a full social life continued undisturbed" (12). Violet Swift also denied her children's disabilities. April is almost deaf; May lacks three and a half fingers on her right hand; Jasper lost an eye when June accidentally shot him when they were children; June is dyslexic. When they were young, "an obstinate mist of love clouded over their disabilities, accepting them and accepting an impotence towards any change in their condition. Mummie had indulgence for everything. From Baby June's dyslexia ('she'll outgrow it, darling'), past Jasper's mortifying eye, and beyond their father's tragic accidental death, she never yielded in her over-looking" (102). She shrouds everything, her husband's infidelity, even her own cancer, in euphemism and silence. [9]

Violet Swift teaches her children well. With the notable exception of June, they live by her example. The deaf April converses as if she hears what others say, making for some hilarious dialogue. Jasper covers his "filthy" eye socket with a patch, which he removes only when behind his locked bedroom door. And "Nothing," Keane writes, "was beyond [May's] will to prove super-normal dexterity" (Keane 1983, 16). She works obsessively at handcrafts, "smother[ing her hand] with her industries" (154). And with petty thievery—"her ultimate protest against her infirmity" (132). Like their mother, the Swifts deny all that is painful and unpleasant, particularly the past. Jasper articulates this motto: "'Oh, never look back, . . . Keep yourself up to date if you can'" (61). June is the only Swift to defy this motto, to the others' disgust. When she voices her memories, especially of their mother, whose long ago death still causes anguish, they unanimously condemn her "poor taste."

The standard of good taste is another component of familial and cultural belief that Keane indicts. She launches her most sustained critique in Jasper, the standard's most vocal apologist. It is one of his worst moments when, hoping that cousin Leda will refrain from talking about her dark past, he calls the Nazi camps in which they all presumed she had died "embarrassing" (Keane 1983, 87). In Jasper, Keane shows how the standard of taste can reduce concentration camps and picking at your food to one dead level. No standard of value at all, it can in fact occlude, or mask the lack of, moral judgment, as in Keane's dramatization of May's final theft. Trying to flee a shop after stealing a porcelain rabbit, May notices "that a very new type of lock had been fitted to the old shop door, in place of the original heavy mortice. In very poor taste, too, she considered, before calling out in her clear upper-class voice, 'Would someone, please, open this door'" (226–27, italics Keane's).

In addition to critiquing such bourgeois standards, *Time After Time* refuses to live by them, rubbing readers' noses in facts Anglo-Irish propriety would repress, thereby revealing its repressiveness. Keane inscribes what the habit of not knowing and the standard of good taste would erase. For instance, she places economic realities center stage. The Swifts' accounts are in the red; Jasper doesn't know how the family would survive should the moneyed April, who pays to stay at Durraghglass, decide to leave. Keane unveils the family's sexual secrets, such as Valentine Swift's liaison with his young niece, and the sexual escapades of April's husband. Violet Swift had admired April's husband as "a man from the right family, popular in the Regiment, who went well to hounds"; now that he is dead, April values her bodily autonomy and her freedom to read Jane Austen, "less for pleasure than as a counteraction to those French books and Chinese and Egyptian prints and pictures which Barry liked her to study before he tried to follow out their instructions and illustrations in bed" (Keane 1983, 49–50).

But Keane's most potent affronts to good taste come in the form of her insistent focus on the body and its functions. Vomit, spit, excrement, urine, flatulence—all figure prominently in this novel. In unforgivingly vivid descriptions, Keane's characters are emphatically embodied. Leda has a "heavy undisciplined body" and "swollen ankles that made her shoes strain and tighten at the insteps" (Keane 1983, 97). April "pour[s] her tubes of bosoms into the cups provided for them at considerable expense" (23). Chain-smoking May has a persistent smoker's cough; hair "the same grey as cigarette ash and stained with nicotine like her fingers" surrounds her "cheesy-looking face" (25, 26). June "was the shape and weight of a retired flat race jockey—too heavy for her height" (10). The characters' disabilities strengthen Keane's emphasis on the body, as do her detailed accounts of their pets' sex lives and smells, which highlight the ties that bind these Anglo-Irish men and women to beasts.

Needless to say, Keane's focus on the body challenges the myth of essential Anglo-Irish grace that Yeats, among others, sometimes promoted. If Anglo-Ireland has a body, as *Time After Time* insists it does, then stereotypical associations of Anglo-Ireland with "civilization"—the ideological opposite of categories like "nature" and "the body"—

do not hold. And if Anglo-Ireland has the body *Time After Time* says it does (a urinating, defecating, decaying body), associations of Anglo-Ireland with inherent refinement collapse, urging concomitant notions of an essentially bestial Ireland to crumble with them.[10]

Indeed, as Ellen O'Brien argues, Keane's representation of the body and its functions implicates Anglo-Ireland in Bakhtin's grotesque, Kristeva's abject: "that which disturbs identity, system, order. What does not respect borders, positions, rules" (Kristeva 1982, 4), and what thereby expresses "the danger to identity that comes from without: the ego threatened by the non-ego, society threatened by its outside, life by death" (71). Keane's bodies manifest Lacan's "Real," which (in the words of Slavoj Žižek) constitutes "corporeal contingency" and "logical contingency," providing "a shock of a contingent encounter . . .; a traumatic encounter which ruins the balance of the symbolic universe of the subject" (Žižek 1989, 171). In "present[ing] the Anglo-Irish ideal beset by bodily abjection," O'Brien concludes, "Keane revises the Big House genre so that the fall transpires not because of outside forces or new ideologies, but because the Anglo-Irish, despite their facade of rituals and props, embodied the Real all along" (E. O'Brien 1999, 44, 40).

Keane further denaturalizes the idea of innate Anglo-Irish grace by displaying the labor that Anglo-Irish myth denies. Refinement is manufactured, Keane insists. April's ageless beauty is the product of exercise, deprivation, and other "tortures." "She considered and pushed and moulded every garment to her body's best advantage" (Keane 1983, 23). Her clothes "had ease and length and fullness" because "Some contrivance nipped them always in the right and prettiest directions" (5–6).

If the feminine ideal of beauty rests on work, so does the day-to-day operation of the Anglo-Irish estate. In the old days, we learn, the estate's centers of labor were invisible. "Far along a driveway the farmyard was held at a distance from the more civilized policies of Durraghglass" (Keane 1983, 18); "kitchens in the afternoon held their distance. Cooks and kitchenmaids used to tidy up. . . . Not any more, naturally. Times change" (4). But sites such as these provide the setting for much of this novel's action. Unable to pay servants, the Swifts do the work themselves. Jasper cooks, hauling meal after meal to the dining room, hauling dirty dishes to the kitchen for washing. Baby June mucks out stables, gathers eggs, births piglets and trains horses, while May clears tables, makes beds, airs rooms.

Only April, with her money, is exempt from labor.[11] The house that Yeats wanted to portray as a symbol of "traditional sanctity and love-liness" and that Bowen tried to see as an embodiment of "the European idea— . . . what was humanistic, classic and disciplined" (Bowen 1940, 27) is, in *Time After Time*, a functioning workplace de-manding long hours of hard labor.[12] Keane goes so far as to display its plumbing: "A lavatory clattered and shushed. Obedient to its plug and chain the contents went down the perpendicular drain to the open water [of the river]. Faint pieces of paper floated among the starred weeds and iris leaves of flags. Very fat trout swam there" (Keane 1983, 22).

Much of this novel's comedy derives from this tension: the Swifts struggle to uphold their mother's values—denial, taste, civility—while behaving in ways that defy them. In a typical scene, Jasper appears in the dining room one evening, ready to serve dinner. "Waiting courteously for [his sisters] to pass through he looked dis-tinguished and charming, standing there in his blue velvet dinner jacket, white silk shirt and dark foulard scarf, pulled through a signet ring—all a bit greasy and spotted from kitchen work." He serves a pigeon pie that he cooked in the same oven June used to in-cubate a newborn piglet. The Swifts feed in silence: "The pie was ex-cellent beyond words. The pigeon breasts married beautifully to the beef from the dogs' dinners, the old rashers of bacon and the eggs. A pile of purple sprouting kale sat on the hot-plate to one side of the pie and pommes-de-terre Anna on the other—all three dishes largely depleted when the ladies had helped themselves" (Keane 1983, 30). The passage's tone, governed by the ideal of grace and re-finement, proceeds oblivious to content, displaying at once the ob-solescence and the extraordinary tenacity of Anglo-Irish systems of value and belief, as well as their dangerous power to mask vivid con-tradictions.

Such moments in *Time After Time* accrue into an exposé of Anglo-Ireland that is both broad and biting. But this is just part of Keane's story. Her novel does not cohere as unequivocal critique or stable satire. Consider Keane's own bad manners. Her energetic focus on the body calls to mind the behavior of an adolescent who deliber-ately misbehaves in order simultaneously to refuse and reinforce parental authority. Keane's critique of Anglo-Irish culture signifies more than simple rejection of that culture, expressing too, as we shall see, a continued and complicated bond.

II

I have been considering Keane's inclination to tell about Anglo-Ireland. In exploring her companion inclination *not* to tell—the impulse to endorse, embrace, and enact home culture—I will focus first on tensions, even contradictions, in attitude and perspective that span *Time After Time*. Such tensions emerge with particularly expressive power in two arenas: in Keane's renderings of her Anglo-Irish characters, and in her representations of habits of mind (other than taste, denial, and so on) that are central to the Anglo-Irish problematic.

Reviewers have commented on the disconcerting generic and tonal tensions that often characterize Keane's novels. Mary Breen asserts (overstating the matter, I think): "The most difficult task when discussing Keane is to find a genre into which she can fit comfortably" (Breen 1997, 206). As Ann Owens Weekes observes, Keane's novels "jolt the reader with their mix of the mundane and the shocking, the comic and the tragic" (Weekes 1997, 151). James Lasdun writes: "part of the charm of [*Time After Time*] is that just when you think you have the measure of it you find you've been outwitted" (Lasdun 1984, 73); just when you think you have come to a relatively stable conclusion, you find the text qualifying, or supplementing, or overturning it.

Keane's characterizations are implicated in—indeed, dominant carriers of—this indeterminacy. Taken together or considered one by one, *Time After Time*'s Swifts elicit conspicuously mixed reader responses. As if drawn from the cold distance of a satirist *and* the sympathetic proximity of an authorized biographer, they seem both broadly rendered caricature and compassionately rendered character. Neither perspective finally coheres.[13] Vera Kreilkamp provides this nuanced description of this attitudinal indeterminacy: "in spite of Keane's chilling tone towards the Swifts, she writes with a curious affection for the very nasty characters she creates and for the dying culture she dissects with such pleasure. . . . Although amused and sometimes appalled by the Swifts, Keane never allows herself to hate or pity them" (Kreilkamp 1987, 460). As Ann Hulbert observes: "The brittle caricatures are still capable of surprising themselves, Keane convinces us—and curiosity thus roused can lead unexpectedly near to sympathy" (Hulbert 1984, 40).[14]

It is worth examining this aspect of the novel in some detail, for it exemplifies the divided and uncertain sympathies, the anarchy in the mind and in the heart, that is written out so frequently in Anglo-Irish fiction.

The Swifts are not an appealing bunch. Hopelessly divided by old jealousies and hurts, they bicker endlessly: over whose dog smells worst, over which one of them will drive their one car. They are all grotesquely devoted to their pets: the women to their dogs, which fill "the empty places of lovers and babies" (Keane 1983, 132), and Jasper to his cat, Mister Minkles. *Time After Time* might be read as a sequel to Bowen's *The Last September.* If Lois Farquar and Laurence Naylor are anxious, in 1920, to find a viable locus of meaning in the face of Anglo-Ireland's demise, the Swifts have found meanings: paltry ones. April is obsessed with health food and fine clothes; May serves as the self-important President of the Flower Arrangers Guild, and is devoted to handcrafts: a "deviser and maker and restorer of so many lifeless pretty things" (132); Jasper plans an exotic wood. With the exception of June's farm work, the Swifts' activities can, from one point of view, seem little more than petty distractions from past pains and present anxieties.

But *Time After Time* also casts these pastimes as sympathetic, if not a touch grand, insofar as they function as hedges against the vacuum left by the disappearance of the world in which the Swifts were reared. Keane's detailed descriptions reveal something lovely about the exquisite Italian fabrics April cherishes. April's girlishness is grotesque, but she does have admirable style. Jasper's horticultural expertise, though pointless, can, still, impress. And his cookery, despite its origins in his grimy, stinking kitchen, is a product of care and skill.[15]

Keane plants seeds of compassion in readers, which likewise prevent us from viewing the Swifts as merely absurd. We learn that all were subject to wrenching rejections and betrayals as children—the sad subtext of the petty arguments and competitions that divide them today. Their disabilities, as Keane represents them, generate additional sympathy from readers, though not among the Swifts themselves. Moreover, the novel's contrapuntal structure—which shows us the Swifts alone, the Swifts used and abused by cousin Leda, and then again the Swifts alone—varies reader response to its focal characters. If the Swifts can seem laughable when going about their business alone, once the Machiavellian Leda arrives, that changes. Leda generates feeling for and even among the Swifts. Under Leda's siege, they appear vulnerable—even (comparatively, at least) noble. Their good behavior, so ridiculously evasive in some contexts, appears a sign of admirable self-possession when compared to Leda's conduct; when they see Leda off, their restrained civility is a welcome relief from her hideous spitefulness. Leda's threatening, brutalizing presence thus precipitates in readers an impulse to champion the Swifts, an impulse echoing what Keane herself seems to feel for Anglo-Ireland when she indicts it in her text. These and other uncertainties inherent in and generated by Keane's labile characterizations express the nature of the project of narrating Anglo-Ireland, evoking both the difficulties of giving "Anglo-Irishness" conclusive narrative form, and the historical indeterminacy of Anglo-Ireland "itself."

If *Time After Time* gives readers unsettled portraits of its Anglo-Irish characters, it offers similarly undecided representations of habits of mind and systems of value historically central to Anglo-Irish culture. At times, as I argue above, the novel unmasks and refuses ancestral assumptions. But at times it embraces them. And sometimes it oscillates inconclusively between these attitudinal poles, so that the novel constitutes and is constituted by a range of incongruous perspectives.

One of the most striking manifestations of Keane's oscillating point of view emerges in her handling of a stock feature of Anglo-Irish fiction: the nostalgic *ubi sunt* motif mourning the lost past and comparing current decline to former grandeur. At its most typical, the convention calls for a character or narrator to contemplate some aspect of a run-down estate—the shabby drawing room, the untended demesne—and reflect somberly upon its decay. At the beginning of *Time After Time*'s second chapter, Keane plays mischievously with this literary cliché. After beginning in a manner consistent with the convention, Keane goes on to dispel the conventional perspective by yoking it to anomalous content, wryly subverting the elegiac contrast between now and then in parody. We have seen part of this passage before:

Late in the evening there came a civilised pause before dinner. Servantless and silent, the house waited for the proper ceremony it had always expected and still, in a measure, experienced. The utter cold of the spring light shrank away from the high paned windows. A steep distance below the house the river gave up an evening daze of fog. A lavatory clattered and shushed. Obedient to its plug and chain the contents went down the perpendicular drain to the open water. . . . Once there had been an open, not a covert, drain. Every morning housemaids lifted a grille and sluiced buckets into a sloped stone spout from which the doings of the night flowed down their paved way to the river. Not any more, of course. Those were the days of tin baths in front of bedroom fires, of mahogany commodes containing pos or bidets, commodes with three steps for the ascent to bed—the days of lots of money. (Keane 1983, 22)

Elsewhere, though, Keane's ironic distance from the conventionally wistful point of view is less complete. Take, for example, May's extended recollection of her mother's garden. For much of this long passage, the narrative seems to join in May's nostalgia; Keane seems with May to celebrate Violet Swift's refusal of "the present snobbish form of gardening, of balancing and landscaping even a small area. She planted exactly where her plants would do best." The energy and detail of the prose suggest that May's impassioned recollection is, also, Keane's (she was in fact an avid gardener). Yet toward the passage's end, Keane dispels the elegiac mood. She names the time that May recalls "Better Days," objectifying the nostalgic cast of mind and chiding it with capital letters. But she then goes on to recall, from within the nostalgic point of view once more: "There was little or no planting of shrubs round a country house. Instead there were acres of mown grass; a pony, shod in leather, for their mowing; wide dappling of tree shadows smooth on their surfaces. The gravel sweeps were weedless and stone pineapples had not toppled off the pillars of the steps going down to the river. It was definite as any photograph to May" (Keane 1983, 119–20). And it is, by way of Keane's narrative, now definite to us. The passage brings Anglo-Ireland to life, rescuing it from time and loss.

Keane sometimes writes with what seems undiluted elegiac feeling. Just three pages before her cheeky comparison of past and present plumbing, Keane describes June's daily walks up and down the Durraghglass drive:

June walked the distance, back and forwards several times a day. She was familiar with its potholes and long, stony depths and she ignored the riot of briars and nettles on its once orderly verges. Close to the back of the house, a different and more precise archway from that of the farmyard led to the stableyard; a now derelict clock in the archway's face had once told the time. It still looked pretty. The stableyard was built round rather a grand semi-circle. Loose-boxes, weedy cobblestones to their doors, were empty—all but one. June's brown hens scratched about on the wide central circle of grass round which horses had been ridden and led and walked and jogged, or made to stand as they should, to be admired by afternoon luncheon guests on Sundays. (Keane 1983, 19–20)

As elsewhere in the novel, point of view is hard to locate. Is this June's train of thought? Is it authorial? Is Keane critically dramatizing a frame of mind? Is she enacting it herself? Might she be doing both? Such questions thwart a reader's conclusive assessment of the passage, preventing one from determining the text's relation to this literary convention and, by extension, the culture from which it grows. What a reader *can* conclude is this: like the finale of May's remembrance of gardens past, the passage recreates the past and invites the reader into the nostalgic point of view. Of course, nostalgia on Keane's part is not remarkable, given her roots in Anglo-Irish culture. What *is* remarkable is that her novel also contains passages like that parody on sewage, and passages like those repudiating other Anglo-Irish habits of mind. It is a striking disjunction.[16]

If Keane's handling of the *ubi sunt* motif evokes a struggle to fix her relationship to Anglo-Irish literary culture, her handling of landscape suggests a struggle that may have been more intense. At times, Keane represents the land with brutal realism, challenging the sentimentalized view embodied in May's trite tweed pictures of a pretty cottage here, a ruined tower there. As the local antique (and marijuana) dealer points out, May's pictures are "'perfect tourist stuff'" (Keane 1983, 230), calling to mind the most saccharine failings of the Celtic Twilight. Keane distances herself from such failings in, for instance, this wry description of the Durraghglass farmyard: "The mountainy fields rose quietly outside it towards gorse and heather. Below its nearly slateless cow-sheds and tumbling iron-gated piggeries, a steep slope drained liquids from all ordure down to the pretty river" (18).

But Keane also composes romantic portraits of the countryside, the farmyard, and the work done there. For instance, carrying "three white eggs, misted in their own freshness," the Swifts' Irish farmhand, Christy Lucey, walks toward June, his hands "cupped and

stretched in front of his advancing steps . . . as though he approached a temple with an offering" (Keane 1983, 90). Often, the
farmyard is less a vivid reality than, for June, a quiet refuge from the
"fractious living" of the house (29) and, for Keane, a trope for primal peace. Keane's representations of the farm oscillate, making it,
at times, a site of grueling, stinking labor and, at others, a site of
sacral presence.

This tension reflects more than the debatable aesthetics and thematics of landscape. It reflects the historical Anglo-Irish relation to
land and that relation's perceived impact on Anglo-Irish legitimacy
and identity. Representing the Irish landscape is a charged project
for the Anglo-Irish writer. Metaphorize, romanticize, or idealize the
land, and the writer risks enacting a colonialist's hopeless alienation
from it, or whitewashing the harsh material realities of it, or co-opt-
ing what has been cast as the native Irish relation to it. Write realistically, and the writer risks alienation from Anglo-Ireland which, as
Time After Time shows, did not typically acknowledge harsh realities,
and often represented place as a metaphor for its political power.
Caught between the rock and the hard place bequeathed it by Irish
history, Keane's narrative does not finish the narrative business of
formulating a unified and coherent representation of landscape. It
remains in search of one.

III

In addition to such novel-wide tensions and inconsistencies, *Time
After Time* contains discrete sites at which Keane's encounter with her
cultural inheritance reveals itself at its most intense. The figure of
May Swift is one such site. The most willful of all the Swifts, the most
insistent on order, obedience, discipline, and control, May seems
closely associated with Ireland's conquerors in Keane's mind.

Not unlike the Anglo-Ireland I describe in my opening chapter,
May exhibits a tyrannical will, along with its shaky underside. We are
reminded throughout the novel that her brave shows of confidence
mask a fundamental lack: "Only May could guess at the cringing second self she must defend so long as they both should live" (Keane
1983, 70). Also like Anglo-Ireland, May is precariously placed. Her
rights of residence at Durraghglass are tenuous, since she con-
tributes less to the estate's upkeep than her brother and sisters do;
Jasper confides to Leda, "'April pays quite a bit. June works like a

slave.'" But May? "'Don't let's talk about May'" (140). May's kitschy tweed pictures call to mind a conqueror's stereotypically distorted understanding of a conquered land. Made not just of tweed, but of bits and pieces of the countryside itself (heather, bird feathers, snail shells), these pictures entail an erroneous imaginative appropriation of the landscape, and a trivializing physical appropriation as well.

Of course, the most remarkable of May's exercises of will is her kleptomania. Her flower arrangements, china restorations, and tweed pictures give her comfort, but "[b]eyond these things it was her secret vagrancies that lent her a power outside herself," Keane writes, "a power that she accepted questionless. It was her ultimate protest and defence against her infirmity" (Keane 1983, 132).

Keane's etiology of May's kleptomania is revealing. May starts stealing at age seven, "when Leda and April shut her out from their giggling best-friendship." Jealous of their intimacy, May "hung and listened on the outskirts of their talk, longing to know more about the cream cakes and chocolate of Austria" about which Leda raves. One day, her longing reaches a decisive pitch. Hiding in her "secret house" in the laurel grove for a "quick out-of-doors pee," May peers out at the two girls playing with Baby June on the lawn. "Far off in her laurels, May was possessed by an immense wish to join them, welcome or not, to belong to the group so near and so divided from her." Her passion for inclusion is so intense that she rushes out of the bushes, forgetting to pull up her underwear. The other girls see her and laugh. "Trembling in a hot brew of embarrassment, May went back again to hide in her dark house. . . . Her love changed, a septic wound remaining. Hidden and comfortless, she watched them through the laurel leaves, heads together, talking, talking." As they leave the lawn, May sees something fall from June's hand. Later, she scours the site and discovers a small toy fox, "Leda's mascot and treasure," which she then buries in her kitchen garden. "When she had buried Fritz-Max-Hans she felt better, stronger. Even tonight she was happy to remember she had yielded nothing" (Keane 1983, 40–42).

Given this novel's Anglo-Irish provenance, it is impossible not to associate May's chronic kleptomania with the historical conquest of Irish land—an association that this important scene corroborates. Colonizer-like, May feels an outcast in her own home. Her relation to the exclusive group on the lawn is figured in terms that echo the historical relation of Ireland and Anglo-Ireland: two groups "so near and so divided." May experiences her exclusion from the other group as an exclusion from their talk, as Anglo-Ireland (and other colonizing cultures) often expressed its distance from those whose land it appropriated: in terms of linguistic difference; elsewhere in the novel Keane herself expresses difference in just these terms, contrasting Irish women's "sweet Irish voices" to "Lady Alys's voice, from a different Irish world" (Keane 1983, 76).[17] When May tries to join the others she is repulsed, prompting her expression of a complex love/hate that echoes the colonialist's stereotypical mixture of longing and loathing for a conquered population.

May's repulse takes an intriguing form. She is rejected when April and Leda see what she believes she should hide; she is rejected when that most abject portion of her body has been revealed.[18] Of course, Anglo-Irish men and women would have felt that they had much to hide from Ireland's indigenous population, on whose conquered land they prospered. Keane here imagines for May a nightmarish exposure before that group to which it is most painful, most lethal, for her to be exposed. The scene thus at once reveals and conceals a powerful sense of guilt regarding the Irish Other, a powerful anxiety about the revelation of that guilt, and, with the logic of nightmare, a powerful anxiety that the Other already sees.

Revealed, May retreats. It is significant that May emerges from and returns to what Keane calls a dark and secret house. Anglo-Irish history and fiction repeat this image of the protective house from which the Anglo-Irish rule and in which they are imprisoned, as well as this scene's pattern of departure and anxious return. And it is significant, finally, that the career of petty thievery launched by this furtive plantation garners May "a colony" of china rabbits (Keane 1983, 27). In this scene, then, Keane imagines Anglo-Irish history in terms of a painful childhood hurt with which the reader is hard pressed not to empathize. And the scene sympathetically reenacts a time-worn conception of Anglo-Ireland's sociohistorical status as the wronged and wounded outsider.

But this is not Keane's only word on May and the social formation she evokes. Keane's point of view toward May, as toward all the Swifts, shifts. Needless to say, it's hard to like May. She is hypocritically self-righteous and pathetically self-promoting. We cringe with the ladies of the Countrywomen's Association: " 'Poor Miss Swift— she shouldn't take it so seriously'" (Keane 1983, 77). Her thefts are outrageously audacious and miserably petty. Her will is appalling, her tweed pictures horrible. But as in Keane's portraits of all the Swifts, her persistent representation of May's pain takes the edge off our dislike. And Leda's presence, particularly her brutal revelation of May's kleptomania, enhances our sympathy, as does that revelation's aftermath, in which we watch May struggle to regain her balance after having had her primary self-definition destroyed.

Along with her sympathetic etiology of May's kleptomania, Keane offers sympathetic diagnoses. Seeming to want to explain if not to justify it, Keane writes again and again of its psychological function. It is a sublimation of May's sexual energy, "taking the place of wild moments she had never known" (Keane 1983, 164). It is a function of "the wish and impulse to assert herself dangerously against a loveless world." "[H]er nerve and dexterity left her equal again with others. She would be more than equal—triumphant, heedless of anybody's love, in a haven of fulfillment" (74). Without her secret knowledge of her secret thefts, Keane writes, May is "entirely disestablished. . . . She was back where the efforts had started, in the time when they fed her with a spoon until she was six; when Jasper, so much younger, had his own fork and silver knife" (177). Keane casts kleptomania as the foundation of May's terribly tenuous adult identity.

Keane's representation of May's kitchen garden enriches her narrative conflation of May and Anglo-Ireland. Recall that it is in this garden that May buried (planted) that first theft, Leda's fox. As if that act somehow marked this plot of land as hers, the garden becomes May's one sovereign realm:

> [May] resented the present overgrowth and hated the ash saplings taking over the tennis courts—like letting in the tinkers, she thought.
>
> The kitchen garden was a different matter—it was enclosed. Ivy might cloak and drag at its walls, docks and nettles invade its distances, but those parts maintained by her vigilance were May's thrust into a conceit of happiness. Every foot of the walled wilderness that could be kept under cultivation was of vital importance to May. It was her province. She fought for its maintenance with all the strength of her immense will. The rotations of peas, beans, spinach; the triumphant hatchings in battered frames of new potatoes for Easter; the continual supplies of parsley, chives, mints (in choice varieties), thymes, oregano and basil were the successes May brought to birth, properly in their seasons or their perpetuities.

... The lock on the wooden door had a big smooth keyhole and the easily turned key made its own possessive sound as May turned it and went in, like a robin or a fox, to possess her territory. (Keane 1983, 120–21)

The passage is rich in historical undertones. May's garden emerges as a figure of a walled estate or the Old English Pale, that varying portion of territory around Dublin that the Anglo-Normans at least nominally conquered and governed. Like them, May fights back the apparent disorder that threatens beyond the Pale. Like them, she orders nature, makes it productive, subdues it to what she considers civilized use. Keane celebrates May's conquest. Clearly Keane loves gardening, and relishes her long list of vegetables and herbs. The passage's jubilant tone (May's "hatchings" are "triumphant," her crops "successes") seems at least in part authorial. The repetition of the affirmative trope of birth, like the comparison of May to bird and beast, naturalizes May's cultivation of her territory. Keane here provides an image that competes with her critical representation of Ireland as Anglo-Ireland's tweed picture: here, Ireland prospers as Anglo-Ireland's fertile garden.

But complicating this reading is the fact that here, as elsewhere, it is not certain whose perspective the passage transcribes. As is often the case, it is difficult to determine where authorial narration leaves off and indirect discourse begins. Perhaps the celebration is May's, a celebration which Keane is exposing to critique. Certainly Keane's appreciation of May's produce is countered by distaste for "her immense will" and critical distance from her extreme responses (resentment of overgrowth, hatred for ash saplings, the idea of ivy dragging and nettles invading). Perhaps we are meant to smile at the grotesque image of potatoes as triumphant hatchings. We certainly flinch at May's comparison of invading overgrowth to "tinkers."[19] And if the images of robin and fox naturalize May's relation to this land, the image of the fox also implies a rapacity carrying distinctly imperial overtones. Once more, Keane's portrait of May *qua* Anglo-Ireland refuses to cohere.

Christy Lucey's appearance in May's garden augments this irresolution. Throughout *Time After Time*, May voices colonialist assessments of this Irish Catholic farmhand: he's shiftless, he's wily, and he's not worth the salary June pays him. Having persuaded June to let him work for her one afternoon, May enters her garden looking for him. "As she expected, Christy Lucey, the unwilling slave, was dreaming over a barrow-load of manure." She instructs him to dig a trench deeper. "'Excuse me, Miss, but I'm killed from digging,' Christy stated gently." As hungry for obedience as ever, May insists, "'Dig deeper, Christy, and don't fill in the manure until I tell you.'" Not surprisingly, "Christy looked less than gentle as he took up his spade. You couldn't satisfy that one, he thought and wished that he was out schooling the Wild Man [June's horse] with Miss Baby to instruct and admire him. Even cleaning out the pigs without a vigilant eye on his short rest periods would be preferable to the heavy employment of this long afternoon" (Keane 1983, 121).

This representation of Christy and his relationship to May is ambiguous. On the one hand, it seems to validate the stereotype of the dreamy, lazy Irishman; it seems to condescend to Christy's unthinking preference for June's admiration over May's "heavy employment." On the other hand, his recalcitrance seems justified. He's right; you can't satisfy May. And it makes sense for a "slave" to be "unwilling." Perhaps, on balance, Keane here chastizes May for her treatment of this Irish man who works her land against his will. But as in the garden passage quoted above, the possibility of competing readings remains. Does Keane's portrait of Christy demystify imperialist attitudes? Does it perpetuate them?

Keane's representation of May's final theft is crucial in establishing and communicating the complexity of her attitude toward May and, by extension, Anglo-Ireland. As the theft approaches, Keane seems to verge beyond explaining May's kleptomania to justifying it. She calls it "an adventurous travesty of dull morals," as if May were a rebellious challenger of convention, as if stealing porcelain rabbits paralleled writing *Time After Time* (223). She labels it a function of May's aesthetic sense, "her feeling for all pretty things and the importance of their preservation" (Keane 1983, 223). Keane goes so far as to justify not just May's thefts but her characteristic failure to admit them, even to herself: "she was unconsciously arrogant in her lack of repentance: who repents adventure?" (223).

Perhaps Keane's explanations verge toward justifications here because it is here that May gets caught. Perhaps they do so because it is here that Keane makes explicit the charged issue at stake in her representation of May's kleptomania, despite May's and perhaps Keane's effort to call it a "small private guilt." Through a two-way mirror, shop owner Ulick Uniacke watches May shoplift a porcelain rabbit. While Ulick maintains his good manners during most of the subsequent confrontation, he refuses to overlook May's crime. After whittling away at May's denials, he retrieves the stolen piece, and insists on searching May's bag. "'Let go,' she ordered, 'at once. Everything in this basket is my own private property.'" Ulick then names the explosive topic to which May's kleptomania alludes: "'Our ideas on private property don't quite match up'" (Keane 1983, 229).

Keane keeps our attitude toward May characteristically unsettled for a while. Ulick's frankness is refreshing. It can seem as if May is finally getting what she deserves. But as in her encounters with Leda, May also looks painfully vulnerable:

> May loosed her grip on the bag. She bent her head. Her need for a cigarette was beyond endurance. And, at this moment of her greatest need, her hand failed her. Her thumb and finger were shaking so shamefully they were past any obedience; they could not open her cigarette case; it was as if their life was ending. She laid her cramped hand on the edge of the table and stared at it, and touched it with her left hand, inattentive to what Ulick meant to do to her, or say to her. Or say to others. (Keane 1983, 230)

When, after this passage, Ulick's politeness turns to glib mockery, sympathy shifts decisively from him to May, who appears his helpless victim.

May's capture at Ulick's completes the process that Leda's betrayal of May begins: it destroys May's capacity to deny her kleptomania. It also forces her to acknowledge her disability: "She laid her cramped hand on the edge of the table and stared at it, and touched it with her left hand." It is important that it is both criminality and disability that Keane has May acknowledge in this climactic scene. For her criminality we probably condemn May. But with her disability, as Keane represents it here, we probably sympathize. By insisting that we see May's hand—which (Keane has emphasized) May conceives as the primary source of her need to steal—as a point of excruciating vulnerability in this May's direst, most dramatically guilty moment, Keane tempers reader condemnation of May's thievery.

But this is not *Time After Time*'s final word on May, either. To paraphrase James Lasdun, just when you think you have the measure of this character, you find you need to refine it, again. For one might read the remainder of May's career as an allegory of Anglo-Irish redemption. After witnessing her crime and holding her accountable,

Ulick offers May a job in his restoration business, which she accepts. May's employment is part of a broader trend in the novel. In a series of parodically comedic endings, *Time After Time* provides all the Swifts with new companions and occupations. Jasper has Brother Declan and their horticultural plans, June has a new farmhand, the "wild tinker boy." April, thinking a comfortable convent preferable to dirty, drafty Durraghglass, will move there with her still-loved Leda. All the Swifts express and find some satisfaction for desire. But in May's case, the change has a reformative dimension. The thief becomes a legitimate wage-earner. The noncontributing resident of Durraghglass finds the means to pay her way.

Yet May's last appearance in the novel complicates this happy allegory. Having, as she puts it, "undertaken such a full-time job in the Antique World," May is, suddenly, preternaturally aware of business opportunities. The new May is not just a legitimate wage-earner; she is an ardent capitalist. On her way home from work one evening, she finds herself obliged to enter a Travellers' caravan to retrieve her dog, the errant Gripper: "May climbed the steps leading to the squalor that she expected and deplored. As the door shut behind her, she was surprised to find herself in a smugglers' cave of old lamps. . . . May swallowed a gasp of wonder and delight at the prospect of such an exchange and mart at her gate. Near to dreaming, she considered how, one by one, these peerless objects might be bought, re-conditioned and re-sold, by her to Ulick" (Keane 1983, 241). After deciding to haggle with the Travellers for their lamps, she goes outside and announces to Jasper, "'They've got some pretty things. Stolen property, obviously'" (242).

Keane's response to May's hypocrisy is swift and harsh: "Jasper stared at her. How, after Leda's revelations [of May's thefts], could she pronounce the word 'stolen' in a way suggesting that it was only tinkers who stole?" (Keane 1983, 242–43). Keane displays May's impulse to project her own dark side onto the Other, even in the wake of her recent exposure. And she replaces May's bald thievery with an exploitative capitalist aggression—a development that mirrors neocolonial political and economic realities.

So May's redemption is far from complete. The recognitions that Ulick forces upon her are fleeting. In this final scene, Keane reinvigorates reader condemnation of May. She revises her (and our) sympathetic alliance with May with a last word that denounces the thief's blindness to her own continued (if sublimated) criminality.

Keane's own representations of the Travellers effectively destabilize even this "last" word. Throughout the novel, Keane distances herself from May's prejudicial assessments of Christy Lucey and the Travellers. We are clearly meant to reject comments like the one May makes when driving past the Travellers' encampment. In the spirit of that other Swift's "A Modest Proposal," May mutters, "'those ghastly children . . . we could do with less of them actually . . . all the same, take care, awfully expensive to kill one'" (Keane 1983, 65). Likewise, Keane seems to urge reader resistance to May's expectations regarding the inside of the caravan, quoted above. And her representation of May's hypocrisy in that scene effectively grants the Travellers the moral high ground, if only by default.

But Keane herself appears to participate in prejudicial attitudes toward the Travellers. Unlike June, who expresses keen sympathy for those whom she calls the "travelling people," Keane employs the term "tinkers" in authorial narration. And her representation of the Travellers in this final scene echoes representations of the colonized Other. Associated with wildness, death, sexuality, and nature, Keane's "tinkers" gather around them just those attributes that are spawned by oppositional hierarchies subordinating oppressed to oppressor. If May projects her own dark side onto the Travellers, so, it seems, does Keane.

So Keane reproaches May for an attitude that she herself, at least intermittently, seems to hold. And she duplicates another of May's gestures. May censures the Travellers for stealing, in spite of her own thefts; Keane censures May for colonialist attitudes, in spite of those that may linger in her own heart and mind. This complex character, from which Keane seems to try to distance herself at the novel's end, is, in the end, Keane's secret sharer.

IV

Keane's representations of the June–Christy dyad is the other primary site on which her encounter with Anglo-Irish culture unfolds with particular intensity. Like her contingent representations of May, her representations of June and Christy mark her undecided relation to home culture. On this site, however, interpretability—the power of Keane's language to generate multiple, at times incongruous readings—plays a central role in the proliferation of uncertainty. These representations not only leave the reader with a strong impression of Keane's agitated process of reckoning with Anglo-Ireland; they require the reader to engage in the process too.

Keane's portrait of June seems part of a novel-wide effort to challenge the historical hierarchy opposing Anglo-Ireland and Ireland. One means by which the novel delivers this challenge is by mapping the two groups' common ground. Thus, for instance, if Christy Lucey is ruled by a potent matriarch, as the stereotypical Irishman is, so are the Anglo-Irish Swifts. More often, Keane actually opposes Ireland to Anglo-Ireland, but in terms that invert the traditional hierarchy. For example, it is to the Swifts' Irish dairymaid great-grandmother that April and her father owe their beauty (Keane 1983, 198). What physical grace the Swifts have can be traced to Irish blood. Similarly, the neighborhood monks have a power over the land that Jasper does not. Jasper may look the part of "the ex-landlord, and gentleman at ease on his own property," but he covets "the monastery tractor . . . —a clean and opulent object, redolent of good care and good money" (208). When Jasper seeks an alliance with the monks, hoping that they will replicate on his ill-husbanded land what they have accomplished on theirs, he courts them with the stereotypically indirect methods of the oppressed. He softens them up with sandwiches, broaching his precious subject slowly.

But it is the figure of June that does the lion's share of depolarizing Ireland and Anglo-Ireland. If May emerges as a deeply complicated figure of Anglo-Ireland, June functions (for a time) as a simulacrum of Ireland. Her situation systematically replicates that of the dispossessed. June works the land; "she worked harder and more faithfully for [the estate's] life than anyone else in the family" (Keane 1983, 38). As Vera Kreilkamp puts it: "She has become, virtually, the family's tenant farmer" (Kreilkamp 1998, 191). By working, she accumulates what Keane suggests are real accomplishments. Jasper wonders "how it was that so utterly silly a woman and so small a person was able to drive a tractor; deliver a calf; perhaps, if absolutely necessary, kill a lamb. He had seen her glittering, satisfied eyes after an assistance at some birth, blood on her hands and on her clothes. The thought of her versatile abilities, while he accepted their usefulness, made him shudder" (Keane 1983, 12). To Jasper, June is a figure of capability, the flip side of the image of Irishness that May invariably projects onto Christy. Jasper harbors a colonialist's typical ambivalence toward his youngest sister: as this passage shows, despite his efforts to demean her, he finds her useful. And he finds her terrifying, not just because of her contact with what Anglo-Ireland would repress (birth, death, sex, the body), but because he is awed by her effectiveness, humbled at its contrast to what he fears is his own ineffectuality.

Like the conquered Irish, June is practically illiterate. Christy reads to her—another inversion of the colonial relationship. And "[s]he was the only Swift who spoke like the people" (Keane 1983, 11). "For her education she had never gone further than the convent school in the village. Mummie was too conscious of her disability in reading or writing to send her away to that famous school for the upper classes that educated her elder daughters" (45–46). Much more routinely than Jasper (who has what power of the purse there is at Durraghglass), June survives by way of the tactics of the oppressed. Her strategy is to "'Play the buggers along.' 'The buggers' was her collective name for her family, or for any group unsympathetic towards her" (44). She tiptoes around them, especially Jasper, who can determine unilaterally the future of the land she loves. She cajoles him into letting her incubate a newborn pig in his oven, promising fresh eggs if he complies. She soothes him with white lies, insisting that she will remind Christy to return a missing ladder "as forgetfulness settled purposefully on her memory" (33). Her tactics gain her isolated victories, but her situation remains tenuous, as Jasper's plot shows. He plans to sell the land out from under her, despite "the harsh problem of [her] heartbreak" (211).

So it is not surprising that June is the only character to express sympathy with other disenfranchised Others: the Travellers. "June defended the tinkers conclusively," Keane tells us. "She was fond of a chat with the travelling people. Their cures and charms for horses' ills interested her keenly" (Keane 1983, 62). June thus functions, for a while, as a mediating figure, linking Ireland and Anglo-Ireland via plot (in her relationship with Christy) and in and of herself.

But this revision of the relation of Ireland and Anglo-Ireland hits this considerable snag. Keane assigns June some "Irish" traits that are not matters of historical fact, as illiteracy and dispossession are, but symptoms of imperialist myth. We learn, for instance, that June "was a true part of the land" (Keane 1983, 47). By virtue of her unity with nature, June enjoys "essential knowledge" that the other Swifts lack (45). Likewise, June does not repress the past; "June had the whole memory of the illiterate" (32), which frees her from the linear conception of time to which her siblings cling; she is, still, "Baby June."

In such moments, June accrues traits generated by the hierarchical opposition of Ireland and Anglo-Ireland—the conceptual structure that Keane elsewhere undermines. Though Keane may try to collapse that structure in June—she does put "Irishness" squarely within the Big House—in associating June with such attributes as childishness, timelessness, intuition, and the primal, Keane's attempts to collapse distinctions collapses itself. "Irishness" remains Other.

The text contains additional manifestations of Keane's quandary. In keeping with her sometimes romantic portraits of the land, she depicts June's farmwork in terms of a Carlylean romanticization of work, replete with idealized notions of a simple life on the land and the simple pleasures it affords. June's labor gives her beatific satisfaction. The end of a long day finds her "happy and not even tired" (Keane 1983, 89). Her farming is impractical and "loving" (36). And June goes to the farmyard not just to work, but to find comfort and peace among "the true importances of her life" (42).

Keane's portrait of June's work is not simply sentimental, however; the aforementioned representation is itself disrupted. June is, after all, a tough-minded realist. Looking at an unproductive hen, she thinks, "'Useless old bitch—you're for the chop'" (Keane 1983, 89). Sweetheart, June's pig, may heave in fulfillment as she suckles her piglets, but June "calculates possible profits—monies to come from the happy family" (90). Keane writes, "On the farm, birth, death from natural cause, or from slaughter, took their inevitable turns and were dealt with as their turns came round" (63). But these liberal doses of realism do not conclusively rescue June the farmer from idealization. Far from it. Neither idealism nor realism conclusively governs the novel's mutable portraits of this hard-working Anglo-Irishwoman.

And the complications continue to proliferate. Keane's treatment of June's stereotypical Irishness at times challenges imperialist stereotypes. Most notably, Keane insists Baby June is no baby. "There was nothing babyish about her," Keane tells us. "She could do the work of two men" (Keane 1983, 10). And it is not just her productivity that prevents her from being called childish. June is the wisest, most stable, most fully realized adult around. She is the only Swift able to sympathize with others—even with her hostile sisters and brother. Unlike them, she has some core strength that prevents her from needing to fight for herself. She maintains careful watch over her material situation, but need not keep defensive watch over her ego or her pride. Importantly, she is the only Swift to remain unmoved by Leda.

But does this portrait of an able, self-possessed June in fact challenge stereotypical formulations of Irishness? Or is it of a piece with them? One might read Keane's celebration of June's ability—which constitutes Keane's proof that June is not babyish—as part and parcel of her romanticization of June's work, in which case it would seem that Keane has dislodged one stereotype with another. Indeed, Keane seems to have a generally idealized vision of June *qua* Ireland. Overall, the narrative values June. She is the object of almost none of the satire that Keane levels at the other Swifts. Her equanimity in the face of Leda's revelations is perfect, her understanding prescient. Further complicating the claim that Keane revises stereotypes in her representation of June is the fact that much of June's lauded strength and stability are grounded in her work, and in her strong ties to the land. She need not fight with her family and is able to resist Leda, we are given to understand, because of the satisfaction she gets from farming. And her ability to see Leda more clearly than the others stems from her "peasant" memory of Leda as a pinching, betraying child. So those capacities that encourage us to read June as other than stereotypically Irish stem from stereotypically Irish traits: unity with nature and long memory.

In her representation of June, then, Keane's challenges to stereotypes of Irishness are entangled with fidelity to them. Orthodoxy and heterodoxy are inextricably intertwined. Keane's attitude toward this "Irish" Anglo-Irishwoman is multilayered, jittery, and very hard to fix—not surprising, since in broaching the topic of the Irish Other, Keane broaches a powerful tribal taboo.

The novel's third chapter contains a passage that exemplifies Keane's dramatically unsettled stance toward June. It is rich in reversals and disjunctions:

She was a true part of the land, but her farm accounts, almost a tally of stones, were intelligible to herself alone. She could, however, translate them with minute accuracy for the income tax forms, over which Jasper fought a sick delaying action with the accountants. It was her illiteracy that gave June a peasant's clarity of memory. She

> forgot nothing. The past was hers, and its voices. Only the future, with its hazards and terrors, ran back and forwards through her mind, the mind of a cute little animal. (Keane 1983, 47)

This passage marks a difficult intellectual and emotional journey. Conflicting perspectives jostle for precedence. The passage seems to throw descriptions at its subject, as if the need to articulate a conception of June and, by extension, Irishness, overwhelms the requirements of coherence. The hazy romanticization of June's work with which the passage begins is displaced by a critical observation on her intellectual limitations which is displaced, in turn, by respect for her practical ability. This matter-of-fact admiration for June's competence is then dislodged by more lyrical stereotyping, which is displaced by another observation on her limitations. The passage ends in a condescending dismissal of June as cute, little, and bestial.

Keane's representation of Christy Lucey does not manifest such instability. Keane's dominant attitude toward Christy is patronizing and indulgent.[20] She seems to wink at us, urging tolerance of his quaint saints, holy days, and rosaries. She seems to want to portray his prayers for the new piglets as evidence of a silly but endearing mysticism; or of an inability to distinguish situations that call for prayer from those that, inconsequential, do not; or of a naive failure to make such hierarchical distinctions. Keane seems unaware of the similarity between Christy's praying for pigs and Jasper's inability to distinguish bad manners from bad morals, a likeness which shows Christy to advantage. And sometimes Keane's indulgence toward Christy has an ugly bite, as in her allusion to the saint Christy "had been propositioning through the whole affair" of Sweetheart's delivery (Keane 1983, 19). Such moments stand at a striking distance from the novel's many challenges to colonialist perspectives.[21]

It is crucial, in examining Keane's representations of Irishness, to consider her representation of Christy's body. We learn that Christy has "dark, nervous good looks" (Keane 1983, 44), and a "lovely dark head" (19). His legs are "long and useful on a horse"; he has "wide shoulders and light hips," and an overall "gracious maturity" (91). Such descriptions are remarkable. Their abundant specificity contrasts sharply with the silence surrounding the body of the novel's other man. If Leda, April, May, and June are insistently embodied, Jasper is not. The narrative barely grazes his body, in a euphemistic reference to hands "clasped, embarrassed and protective, over the somnolence of his private person" (166). Christy's body, by contrast, is the object of a lingering and idealizing gaze.

Perhaps Keane's imagination of Christy's physical beauty, as of the beauty of the Swifts' Irish great-grandmother, marks an impulse to represent Irish, as opposed to Anglo-Irish, grace. But what is most striking about this portrait is its full and, in this novel, anomalous sexuality. If Jasper's body is absent, shrouded in euphemism, Christy's is vividly present. And if Jasper is sexually impotent, Christy is sexually enthralling, as we surmise not simply by way of Keane's descriptions, but by way of June's relation to him. Despite Keane's willingness to expose Jasper, on other counts, as no more than a mock-patriarch, she retains a reticence worthy of Violet Swift about the mock-patriarch's body. The body of the Irish farmhand, on the other hand, like the bodies of women, is legitimate narrative material: it is the text's single locus of viable sexuality (though Jasper's sometime friend, Brother Anselm, is "pretty" too).[22]

While Keane's representation of Christy seems, on the whole, closed and stable, her narrative does leave open to question just how one should evaluate this Irishman's work. Is Christy indolent and overpaid, as Jasper and May repeat? Is he a priceless assistant, as June insists? On the one hand, Keane highlights the extent to which this Anglo-Irish estate rests on Christy's labor. We overhear June think: "He was the support and stay of her every farming activity—without him, what should she do?" (Keane 1983, 19). The narrative challenges negative assessments of him as "'more utterly useless every day, every hour'" (11). We watch Christy work with June. We see him work wonders with her horse, the Wild Man. Beyond the call of duty, he returns to Durraghglass the night the piglets are born, to check the farrowing light.

But the narrative also counters this portrait of the Irishman as a conscientious worker. June is required time and time again to let Christy leave work early, so that he can tend to his mother or go to church, errands that are never confirmed to be real. Keane undercuts his generous attention to the piglets: "in her pleasure at tonight's devotion to duty June was happy to forget how often Christy might neglect his work in hand at Durraghglass to cycle home" (Keane 1983, 44). The gutters remain unrepaired, and Christy never does return Jasper's ladder. June's hard worker is also May's delinquent employee.

But to conclude that Christy conforms to Irish type is to agree with Jasper and, worse, May, whose sniping about Christy appears invariably vindictive. And it is to disagree with June, the character with whom we sympathize most consistently and whose vision seems, on the whole, most clear. Yet Keane does suggest that when it comes to Christy, June's vision may blur. June's estimation of Christy seems colored by sexual as well as maternal interest, and by her need for companionship. Christy's worth to June may be more emotional than economic, which reinforces the possibility that Christy is indeed a lax Irishman. And so on. Keane's representation of Christy is essentially ambiguous.

Keane's rendering of June's relation to Christy constitutes a similarly indeterminate representation of interclass relations. For all June's identity as a mediating figure in the novel and for all her figurative "Irishness," she is at the same time Christy's employer, whom he calls "Miss Baby." Keane proposes several models of relationship to express their bond, models that may be read as either revisions or rehearsals of colonialist conceptions.

Keane's portrait of the relationship as a harmonious collaboration is part and parcel of her romanticization of work on the land. After the birth of Sweetheart's piglets, "in a warm corner of a sound old cow-shed, Baby June and Christy Lucey looked with happy satisfaction at Sweetheart. . . . and her eight piglets, safely delivered. Outside the shed spring rain was falling coldly on wild cherry blossom and through the evening songs of birds. Christy Lucey and June had neither eyes nor ears for these other springtime events" (Keane 1983, 18–19). Snug in the womblike shed, June and Christy join in awe at the product of their labor. We see them later that evening, united again in concern for the piglets. Especially given its contrast to the Swifts' quarrelsome dinner and to the night that is falling outside, the scene stands as a rare and vivid image of peace, accord, and warmth: "Together they turned the light of their torches . . . on the long pale sow and her piglets"; "They had a second agreement over the fizz and murmur in the farrowing light"; Christy "stood with June and Tiny and his leaning bicycle, all together in the deepening night" (42–43).

Other models of the relationship also emerge. Contemplating the possibility of losing Christy's help on the farm, June panics in the terms of love, not utility: "without him, what should she do? Life would fail her—she would be so deprived the beat of her heart would stop" (Keane 1983, 19). Jasper is right: "'Baby's world spins round Christy Lucey'" (139). But the precise nature of her attachment is difficult to ascertain. Partly because so many Anglo-Irish novels involve sexual mésalliance, partly because Keane cultivates its appearance by way of the gossip of Lady Alys and Leda, we can't help but wonder if June's connection with Christy is cemented by sexual attraction. It is, after all, June's gaze that generates descriptions of Christy's body. But Leda also observes: "'Baby is like a lioness with her cub on the subject of Christy Lucey'" (155). And June calls the young man who replaces Christy "'my new little boy'" (246). Her attachment is also maternal.

How are we to read these representations of harmonious interclass relations, sexual and/or familial? Perhaps they constitute an attempt to revise the hierarchy that historically divided landlord and tenant, employer and worker. By replacing hierarchy with equality in work, by replacing the employer-employee relation with that of parent and child or lover and beloved, Keane may attempt to reverse old wrongs. The fact that Keane's Anglo-Irish participant in this interclass relation is cast as "Irish" brings the two characters even closer, reinforcing the possibility that Keane seeks to cancel hierarchy in her portrait of their bond. Indeed, the narrative reiterates the relation's egalitarianism: "She could translate [her skills and courage] for him. They had the same use of words. There was an equality between them" (Keane 1983, 91).

But one might also read Keane's portrait of this relation as an attempt to evade a dark past. One might argue that replacing the economic bond with an emotional one represses the historical violence of the Irish social order. Certainly Keane's representation of the pair as mother and son coincides with the familial metaphor historically deployed to mask oppression. And it upholds the stereotype aligning Irishness with childishness. Perhaps in painting this picture of irenic, even familial relations, Keane is trying not to reverse but to erase the wrongs Anglo-Ireland committed, and conserve what status it yet enjoys.

Perhaps Keane subverts traditional systems of value and belief. Perhaps she perpetuates them. Different readers may discern different "truths." Interpretability sanctions none, or all.

In any case, this harmonic union—maternal, sexual, collegial—does not last. Christy gives June picturesquely roundabout notice that he is leaving Durraghglass for a better job. Lady Alys, he informs

June, has offered him the chance to ride in the prestigious Dublin horse show; June had been grooming him to ride only in Cork. And while June had been able to compensate him with only the old gate lodge and Jasper's Huntsman jodhpurs, "'There's a house and electricity and a toilet going with [Lady Alys's] job'" (Keane 1983, 192).

Keane's handling of this development is uneven. She initially keeps her distance from June's distress. June's heart is "shocked" at the news; she feels a "chill of despair" (Keane 1983, 191). Feeling wronged, she scolds Christy: "'And the hours I gave schooling you to ride in a show'" (191). This distance shrinks, however, when Christy returns that same afternoon to ask June for his job back. Calling June a "victim of a betrayal" and Christy's action a "worthless betrayal and light departure," the narrative seems to corroborate June's vengefulness, and aligns Christy with the novel's true traitor, Leda (245). Keane's former indulgence of Christy turns to angry disdain. Now he is not picturesque but "shamelessly pathetic." Keane conclusively names Christy's "frequent failures from duty" and his "pretensions to a religious discipline with which he excused his early departures and late arrivals" (245). She concludes "he had not only justified May's endless spyings and steely criticisms, but, without a thought, he had left June to chill and sicken in a bitter wind of fear" (245).

Late in the scene, both June and Keane temper their harsh assessments. But Christy remains more mocked than indulged. If we had doubts about Keane's estimation of Christy before, we have few now. At the end of the novel, Christy resolves into the stereotypical Irishman: a thoughtless shirker of duty, a short-sighted traitor, a naively self-confident and perpetually childish man. He exits the novel, contrite and purely picturesque: "Christy bowed his head and crossed himself gently before he rode away towards his church and his mother" (Keane 1983, 247). He could be a figure in one of May's tweed pictures.

As Christy conforms to type, so does June. No longer a figure of Irishness, June resolves into a figure of condescending Anglo-Ireland. Jasper-like, she condemns Christy's decision to leave Durraghglass as an instance of bad manners. Her sympathy with Christy becomes, at best, forbearance. And their former equality becomes hierarchy. Keane gives June the moral high ground, having her dismiss Christy with an elitist arrogance which elsewhere Keane repudiates and before which Christy appears rightly humbled. The relation between these two former partners ends on a note of sheer difference, with Christy playing the amoral traitor to June, the righteous victim.

So this final scene stands startlingly at odds with the novel's preceding subversions of colonialist formulations of Irishness and oppositional notions of interclass relations. And it startlingly reverses Keane's preceding portrait of June. The collapse of difference reverts to its bitter reinstatement.

V

At the beginning of this chapter, I compared May's ambivalence about telling her secrets, to Keane's about telling what she might consider Anglo-Ireland's, suggesting that May's ambivalence may imply some of the hopes and fears Keane attaches to narrating Anglo-Ireland. In the end, though, it is not May but in fact Leda who emerges as *Time After Time*'s most conspicuous storyteller figure, with important implications for our understanding of Keane's relationship to her narrative project.

Keane explicitly aligns Leda, the novel's abhorrent traitor, with the novelist generally and a Keane-like novelist more specifically. Having learned about May's thefts Leda exults, "Such a good story—who should she tell it to?" (Keane 1983, 165). Commenting on Leda's malicious accumulation of the Swifts' guilty secrets, Keane remarks, "Leda might have been wanting to write a book about her cousins" (145). If Keane generates a narrative that manipulates and misleads (leading us to worry toward the end of the novel, for instance, that June is dead) so does Leda, though her mischief is decidedly more treacherous.[23] Moreover, Leda, like Keane, tells "tales of terror and filth" (109), defying social constructions of decency. Ellen O'Brien observes: "Leda's use of excrement as a signifying practice, coded as the undeniable subversion of ritualized civility, mimics Keane's use of abjection . . . for clearly Keane uses excessive 'nasty stuff' to concentrate our attention on the delicacy and descendancy of Anglo-Irish culture" (E. O'Brien 1999, 49). If Leda is, as O'Brien goes on to suggest, an embodiment of "the Real" ("the repressed material left over which [the Swifts] hitherto have been identifying as a properly disappeared and completely abject corpse" [E. O'Brien 1999, 48]), then Keane's self-alignment with this character is all the more daring and dangerous.

The consequences of Leda's tales are dire. We witness firsthand their devastating impact on the Swifts, particularly on May. But the outcome of narratives that Leda told long ago, in the past that precedes the text's present, was even more grave. Her apparently exaggerated accounts of her affair with Uncle Valentine helped precipitate his suicide. "A man had died *on her account*," Keane's narrator puns (Keane 1983, 130, italics mine). And as we learn late in the novel, the tales Leda told as a Nazi collaborator, like those she continues to tell to authorities about her Nazi ex-lover, are similarly fatal. In the world of this novel, telling can kill. [24]

The figure of Leda expresses Keane's deepest anxieties about her narrative project, revealing how much Keane must have felt was at stake. As if to help assuage her misgivings regarding her narrative's fearful power, Keane disqualifies Leda's narratives, emphasizing her tendency to exaggerate and tell "fairy stories" (Keane 1983, 182). By the end of the novel, she revokes Leda's authority altogether: Leda's only audience is the deaf April, to whom Leda's handwriting is indecipherable (248).

Perhaps Keane seeks to temper her own text too. One might read *Time After Time*'s many comically ironic narrative gestures as traces of such an impulse. Again and again Keane alludes broadly to the Anglo-Irish literary tradition, especially to Swift and to Yeats, by way of Leda and many swans. She overdoes her images, as in her reference to May's immature pussy willows and Jasper's clipped filberts, and as when Jasper and Leda consummate their friendship while Jasper furiously creams butter. Like Bowen in *The Last September*, she gives her chapters tidy, anachronistic titles: "In the Dining-Room," "Bedtime," "Separate Pursuits." Such gestures highlight *Time After Time*'s artificiality, as if to establish its status as (mere) narrative, story, text.

The many tensions and instabilities I have charted in *Time After Time* might also be read as traces of the uneasiness that the figure of Leda expresses. Unlike Leda's final texts, though, Keane's is far from indecipherable. It is complex, undecided, interpretable. And it is all the more powerfully expressive therefor. Far from an univocal apologia for an heroic culture, far too from an indiscriminate accomplice with a dominant ideology, *Time After Time* entails an unfinished process of interrogation, a dynamic conversation with itself over how to narrate Anglo-Ireland. David Lloyd has written: "history is written from the perspective of and with the aim of producing a non-contradictory subject" (Lloyd 1999, 17). Delineating one writer's emotional, intellectual, and linguistic responses to Anglo-Ireland's tight spot, *Time After Time* rebuts the monolithic model of unified and coherent, clear and distinct identity, political or personal, that can so constrain one's reading of a literary text, and has proven so dangerous in Ireland, as elsewhere.

4

Elizabeth Bowen's
The Last September:
Gendering Anglo-Ireland

"I think being a woman is like being Irish . . . Everyone says you're
important and nice, but you take second place all the same."
—Iris Murdoch, *The Red and the Green*

"I hate women. But I can't think how to begin to be anything else."
—Elizabeth Bowen, *The Last September*

E LIZABETH BOWEN'S ANGLO-IRISH HERITAGE HAS BEEN WELL DOCU-
mented. Born in Dublin in 1899, the only child of Henry Cole Bowen
and Florence Colley Bowen, her roots stretched deep into Anglo-Ireland. Her mother's family arrived in Ireland in the time of Elizabeth I. Her father's traced its Irish origins to 1653, when Colonel
Henry Bowen, a Welshman, received a grant of land in southeastern
County Cork in return for his service in Cromwell's Irish campaign.
Bowen's Court, the estate built on that land, where Bowen spent
many childhood summers and more sustained time after inheriting
it in 1930, dates to 1775.

The geography of Bowen's life is suggestively unsettled. As a
young child, Bowen was shuttled back and forth between Dublin and
Bowen's Court. Her father anchored the family in the city where, to
his father's chagrin, he had taken up a career as a lawyer rather than
manage the family estate; he later worked for the Land Commission,
implementing the land reforms that would so drastically reduce
Anglo-Irish holdings. By the time she was seven, Bowen was shuttled

more frequently between Ireland and England, where she and her mother lived near Anglo-Irish relatives in Kent—an adjustment in family life her father's doctors had encouraged. Bowen's mother died when she was thirteen, leaving her in the care of aunts in England. They enrolled her in school: first Harpenden Hall, then Downe House. In 1917, Bowen returned to Ireland to live with her father and stepmother at Bowen's Court.

When Bowen was twenty she took two terms at the London County Council School of Art. But she soon returned to Ireland and to writing, publishing her first collection of stories in 1923. That year also saw her marriage to Alan Cameron, an Englishman, with whom she lived thereafter in England, first near Oxford and then in London. When her father died in 1930, Bowen inherited Bowen's Court. She and Cameron spent summers there until 1952, when they returned to Ireland, planning to live at Bowen's Court year-round. But after Cameron died that August, Bowen spent most of her time lecturing in Europe and the United States. She managed to retain Bowen's Court until 1959, when financial pressures finally forced her to sell it to a farmer who soon razed the house. Bowen returned to England: first to Oxford, then to Kent. She died in London in 1973 and was buried near her old home in County Cork.

As Hermione Lee has argued: "It is not essential to approach Elizabeth Bowen as an 'Anglo-Irish' writer. One might be as much entitled to introduce her in her relation to Forster and Virginia Woolf, or in company with a group of English contemporaries—L. P. Hartley, Henry Green, Rosamond Lehmann. Some of her best novels, *To the North, The House in Paris,* and *The Death of the Heart,* are not—or are only incidentally—about Ireland. She was quite as much a London literary figure as she was a member of the County Cork Protestant gentry" (Lee 1981, 19). She lived "the most Anglicized kind of Anglo-Irish life" (42). But more deliberately than most other writers in the Anglo-Irish tradition, Elizabeth Bowen confronted Anglo-Irish culture and history head on, in both imaginative and expository prose. A proto-culture critic, she returned again and again to the project of historicizing, textualizing, and contextualizing Anglo-Ireland.

The work that grew out of this project bears pervasive marks of those tendencies that I have argued are endemic to fiction in the Anglo-Irish tradition. How shall I assess my home culture? How shall

I account for its relation to Irish men and women, Irish land, Irish history? Driven by competing loyalties and contradictory motivations, by what Lee has described as a "kind of double vision" in which "[r]etrospection, 'repining,' had always to be balanced with some kind of ironic distancing" (Lee 1981, 18), Bowen's texts offer inconclusive answers to such questions, at once authenticating and demystifying Anglo-Ireland.

In her expository work—essays like "The Big House" (1940) and her massive account of her ancestral home, *Bowen's Court* (1942a)—frank criticism of Anglo-Ireland plays with frank defense; cool judgments of Anglo-Ireland's moral blunders transform themselves into apparently unself-conscious enactments of them; statements of ambivalence toward Anglo-Ireland and its Others, Ireland and England, jostle professions of love and near hate. As Ann Owens Weekes describes *Bowen's Court*, it is "an attempt to explain, to gain understanding and sympathy for ancestors of whose injustice she is always aware" (Weekes 1990, 86). While Bowen mourns and even idealizes her home culture, she admits again and again: "my family got their position and drew their power from a situation that shows an inherent wrong" (Bowen 1942a, 453). She acknowledges, in an incriminating present tense, "Cromwell's portrait hangs at the top of our front stairs" (68).[1]

The Last September (1929a) is similarly rich in double vision. Set deep in the Irish countryside during the guerrilla war between the Irish Republican Army and Britain's notorious Black and Tans, the novel draws on Bowen's own experience of that difficult time, recounting the decline and fall of a Big House she calls Danielstown. As Bowen reveals in the novel's preface, the central character, Lois Farquar, "derives from, but is not, myself at nineteen" (Bowen 1929b, xii). Like other novels in the Anglo-Irish tradition, *The Last September* chronicles its author's inconclusive attempt to reckon with the twin problems of Anglo-Ireland's place in Irish culture and the writer's place in Anglo-Ireland. But *The Last September* also offers this distinctive contribution to the tradition. By placing the category of gender at the center of her Big House novel, Bowen provides a vigorous and systematic challenge to prevailing masculinist representations of Anglo-Ireland. Bowen effectively genders Anglo-Ireland, offering the first sustained interrogation of the Anglo-Irish construction of femininity and its costs.[2]

I

The Last September opens in a series of descriptive paragraphs the equivocal manner and content of which announce its Anglo-Irish provenance. The arrival of Mr. and Mrs. Montmorency at the Big House called Danielstown is described with both reverence and venom, sincerity and sarcasm, in a jumpy overture that is at once ruthlessly sardonic and nostalgically precise:

> About six o'clock the sound of a motor, collected out of the wide country and narrowed under the trees of the avenue, brought the household out in excitement on to the steps. Up among the beeches, a thin iron gate twanged; the car slid out of a net of shadow, down the slope to the house. Behind the flashing windscreen Mr and Mrs Montmorency produced—arms waving and a wild escape to the wind of her mauve motor-veil—an agitation of greeting. They were long-promised visitors. They exclaimed, Sir Richard and Lady Naylor exclaimed and signalled: no one spoke yet. It was a moment of happiness, of perfection.
>
> In those days, girls wore crisp white skirts and transparent blouses clotted with white flowers; ribbons, threaded through with a view to appearance, appeared over their shoulders. So that Lois stood at the top of the steps looking cool and fresh; she knew how fresh she must look, like other young girls, and clasping her elbows tightly behind her back, tried hard to conceal her embarrassment. The dogs came pattering out from the hall and stood beside her; above, the vast facade of the house stared coldly over its mounting lawns. She wished she could freeze the moment and keep it always. But as the car approached, as it stopped, she stooped down and patted one of the dogs. (Bowen 1929a, 7)

Bowen describes a would-be nineteenth-century scene from an intermittently modernist point of view. Some of the imagery is patently lovely: a tree-lined avenue, a mauve veil. But some is mechanistic and grotesque: the sound of a motor "collected," the "twang" of an iron gate, the sight of a blouse "clotted" with flowers. Bowen's prose invokes and then refuses sentimental loveliness, only to revert to loveliness, and to further ironic refusals. The passage bespeaks a wry awareness of the calculated nature of the scene's effects—the requisite exclamations, young Lois's artificial-flower-fresh look. Social grace is a function of crass cause and effect, the passage announces.

And yet the narrator concludes, "It was a moment of happiness, of perfection," to be echoed by the self-conscious niece of the house who, despite her embarrassment at the false notes struck by the scene's fabricated excesses, "wished she could freeze the moment and keep it always." Bowen drapes the event in offhanded satirical coldness, and labels it a moment of perfect being, at once preserving and parodying the age-old ritual of arrival.

This tonally complex opening scene anticipates the unsettled stance of the novel as a whole. *The Last September* is riven with generic, perspectival, tonal, and stylistic tensions that keep it teetering dynamically among styles and modes. In her preface Bowen asserts: "The mood and cast of my characters, and their actions, were to reflect the glow of a finished time, ... so I opened my second paragraph with a pointer: '*In those days*'"; "Yet I wished [the reader] to *feel*: 'But see, our story begins!'" (Bowen 1929b, ix). This perception of the past as definitively past ("In those days") and the sensation of the past as palpably present contend throughout. Accordingly, the text straddles fences that would separate a nineteenth-century sensibility from a twentieth, and nostalgia for Anglo-Ireland from critique of it. Thus the sociable titles of its three neat parts—"The Arrival of Mr and Mrs Montmorency," "The Visit of Miss Norton," "The Departure of Gerald"—along with the cleanly linear and ritual-laden narrative as a whole, suggest a stably conventional novel of manners. But the stark tension between those three parts' titles and their chaotic, disrupted content—in which, one feels, *Pride and Prejudice* meets *Women in Love*—implies a modernist text of alienation and breakdown. Such tensions make it difficult to categorize this text except by way of hybridized descriptions. *The Last September* is a late nineteenth-century novel of manners that registers awareness that it is falling apart. It is a demythologizing modernist text that takes as its topic the still-alluring certainties of a previous age. It is at once a cool deconstruction and a loving preservation of Anglo-Ireland, burning the Big House down and encasing it safely in narrative.[3]

The Last September's representations of Anglo-Ireland's stereotypical habits of mind—its intellectual and literary styles—exacerbate the novel's indeterminate literary identity and tone. The narrative repeatedly disrupts its own intermittently complacent lyricism with surreal grotesquerie. So of Lois's friend Livvy on her way home from a trip to the dentist's just after becoming engaged, Bowen writes, "All in a dream she had sat and bled from the gums in a train" (Bowen

1929a, 110). Satire shifts toward sentiment and back. Realism displaces surrealism, which displaces idealism, and so on. The effect is kaleidoscopic—a trace of, among other things, Anglo-Ireland's geopolitical and ontological uncertainty during these troubled political times, and of this writer's debate with herself over how to situate herself in relation to her home culture. Bowen at once embraces and dismisses Anglo-Ireland as it was, as she wishes it were not, and as she longs for it still to be.

Like other novels in the tradition, *The Last September* mixes conservative reenactment and radical critique in its representation of the requisite Anglo-Irish topics. One of the most focal, in Bowen and in the Anglo-Irish tradition more broadly, is Yeats's "ceremony of innocence," that myth of inherent civility and grace which, as I have argued, Molly Keane also confronts in *Time After Time*. In her intermittently Yeatsian essay, "The Big House," Bowen celebrates—or tries to—"the routine of life," "the order, the form of life, the tradition to which big house people still sacrifice much" (Bowen 1940, 28–29). The big houses "were planned for spacious living—for hospitality above all," she writes (26). They

> contributed to society, . . . raised life above the exigencies of mere living to the plane of art, or at least style. There was a true bigness, a sort of impersonality, in the manner in which the houses were conceived. After an era of greed, roughness and panic, after an era of camping in charred or desolate ruins (as my Cromwellian ancestors did certainly) these new settlers who had been imposed on Ireland began to wish to add something to life. The security that they had, by the eighteenth century, however ignobly gained, they did not use quite ignobly. They began to feel, and exert, the European idea—to seek what was humanistic, classic and disciplined.
>
> It is something to subscribe to an idea, even if one cannot live up to it." (Bowen 1940, 27)

At the center of the social idea for which the house stands, Bowen suggests, is "the subjugation of the personal to the impersonal. In the interest of good manners and good behaviour people learned to subdue their own feelings. The result was an easy and unsuspicious intercourse" (29). "Well, why not *be* polite" Bowen queries, as if answering her own unspoken objections to the "impersonality" she has just praised; "are not humane manners the crown of being human at all? Politeness is not constriction; it is a grace" (29).

Like "The Big House," *The Last September* is divided on the topic of gracious, well-mannered social intercourse. At one pole we have the novel's pervasive narrative voice, which is nothing if not polite. Lady Naylor–like, it approaches sexuality, money, the body—topics that Keane and Beckett delight in confronting head on—only obliquely. But as the novel's opening scene reveals, the narrative also drives home the fact that Anglo-Irish social forms—good manners, polite sociability—are anything but natural or innate, essentially good or polite. They are in fact self-conscious and strategic, often awkward and repressive, and they wield a terrible capacity to do harm.[4]

The exchange that follows on the heels of the Montmorencys' arrival introduces the reader to Bowen's critique of "humane manners" (Bowen 1929a, 7–8). Francie Montmorency opens the conversation with a series of incoherent fragments: "'And this is the niece! . . . Aren't we dusty! . . . Aren't we too terribly dusty!'" "'She's left school now,' said Sir Richard proudly." "'I don't think I should have known you,' said Mr Montmorency," conventionally. Francie interjects, "'Oh, *I* think she's the image of Laura—.'" "'—But we have tea waiting!'" Lady Naylor interrupts, skirting the dangerous topic of Hugo's youthful infatuation with Lois's mother. "'Are you really *sure*, now, you've had tea?'" she presses—as if she has already asked if they want tea, and in fact presuming that they don't. Hugo aids Lady Naylor's attempt to wrench the conversation back on the rails of clichéd exchange: "'Danielstown's looking lovely, lovely. One sees more from the upper avenue—didn't you clear some trees?'" Sir Richard responds: "'The wind had three of the ashes—you came quite safe? No trouble? Nobody at the cross-roads? Nobody stopped you?'" Though his ritualized inquiries about the travelers' journey darken momentarily, they remain safely subsumed by convention, at once admitting and denying the possibility of the Montmorencys' having stumbled upon the guerrilla war (7–8).

In this scene as elsewhere in the novel, characters talk at each other, or, interrupted and interrupting, hurl sentence fragments, their "conversations" entailing parallel strands of talk that do not meet. Suppressing its own internal disruptions, not only does the language of polite exchange fail to perform its ostensible function as social lubricant (reality intrudes and derails it); it proves an agent of coercion and evasion that forcefully represses meanings that swirl unsaid, perhaps unsayable, around it.

Laurence's deadpan account of a subsequent exchange high-lights the absurdity of conventional social interaction. It is a passage Beckett would have relished:

> "Mr Montmorency has gone for a walk. . . He had to take an um-brella. Apparently he does not usually take an umbrella, but when he was half-way down the avenue Mrs Montmorency suddenly said he must, because it had never rained like this before. So she took an umbrella and one for herself and started off down the avenue after him. Aunt Myra said she should not have done this because of her heart and looked round for me, but I had gone quickly into the din-ing-room, which is the last place anybody would look for one be-tween meals. So she found Uncle Richard and he took another um-brella and ran quickly down the avenue after Mrs Montmorency, telling her not to run like that. When he had caught her up he took the umbrella from her and went still more quickly, shouting, after Mr Montmorency, who pretended not to hear and walked on with a back view of positive hatred." (Bowen 1929a, 104)

With more realism and restraint than Beckett, Bowen unveils socia-bility as, in Laurence's words, "a rather perplexing system of niceties . . . ; an exact and delicate interrelation of stresses between being and being, like crossing arches" (93). It entails "asking questions, and ignoring the answers as far as possible" (54). It constitutes a fre-quently vapid form, a falsely self-evident style that lacks content, or a style laden with camouflaged content, an abstract, obsolete system—hardly, as Bowen tried to argue in "The Big House," "the crown of being human."

Elsewhere Bowen explores a contiguous, more potentially dam-aging phenomenon: the deliberate gap between social language and fact, word and thing. There is, for instance, the art of hypocritical hy-perbole. Long ago, when Francie failed to accompany Hugo to Danielstown, "The Naylors sent her out wails, injunctions and decla-rations. They would never, *never* be happy till she was with them also" (Bowen 1929a, 15). At the start of the current visit, Francie sees Myra's face in a mirror and thinks, "'Myra's aged!'" but then says, "'You look wonderful, you know'" (16). Lois has learned this social practice. When Marda announces she is engaged, Lois responds, "'Oh, how lovely!' Lois had a shock of flatness" (96).

Misrepresentations by way of understatement accompany such lies of overstatement. At a tennis party, the Naylors and their guests discuss an I.R.A. attack on a barracks in which, the narrator reveals, "[t]wo of the defenders were burnt inside it, the others shot coming out. The wires were cut, the roads blocked; there had been no one to send for help, so there was no help for them." The conversation tames and sanitizes the incident, reducing it to small talk, as it does other eruptions of the war into Anglo-Ireland; "It was this they had all been discussing, at tea, between tennis: 'the horrible thing'" (Bowen 1929a, 47).

Such dilutions of harsh realities stem as a matter of course from the Naylors' tribal habit "of not knowing": "'One cannot help what people say,'" Lady Naylor says, "'though it is always annoying. Not that I ever do know what they say: I make a point of not knowing'" (Bowen 1929a, 57). Lady Naylor prohibits some truthful exchanges outright. When Hugo asks Laurence, "'And what do you think of things?'"—"things" being his euphemism for the worsening Troubles—the forthright Laurence responds, "'Seem to be closing in, . . . rolling up rather.'" Lady Naylor rebukes him: "'Ssh! . . . Now you mustn't make Laurence exaggerate. All young men from Oxford exaggerate. All Laurence's friends exaggerate: I have met them'" (24–25). She will go only so far as to admit, "'From all the talk, you might think anything was going to happen, but we never listen'" (26).

The proximity of war is the novel's most decisive deflator of ritual social exchange. Polite language wilts and shrivels, rings false under pressure from violent content it cannot contain. After lunch one day Lady Naylor quizzes Gerald Lesworth as if pressing him to divulge the latest gossip: "'Now I want to know, Mr Lesworth, what Colonel Boatley really thinks of reprisals. Of course it will go no further, though you mustn't think I want you to be indiscreet'" (Bowen 1929a, 94). At Danielstown, drawing-room values presume to supersede military ones. By the end of the afternoon, "The drawing-room became to Gerald fantastic and thin like an ice-palace, and, reflected backwards and forwards in tall mirrors, seemed like a chain of galleries at Versailles" (95). The visit ends on a surreal, mock-gracious note: "An armoured car called for Gerald at four o'clock. . . . The last they saw of him was a putteed leg being drawn in carefully. Something steel slid to; they waved, but never a hand came out" (95).

Bowen gives us "humane manners" at their most brutal in the quietly violent interview Lady Naylor conducts with Gerald, in which she "manoeuvre[s] more or less openly for position" (Bowen 1929a,

178) to engineer the end of his relationship with Lois (178–83). Myra Naylor's impeccable manners mask a tyrannical will, at once camouflaging and expressing her contempt for this titleless, landless Englishman. Gerald emerges from the exchange "stunned, bruised, a little craven from shock" (181). Lady Naylor, by contrast, "got up, looked at herself in a mirror, arranged her boa and pulled down the brim of her hat. Then she shook hands with Gerald warmly, saying how much she had enjoyed their talk" (183).

As in other Anglo-Irish novels, the centerpiece of Anglo-Irish iconography—the house and its relation to Irish land—proves a significantly unsettled topic. Bowen opens her description of the ruined mill into which Marda Norton and Lois venture late in the novel in the stereotypically elegiac, even anthropomorphic terms other writers use to describe ruined houses—perhaps deflecting utter ruin from the totemic Big House onto a less-charged site of long-defunct commercial production. What ensues is a passage rich in the rhetorical jitters and incoherent reversals that typify narrative representations of the Anglo-Irish estate:

> The river darkened and thundered towards the mill-race, light came full on the high facade of decay. Incredible in its loneliness, roofless, floorless, beams criss-crossing dank interior daylight, the whole place tottered, fit to crash at a breath. Hinges rustily bled where a door had been wrenched away; up six stories panes still tattered the daylight. Mounting the tree- crowded, steep slope some roofless cottages nestled under the flank of the mill with sinister pathos. A track going up the hill from the gateless gateway perished among the trees from disuse. (Bowen 1929a, 123)

Having evoked the scene, the narrative moves on to a chaotic attempt to interpret it. It first neutralizes the potentially tribe-incriminating admission of the ruined cottages' "sinister pathos," suggesting that there is in fact nothing sinister here, just a banality turned into a melancholy *memento mori*: "Banal enough in life to have closed this valley to the imagination, the dead mill now entered the democracy of ghostliness, equaled broken palaces in futility and sadness." In its most interesting and contorted turns, the passage admits and immediately retracts what it implies by its reference to the cottages' "sinister pathos": the mill's "meanness"—an evocative noun that conjures not just commonness but also ruthlessness, callousness, wickedness, greed. The ruin, the narrative proposes, "was transfigured by some response of the spirit, showing not the decline of its meanness, simply decline." Finally, in its last clause, the passage reverses itself once more: the mill "took on all of the past to which it had given nothing." The mill stands momentarily as a universal emblem of inevitable decline (it "took on all of the past") but then again it turns "mean"—not, in this context, banal, but contemptibly ungenerous ("the past to which it had given nothing") (Bowen 1929a, 123).

Bowen's representation of the Big House itself is comparably jumpy. She has little trouble evoking the oblivious vulnerability of a neighboring house, the Careys' Mount Isabel: "the cream facade of the house was like cardboard, high and confident in the sun—a house without weight, an appearance less actual than the begonias' scarlet and wax-pink flesh. . . . [A] maid leaned out from the dark through the drawing-room window sounding the brass tea-gong: a minor note" (Bowen 1929a, 115–16). But the narrative rather shies from confronting the contingency of its own Big House. Danielstown and its grounds are, in comparison to Mr. Knott's nameless estate, as we shall see, fairly carefully preserved. And Bowen sanitizes her Big House. Keane details Durraghglass's plumbing in *Time After Time*; Beckett's Watt prepares Knott a repulsive meal and empties his slops. Such facts of Danielstown life remain resolutely offstage. We do not witness labor in *The Last September*. Servants make their presence known by the products of their apparently authorless work: a sideboard laid with breakfast, a table set for tea. As in the archetypal houses described in "The Big House," (and in the estates of so many English country house poems), "The functional parts . . . —kitchens and offices, farm-buildings, outbuildings—were sunk underground, concealed by walls or by trees" (Bowen 1940, 26).[5] Thus, while this text unmasks the myths of civilized sociability and, as I will argue, innately gracious Anglo-Irish femininity, it perpetuates the age-old image of leisured, effortless living. Threats to that image always originate in historical developments occurring outside Danielstown's gate—in Irish nationalism, in economic change—as when, after tea one day, a

sense of exposure, of being offered without resistance to some ironic uncuriosity, made Laurence look up at the mountain over the roof of the house. In some gaze—of a man's up there hiding, watching among the clefts and ridges—they seemed held, included and to have their only being. The sense of a watcher, reserve of energy and intention, abashed Laurence, who turned from the mountain. But the unavoidable and containing stare impinged to the point of a transformation upon the social figures with their orderly knitted shadows, the well-groomed grass and the beds, worked out in this pattern. (Bowen 1929a, 119)

When the narrative addresses the possibility of decline at Danielstown proper, it just barely grazes it, as in this delicate description of the anteroom:

The high windows were curtainless; tasselled fringes frayed the light at the top. The white sills, the shutters folded back in their frames, were blistered, as though the house had spent a day in the tropics. Exhausted by sunshine, the backs of the crimson chairs were a thin light orange. . . . There were two locked bookcases of which the keys had been lost, and a troop of ebony elephants brought back from India by someone [Lois] did not remember paraded along the tops of the bookcases. (Bowen 1929a, 9–10)

When the narrative intimates the estate's futility and susceptibility— its "vacancy," to use one of Bowen's recurring terms—it tends (except at the novel's end) to quickly refurbish the house with an influx of presence. Thus Gerald arrives at Danielstown unannounced for lunch, and finds the house disconcertingly empty—not unlike the house of Knott that so perplexes its newcomer, Watt:

Something had now been wiped from the place with implied finality. Gerald told himself it was all very queer, quiet. . . . He tugged the bell, a maid appeared in surprise, did her hair back hastily, encouraged him in with a smile and left him. . . . He listened, took off his trench-coat, stepped to the drawing-room door. The five tall windows stood open on rain and the sound of leaves, rain stuttered along the sills, the grey of the mirrors shivered. Polished tables were cold little lakes of light. The smell of sandalwood boxes, a kind of glaze on the air from all the chintzes numbed his earthy vitality, he became all ribs and uniform. (Bowen 1929a, 87)

Like Betty Vermont and her friend, later in the narrative, Gerald surprises the Big House with its hospitality in abeyance, its civilized performance on hold, and confronts the absence that its social productions mask. Finally, Lois appears, lunch is produced, and Lady

Naylor commandeers him into the drawing room for a spate of mind-numbing talk.

As far as the protagonist's attitude toward this Big House is concerned, it, like her attitudes toward much else, entails an open-ended mix of attraction and repulsion. Working from Ellen Moers's *Literary Women*, Gilbert and Gubar's *The Madwoman in the Attic*, and Gaston Bachelard's *The Poetics of Space*, R. B. Kershner argues: "Although the house in Bowen's work certainly shares the psychological intensity [found] in the image's use by other women writers, it falls neither into Bachelard's category of felicitous space nor into the feminists' nightmarish space" (Kershner 1986, 411). He refers, here, to Bachelard's "house of dream-memory, that is lost in the shadow of a beyond the real past [sic]" (Bachelard 1969, 15), and to the sinister patriarchal structure associated with feminine entrapment. *The Heat of the Day*'s Mount Morris resembles the patriarchal house: Stella muses, "Was it not here in this room . . . that Cousin Nettie Morris—and who now knew how many more before her?—had been pressed back, hour by hour, by the hours themselves, into cloudland? Ladies had gone not quite mad, not even quite that, from in vain listening for meaning in the loudening tick of the clock" (quoted in Seward 1956, 36). Lois's experience of Danielstown, by contrast, fits Kershner's description of Bowen's typically ambiguous house.

As Lois and Hugo return to Danielstown one evening, Bowen generates this agitated portrait of the estate, her most daring and sustained engagement with a vision of her ancestral home's and, by association, her home culture's contingency:

> To the south, below them, the demesne trees of Danielstown made a dark formal square like a rug on the green country. In their heart, like a dropped pin, the grey glazed roof reflecting the sky lightly glinted. Looking down, it seemed to Lois they lived in a forest; space of lawns blotted out in the pressure and dusk of trees. She wondered they were not smothered; then wondered still more that they were not afraid. Far from here too, their isolation became apparent. The house seemed to be pressing down low in apprehension, hiding its face, as though it had her vision of where it was. It seemed to gather its trees close in fright and amazement at the wide, light, lovely unloving country, the unwilling bosom whereon it was set. From the slope's foot, where Danielstown trees began, the land stretched out in a plain flat as water, . . . till the far hills, faint and brittle, straining

against the inrush of vaster distance, cut the droop of the sky like a glass blade. Fields gave back light to the sky—the hedges netting them over thinly and penetrably—as though the sheen of grass were a shadow on water, a breath of colour clouding the face of light. Rivers, profound in brightness, flowed over beds of glass. . . . Down among [the trees], dusk would stream up the paths ahead, lie stagnant over the lawns, would mount in the tank of garden, heightening the walls, dulling the borders like a rain of ashes. . . Seen from above, the house in its pit of trees seemed a very reservoir of obscurity; from the doors one must come out stained with it. . .

But as they drove down the home-sense quickened; the pony, knowing these hedges, rocketed hopefully in the shafts. The house became a magnet to their dependence. And indeed it was nice, they felt in this evening air, to be driving home, with all they would have to tell of the Mount Isabel party, to all they would have to hear of Sir Richard's day in Cork. Friendly women smiled at them over half-doors of cabins. And they both felt approached, friendlier, turning in up the avenue under the arch of the trees; he accepting her with philosophy as though she were his daughter, she comforted in her fancy, as though he had wept coming over the mountains and told her his life was empty because she could never be his wife. (Bowen 1929a, 66–67)

At the outset of this long passage, Lois experiences a sudden dissociation from and objectification of the estate, which leads her to perceive it and its relation to Ireland in a frightening new way. It is, suddenly, nothing more than "a dark formal square like a rug," "a dropped pin," a minute and artificial construct placed by humans, in time, upon a wild "forest" terrain which opposes and ominously threatens it. It is a small dot on a vast landscape, unreal and ephemeral, obliterated, in imagination, by water and dusk. Bowen's language ominously liquefies the ground on which the house rests.

Yet this vision of contingency gets shouldered out of the way by the quickening "home-sense." The narrative returns to business as usual, leaving this disconcerting, disheartening vision—this rupture in "some contact between self and sense perilous to the routine of living"—quite resolutely behind (Bowen 1929a, 67). But the narrative does undermine this reversal by making readers aware that Hugo's and Lois's comforting vision of a stable home is as deluded as Hugo's fantasy that Lois is his daughter, and Lois's that he is her lover. Bowen's Big House keeps shifting: from an isolated, vulnerable structure, to a solid homeplace, to what the text intimates is a hollow illusion, to emerge, in the end, as a structure constituted by a fluctuating play of absence and presence.[6]

In the end, the narrative confronts the house's dramatic demise, but again, agitatedly, in a passage rife with conflicting responses to and interpretations of the climactic event (Bowen 1929a, 205–6). The narrative represents Danielstown's burning, but from a protective, protected distance, as it winds down and pulls away from the landscape, and takes a long withdrawing view. The passage revises its metaphors for the house's fall, casting it first as a "death," an organic, inevitable and natural event, but then as the result of culpable aggression: "For in February . . . the death—execution, rather—of three houses, Danielstown, Castle Trent, Mount Isabel, occurred in the same night" (206). The passage gestures toward uniting Anglo-Ireland and Ireland, or perhaps imposing the former on the latter's "unwilling bosom": "It seemed, looking from east to west at the sky tall with scarlet, that the country itself"—not the Big Houses erected there—"was burning" (206). Bowen imagines cabins "pressed in despair to the bosom of the night," as if they are mourning the houses' passing. The narrative admits, however, that the scene is one of both "order and panic"; indeed, the neat symmetry of the novel's closing and opening scenes—the echoing twang of the iron gate, and the parallel arrivals and departures of cars in the drive—implies the logic and inevitability of this violent outcome. Still, the passage ultimately labels the agents of the house's destruction "executioners." Point of view returns to a now patently delusional solipsism—"The sound of the last car widened, gave itself to the open and empty country and was demolished"—perhaps mocking, perhaps enacting the point of view Bowen explains in "The Big House": the "very great feeling of independence: in the big house one does not feel overlooked; one lives by one's own standards, makes one's own laws and does not care, within fairly wide limits, what anybody outside the demesne walls thinks" (Bowen 1940, 28).

The novel offers one last ironic reference to the myth of civilized hospitality—"Above the steps, the door stood open hospitably upon a furnace"—and then closes in this terse, equivocal paragraph: "Sir Richard and Lady Naylor, not saying anything, did not look at each other, for in the light from the sky they saw too distinctly" (Bowen 1929a, 206). Certainly these lines chastise Anglo-Ireland's tendency to grasp the obvious only too late. But do they implicitly applaud the Naylors' stoic witness-bearing, the restrained civility that elsewhere the narrative debunks? (In "The Big House" Bowen writes, "It is, I think, to the credit of the big house people that they concealed their struggles with such nonchalance" [Bowen 1940, 28].) Or do they critique the Naylors' unflinching attitude, casting it as residually evasive, fashioning these landowners as emotionally inadequate to the events at hand? Interpretability keeps such questions unanswerable. In any event, the novel's closure shares the Naylors' stolid, implacable restraint.

II

At the core of Bowen's unsettled and open-ended representations of the Anglo-Irish problematic stand her dynamic representations of her English, Irish, and Anglo-Irish characters and their tangled relations. It is these shifting portraits of the players on *The Last September*'s stage that perhaps do most to communicate Bowen's blurred assessment of Anglo-Ireland and those Others, English and Irish, against which it historically defended and defined itself.

Of course, "character" is a problematic category to use in connection with Bowen's fiction. As Bennett and Royle argue, "the notion of character (that is, people, real or fictional), is fundamentally transformed in Bowen's writing: her novels derange the very grounds of 'character,' what it is to 'be' a person, to 'have' an identity, to be real or fictional" (Bennett and Royle 1995, xvii). In W. J. McCormack's view, Bowen's narrative "constitutes not only an interrogation of fictional character as a realistic device but also an exposé of (Irish or English) identity as a fiction" (McCormack 1993, 210). While *The Last September* does not destabilize the notion of character as drastically as her later work does, its shifting portraits do indeed attenuate the firm boundaries ostensibly separating "selves" and, concomitantly, social formations. As a result, as McCormack suggests, they wield a significant sociopolitical charge, suggesting that Anglo-Ireland's relations with Ireland and England constitute neither the stark opposition nor the monolithic complicity that prevailing cultural stereotypes might imply. In Bennett's and Royle's words: "The dissolution of the boundaries of the self is mapped onto the problematic construction of political boundaries in the Ireland of 1920" (Bennett and Royle 1995, 18). Perhaps Bowen's conflicting loyalties endowed her with a roving, labile empathy that was negatively capable of breaching historical and cultural boundaries. In any

event, her shifting and indeterminate representations of character—
her portraits of what she called human "amorphousness, the amorphousness of the drifting and flopping jellyfish in a cloudy tide"
(Bowen 1950, 58)—helps make this novel an inconclusive meditation on the competing moral claims of all.[7]

The Last September's Anglo-Ireland is internally divided. It is comprised of a modern camp (Laurence, Lois, Marda) and an old guard
(the Naylors and Montmorencys), each of which criticizes the other
with conviction and force. Moreover, as Margaret Scanlan has ob-
served, the Anglo-Irish woman, not the Irish Other, functions as the
dominant carrier of Otherness—chaos, disruption, blood, sex, death
—in the text. Scanlan argues, "The political activities of the time are
figured to some extent in the disruptions caused by the arrival of
Marda" (Scanlan 1985, 76). In these ways, and in others I will discuss
below, Bowen fractures her Anglo-Ireland from within, challenging
notions of this social formation's stable identity, and prohibiting the
impulse to presume congruency between the "identity" of a social
formation and the identities of its nominal members.

But it is Bowen's shifting portraits of Anglo-Irish men and women
that most consistently interrogate fictional character as a realistic device and most forcefully expose identity, and identity politics, as fictions. With the exception of Lady Naylor, the "amorphous" men and
women of Danielstown (like their counterparts at Keane's Durraghglass) prompt fluctuating mixtures of sympathy and disdain, and
many responses in between, making it difficult for the reader to conclusively assess them. Lady Naylor is, with Keane's Lady Alys and
Beckett's Lady McCann, the novel's apparently requisite female
scapegoat, the object and vehicle of undiluted distaste for Anglo-Ireland. By contrast, Lois and Marda, Hugo and Francie Montmorency,
and Sir Richard if not Lady Naylor are each alternately pitiable,
laughable, compassionate, narcissistic, oracular, deluded—the list of
adjectives goes on.

For instance, Sir Richard remains willfully, culpably blind to political realities. But he is no dissolute, negligent landowner. He is
committed to the welfare of his land. He makes the rounds on his estate each morning, and with particular eagerness one morning after
a storm. "[H]ow much of his corn had been 'laid' by the rain last
night he did not like to imagine; it was better to know" (Bowen
1929a, 79). He is genuinely if ineffectually disheartened by the military activity of the British, exclaiming, "'This country . . . is alto-

gether too full of soldiers, with nothing to do but dance and poke old women out of their beds to look for guns. It's unsettling the people, naturally. The fact is, the Army's got into the habit of fighting and doesn't know what else to do with itself'" (25). While his analysis of cause and effect is deeply flawed, the direction of his sympathies is clear. Upon learning that Gerald has captured Peter Connor, the son of a family whom Danielstown has known and probably employed for years, he "flush[es] severely and responds, 'I'm sorry to hear that. . . . His mother is dying. However, I suppose you must do your duty'" (91–92). Such nuanced, open-ended characterization ripples outward to make *The Last September* the satirical elegy or elegiac satire it is, ensuring that though we perceive Anglo-Ireland's limitations, we feel some sympathy for its predicament and perhaps for its loss.

More dizzying still is Bowen's manipulation of reader response to characters of historically opposed geopolitical identities. As John Coates has shown, *The Last September* is a symmetrical narrative, with an architecture that encourages comparison of characters and pairs of characters (Coates 1990).[8] It is a dialogic text in which event comments upon event, character upon character, in a pervasive pattern of judgment-destabilizing juxtapositions. Thus, if the narrative condemns Anglo-Ireland as myopic and oppressive, particularly in the figure of Myra Naylor, it also gives Anglo-Ireland fierce critics, critics so fierce that they and their critiques are themselves implicitly condemned. The urbane Leslie Lawe, Lois's cousin Laurence, the petty Betty Vermont (who "had never before been to so many large houses with so small sense of her smallness," Bowen chides [Bowen 1929a, 36])—these characters' antagonistic assessments of Anglo-Ireland are at times so extreme as to garner reader sympathy for the Anglo-Ireland that they (and elsewhere Bowen) malign. But this sympathy is itself unstable. For some of these critiques prove equivocal. For instance, Laurence's verbal swipes at Anglo-Ireland are the mark of both the smart-alecky undergraduate and the desperate seer: "'This is an unreal party'"; "'I should like to be here when this house burns'"; "'Tea will be coming, never forget tea'" (43–45). His observations are both cruel and right.

Both the English and the Anglo-Irish wield words and preconceptions as tools for defining and subordinating the Other by which they are subordinated and defined. Each earns readers' censure and sympathy in the process, moving readers to defend and to condemn each of these historically opposed parties, as each judges and is judged. Thus if Betty Vermont and her English friends earn our disapproval for patronizing Anglo-Ireland, the Anglo-Irish earn a symmetrical reaction for condescending in like fashion to the English. Upon bringing a friend to Danielstown, Betty explains, "'I did want Denise to see a lovely old Irish home.'" ("'Yes, we are quaint, really,'" Laurence responds). Betty squeals: "'Oh, darling, look at those teeny black cows. Those are Kerry cows. They farm, you know; they have heaps of cattle'" (Bowen 1929a, 195). The Naylors are as much as part of the scenic spectacle as the "darling cows" (196): "'Ssh, there's Sir Richard writing in the library,'" Betty exclaims. "'Denise *just* look through, sideways. He's such a type'" (195). Yet by the same token Lady Naylor proclaims: "'I think all English people very difficult to trace. They are so pleasant and civil, but I do often wonder if they are not a little shallow: for no reason at all they will pack up everything and move across six counties. . . . Of course, I don't say Gerald Lesworth's people are in *trade*—I should never say a thing like that without foundation. Besides if they were in trade there would be money, money in English people shows so much'" (58). Struggling to look on the bright side of Marda's impending marriage to a man of whom "nothing . . . was Irish except his aunts," Lady Naylor muses, as if inventing a comforting anthropology of a distressingly foreign tribe: "'of course it will be lovely for you being so much nearer everything. And you will have no neighbours, one never has, I believe. . . . I always find the great thing in England is to have plenty to say, and mercifully they are determined to find one amusing. But if one stops talking, they tell one the most extraordinary things, about their husbands, their money affairs, their insides. They don't seem discouraged by not being asked. And they seem so intimate with each other; I suppose it comes from living so close together'" (134). Indeed, Bowen herself disparages her English characters for what she might term their commonness, as in that biting reference to Betty Vermont's "smallness," and as when Betty informs Laurence, "'I have a boy cousin at Reading University. That's quite near Oxford, isn't it?'" (194). She participates in the England-bashing she elsewhere derides.

Such portraiture does more than destabilize the reader's assessment of the juxtaposed parties; it suggests the complexity of Anglo-Irish sympathies. Though they historically looked to England for their young men's educations and careers, Bowen's Anglo-Irish men and women condemn imperial militancy in Ireland. They express class-bound repugnance for what they take to be English vulgarity. Like their Irish neighbors, they at times look upon the English with a spontaneous fear. When Daventry's convoy stops outside the Danielstown gate to let him take news of Gerald's death to Lois, the cottagers become alarmed (Bowen 1929a, 200); likewise, even after learning of the reason for his visit, the Naylors "did not at all care for the look of Mr Daventry. They felt instinctively that he had come here to search the house" (202).

Anglo-Irish attitudes toward Ireland are comparably fraught in Bowen's text. Bowen assigns the worst clichés of Irishness to the English, implying that offensive stereotypes belong to England, not Anglo-Ireland. Betty Vermont tells how her mother "'had brought us all up as kiddies to be so keen on the Irish, and Irish songs. I still have a little bog-oak pig she brought me back from an exhibition. She always said they were the most humorous people in the world, and with hearts of gold. Though of course we had none of us ever been in Ireland.'" Betty finds the country "'so picturesque with those darling mountains and the hens running in and out of the cottages just the way Mother always said'" (Bowen 1929a, 46–47).

But the charged exchange among Lois, Hugo, and Michael Connor at the Connor farm suggests Anglo-Ireland's equivocal participation in those attitudes Bowen tries to attribute to the likes of Betty Vermont (Bowen 1929a, 64–66). The rhetorically complex passage —Bowen's most sustained exploration of the equivocal relation between Anglo-Ireland and Ireland—opens with a description of the farm that rivals Betty Vermont's mother's saccharine portraits and May Swift's tweed pictures. We are given a quaint caricature of a farm, peopled by a teeming mass of indistinguishable Irish children:

> Michael Connor's farm first announced itself by some pink little silky pigs running along the roadside. A sow got up, like a very maternal battleship. Connor children looked, shrieked, fell from a gate and fled to the farmhouse, skirting a pool of liquid manure in the front yard. It was a nice farm, Lois pointed out, it had the door and window-frames painted blue, the colour of all the cart-wheels. The Connors were darling people. (Bowen 1929a, 64)

As at comparable moments in other Anglo-Irish novels, point of view is difficult to determine. Does the passage embody a mind set, perhaps Lois's, that Bowen holds up for our disapproval? Is the problematic point of view Bowen's own? These questions hover over the scene, unanswerable.

What follows is a ritualized, near-feudal exchange between castle and cabin, the kind of exchange we will see Beckett parody in *Watt*. "Michael Connor came out from a furze-thatched shed at the side. He took off his wide straw hat and shook hands with them both. . . . 'It's a grand evening,' said he with a melancholy smile." Lois inquires, as conventions dictate she should, after the ailing Mrs. Connor. Connor responds, "'Ah, the poor woman . . . the poor woman!' Michael looked away from them, nobody spoke. Lois said at last, 'Give her my love.'" "'I will,' said Michael, 'and proud she will be. And yourself's looking lovely, Miss Lois; a fine strong lady, glory be to God.'" When Lois asks if he remembers Hugo, Connor exclaims, "'Sure indeed I do! . . . And very well I remember his poor father. You are looking grand, sir, fine and stout; I known you all these years and I declare I never seen you looking stouter. And welcome back to Danielstown, Mr Montmorency, welcome back, sir!'" (Bowen 1929a, 64–65).

The conversation turns to the Troubles. Connor seems to assume Lois and Hugo will agree with him on the poor behavior of the marauding British: "'the military Carveen have the hearts torn out of us nightly, and we stretched for sleep, chasing and charging about in the lorries they have. Sure you cannot go a step above in the mountains without them ones lepping out from your feet like rabbits. Isn't it the great pity they didn't finish their German war once they had it started?'" (Bowen 1929a, 65). Connor seems to assume Irish and Anglo-Irish comprise an "us" opposable to a disparagable English "them." And Lois seems to bear his assumption out, explaining to Hugo, after they have resumed their homeward journey, that Connor's son Peter "'is on the run—'Proscribed' don't they call it? He could be shot at sight. He is wanted over an ambush in County Clare; they got him once, but he escaped again—I was so glad. I shouldn't wonder if he was up the boreen at the moment. I know he is home, for Clancey saw him three days ago. But don't speak of it—one cannot be too careful'" (66)

But in her interaction with Connor, she does not express this attitude quite so purely. "'And no news at all of Peter?' Lois asked, diffident," as if leery of broaching a topic that she knows he might resent, a topic on which he might rightly mistrust her. She is, after all, the lover of an English soldier. "'We have not,' said Michael, expressionless," his sudden impassivity implying the falsity of his response. The in-group dialogue transforms itself, at this moment, into a tensed and wary exchange between members of opposing factions who only intermittently behave and perhaps only intermittently see themselves as such. The moment passes quickly. "'And I don't know what is to be the end of it,' resumed Michael, with a return to his conversational manner. 'I couldn't tell you what will be the outcome at all. These surely are times that would take the heart from you. And thank you, Miss Lois, and you too yourself, your honour'" (Bowen 1929a, 65).

One might argue that this conversation is, on the whole, an exchange among like-minded if socially unequal countrymen and women that is interrupted by an apparently anomalous blip of divisive wariness—as if Connor himself remains committed to sustaining the "us." But is this exchange what it seems? Or is Michael Connor acting the part of the submissive serf to camouflage his family's republicanism? Is his end of the dialogue, which a reader reading for Bowen's identity politics might condemn as gross "stage Irish" caricature (his grandchildren "'do be stravaging about always and not contented at all. They are a great distress to herself'" [Bowen 1929a, 65])—is his end of the dialogue Bowen's rendition of his *rendition of* "Irishness," a manifestation of tribal camouflage? Certainly Bowen raises this possibility when Lois explains to Hugo: "'Mrs Michael is dying, you know: she has been dying a long time. The last time I went up they wouldn't let me see her because of the pain. . . '" (66, ellipsis Bowen's). This text's many references to the republicans' guerrilla tactics, along with Bowen's provocative ellipsis, suggest that though "Mrs Michael" may in fact be ill, Lois might well have been prohibited from seeing her to prevent her from stumbling on someone else, perhaps the proscribed Peter himself. Certainly the end of the encounter corroborates the possibility that it is something other than the conventional feudal exchange it may seem. Lois and Hugo drive off and Connor turns away, leaving a flock of geese to attend their departure. Eventually, even the geese "went straining off in the other direction. Their backs were more than oblivious; they made the trap, the couple in it, an illusion. And indeed Lois and Hugo both felt their pause, their talk, their passing had been less than a shadow" (65).

In the end, the scene remains interpretable. It repeats the questions that it perhaps set out to answer: What *is* the nature of the relation between Ireland and Anglo-Ireland? And what, then, is Anglo-Ireland?

These questions persist as the incident draws to a close. Driving home, Lois fills Hugo in on all she knows about the farm's environs, knowledge obtained and confirmed by way of her connections to men on both sides of the conflict: "'There are young men gone from three of the farms up here—Captain Carmichael told me; he is Intelligence Officer. And I know it is true, because Clancey told me too.'" Lois's sympathies do not reside exclusively, or intelligently, with the Irish, as some of her more impulsive utterances might suggest. She muses, "'I say, supposing Gerald had happened to be with us and Peter Connor had come down the boreen, would Gerald have had to have shot him, or would he have been off duty?'" Hugo points out, "'Peter might have shot Gerald.'" Assuming she rests safe in the nest of feudal loyalty, Lois responds, "'Oh no, not when he was with me'" (Bowen 1929a, 66). Her express sympathy for the rebels is, perhaps, little more than skin deep, little more than youthful hankering for melodrama.

Bowen's representations of relations between Anglo-Irish characters and their English and Irish Others, then, create a fluctuating narrative of contestation and debate over how to assess these historical antagonists. Another way of understanding this aspect of Bowen's text is by way of Foucault's notion of immanent power, in which, in Jenny Sharpe's words, "Power is not the right or privilege of a few but a strategy that everyone undergoes and exercises" (Sharpe 1993, 9). In *The Last September* as for Foucault, power is not a discrete state or fixed entity which may be set against a flat opposite called "powerlessness." Rather, power has an alternating structure, in which "having power" and "lacking it" are positions in an ongoing circulation of authority and control. This is not to suggest that power is illusory, or to minimize power's deleterious potency. As Steven Connor writes: "The effect is not to elide or abolish power. Rather, it is to point to power as centreless and unfixed, as consisting in exchange rather than in permanence" (Connor 1988, 180). Power "is everywhere; not because it embraces everything, but because it comes from everywhere" (Foucault 1980, 197).

Thus if Gerald Lesworth snares Peter Connor, Lady Naylor vanquishes Gerald; as Lassner observes, "He is, in effect, treated like the Irish revolutionaries" (Lassner 1991, 34). In the end Lady Naylor, too, is vanquished, her house burned by the I.R.A. If Gerald is, in his interview with Lady Naylor, a victim of Anglo-Ireland's elitist disdain, he is, in a conversation with Laurence, an ethnocentric proponent of Empire who mistakes the English way of doing business—conditioned by history, motivated by self-interest—for Civilization (Bowen 1929a, 92–93). Bowen assigns Gerald an ugly attitude toward the Irish; they are "'blighters'" (91), "'beggars'" whom he would like to "'clean . . . out in a week!'" (38). And Bowen counterbalances his attitude with Lady Naylor's proprietary stance toward "'the people,'" "'our people'" (26). Likewise, the apparently obsequious Michael Connor who scrapes and bows to "Miss Lois" (64) is also the potent father of an I.R.A. man (and perhaps his skillful protector). The Black and Tans stationed in Clonmore are the effective agents of imperial power, and they are, also, its victims, as Bowen dramatizes most vividly in the shell-shocked Mr. Daventry, who "'had a company in France in 1916.'" Hardly fortified by the power he wields in Ireland, he is clearly afflicted by what he experiences as yet another demoralizing, dehumanizing mission. At the Rolfes' dance:

> He kept shutting his eyes; whenever he stopped dancing he noticed that he had a headache. He had been out in the mountains all night and most of the morning, searching some houses for guns that were known to be there. He had received special orders to ransack the beds, and to search with particular strictness the houses where men were absent and women wept loudest and prayed. Nearly all beds had contained very old women or women with very new babies, but the N.C.O., who was used to the work, insisted that they must go through with it. Daventry still felt sickish. (Bowen 1929a, 144)

Empire is an absent cause that turns all characters into its pawns.

Bowen's conception of power destabilizes stereotypical conceptions of dominance and subordination and counters notions of sociopolitical relations as statically hierarchical. In the knotty relations of England, Ireland, and Anglo-Ireland, as Bowen narrates them, shifting power dynamics preclude clear-cut assignations of empowerment and disempowerment, or steady assessments of innocence and guilt. Far from championing Anglo-Ireland's historical power, far from merely lamenting its loss, *The Last September* goes so far as to dispel the model of hierarchy on which a Yeatsian mourning for Anglo-Irish authority would have to rest. In the end, *The Last September*'s rendering of power denaturalizes all political hierarchies that pretend to be essential or absolute, dramatizing power's inevitable fluctuation within circumstance, context, and time.

The mill scene constitutes perhaps the novel's most entangled representation of power's operations (Bowen 1929a, 122–26). Out for a walk with Hugo, Marda and Lois come upon the ruined mill, which the adventurous Marda urges Lois to join her in exploring. "The mill startled them all, staring, light-eyed, ghoulishly, round a bend of the valley" (122). "Those dead mills—the country was full of them, never quite stripped and whitened to skeletons' decency: like corpses at their most horrible" (123). This site gathers together all the hierarchical relations and historical oppressions that this novel's postcolonial scene evokes, casting power and hierarchy as fluid and unfixed. On the one hand, the mill alludes to Anglo-Ireland's one-time economic and territorial power; it was Protestants, backed by Empire, who built, ran, and profited from such industries. In ruins, the mill also emblematizes Anglo-Ireland's decline, evoking Empire's indifference if not hostility to Anglo-Irish industries, most specifically, and its economic interests, more broadly. It represents "'Another,' Hugo declared, 'of our national grievances'" (123). As we have seen, the mill prefigures the burnt houses that will soon join it, "ghoulishly," on the Irish landscape. Now, though, it serves as a hideout for an armed I.R.A. man, who threatens the two Anglo-Irish women ("'It is time . . . that yourselves gave up walking. If you have nothing better to do, you had better keep in the house while y'have it'" [125]) and wounds Marda with his gun. On this site, as in the broader social and political world of *The Last September*, the positions of contending social groups shift among exploiter and exploited, oppressor and oppressed. Power as Bowen represents it proves her novel's great leveler.

III

While *The Last September* is indeed, as I have been arguing, another in a series of equivocal novels in the Anglo-Irish tradition, this novel's emphasis falls on the young woman's place in the Anglo-Irish social formation and her gendered response to its twentieth-century demise. Lois Farquar is the novel's focal character, the pivot on which the plot turns. The text is, as Ann Owens Weekes has argued, Lois's *bildungsroman*, a chronicle of her quest for viable identity. As she gropes toward this elusive goal, Lois makes this pained admission to Marda Norton: "'I hate women. But I can't think how to begin to be anything else'" (Bowen 1929a, 99). Lois does not mean that she hates females. Indeed, she comes close to falling in love with Marda and speculates, "'I think . . . I must be a woman's woman'" (100). What Lois hates, rather, is the phenomenon of women as she knows it. She hates, in other words, the prevailing construction of femininity, and her *bildungsroman* is Bowen's attempt to analyze why.[9]

Writing on "Feminism and the 'New Historicism,'" Judith Lowder Newton has called attention to: "a tendency still familiar in much cultural materialist work, a tendency to define class in terms of men's economic and social relations with each other, a tendency to define class consciousness in terms of men's values and interests, and a tendency to associate the development of class identity with events in which men played the central role or in which women's participation has not been fully explored" (Newton 1989, 159). Molly Mullin has discussed this tendency in the Irish context, contending that "there have been relatively few studies of the way in which assumptions about tradition and public representations of national pasts relate to *gendered* subjectivities," and urging that we "no longer assume that there is only one proper past, one history, but rather multiple and always selective versions of histories" (Mullin 1991, 32–33). This assumption of "one proper past, one history" has prevailed in the study of Anglo-Ireland as well. Anglo-Irish history and identity have been constructed, and critical accounts of literary encounters with that history and identity have largely proceeded, from a masculine point of view.

In her preface to *The Last September*, Bowen herself provides a masculinist definition of Anglo-Ireland's ambiguous geopolitical identity that provides a fine example of the tendency Newton describes: "Inherited loyalty (or at least adherence) to Britain—where their sons were schooled, in whose wars their sons had for generations fought, and to which they owed their 'Ascendancy' lands and power—pulled them one way; their own temperamental Irishness the other" (Bowen 1952a, 125). In *The Last September* proper, however, Bowen interrogates such definitions, emphasizing how differently women and men were placed in Anglo-Irish culture. Her interrogation proceeds in the spirit of the claim Virginia Woolf makes in *A Room of One's Own*: "If one is a woman one is often surprised by a sudden splitting off of consciousness, say in walking down Whitehall, when from being the natural inheritor of that civilization, she becomes, on the contrary, outside of it, alien and critical" (Woolf 1929, 91). Barred access to English schools, prohibited from serving in the legions of Empire abroad, enjoying a severely diluted relation to "'Ascendancy' lands and power," Anglo-Irish women bore relations to England, Ireland, Empire, authority, land, property, servitude—all those components of what I have called the Anglo-Irish problematic—that were profoundly different from the relations Anglo-Irish men enjoyed and endured.[10]

The diluted feminine relation to Protestant land and power is announced by the masculinist metaphors historically used to describe Anglo-Ireland's relation to Ireland. In her 1919 novel *Mount Music*, Edith Somerville describes the landowner's "feudal feeling that the Mount Music tenants were his, as they had been his ancestors', to have and to hold, to arbitrate and stand by, as a fond and despotic husband rules and stands by an obedient wife, loving and bullying her (but both entirely for her own good)" (quoted in Flanagan 1966, 70). Bowen herself deploys such metaphors when she refers to Danielstown's having been imposed on the "unwilling bosom" of the Irish landscape and, in "The Big House," when she refers to Anglo-Ireland's "divorce from the countryside in whose heart their struggle was carried on" (Bowen 1940, 27).[11]

Of course, such metaphors are not unique to Anglo-Irish literature or to the Irish situation. Andrew Parker, Mary Russo, Doris Sommer, and Patricia Yaeger show "how deeply engrained has been the depiction of the homeland as a female body whose violation by foreigners requires its citizens and allies to rush to her defense," recalling that "this trope of the nation-as-woman of course depends for its representational efficacy on a particular image of woman as chaste, dutiful, daughterly or maternal" (A. Parker, et al. 1992a, 6). And in the Irish context such metaphors are not exclusively Anglo-Ireland's. As Weekes explains: "The practice of seeing the conquered country as female goes back to the early Gaelic poetry, to the perception of Ireland as 'Mother Ireland,' 'Dark Rosaleen,' or the most insidious image, 'Kathleen Ní Houlihan,' the old woman restored by the warrior to youthful beauty. England, the conqueror, is always male in this paradigm" (Weekes 1990, 90). The femininization of Ireland has served both nationalistic and imperial agendas, with adverse implications for women. As Toni O'Brien Johnson and David Cairns argue, where a female figure "stands for the land, the earth/body analogy becomes the burden of the woman, with an inevitably reductive effect which tends to undermine any notion of the woman being something more than her mere body." A reflection of a "masculinist drive to invest the female figure with the meaning it favours and fix it," "the woman is being used to reproduce an idea" (Johnson and Cairns 1991, 4). Or as Nuala Ní Dhomhnaill asserts, "there is a psychotic splitting involved where, the more the image of woman comes to stand for abstract concepts like justice, liberty, or national sovereignty, the more real women are denigrated and consigned barefoot and pregnant to the kitchen" (Ní Dhomhnaill 1996, 16).

What impact might such metaphors have had on Anglo-Irish women's relations to their home culture? For better or for worse, masculinist mythologies of a feminized Ireland might have inhibited Anglo-Irish women from conceiving of the kind of "union" with Ireland that the mythology sanctioned for Anglo-Irish men. The myth might thus have reinforced women's legalized exclusion from the stereotypical Protestant relation to the land. Weekes argues that the myth might also have promoted a bond of empathy with the feminized landscape so fondly ruled—a bond leading to the kind of quip I quote from Iris Murdoch's *The Red and the Green*: "Being a woman is like being Irish." Allegations of such bonds are problematic, as we shall see.

Bowen's focus on gender in *The Last September* has a critical impact on her representation of Anglo-Ireland. By foregrounding gender, *The Last September* challenges the myth of an inherently gracious Protestant Ascendancy in terms other than those of novelists who focus on the bankruptcy of Anglo-Ireland's relations to "Irish-Ireland," or those of historians, like J. C. Beckett and W. J. McCormack, whose accounts of Anglo-Ireland's internal discontinuities emphasize class. Though, as I have shown, *The Last September* participates in many of the tradition's habitual concerns, it also reframes questions of hierarchy and authority, which Anglo-Irish fiction typically explores in the context of Protestant-Catholic relations, in terms of gender. Gender in this novel is, in Carroll Smith Rosenberg's words, "a fault line undercutting the solidity of class identity" (Rosenberg 1986, 33), revealing Anglo-Ireland to be an internally hierarchized social formation where tyranny reigns not just without but also within the Big House. *The Last September*'s Anglo-Ireland is not just that "anarchy in the mind and in the heart" which we may trace in other Anglo-Irish texts. It is, also, that which is "experienced differently by individuals who were positioned differently within the social formation [and] . . . articulated differently by the different institutions, discourses, and practices that it both constituted and was constituted by" (Poovey 1988, 4). Attending to women's placement in Anglo-Irish culture, *The Last September* unveils (paraphrasing Newton) deep-seated and potentially destabilizing tensions within Anglo-Irish ways of imagining the world (Newton 1989, 161).

Ann Owens Weekes's groundbreaking study, *Irish Women Writers: An Uncharted Tradition,* precedes my thinking about Bowen in emphasizing the importance of the category of gender to discussions of Irish literary culture. But Weekes underemphasizes the extent to which varying social and economic pressures have interacted with gender to foster significantly different experiences for Irish and Anglo-Irish women. As Andrew Parker et al. remind us, "One of the gains of academic feminism has been its hard-won recognition that gender relations cannot be 'understood in stable or abiding terms' either within or between the borders of nations, and that while patriarchy may be universal, its specific structures and embodied effects are certainly not."[12] Though both Anglo-Irish and Gaelic-Irish cultures (as Weekes calls them) were indeed patriarchal, as she argues, prevailing economic and legal systems made them patriarchal in very different ways. Weekes minimizes these differences, contending that colonization "makes female both country and people, ironically bonding both the women 'of' the colonizers and the peoples colonized" (Weekes 1990, 15). Thus she goes on to claim, "By 1800 . . ., despite the number of Gaelic-Irish women engaged in manufacturing textiles, Irish women's lot on the whole—their economic, social, and legal statuses, those important determinants of personality and perspective—was, unlike men's, different in degree rather than in kind" (16–17). One need only point out how dramatically, up until the twentieth century, Anglo-Irish women outnumber Irish women in the ranks of published writers to suggest the limits of this analysis.[13]

Due in part to her reading of Irish women's history, Weekes's claims for a women's tradition of writing in Ireland—"a unified tradition of subjects and techniques, a unity that might become an optimistic model not only for Irish literature but also for Irish people" (Weekes 1990, 219)—seem forced. Surprisingly, her final chapter, "Irish Women Writers: The Experience of the Mass," draws distinctions between social formations that counter both her readings of individual texts and her totalizing claims for a women's tradition; for instance: "I suggest that the childhood training of girl children in the relatively wealthy group of Anglo-Irish Protestants was closer to that Chodorow characterizes as male than was the training of girl children in the Gaelic-Irish Catholic homes" (217). Clearly, the time is ripe for an extensive study of literature by Anglo-Irish women from the point of view of gender, class, and postcoloniality. Such studies of writing by women from the nationalist tradition have, of course, already begun to proliferate.[14]

In exploring the impact of gender, *The Last September* shares common ground with the novels of Molly Keane, and Edith Somerville and Martin Ross, which also attend to Anglo-Irish women's places in and perspectives on their home culture. But other Anglo-Irish women writers tell the truth a bit more slant than Bowen does. A brief consideration of their work is in order, to isolate just how distinctive and significant a departure *The Last September* is.

Any discussion of Anglo-Irish women writers must begin with Maria Edgeworth. Here, as elsewhere, I will use Weekes's reading of a central text as a starting point, as Weekes's concern throughout *Irish Women Writers* is to demonstrate how critical analyses of gender politics unite Irish women's work across centuries, borders, and cultures. Her reading of *Castle Rackrent*'s treatment of gender has two prongs. She argues, first, that the 1800 novel explores "the contradictions in the landlord-tenant relationships and the uncertainties and potential dangers in the marriage contract" (Weekes 1990, 39). In her view, "Edgeworth draws clear parallels between the behavior of the Rackrents as landlords and of the Rackrents as husbands" (42). She concludes, "Ignoring the mutuality of commitments implied by the words *husband* and *landlord*, the Rackrents, while insisting on their legal positions, reduce and destroy the 'natural' basis of semantic and legal definitions. Their own barren natural conditions symbolize their true standing as both husbands and landlords" (55). The second prong of Weekes's analysis rests on an examination of narrative technique. While the novel's narrator, Thady Quirk, "dismisses the Rackrent women's problems," Weekes contends that "the persistent jettisoning of the women's, or domestic, plot into the lacunae created by Thady's parataxis calls attention to the discarded plot, an instance of the italicizing by underemphasizing that Nancy Miller discusses" (32).[15]

Weekes uses these readings as a platform from which to claim gender awareness for Edgeworth and gender focus for *Rackrent*, and to find a full-blown feminism in an at best ambivalently protofeminist text. Edgeworth's portraits of the Rackrent marriages do not amount to a critique of marriage *per se*, they remain more critiques of particular marriages than, as Weekes concludes, a "subversive domestic plot." And as Marilyn Butler has argued, Edgeworth's use of Thady as narrator "certainly does not allow the story to speak for her" (M. Butler 1972, 306). Rather, it highlights a male servant's shifting assessment of his Anglo-Irish employers. The Anglo-Irish woman's point of view on feminine experience remains muted.

Weekes's most compelling reading emerges in her examination of how women's stories end in *Castle Rackrent*: "In terminating women's stories with their marriages, the structure as well as the content [of traditional narrative] signals that marriage is the end of women's lives and of their interest as narrative subjects. Edgeworth reverses the schema, opening her sequences with the women's marriages and closing with their escapes" (Weekes 1990, 57). Still, *Castle Rackrent*'s women are not its focus. The narrative spotlight remains trained on Rackrent men, and the Rackrent women are less characters than props and thematic vehicles in the text.

Like those of other Anglo-Irish writers, Edith Somerville's and Martin Ross's texts indict while enacting many of Anglo-Ireland's most unsympathetic colonialist gestures.[16] Weekes's reading of their most critically acclaimed novel, *The Real Charlotte*, like her reading of *Castle Rackrent*, identifies a solid feminist agenda where the text at best intimates an uncertain one. For instance: "The authors' names on the title page, the male-sounding E. Œ. Somerville and Martin Ross, complicate, as does Edgeworth's male narrator, the narrational stance and allow us to read all the narrational insensitivities and acceptances of female victimization as the representation by two women authors of women's views of the contemporary male perspective" (Weekes 1990, 70–71). She offers this reading of Charlotte Mullen's gender-bending cat Susan: "the confusion of Susan's gender calls attention to the arbitrariness . . . of gender roles, roles that confer, among other privileges, the right, or at least the option, of pursuit to tomcats and men" (Weekes 1990, 73). Her most elaborate contention proceeds: "In depicting the crumbling of the Anglo-Irish ascendancy, Somerville and Ross reveal the connections between the society and the patriarchal family on which it is modeled; the source of disintegration in their beloved society mirrors and can be seen as a logical extension of the source of injustice in the equally beloved family. The arbitrariness of the access to power—political, economic, and social—which membership in the ascendancy ordained, reflects the arbitrariness of gender-specific roles ordained by membership in the patriarchal family" (61). Such aspects of *The Real Charlotte* would constitute decidedly oblique critiques of gender compared to Bowen's.

In making such arguments, Weekes seems to work from Somerville and Ross's autobiographical writings and to ground her analysis of the "tyranny of gender" (Weekes 1990, 73) in *The Real Charlotte* on them. The autobiographical texts do indeed reveal a disastrously cramped and painful construction of Anglo-Irish femininity. Somerville complained: "Daughters . . . were at a discount, . . . permitted to eat of the crumbs that fell from their brothers' tables, and if no crumbs fell the daughters went unfed" (Somerville and Ross 1917, 52). But the interpretations of the fiction to which such autobiographical revelations lead Weekes—regarding, for example, "how the accident of gender determines one's life, creating another, more fundamental, political disease at the core of the social order" (Weekes 1990, 77)—are more in the spirit of *The Last September* than *The Real Charlotte* or *The Irish R.M.* To be sure, "as a woman Charlotte is not considered for the agentship of Bruff, whereas masculinity alone qualifies the mediocre Lambert" (77); to be sure, "Charlotte's is the tragedy of gender. Born female, she cannot employ her 'male' talents; born plain, she cannot compete in the only business open to women"—marriage (79). But Charlotte is hardly representative of Anglo-Irish femininity; she is in fact excluded from that social order, and disdained by the narrator for her Irish-seeming vulgarities. In Rudiger Imhof's words, "Charlotte Mullen is the descendent of Jason Quirk" (Imhof 1992b, 96). So to look to her career as a litmus test for how women fare in Anglo-Ireland is problematic. This text leaves the Anglo-Irish construction of femininity as Somerville and Ross themselves might have experienced it all but untouched.

The point is worth emphasizing: *The Real Charlotte* does not address the fate of women who are poised to "succeed" in Anglo-Ireland. As Virginia Beards writes in her introduction to the 1986 Rutgers edition: "The novel is about the fates of different sorts of women in a particular patriarchal, materialistic society"—a society in which "marriage constitutes a natural selection principle guaranteeing a female's survival" (Somerville and Ross 1894, xi). "In a society that places such a high value on women's looks," Beards observes, "it is no wonder that Francie and Charlotte suffer as they do" (xvi). Neither woman has the pedigree nor the manners she needs to prosper on the marriage market. Unlike Bowen's Lois Farquar, Charlotte doesn't hate being a woman. She hates being an unattractive woman; she envies Francie's beauty. As Sean McMahon argues, "Her ideal is to be lady of a more substantial house than her modest legacy Tally-ho, and to live in it as the loving wife of Roderick Lambert" (McMahon 1968, 129). Charlotte and by extension Somerville and Ross seem not to get on the outside of patriarchal values to the extent that Bowen does in *The Last September*. Their real Charlotte longs to be patriarchy's ideal woman. As I will argue, Bowen's critique of gender cuts deeper.[17]

In *Good Behaviour* as throughout much of her work, Molly Keane's abiding concern is less gender politics than family politics. Family dysfunction and devotion to the refined savagery of "good behaviour" are the crucial agents that make Aroon St. Charles who she is. Certainly her big body's failure to conform to the prevailing ideal of feminine beauty plays a part in her fate; the narrating Aroon, aged fifty-seven, muses: "Sometimes I think (though I would never say it) how nice that bosoms are all right to have now; in the twenties when I grew up I used to tie them down with a sort of binder. Bosoms didn't do then. They didn't do at all" (Keane 1981, 4). And Aroon bemoans her social status as "the unmarried daughter who doesn't play bridge, letting out the dogs for evermore" (219). But she frames these complaints not as objections to a limiting patriarchal order but as objections to her continued thrall to her mother: "Mummie and Rose would be in power over me, over Temple Alice, until I was old, or middle-aged at best, beyond even the remembrance of time past" (219); she is "a child of the house living in the grace and favour of unexplored obedience" (164). How family circles form and close against Aroon; how her mother suppresses her every urge to flourish and grow, enlisting the allegiances of Papa, Hubert, and finally Rose in the effort—these are Aroon's primary determinants and Keane's main focus. Like Bowen, Keane unveils division and strife within the ostensibly civilized Big House, but it is, in the end, a family and not a patriarchal affair. Temple Alice is, after all, a vehemently matriarchal structure.

The narrative regrets Aroon's status as the unmarried daughter of the house, and sympathizes with that plight. But, like *The Real Charlotte*'s assessment of Charlotte's situation, it grants that that status is a plight, never venturing beyond the confines of the domestic space or the marriage plot to entertain other modes of being, or hypothesize other categories by which to live. Aroon doesn't ask Lois Farquar's question—"'What am I to do?'"—until her father dies, at which point she is given the domestic and, as such, financial power she craves. Weekes argues: "Economic independence is the actual liberating, empowering force that allows Aroon to control her life through controlling the narrative" (Weekes 1990, 173). But what social power Aroon gains remains severely circumscribed, essentially domestic. It has the effect of keeping her enclosed in the domestic sphere, where she merely perpetuates her mother's brutal power politics, inverting the old hierarchy and torturing, finally killing her "Mummie." Certainly the present tense voice of the narrative's first chapter—querulous, beleaguered—suggests that Aroon has not grown over the years, that she retains profound and persistent self-doubts, despite her domestic power.

The most notable by-product of Aroon's autonomy is indeed her narrative, through which she may lay claim to a relatively free-standing identity. But like its author, this narrative remains enclosed in the enveloping familial, domestic space. And it ends without a return to the present tense in which it begins; the novel ends in Aroon's recreated past, as if her present tense narrative is overwhelmed by her narrative of the past. This truncation of the narrative frame closes the text on a fragmented, off-balance note, suggesting the extent to which Aroon remains marooned in her constricting past, and perhaps suggesting, too, her difficulty in asserting and sustaining a viable, distinctly present-tense identity. If narrative equals control, Aroon seems not to know it. In the end, what power Aroon does gain in the course of her story—domestic, psychological, narrative—appears deeply provisional.[18]

Perhaps only George Moore's *A Drama in Muslin* (1886)—a novel which, given her focus on women writers, Weekes does not consider—equals *The Last September* in the directness and intensity of its confrontation with gender inequities. As Klaus Lubbers argues, in Moore's novel, "the doings of the Land League and the decadence of the gentry are subordinated to the exposure of the 'elegant harlotry' [p. 184] of the marriage market and the sacrifice of 'the poor muslin martyrs' [p. 291], i.e. the daughters of a gentry burdened with a surplus of females, at the Shelbourne Hotel and at the Castle balls" (Lubbers 1992, 26). The trajectory of Alice Barton's life adumbrates Bowen's own: she escapes this martyrdom and becomes a writer.

I provide this survey of selected novels by other Anglo-Irish women neither to impugn their feminist credentials nor to applaud Bowen's, but to highlight just how different Bowen's handling of gender is. Although Bowen resisted the idea of the "feminist writer" and even denigrated her friend Virginia Woolf's feminism as an "obsession," "a bleak quality, an aggressive streak, which can but irritate" (Bowen 1949a, 81), in the majority of her fiction, as Lassner argues, "women are exemplars of social and economic oppression as well as harbingers of alternative strategies for survival" (Lassner 1991, 8). In *The Last September*, Bowen tackles the issue of gender head on, without the "italicizing of demaximation" of Edgeworth's "discarded" domestic plot, or the "muted voice of a double discourse" of Edgeworth and Somerville and Ross (Weekes 1990, 197). She does not write under a male pseudonym, nor does she deploy a male narrator. Bowen scrutinizes Anglo-Ireland's dominant construction of femininity directly. Lois Farquar's story is not muted, nor is the novel's interest in the workings of gender in the Big House masked; if anything, it is Irish politics and culture that Bowen places on the sidelines. *The Last September* expands on insights of other Anglo-Irish women writers, offering a sustained and unflinching interrogation of the Anglo-Irish construction of femininity and its costs.

Moreover, Bowen focuses her narrative on women who enjoy what little power Anglo-Irish women had: the power to attract men. Lois and Marda are fully eligible to receive what "benefits" Anglo-Irish culture had to offer them. In focusing not on characters that reigning constructions of femininity would have defined as deficient (physically non-ideal, or inadequately moneyed or related) but on those who approximated the cultural ideal, Bowen's critique of Anglo-Irish patriarchy cuts both deeper and wider than those of Somerville and Ross and Keane. It goes beyond re-evaluating patriarchy's ostensibly inferior woman to interrogate and disqualify even its beloved ideal. This ideal is not workable for the women of *The Last September*. It comprises a collection of roles in which the women of this novel chafe. Possessing what power Anglo-Ireland granted women, these women question that power's sufficiency, making Bowen's novel a forceful plea to escape the patriarchal value system altogether.

IV

The Last September demystifies received ideas of femininity. The demystification begins on the novel's opening page, with Bowen's sardonic harping on the importance of Lois's appearance, and on Lois's self-conscious compliance with the injunction to look "fresh." Such challenges to ideal femininity's ostensible naturalness permeate the text. For instance, describing a conversation between Livvy and her suitor on the subject of Lois, Bowen writes: "This concern for her friend she put up and twirled like a parasol between them. . . . Her panama hat turned down and light tufts of hair came out in fluttering commas against her cheek-bones" (Bowen 1929a, 39). Bowen dissipates the lady's prop into a surreal, satirical metaphor—a parasol of specious concern—and describes one of the lady's iconographic attributes in an orthographic image bordering on the grotesque. Similarly, at tea one day, the conspicuous Livvy refuses a cigarette, saying, "she would *not* smoke, she would not indeed: they might laugh but she was an old-fashioned girl. Her continued protests attracted a good deal of attention, till she noticed that old-fashioned girls were after all in the majority. . . . So she accepted a strong cigarette of Captain Carmichael's and Smith broke into a howl and said she had sacrificed his ideal of womanhood" (72). During the dance at the English barracks Lois and Gerald venture outside, where a cold wind howls; "'At one time,' said Lois, wrapping her wild skirts round her, 'a girl would have died of this'" (151). Bowen's narrative insists the feminine ideal is a malleable, provisional construction, a text in the process of being rewritten.

As Carroll Smith Rosenberg has argued: "Images of the body and rules regulating its treatment and behavior . . . correlate closely to social categories and the distribution of power. Differences in the rules governing the body (dress and sexual codes, freedom of movement, and so forth) will demarcate social differences and positions of relative power. A concern with social control will dictate a system of rigid bodily and sexual restrictions governing the group to be socially controlled" (Rosenberg 1986, 49). One of the primary means by which Bowen destabilizes the myth of "the lady" is by displaying Lois's unconventionally unrestricted body. "Lois turned in at the back door and pulled herself up to dress by the back-stairs banisters. She sniffed—duck for dinner again" (Bowen 1929a, 70); "Lois sat on the hall table to look at the *Tatler*" (76); Lois comes upon Marda, "engaged in manicure. Little pots, pads and bottles paraded. . . . 'The most I can do,' said Lois, intent, 'is to keep mine clean'" (95). Toward the end of the novel, Lois arrives at the Rolfes' dance, which is already in full swing. "But one hadn't yet made one's official appearance: Lois blinked and began to tug out her silver shoes from her pockets; somebody pulled her on down a passage to change" (148–49). Certainly Bowen is not vehement about Lois's body, as Keane is about her aging ladies' in *Time After Time*. And Bowen refrains from that Swiftian focus on bodily functions and imperfections that we witness in Keane and in Beckett. But she does insist, politely, that we observe the gap between the idealized young lady as she ought to appear and this young woman as she physically, often awkwardly, is. She reminds us that the lady's "official appearance" is, like Anglo-Ireland's, a construction engineered to secure a premeditated effect, to satisfy a preconceived idea.

But Bowen does more than scrutinize traditional constructions of femininity. *The Last September*'s narrative structure deliberately isolates the workings of gender by juxtaposing the young Anglo-Irish woman's career to the young Anglo-Irish man's. Like Woolf in *A Room of One's Own*, Bowen invents a bleak parallel case.[19] As if determined to demonstrate how "Anglo-Irishness" takes different forms across gender lines, *The Last September* systematically contrasts Lois Farquar's story to Laurence Naylor's, driving home the phenomenon of gender difference within this supposed "unity of culture."

The novel opens and closes on scenes that link the cousins. After the Montmorencys arrive at Danielstown, Laurence and Lois whisper and reconnoiter, like naughty children conspiring against adults (Bowen 1929a, 8–13). At the novel's end, the two exchange what last words they can regarding the story's harrowing conclusions (203–4). After hinting, during this encounter, that she would like to be left alone, Lois tells Laurence, "'Though if it has to be anyone, you'" (204)—an equivocal acceptance of his company that constitutes as sturdy a bond as any in the novel.

Like Judith and William Shakespeare's, Lois and Laurence's circumstances are neatly symmetrical. About the same age, members of the same class, both are orphans, dependent on aunts and uncles for a semblance of family and home. Neither has money. Neither really belongs at Danielstown. Each stays there for lack of anywhere else to be. But here the similarities end.

Bowen's portrait of Lois reveals a painfully marginalized young woman.[20] Lois's marginalization is partly a function of Anglo-Irishness. All the Anglo-Irish, as Bowen maintained, "were really only at home in mid-crossing between Holyhead and Dun Laoghaire" (Glendinning 1977, 11); thus Lois marvels at the purposeful Irishman she spies striding across her uncle's land: "It must be because of Ireland he was in such a hurry. . . . Here was something else she could not share. She could not conceive of her country emotionally" (Bowen 1929a, 34). Her alienation is partly a function of generation; Lois could not participate fully in the conversations of the Naylors and the Montmorencys, based in years of mutual knowledge, even if she wanted to. Moreover, Lois remains "niece always, never child, of that house" (126). As Lois tells Daventry late in the novel, "'I don't live anywhere, really'" (157). Her family membership is, like May Swift's, tenuous, contingent.

But at bottom, it is Lois's status as a nascent "lady" that gives her alienation its depth and Bowen's critique of gender its charge.[21] Bowen calls attention to Lois's gendered marginalization in the novel's first scene. After exchanging their greetings in "the yellow theatrical sunshine" (Bowen 1929a, 7), the Naylors and the Montmorencys

> swept in; their exclamations, constricted suddenly, filling the hall. There was so much to say after twelve years: they all seemed powerless. Lois hesitated, went in after them and, as nobody noticed, came out again. The car with the luggage turned and went round to the back, deeply scoring the gravel. She yawned and looked out over the sweep to the lawn beyond, where little tufts of shadow pricked like reeds from water out of the flat gold light. (Bowen 1929a, 8)

Beside the point, like the chauffeur with the luggage, Lois is left contemplating the details of the familiar landscape while the social transaction of the moment goes on without her. "She yawned with reaction" (8). "Her cousin Laurence," meanwhile, "had gone upstairs with a book when he heard the motor" (8).

We learn immediately thereafter of Lois's penchant for Danielstown's anteroom, "though it wasn't the ideal place to read or talk. Four rooms opened off it; at any moment a door might be opened, or blow open, sending a draught down one's neck. People passed through it continually, so that one kept having to look up and smile. Yet Lois always seemed to be talking there, standing with a knee on a chair because it was not worth while to sit down" (Bowen 1929a, 9). Her favorite place is not a room of her own but a liminal, transitional space that keeps her unsettled and unplaced, and drags her attention to the apparently more purposeful agendas of the others in the house—a vivid emblem of her relationship-based placelessness.

Lois's activities are restricted and rigidly defined. She arranges the flowers. She goes to dances. She plays tennis and takes tea. Meanwhile, the Black and Tans skirmish with the I.R.A. Men are killed in ambush. She marvels to Gerald Lesworth: "'Do you know that while that was going on, eight miles off, I was cutting a dress out, a voile that I didn't even need, and playing the gramophone? . . . How is it that in this country that ought to be full of such violent realness, there seems nothing for me but clothes and what people say? I might just as well be in some kind of cocoon'" (Bowen 1929a, 49).

When Lois seeks advice on how to escape her cocoon, she is directed toward dilettantish pursuits: the study of Italian, or German, or drawing. Lady Naylor resolves, "'I shall talk to Lois seriously about her future. She draws very nicely; I often think that she might take that up'" (Bowen 1929a, 59). In her opinion, "'girls needed interests . . . and I've always thought that music or drawing, or writing a little, or organization of some kind—'" (164). Marda suggests vaguely, "'Why can't you write, or something?'" (98). Lois complains, "'If I learn German, they say, why not Italian? And when I learn Italian they take no interest'" (187). The day of Marda's departure from Danielstown provides bleakly comic images of Lois's gendered aimlessness: "she was bouncing a tennis ball on the dining-room wall between the portraits. She says she has not much to do at present . . . [S]he had been sorting out some packs of old playing-cards in the drawing-room and seemed very busy" (131).

Lois's trouble in getting people to take interest in what she does is part of the larger problem of getting them to acknowledge her subjectivity. Few of her companions listen when Lois speaks, whether she is suggesting that they sit out on the steps after dinner or whether she is desperately asking, "But what am I for?" "'What they never see,'" she complains, "'is, that I must do something'" (Bowen 1929a, 186). "And because no one answered or cared and a conversation went on without her, she felt profoundly lonely, suspecting once more for herself a particular doom of exclusion" (23). When people do attend to her, they make her the object of appropriative talk. Again and again, characters pair off and discuss Lois—one of Bowen's many female figures who, in Harriet Chessman's words, "become objects of narration," "but who themselves have no language, and who therefore cannot generate other texts. These figures haunt [Bowen]" (Chessman 1983, 70, 71).[22]

Lois senses the violation such conversations entail when she overhears her aunt and Francie Montmorency from outside her bedroom door. She "heard 'Lois . . . Lois . . . Lois'" in the hall. She discerns "a keen hunting note" in their voices. Their voices "came after her. She flung herself on her bed with a squawk from the springs and pressed her ear shut till the lobes and her finger-tips ached; also she pulled the pillows over her head. . . . [S]till the voices penetrated. They came on steadily, like the Hound of Heaven. It was hard, really, the way they both kept at it." When Francie is about to conclude, "'Lois is very—'", Lois erupts. Bowen's narrator explains: "Was she now to be clapped down under an adjective, to crawl round life-long inside some quality like a fly in a tumbler? Mrs Montmorency should not!" To make her presence known and put a stop to their conversation, Lois "lifted her water jug and banged it down in the basin: she kicked the slop-pail and pushed the wash-stand about." Significantly, Lois's rebellious interruption is inchoate. And it is, the narrative makes clear, only ironically successful: "It was victory. Later on, she noticed a crack in the basin, running between a sheaf and a cornucopia: a harvest richness to which she each day bent down her face. Every time, before the water clouded, she would see the crack: every time she would wonder: what Lois *was*—She would never know" (Bowen 1929a, 60). Lois's identity is constituted, the passage suggests, by a kind of fracture or gap.

In Lois, then, Bowen creates a haunting portrait of a young woman yearning to become an audible, visible, viable subject. None of the available forms of being seems right. It is precisely the phenomenon Woolf isolates in her essay on Geraldine Jewsbury and Jane Carlyle. Geraldine writes to Jane: "We are indications of a development of womanhood which as yet is not recognised. It has, so far, no ready-made channels to run in, but still we have looked and tried, and found that the present rules for women will not hold us—that something better and stronger is needed. . . . There are women to come after us, who will approach nearer the fullness of the measure of the stature of a woman's nature" (quoted in Lee 1997, 513).

Though she is not conscious of her dilemma, as Geraldine is, Lois clearly chafes at her marginal role. She cannot or will not perform her duties well. She arranges the sweet peas atrociously (Bowen 1929a, 8). She places geraniums on a dressing table where Hugo knocks them over (20). She forgets how many guests she invites to tea, causing an inhospitable shortage of raspberries (36). She resists Lady Naylor's injunction to socialize, insisting: "'I've got nothing to say and I'm sick of always having to keep on saying it'" (134). She refuses to parrot sentimentalized constructions of femininity and masculinity as when, in a flurry of worry that their suitors might be sick, Livvy reflects, "'I often think it is only when a man is ill that he understands what a woman means in his life.'" In response, "Lois said that her own impression of a man ill was one of extreme crossness and of inability to find the nicest woman attractive at all. She pointed out that there was an excellent military hospital at Clonmore, so that they need not imagine David and Gerald tossing feverish and untended" (68). And Lois resents the lady's requisite asexuality: "She did not mind being noticed because she was a female, she was tired of being not noticed because she was a lady" (99).

She complains to Marda: "'Being grown up seems trivial, somehow. I mean, dressing and writing notes instead of letters, and trying to make impressions. When you have to think so much of what other people feel about you there seems no time to think what you feel about them. Everybody is genial at one in a monotonous kind of way. I don't seem to find young men inspiring, somehow. I suppose I shall. Did you ever have any difficulty about beginning?'" (Bowen 1929a, 97). Cocooned off with only fatuous activities to occupy her, Lois repeats: "But what can I do?", "But shall I never do anything?" (20, 168). Worried that "a particular doom of exclusion" awaits her (23), she feels "quite an outcast," "she must clearly be outside life" (197).

Of course, Lois is not alone. Laurence shares her *Godot*-like "sense of detention, of a prologue being played out too lengthily, with unnecessary stress" (Bowen 1929a, 118). Ensconced in the Big House, they resent "giving so much of themselves to what was to be forgotten . . . while, unapproachably elsewhere, something went by without them" (118). Their sense of exclusion and futility is due in part to an archetypal generational shift, exacerbated by the rapid pace of change in the early twentieth century; it is due in part to the dislocations of twentieth-century Irish history. As Phyllis Lassner argues, Anglo-Ireland sequestered all its members, male and female, in a last ditch effort to stave off its annihilation (Lassner 1986, 46–47). Lacking their elders' unquestioning relationship to Anglo-Irish culture, sensing the feasibility of competing ideologies (modernity, democracy, socialism), both men and women of the younger generation sense that the time-honored Anglo-Irish way of life is on its way out. Still, gender decisively intensifies Lois's sense of being passed by. Her identity as a would-be lady supplements her other displacements, to make her marginalization the most intense in the novel. For unlike Laurence, on top of being an orphan, and on top of being sidelined with her culture, she is sidelined by it. Of all the characters on this scene, it is the young woman for whom Anglo-Irishness is most desperate and bleak.

Ann Owens Weekes would disagree. In her view, Bowen's "representation of dislocation and dispossession as a natural condition of life" for women "is not seen as tragic. It is difficult, yes, but preferable in fact to the comfortable serenity of her peers, whose complacence, Bowen suggests, springs from ignorance, not knowledge, from a naive acceptance of the doctrines and illusions of their particular Edens" (Weekes 1990, 83). Reading *The Last September* by way of the Christian myth, Weekes casts Lois as "Milton's Eve, alive with curiosity, [exploring] the tree and, wishing, as she says, to 'grow mature / In knowledge, as the Gods who all things know'"; "Lois balances on the walls of Eden, capable of looking wither back toward innocence or forward into the unknown. . . . [S]he opts for the future" (93, 97). As Weekes sees it, Bowen gives us a happy story of a young woman's decisive rejection of patriarchal blinders, a "novel of Lois's awakening" (90).

Weekes admits: "Despite her questioning of specifics, . . . Lois does not question the underlying pattern but in seeking to fit in, to be secure, follows in Eve's footsteps. She finds the lure of a secure marriage to the tame Gerald difficult to resist." The mill scene is decisive for Weekes: "Asserting her sexual and political independence simultaneously, Lois bars Hugo's entrance to the mill. In preserving the women's and the Irish rebel's secret, Lois symbolically asserts the mutuality of women's and rebels' interests. . . . The bandaging of Marda's hand . . . is an intimate sororal ceremony of adulthood. . . . Having discarded the old conceptions, Lois discovers that she has also lost her old fear; illusion and fear are truly symbolic" (Weekes 1990, 102). Weekes concludes, "The last picture of Lois is that of a mature woman, one who understands the forbidden knowledge" (105).

In fact, the narrative whisks Lois away to France—"'Tours. For her French, you know. And to such an interesting, cultivated family'" (Bowen 1929a, 204)—without according her a final word, enacting the same indifference to Lois that its characters do throughout. Weekes maintains, "[s]ignificantly we do not see Lois again, but we hear from Lady Naylor that she left Ireland, refusing to be accompanied, or protected, by her male cousin" (Weekes 1990, 105). Lois seems, rather, to have been shuffled off to undertake another phase in her training to become a sort of Myra Naylor—"Myra was 'interesting,' cultivated, sketched beautifully, knew about books and music. She had been to Germany, Italy, everywhere that one visits acquisitively" (Bowen 1929a, 14)—just the kind of woman *The Last September* has shown us is obsolete.[23]

Gender impinges upon the young Anglo-Irish woman in yet another way in Bowen's narrative. If gender confines her within Anglo-Ireland, it also undermines her capacity to weather Anglo-Ireland's demise. In *The Last September,* as in other twentieth-century Anglo-Irish texts, this social formation's decline triggers a locally inflected version of the modernist crisis. As their culture of origin dissipates, Anglo-Irish men and women feel the ground slipping out from under them, certainty receding and the abyss looming. Like the novels of Conrad, Lawrence, Joyce, and Woolf, *The Last September* documents what is finally a "crisis of meaning and order" (Coates 1990, 210).[24]

Lois's gendered marginalization robs her of means for meeting this crisis. The Naylors can ignore the shaking of the foundations. They continue their social regimen, chatting about ambushes between tennis and tea, until Bowen's comedy of manners approaches black humor and the literature of the absurd in its repeated juxtaposition of polite society and war. Though the Montmorencys receive intimations of absence that the Naylors do not, they too can mask them—Hugo with "manly talk" (Bowen 1929a, 44), Francie with her belief in love—and allow the pattern of arrivals and departures, and the interim routine of meals, walks, and tea, to conjure an illusion of stability and presence. Lois, by contrast, cannot retreat to the myths and rituals of a cohesive Anglo-Ireland. They are too constraining.

Lois's contrast to Laurence, on this count, is critical. The gentleman, like the lady, is fast becoming obsolete, and Laurence, like

Lois, lacks purpose. "'I live,' he used to say, 'from meal to meal'" (Bowen 1929a, 9). But Bowen's Laurence is a far cry from Somerville and Ross's anomie-ridden Christopher Dysart, who is the focus of their analysis of a waning Anglo-Ireland's futility in *The Real Charlotte*. Profoundly alienated from his culture, Dysart is a self-professed failure at conforming to its masculine ideal. His diplomatic career had no value in his eyes. The duties and pastimes that fall to him as a country gentleman hold no interest. "If only I could read the *Field*," he thinks wryly, "and had a more spontaneous habit of cursing, I should be an ideal country gentleman" (Somerville and Ross 1894, 70). He is most at home when alone in his boat on Lismoyle's lake— a vivid emblem of adriftness in the face of meaninglessness. "He felt disgusted with himself and his own futility" (70).

Laurence is, with Lois, at loose ends. But he lives at Danielstown for the summer only. "'He is with us a good deal, between Oxford,'" Lady Naylor tells Francie (Bowen 1929a, 16); he has no money, and "'[has] to eat somewhere'" (44). October will find him back in England where he cultivates his identity, everyone reiterates, as something of an intellectual. As such, he is able to evade meaninglessness in books and to close the gaps left by his failing culture, at least provisionally, with language. Enjoying perspective and overview, he asserts conclusions about his experience, culture, and era. "'A furtive lorry is a sinister thing,'" he pronounces after dinner one night (31). ("'Laurence, it isn't furtive!' said Lady Naylor. 'Can't you be ordinary?'" [31].) "'This is an unreal party,'" he says at a tennis party (43). ("[T]hat discomfort should be made articulate seemed to [Hugo] shocking" [44].) Laurence has firm opinions about the political situation in Ireland, which his aunt urges him to muffle. Laurence's capacity to conceptualize helps *place* him, so that "What next?" is not the utterly desperate question for him that it is for Lois. To be sure, Laurence is by no means satisfied or calmed. He even feels momentary envy of women: by marrying, he thinks, Marda "would be getting herself a good home and what went with it— money, assurance and scope. He himself only wished he could do so as easily" (119). But even without marriage, he enjoys provisional identity and place—more, in any case, than Lois can construct.

For Laurence's solutions are definitively off limits. As Bowen says, it is their sons the Anglo-Irish send to school in England. If university is not an option for this Anglo-Irish woman neither is a freelance intellectuality. Lois gropes toward this solution, begging: "'Laurence, I wish you would tell me something to read.'" But Laurence (who when Lois "wished to impress him as an intellectual girl" had told her "she should read less and more thoroughly and, on the whole he thought, talk less") suggests she "'should go to sleep'" (Bowen 1929a, 11, 161). She pleads, "'But I want to begin on something; I do think, Laurence, you might understand. There must be some way for me to begin. You keep on looking into rooms where I am with silent contempt—what do you think I am for?'"(161). But lacking encouragement, resources, training, a mentor, Lois cannot build meaning in committed intellectual work.

Like Laurence, Lois does comment on her experience. But her commentary is piecemeal and episodic. She protests against stray symptoms of her culture and its decline—the need to chat, the sense of being passed by—but does not diagnose the whole, as Laurence does (and as Bowen does). In the world of this text, such partial and inconclusive naming affords small comfort. When Lois glimpses the trench-coated man in the Danielstown demesne, she feels the urge to speak—but what to say she is by no means sure. She undertakes a silent survey of the menu of responses available to her. "'It's a fine night,' she would have liked to observe; or, to engage his sympathies: 'Up Dublin!' or even—since it was in her uncle's demesne she was straining under a holly—boldly—'What do you want?'" (Bowen 1929a, 34). Unlike Laurence, she has no center of gravity, no ordered sense of self, allegiances, priorities, or beliefs by which to structure an even provisionally coherent discourse. Of Bowen's *The Death of the Heart* Chessman writes: "Louie's incapacity to use language forces her into a perpetual regression. She can gain no identity without the defining power of words" (Chessman 1983, 72). Similarly unable to define her predicament, Lois remains defined by it.

Indeed, Lois seems virtually volitionless, and not in such a way as to bear out Woolf's dictum: "To be passive is to be active" (Woolf 1938, 74, 107, 119). Bowen writes emphatically of Lois's need to be compelled by others, in relation. "She had never refused a role" (Bowen 1929a, 32), we are told. She tells Marda, "'I can't help getting involved with people. Personal relations make a perfect havoc of me'" (97). Why does she stay at Danielstown?, Marda asks. "'I like to be in a pattern,'" Lois explains. "'I like to be related, to have to be what I am. Just to *be* is so intransitive, so lonely'" (98). In the novel's climactic scene, desperate for Gerald to regain his confidence in their relationship so that she can tap it as her own, Lois begs him to compel her to love him, to cancel "her impotence, her desolation . . . at not being compelled. . . She wanted something to look at, to follow" (190). "'All that matters is what *you* believe,'" she implores (191). But Lady Naylor has shaken him loose from his belief in himself, in their engagement, and (correctly) in Lois's love for him. Probably for the better, Lois cannot make up for his lack.

After one of Lois's most desperate requests for guidance, Laurence perceives her plight with sudden clarity:

> He leaned against the frame of his doorway, looking at her with surprise and a degree of humanity. Today four weeks, Term would have begun again; he did for a moment stretch to an effort of comprehension: there was nothing for *her* to go on with. The vacancy, more than negative to him, which had succeeded Marda made the natural claims of a life on his young cousin. With that concession to fancy one makes for the doomed or the very weak, he suggested she should go on with her German. He gave her two grammars, a dictionary and a novel of Mann's, which she took from him doubtfully. (Bowen 1929a, 161 italics Bowen's)

Anglo-Ireland's decline proves qualitatively different for this young woman than for the others. She is the least well-equipped to meet it. Absence looms larger, a more desperate affair. Bowen writes, in her preface, that Danielstown's burning liberates Lois (Bowen 1929b, xii). *The Last September* proper insists it does not. In the novel, Anglo-Irish decline does not offer a young woman the prospect of autonomy or hope. The horrible paradox, as dramatized by this narrative, is that while the young woman is marginalized within Anglo-Ireland, she is nowhere without it. Powerless to repudiate the marginal and moribund role to which gender and class assign her, powerless to design or embrace a new one, Lois resembles the speaker of Arnold's "Stanzas from the Grand Chartreuse." More hopelessly than any other character in this text, Lois wanders "between two worlds, one dead, / The other powerless to be born."

V

When Lois tells Marda of her penchant for being "related," her desire "to have to be what I am," Marda responds, "'Then you will like to be a wife and mother. . . . It's a good thing we can always be women'" (Bowen 1929a, 98). It is in this context that Lois asserts: "'I hate women. But I can't think how to begin to be anything else'" (99).

"Being a woman"—adhering to the feminine roles scripted by received ideas of love, marriage, and motherhood—can seem to Lois, as it eventually does to Marda, the most obvious route out of the Anglo-Irish margins, and the most probable presence with which to counter modern absence. Marriage was, of course, the socially sanctioned role for Anglo-Irish women—even though this role grew less secure during the period when *The Last September* takes place. Many eligible young Anglo-Irish men had died in the first World War. When money was scarce at the Big House, "daughters, undowered, stayed unwed; love-marriages had to be interdicted because money was needed to prop the roof" (Bowen 1940, 27). As Anglo-Ireland's economic situation worsened, Anglo-Irishmen turned increasingly to England not merely for educations but for brides. Meanwhile, unmarried daughters remained at home, running the households "until the sons returned from England or outposts of the Empire with English or Anglo-Irish wives—to whom the daughter would give her keys" (H. Robinson 1980, 5–6). Such social trends perhaps inform Bowen's portrait of her distressedly directionless young woman.

Such trends notwithstanding, marriage emerges consistently as Lois's default solution to the problem of her painful placelessness. When she feels that "doom of exclusion" descend, when she feels threatened by other men, as at the mill and the Rolfes' dance, "I must marry Gerald" is the remedy that flashes automatically across her mind. "Being a woman" would accord Lois what status is available to her. Thinking of Livvy's engagement, Lois reflects, "Livvy was privileged. If she chose to announce her engagement even Sir Richard must stop and listen. It was a passport at any frontier" (Bowen 1929a, 132). In her autobiographical essay "The Mulberry Tree," Bowen herself recalls: "I and my friends all intended to marry early, partly because this appeared an achievement or way of making one's mark, also from a feeling it would be difficult to settle to anything else until this was done. (Like passing the School Certificate)" (Bowen 1934, 17). Even the free-thinking Laurence sees some sense in this plan of action. "'I don't see why'" Lois should marry, he muses. "'Though I don't see why not. As Lois never does anything or seems to want to, I suppose she must be expecting to marry someone'" (Bowen 1929a, 54). "'At least Gerald is definite,'" Lois tells Francie, "'At least [marriage] may get one somewhere'" (187).

But despite Lois's sense that marriage might, as Marda says, "furnish" her (Bowen 1929a, 101), she resists it. Lois's resistance stems partly from a skittishness about experience generally and about sexuality in particular.[25] But Bowen suggests it is also a function of Lois's good sense that marriage constitutes no safe home but, in fact, another margin. Lois seems to suspect that marriage is "not an act of self-determination, but another trap of sexual identity" (Lassner 1991, 37).

Lois dimly perceives the contradictions that fracture reigning mythologies of love and marriage. Love is what women are for, women are told. Yet "the practice of love" (Bowen 1929a, 60) seems not all it's cracked up to be. Lois is repulsed by its maudlin mind set: "when Livvy said, 'Melisande' was a beautiful poem, wasn't it, something stiffened in Lois: she said she thought it was sentimental. 'All that fuss, if you know what I mean, about just somebody'" (74). And "[l]ove, she had learnt to assume, was the mainspring of woman's grievances. Illnesses all arose from it, the having of children, the illnesses children had; servants also, since the regular practice of love involved a home; by money it was confined, propped and moulded. Lois flung off the pillows and walked round the room quickly. She was angry" (60). Still, she wonders aloud to Marda, "'But surely love wouldn't get so much talked about if there were not something in it?'" "'Oh, there must be,'" Marda tosses back (97).

What Lois seems to sense is gender relations' imperial structure. When she tries to speak of Gerald after his death she thinks: "He loved me, he believed in the British Empire" (Bowen 1929a, 203). Empire is the pervasive metaphor by which Bowen represents gender relations in this text. But if, in Bowen's representation of geopolitical relations, an immanent power circulates, in her representation of gender relations it does not. Though Bowen's narrative casts women as more substantial and sympathetic, and far wiser than their lovers, gender politics inevitably subject them to men. Male vision and voice rule in the world of *The Last September*, not because men wield the power to resist women's subjectivity, but because they do not grant that it exists. With the exception, once more, of Lady Naylor, Bowen's women undergo not enhancement, as the patriarchal ideal of femininity would have it, but diminishment in relation to men.[26] Which is not to say that the narrative points the finger of categorical blame at men; as Lassner maintains, Bowen's men "too, are victimised by codes which they have no power to change" (Lassner

1991, 158). Resistant to binaries, Bowen's narrative carries some compassion for almost all subjects of imperial and patriarchal power, "victims" and "villains" both. Like Daventry in Ireland so Gerald in love: puppetlike, he seems unable to help the manner of his approach to Lois and the havoc it wreaks on her ability to feel for him as he wants her to. But Gerald's primary role in the novel—as the soldier suitor who believed in the British Empire—is predominantly antipathetic.

As if to gloss her young lady's *bildungsroman* and the nature of the gender dynamics by which it unfolds, Bowen gives it an explicitly imperial context. The text is full of references to Empire: India, Ceylon, South Africa, the Colonies, Nigeria, East Africa (Bowen 1929a 10, 31, 91, 99, 113, 117). Bowen underlines her representation of gender relations' imperial structure with the iconography of Irish nationalism. She drapes her marriageable Anglo-Irish women in green, yoking them to the Irish rebels' cause and to "the green country" itself (66). Marda once had, and lost, an emerald engagement ring. "'The jeweller said it must be emeralds because the lady was Irish'"; "'I had had no idea I had such an expensive nationality,'" Marda quips (81). Marda wears a green jumper in the mill scene; Lois wears green tulle to the gunners' dance (108, 145).

Gerald, the novel's primary suitor, is explicitly linked to Empire, most obviously in his status as an officer with the Black and Tans, most damningly in his conversation with Laurence regarding the English military presence in Ireland. Despite his "awareness of misdirection, even of paradox" in the operation, Gerald retains complacent faith in what he thinks of as the British cause. "'[T]he situation's rotten,'" he admits. "'But right *is* right,'" he insists— "'from the point of view of civilization.'" Laurence asks, "'[W]hat do you mean by the point of view of civilization?'" No match for this well-read Oxford man, Gerald responds, "'Oh—ours. . . . I mean, looking back on history—not that I'm intellectual—we *do* seem the only people'" (Bowen 1929a, 92–93).

Courtship, for Gerald, smacks of conquest:

> He did not conceive of love as a nervous interchange but as something absolute, out of the scope of thought, beyond himself, matter for a confident outward rather than anxious inward looking. He had sought and was satisfied with a few—he thought final—repositories for his emotions: his mother, country, dog, schools, a friend or two,

now—crowningly—Lois. Of these he asked only that they should be quiet and positive, not impinged upon, not breaking boundaries from their generous allotment. (Bowen 1929a, 41)

Gerald's kiss resembles a military maneuver: "he meant to go past the hands, to kiss the curve of Lois's cheek as she strained away, then stamp her uncertain mouth with his own certainty" (85). The kiss marks her as his; "she was his lovely woman: kissed" (88). For her part, Lois remembers this kiss, which is linked in conversation with Gerald's capture of Peter Connor, as "his attack" (91). She thinks of it as having been "not exchanged but—administered" (152).

If family and friends aggressively delineate Lois in language, Gerald all but smothers her. He muses: "She had this one limitation, his darling Lois; she couldn't look on her own eyes, had no idea what she was. . . . When he said: 'You will never know what you mean to me,' he made plain his belief in her perfection as a woman. She wasn't made to know, she was not fit for it. She was his integrity, of which he might speak to strangers but of which to her he would never speak" (Bowen 1929a, 49–50). Lois worries, rightly, "'But you never take in a word I say. You're not interested when I tell you about myself'"; "'I don't believe you know what I'm like a bit'" (49, 45). He writes her a letter, the crested envelope of which, "handed in with its air of a claim on her, had austerity, like some limb of an institution" (161). The letter is possessive and domineering: "all that matters is that you are beautifully beautiful," he writes; "you are lovely and simple and all mine"; "All your life I am going to keep you and wrap you up and protect you and never let you be cold again" (162).

So it is no surprise that after they become engaged "[w]hat she had done stretched everywhere, like a net" (Bowen 1929a, 162). To marry Gerald, Bowen emphasizes, would be to subject oneself to a nominally benign master or, in Weekes's words, "to embrace his rule as England wished Ireland to embrace English rule" (Weekes 1990, 100). Lois tries to dismiss her misgivings and ride the wave of Gerald's unreflecting, implacable certainty: "'If this thing is so perfect to anyone, can one be wrong?'" (Bowen 1929a, 163). The pervasive imperial imagery suggests a clear answer to this question, but Lois is unable to access it. "After an anxious glance at the possible"—the possibility of not marrying—"a pang so sharp that it seemed her own forbade recantation. It was inevitable that she should marry Gerald" (166). Internalized codes of feminine behavior overrule her anxious glance. As with the Anglo-Irish social formation as a whole, so with its construction of femininity: Lois is unable to shun the construction that confines her or to author an original response with which to replace it. She is caught between the impulse to adhere to the role that has been scripted for her and the urge to heed her glimpses through the false rhetoric of love and marriage. Interestingly, it is at this moment, the moment of her most passive and self-destructive capitulation to convention, both patriarchal and imperial, that Lois identifies most closely and perilously with her tribe: "she could not try to explain the magnetism they all exercised by their being static. Or how, after every return . . . she and those home surroundings still further penetrated each other mutually in the discovery of a lack" (166).

Marriage threatens other women characters with comparable constraints. Bowen writes of Captain Vermont's having "acquired" his wife Betty (Bowen 1929a, 147). Francie Montmorency is overjoyed at Marda's engagement, "glad as a wife that the net should be flung wider" (105). Leslie Lawe (whose name suggests not just the clamp of The Law but, like Gerald Lesworth's, "less") may offer Marda a sense of arrival, but he may also deprive her of a full and autonomous self. Marda imagines: "walking with him in a clipped and traditional garden, in Kentish light. Under these influences, she would be giving account of herself. Leslie's attention, his straight grey gaze, were to modify these wandering weeks of her own incalculably, not a value could fail to be affected by him. So much of herself that was fluid must, too, be moulded by his idea of her. Essentials were fixed and localized by their being together—to become as the bricks and wallpaper of a home" (129). Though initially cavalier toward marriage—she lost an engagement ring at a tennis party, and broke off an engagement (75)—at this stage Marda, as Weekes observes, "has abandoned her own fight for autonomy and has opted instead for a quintessentially patriarchal marriage" (Weekes 1990, 92). But she doesn't romanticize her decision to marry. She tells Lois: "'I don't know for myself what is worth while. I'm sick of all this trial and error'" (Bowen 1929a, 101). She knows marriage will not be transforming: "'I don't expect I shall be much different'" (86). Marda sees the limits of her course of action and takes it anyway; she perceives the textuality of "being a woman" and decides to follow the text, with no illusions.

The imperial structure of gender relations is so tenacious that gender politics repeatedly trump imperial politics in Bowen's text.

On an unchaperoned drive home from Clonmore, Livvy and Lois just barely escape an encounter with a truckload of drunken Black and Tans:

> they heard a lorry coming. Black and Tans, fortified inwardly against the weather, were shouting and singing and now and then firing shots. The voices, kept low by the rain, the grind of wheels on the rocky road, tunnelled through the close air with a particular horror. To meet in this narrow way would be worse than a dream; before the half-obscured lorry appeared Livvy had turned the pony hurriedly up a boreen. They went up some way and waited under a dripping thornbush; if Black and Tans saw one hiding they were sarcastic. They heard the lorry grind past the mouth of the boreen with apprehension, feeling exposed and hunted. (Bowen 1929a, 75)

The imagery—soldiers' voices "tunneling," the "narrow way," the boreen's "mouth"—underlines the scene's menacing sexual charge. Gender politics endanger the women whose interests these men of the British garrison ostensibly protect and whom, in regulated settings (drawing rooms, tennis courts), they graciously court.

In the scene at the Black and Tans' barracks the Anglo-Irish woman's body and the Irish landscape explicitly converge, blurred in the gaze of the shell-shocked Englishman. Bowen sets the imperial tone early. Gerald invites Lois to dance by approaching her from behind, asserting, "'Mine next'" (Bowen 1929a, 150). Lois's body, buffeted among dancing soldiers, recalls the "passive disputed earth" on which the novel's plot unfolds (34). The scene's climactic conflation of Irish land and the Anglo-Irish woman's body occurs when the desperate Mr. Daventry stands "looking over [Lois's] green frock with his discomforting eyes" (156). "Hers was, he said, a remarkably beautiful country. . . . He stared at her arms, at the inside of her elbows, with such intensity. . . . She moved her arms nervously on the silk of her dress" (156–57). It is no surprise that, by the end of this evening, Lois's green dress is torn (166).

This model of gender relations also regulates Anglo-Irish women's relations to Irish men, in recurring scenes of sexual threats to women's bodily autonomy. Laurence complains about having to drive Lois to Castle Trent for tennis: "'I often wonder whether she really *would* get assaulted by Black and Tans if she went alone, or by sinister patriots'" (Bowen 1929a, 55). The postman relays to Sir Richard news of "how three young women in the Clonmore direction had had their hair cut off by masked men for walking out with the soldiers" (61). Such scenes again place Anglo-Irish women in the position of "the green country," casting them as contested territory over which and upon which forces of Empire and colony wage war.

Most dramatically, Marda (in her green jumper) and Lois are mortally endangered when they come upon the I.R.A man and his pistol in the ruined mill. As we have seen, the man disputes the women's right to roam the Irish countryside, and threatens them with dispossession: "'It is time,' he said, 'that yourselves gave up walking. If you have nothing better to do, you had better keep in the house while y'have it'" (Bowen 1929a, 125). His warning carries a patriarchal valence at least as potent as its nationalistic thrust, urging the women to remain within the house's enclosed domestic space. Bowen makes the scene's sexual threat as clear as her narrative's euphemistic propriety will allow: "'Stay there,'" he orders when he first sees them. "A pistol bore the persuasion out. They were embarrassed by this curious confrontation. Neither of them had seen a pistol at this angle; it was short-looking, scarcely more than a button" (154). The man's apparently tame instrument, this instrument which the narrative voice itself seems to seek to tame, proves powerful: it persuades the women to lie to protect him, and it bloodies Marda's hand. Bowen underscores the gendered nature of this assault subtly but firmly: upon Marda's departure from Danielstown Lady Naylor commiserates, "'it really is a terrible pity about your hand. Especially as it's the left hand, as I'm afraid you will have to be conventional and start wearing your ring again, now you are going to England'" (133).

So *The Last September*'s women are subject to a tangled array of hazards that makes them vulnerable in ways Anglo-Irish men are not. In the end, Bowen's representation of Anglo-Irish women seems more deeply rooted in her imagination of gender politics than in her engagement with Ireland's. It is gender hierarchy that gives the above scenes their frightening charge. Certainly gender dynamics stand at the center of Lois's response to the encounter in the mill: the "revelation" to which it leads her concerns not Ireland and Anglo-Ireland but Marda and Hugo ("'he's being awful about you, isn't he?'"), and Marda and herself ("'Their sex was a stronghold, they had to acknowledge silently'" [Bowen 1929a, 128, 127]). Although *The Last September* lets the reader know that English rule and Anglo-Irish houses have been placed on the "unwilling bosom" of

Irish land, it makes the reader *feel* the clamp of Gerald's kiss and Daventry's eyes, and the force of other gendered threats.

What, if anything, can we infer about Bowen's politics and her attitudes toward Anglo-Ireland from her representation of gender relations? Is *The Last September*'s emphasis on gender an evasion of Anglo-Ireland's implication in the imperialist enterprise? Is it an assertion of Anglo-Irish women's exculpatory distance from that enterprise? One might argue that in representing gender relations as imperialist, *The Last September* implies Anglo-Irish women's affiliation with the Irish. This would seem to be Ann Owens Weekes's point, arguing as she does that colonization "makes female both country and people, ironically bonding both the women 'of' the colonizers and the peoples colonized" (Weekes 1990, 15), and that the mill scene suggests "the mutuality of women's and rebels' interests" (102).

Susan Meyer's *Imperialism at Home: Race and Victorian Women's Fiction* (1996) offers a more nuanced reading of the implications of the imperial or, as she calls it, "racial" metaphor, and the "idea that white women were like, or could be likened to, people of other races." Of course, insofar as "race" is ever more than a trope, it is not a category that pertains to imperial politics in Ireland. As Andrew Murphy has emphasized, the Irish were not one of the "dark races," and were bound to England by culture, geography, and ethnicity.[27] But Meyer's race-based analysis applies; indeed, imperial rhetoric often figured the Irish as "dark," as in nineteenth-century representations of Irishness as simian. Thus where Meyer writes "dark races" we might substitute "colonized (Irish) subjects"; where she refers to the racial metaphor we may understand the colonial one.

Though most recent criticism follows Gayatri Spivak in emphasizing "the implicit imperialism within the feminist literary tradition" (Azim 1993, 145–46),[28] Meyer finds that "since the gender positioning of British women writers required them to negotiate an association with 'inferior races,' their feminist impulses to question gender hierarchies often *provoked* an interrogation of race hierarchies." In Meyer's view, Charlotte Brontë, Emily Brontë, and George Eliot "were necessarily situated differently from their male contemporaries in relation to the idea that white women are like people of other races, and indeed this idea undergoes a transmutation as it appears in their fiction. What links the two terms of the metaphor," in their work, "comes to be not shared inferiority but a shared experience of frustration, limitation, and subordination" (Meyer 1996, 7).

Meyer offers this important qualification: "To say this is not to contend, with the optimistic idealism of the feminism of an earlier era, that an awareness of gender oppression has historically given women an easy, automatic comprehension of oppression on the basis of race or class." She does contend, however, that women writers' "gender . . . positioning produced a complex and ambivalent relation to the ideology of imperialist domination, rather than an easy and straightforward one. It was precisely the gender positioning of these women writers in British society, in combination with their feminist impulses and their use of race as a metaphor, that provoked and enabled an (albeit partial) questioning of British imperialism" (Meyer 1996, 11).[29]

Why would using race relations as metaphor for gender relations enable an only partial questioning of imperialism? Meyer explains:

> The metaphorical use of race by these women novelists has a political double edge. . . . [H]ere, as in any metaphor, the vehicle is in one sense emptied of its full array of meaning. . . . Thus the women novelists who use race as a metaphor are in one sense emptying out the vehicle 'enslaved Jamaican blacks,' 'Jews,' or 'Ashantis,' of its full significance; they are not primarily directing our attention toward the humanity, or even toward the oppression, of the people invoked. Instead their construction of the metaphor draws our attention as readers to the experience of oppression or limitation that white women or girls have in common with the peoples invoked, and draws our attention away from all the other things we might think about were we to think, say, of the people of India without the guidance and restraint of the metaphor. (Meyer 1996, 22–23)

The metaphor "demonstrates only a very partial interest in" the indigenous colonized peoples (56). One could even argue that the anti-imperialist politics carried by the metaphor "are more self-interested than benevolent" (81).

One could offer a kindred reading of Bowen. Though her representation of gender relations implies anti-imperialist politics, Bowen's Irish characters—the Connors, the nameless I.R.A. man at the mill, the trench-coated man in Danielstown's demesne—are granted only cameo appearances, and do not move beyond type to character, do not fully break the bounds of metaphor into a more completely figurative capacity.[30] After reading *The Last September,* Sean O'Faolain chided Bowen to write a novel "that was at least aware of the Ireland outside" the Big House, and "that, perhaps, regretted the division enough to admit it was there" (Glendinning 1977, 108).

However, as Meyer contends, "the nonshared qualities and thus the full signification of the vehicle of metaphor remain present at the margins of our consciousness as we perceive metaphors," which "helps to account for the dual political edge of the metaphorical use of race . . . The yoking of the two terms of this recurrent metaphor, 'white woman' and 'dark race,' produces some suggestion in the text of the exploited or vulnerable situation of the people of the race invoked"; "the fuller existence of the 'dark races' used as the vehicle of the metaphor has a way of pushing back in each novel, of making its presence felt" (Meyer 1996, 23). "Although this figurative strategy does not preclude racism," Meyer argues, "it inevitably produces the suggestion that people of these 'other' races are also oppressed." And it "betrays an anxiety that imperialism and oppression of other races constitute a stain upon English history and that the novel's own appropriation of nonwhite races for figurative ends bears a disturbing resemblance to that history" (66).

Following Meyer, I would argue that *The Last September*'s critique of gender carries a critique of Empire that is equivocal, double-edged. If *The Last September* does not confront Irishness as directly as *Time After Time* does in the figure of June, or as *Watt* does in the master-servant relation, it does evoke Empire's gendered underside. What Meyer writes of *Jane Eyre* holds true for Bowen's text as well: "the novel's relation to imperialist ideology is shifting and conflicted, precisely because of [the] metaphorical use of race" (Meyer 1996, 25); both novels prove examples "of the associations—and dissociations—between a resistance to the ideology of male domination and a resistance to the ideology of imperialist domination" (94–95).

If the imperial metaphor as Bowen uses it is inherently equivocal, Bowen's critique of Empire is also equivocal in and of itself. The scene that so forcefully confirms Bowen's critique of gender hierarchies as imperialist, for instance, is itself entangled in the kind of imperialist attitudes it would seem at the same time to reject. The Irish man upon whom Marda and Lois stumble at the mill "sat looking at them with calculating intentness, like a monkey" (Bowen 1929a, 154)—recalling Reverend Jennings's "jaded and sulky" monkey, in Le Fanu's "Green Tea" (Le Fanu 1869, 95), and many other representations of the Irish Other. In the mill scene, Bowen's critique of gender relations as imperialist implicates itself in imperialist systems of value and belief. Such interminglings may occur in other scenes as well. For one might read the novel's scenes of sexually threatening Irish men as expressions of the fear that the Irish Other will appropriate not just the colonists' land but the colonists' women. As Jenny Sharpe argues in her analysis of the "discourse of rape" in the colonial context:

> The image of native men sexually assaulting white women is in keeping with the idea of the colonial encounter as a Manichaean battle between civilization and barbarism. . . . When articulated through images of violence against women, a resistance to British rule [or, in *The Last September*, Anglo-Irish presence] does not look like the struggle for emancipation but rather an uncivilized eruption that must be contained. In turn, the brutalized bodies of defenseless English [or Anglo-Irish] women serve as a metonym for a government [or social formation] that sees itself as the violated object of rebellion. (Sharpe 1993, 6–7)

So Bowen's critique of Empire by way of gender itself incorporates imperial habits of mind, jumbling resistance to imperial power structures (as enacted in gender relations) with reenactment of imperial belief systems. Interpretability supplements this tangle of attitudes. One might read Bowen's emphasis on Anglo-Irish women's vulnerability as an evasion of Anglo-Ireland's role in Irish history. One might read Bowen's exposed and placeless Anglo-Irish woman as a sympathetic metaphor for twentieth-century Anglo-Ireland; like Anglo-Ireland, the Anglo-Irish woman is doubly threatened, by both colonial "enemies" as well as imperial "friends."[31] Or one might say that *The Last September* evokes all these readings.

In any event, Bowen's gender critique appears all but unequivocal.[32] If geopolitical power circulates in *The Last September*, patriarchal power proves a clear-cut, one-way street to which women are barred access. If this narrative has a villain, that villain is not Empire, but patriarchy—this novel's most urgent absent cause of injustice and suffering. And, since patriarchy spans England, Ireland, and Anglo-Ireland, empowering English, Irish and Anglo-Irish men, the operation of patriarchal power, as Bowen understands it, entails one more challenge to notions of essential difference among these ostensibly distinct social groups. Patriarchy unites them in fracturing them all.

5

Watt . . . Knott . . Anglo-Ireland: Samuel Beckett's *Watt*

Did I wait somewhere for this place to be ready to receive me?
Or did it wait for me to come and people it?
—Samuel Beckett, *The Unnamable*

For to explain had always been to exorcize,
for Watt.
—Samuel Beckett, *Watt*

A WRITER OF WORLD STATURE IN WORLD CULTURE, SAMUEL BECKETT is, it goes without saying, the cosmopolitan author *par excellence*. As Charles Pullen puts it, "Beckett is fundamentally in the central tradition of European art. . . . All that one needs to know in order to understand [him] is the whole history of the Western world" (Pullen 1987, 296). What then are we to do with this much cited fragment from *Watt*'s odd Addenda: "for all the good that frequent departures out of Ireland had done him, he might just as well have stayed there" (S. Beckett 1953, 248)?

Like this fragment's indeterminate "he," the manifestly cosmopolitan Beckett is also a man of the provinces. Beckett's readers have grown increasingly interested in the ties that bind his often surreal work to political and historical realities in Ireland and elsewhere. Though Georg Lukács and Marxist critics after him tended to characterize Beckett's work as culpably apolitical (Lukács 1963, 17–46; Eagleton 1976b, 27–31), others called Beckett a social critic some time ago. Raymond Federman, for one, argued that Beckett's "English" fiction (*More Pricks Than Kicks, Murphy,* and *Watt*) "ridicules and destroys established order, whether social, religious, ethical or aesthetic" (Federman 1965, 18). Ruby Cohn called *More Pricks Than Kicks* a comedy of manners, placing especially "A Wet Night" and "What a Misfortune" in "the tradition of social satire" (Cohn 1962, 22).[1] More recently, John P. Harrington's compendious study, *The Irish Beckett*, (1991) has amply documented Beckett's lifelong and canon-wide engagement with the specifically Irish social order: with Irish history, culture, legend, and literature. As Harrington argues, this engagement was no less Irish for having been based in Paris, where Beckett sometimes enjoyed and sometimes spurned the company of a host of Irish writers-in-exile.[2]

While Harrington and others have examined Beckett's broadly Irish contexts, I am interested in the extent to which Beckett's relation to that social formation called "Anglo-Ireland" informs his work. Of all Beckett's texts, it is *Watt* that is most instructive in this regard. As we shall see, reading *Watt* in light of what we know of Anglo-Ireland opens new ways of understanding not just the Beckett canon, but the tradition of Big House fiction, and the trajectories we know as literary modernism and postmodernism.

Watt traces its title character's peculiar journey from Dublin, where he talks with a Mr. Hackett and a Mr. and Mrs. Goff, to the house of Mr. Knott, where he works as a servant, to, apparently, an asylum, where he meets a fellow named Sam who (we eventually learn) narrates the novel. Watt is, of course, one of Beckett's many Cartesian heroes, on the road to nowhere, possessed by voices, and possessed, despite himself, by a powerful compulsion to know. In *Watt* as in other texts, Beckett explores the problematics of knowledge and the insufficiency of Western tools—reason, language, logic—for seeking it. But, as Harrington has shown, *Watt* is deeply embedded in Irish culture, is "fundamentally focused on the matter of history and ideology," and can be read as a variation on the Anglo-Irish Big House novel (Harrington 1991, 131, 115). Begun in Paris in February 1941 and completed in Rousillon during the Second World War, *Watt*'s "plot" is set in Ireland during the first part of the twentieth century, the time of the final phase of Anglo-Ireland's decline. James Knowlson reports: "The manuscript is even more filled with memories of Ireland, and of Dublin in particular, than is the published novel" (Knowlson 1996, 303).

In *Watt*, Beckett reckons with just that network of charged topics to which Anglo-Irish writers return again and again in their agitated

quests to narrate Anglo-Ireland: history, property, interclass relations, authority, servitude, work. Fraught (like other Anglo-Irish fiction) with the tensions inherent in the effort to give these topics
narrative form, *Watt* (like other Anglo-Irish fiction) ultimately represents Anglo-Irishness as an uneven and open-ended attempt at
self-narration. But while traversing this familiar ground, *Watt* blazes
trails towards which other Anglo-Irish novels incline but do not go.
Probing the linguistic, ontological, and epistemological implications
of the Anglo-Irish writer's project, Beckett lays bare its more broadly
modernist and postmodernist resonances, teasing out the subversive
implications of more traditional Anglo-Irish novels. At once perpetuating and significantly extending the Anglo-Irish literary tradition,
Watt drives home what other novels in the tradition largely imply:
the extent to which the Anglo-Irish predicament echoes—or is itself—the modernist one, spawning narrative without an omniscient
author, narrative in the interrogatory mode.[3]

I

Calling Beckett an Irish writer, let alone an Anglo-Irish one,
means refusing to take him at his word. Beckett claimed again and
again to be averse to the autobiographical impulse in reading and
writing; he professed no interest in writing social realism, Irish,
Anglo-Irish, or otherwise.[4] Yet James Knowlson's 1996 biography has
demonstrated the extent to which "the life material" generally pervades Beckett's work, if "at several removes below the surface"
(Knowlson 1996, 21). And this "life material" is replete with details
of a richly textured Anglo-Irish heritage. Angela Moorjani posits a
relation between the art and the life with which even Beckett might
agree: "Writing . . . entails the process of fraying a path into the embedded archives of the mind consisting of the records of previous
frayings and the inscriptions of the past. . . . And as the writer on his
path through the psychic archives comes upon the first of the series
of embedded archives and begins to transcribe it, he notices that he
can see and hear it only partially and that it too is full of flaws and
gaps through which are noticeable the traces of another text. . . .
and so on to infinity" (Moorjani 1982, 149). Like other Beckett texts,
Watt constitutes a kind of palimpsest, with Anglo-Ireland emerging,
here and there, as one of its foundational underlayers. Or, following
Moorjani: Anglo-Ireland is one of a series of sites on the path

through the "embedded archives" of Beckett's mind; *Watt* is a trace of the text of Anglo-Ireland. [5]

The particulars of Beckett's Anglo-Irish background are as follows. Beckett grew up in Foxrock, an affluent and predominantly Protestant suburb of Dublin. In her 1978 biography, Deirdre Bair reports that riders on the Foxrock train "were proud of the saying that one could ride from the south end of the line into the heart of the city without having to speak to a Catholic, except for the train conductors, who did not count" (Bair 1978, 26). Vivian Mercier corroborates Bair's report: people from Foxrock "were likely to be associating almost exclusively with fellow Protestants—as Beckett did at Earlsfort House School and later at Trinity. Irish Catholics, rich or poor, played walk-on parts in their lives" (Mercier 1977, 28). The Becketts' Foxrock home, called Cooldrinagh after Beckett's mother's family estate, sported croquet lawn and tennis court, and gardens tended by an Irishman named Christy (E. O'Brien 1986, 3).

Beckett's Protestant ancestry is mixed, further testimony to Anglo-Ireland's heterogeneity. Mercier describes the mixture in Anglo-Irish shorthand, calling Beckett the son of "a sporting father and an evangelical mother" (Mercier 1977, 65). William Beckett provided (in the words of Belacqua Shuah) the "grand old family Huguenot guts" (S. Beckett 1934a, 172). Originally "Becquet," this branch of the family migrated from France in the eighteenth century, and worked as weavers in Dublin (Bair 1978, 4; Knowlson 1996, 27). Beckett's grandfather William, a prosperous builder, "went on to concentrate on buying land and building large, impressive houses on it in the city of Dublin and its growing suburbs" (Knowlson 1996, 27–28). Beckett's father, also William, left school at the age of fifteen to enter his father's business, and eventually bought into a quantity surveying firm. It was, Lawrence Harvey explains, "a well-thought of profession in Ireland. Its practitioners occupy an intermediate position between architect and builder, estimating materials and labor required for a given project" (Harvey 1970, 153). Bill Beckett's impatience with books and drawing rooms, and his robust appetite for sports, food, and drink, give him more than a passing resemblance to those sporting men and women we encounter in the novels of Somerville and Ross, and Keane. But the social niche to which he most clearly belonged was that of Yeats and Synge: the urban upper middle class, a category of Anglo-Irishness that (according to W. J. McCormack) Ascendancy myth suppressed.

Beckett's mother, *née* Maria Jones Roe, hailed from an Anglo-Ireland more congruent with Ascendancy myth. Bair explains, in terms derived from that myth, "[H]er family was on a slightly higher social level than [William Beckett's] because they were landed gentry. Her father was Samuel Roe of 'The Roes of Roe Hall' . . . , the leading family in Leixlip, County Kildare, owners of the only grain mill in the village and looked up to by the farmers and peasants to whom they dispensed largesse with a profound sense of duty" (Bair 1978, 7). Beckett's cousin Sheila Roe Page recalled: "They had a big house in those days and my grandfather was rich. I remember going to see the house, biggish, with steps up to the front door. A big gentleman's country house . . . And the boys were all great fishermen. And shots" (Knowlson 1996, 621, note 10). Dating from 1760, the house sat on sixty-five acres along the Liffey and employed numerous servants and gardeners. Though members of the community called it Roe Hall, its proper name was Cooldrinagh House, from the Irish, meaning "the back of the blackthorn hedge" (24).

If William Beckett perpetuated his family's tradition, circumstances prevented May (as Beckett's mother was called) from perpetuating hers, at least for a time. Her father's grain business began to suffer in the 1880s, and his death in 1886 left his family in a tight spot. Beckett told Knowlson, "That's how from the family prosperity they were all brought down" (Knowlson 1996, 26). As a result, May needed to work for a living, and did so as a nurse at the Adelaide Hospital, where she met William Beckett.

After her marriage, however, May reclaimed her former class status, appearing the stereotypical Anglo-Irish lady, "devoted to her husband, her sons, her house, garden and church—in that order" (Bair 1978, 10). She attended the local dog shows; she was devoted to her own dogs (Knowlson 1996, 33). She "ran the new Cooldrinagh with ruthless efficiency and a rod of iron," living by "a rigid code of conduct and a concept of decorum that promised trouble once her second son started to behave in rather wild, bohemian ways" (26–27). Life at Cooldrinagh "reflected *le grand style.* Everything had to be properly done as she attempted to live up to the standards of the big house in which she had been brought up, although with fewer staff" (39).[6] May's commitment to decorum was apparently obsessive. She "aimed to mold her children to her own design" (39). She taught her sons their prayers and on Sundays took them to the Tullow Parish of the Church of Ireland, "where the family, as befitted its status, owned a pew" (Bair 1978, 17).[7] Summers were spent in Greystones, a primarily Protestant holiday destination, and playing tennis at home (Knowlson 1996, 46, 50).

The details of Beckett's schooling are similarly revealing. As a child, he and his brother were cared for by Bridget Bray, a nurse from Meath (Knowlson 1996, 35). He attended a local private school (run by Misses Ida and Pauline Elsner) and the Earlsfort House School, a preparatory day school for boys. Then, like "the sons of Protestant gentlemen from all parts of Ireland for over three and a half centuries" (E. O'Brien 1986, 111–12), he was enrolled in the Portora Royal School in Enniskillen, County Fermanagh. Knowlson maps the sociology of this choice: "The higher landed gentry mostly sent their sons to England, where fees at a top public school were about twice as high as those at Portora"; Beckett's Portora peers were the sons of businessmen, bankers, lawyers, army officers, civil servants, and clergymen (Knowlson 1996, 54). Beckett entered Trinity College, "the educational and spiritual home of the Protestant Ascendancy," in 1923 (Inglis 1962, 122–23).[8]

A hybrid Protestantism joining suburb and semi-profession to the memory, at least, of county and land, Beckett's background was neither clearly "Ascendancy" nor certainly middle class. He claimed he identified with the mercantile Becketts more than the gentrified Roes (Bair 1978, 232), but he sustained vital relationships with his Roe cousins from the time they lived at Cooldrinagh as children. That his family's socioeconomic status kept him on the margins of the mythologized Ascendancy may at one point have troubled him some. When he enrolled at Trinity, Bair reports, he "listed his father's occupation as 'architect,' thus elevating Bill Beckett a step in Dublin society" (Bair 1978, 38). Yet he consistently spurned his mother's attempts to pull him into the Anglo-Irish fold. Such unsettled affiliations might well help spur a writer to embark on the kind of dynamic interrogation of home culture that unfolds in *Watt*.

II

Beckett's first novel, *More Pricks Than Kicks* (1934), breaks ground for that later interrogation. Like other Beckett protagonists, Belacqua Shuah is a "pseudo-self-portrait" (Moorjani 1982, 60). He is sensitively attuned to caste and class, and keenly conscious of his own apparently dubious station. As he wends his way through adventures and misadventures in and around Dublin, he announces his class identity obsessively. It is forever on his mind and always, his obsession suggests, in question. More often than not, he undercuts his affiliations with irony, calling himself a "dirty low-church Protestant," "a dirty low-down Low Church Protestant high-brow," "an indolent bourgeois poltroon," a "young man of good family, so honourable . . . in all his dealings, so spiritual, a Varsity man too" (S. Beckett 1934a, 78, 184, 174, 116). Belacqua is foiled throughout by members of other social groups, making *More Pricks* (among other things) a map of Ireland's intricately stratified social world. He meets weary urban proletarians "at rest on arse and elbow"; "dockers, railwaymen, and vague joxers on the dole"; "the poor and lowly queued up for thruppence worth of pictures"; a liquor-loving Catholic gardener who burns down his Protestant employer's house; a drunken lord in a "superb silent limousine, a Daimler no doubt" (45, 44, 54, 197, 118). Belacqua's attitude toward the different classes remains unclear. Though he roams portions of the city no respectable *haute-bourgeois* would and manifests little patience with the ostensibly refined bourgeois world, he reveals a genteel distaste for the "rough, gritty, almost verminous" jarveys from whom he shrinks, and for his fishmonger: "God damn these tradesmen, he thought, you can never rely on them" (16).[9] *Murphy* (1938), too, is grounded in a world of recognizably Irish social and political realities. H. Porter Abbott has labeled it "a satirical novel," a novel of "direct social criticism" (Abbott 1973, 46).

But it is not until *Watt* that Beckett fixes his gaze squarely on Anglo-Ireland. Some traces of *Watt*'s Anglo-Irish provenance are not at all difficult to spot. An enigmatic landlord-master surrounded by servants and prolific Catholics—the figure is endemic to fiction in the Anglo-Irish tradition. Like that iconic figure, Beckett's Knott is wildly eccentric, and fiercely isolated in "the great mass of the empty house" (S. Beckett 1953, 169). "Mr Knott saw nobody, heard from nobody, as far as Watt could see" (69). He is devoted to time-worn tradition: his ritual meal, the requisite handover of leftovers to the Lynches' dog. More urgently than Bowen's Sir Naylor, he seems to feel beleaguered. He sends his servant Erskine up and down the stairs "perhaps to look out of a top window; to make sure that nobody is coming, or to have a quick look round below stairs, to make sure that no danger threatens the foundations" (119). He has an historically feudal relation to families living nearby, like Mr. Graves':

"Mr Graves had much to say on the subject of Mr Knott. . . . He quoted as well from his ancestors' experience as his own. For his father had worked for Mr Knott, and his father's father, and so on. . . . His family, he said, had made the garden what it was" (143).

Beckett thus invokes the stock-in-trade of Anglo-Irish fiction. Using the language of a tribe, he gives *Watt* an Anglo-Irish signature. But *Watt's* more illuminating connections to the Anglo-Irish tradition emerge in its representations of those topics comprising the Anglo-Irish problematic. The novel's first lines take up one of these topics and instruct us straight away in the kind of Anglo-Irish fiction *Watt* is. The issue at hand is property.

> Mr Hackett turned the corner and saw, in the failing light, at some little distance, his seat. It seemed to be occupied. This seat, the property very likely of the municipality, or of the public, was of course not his, but he thought of it as his. This was Mr Hackett's attitude towards things that pleased him. He knew they were not his, but he thought of them as his. He knew they were not his, because they pleased him. (S. Beckett 1953, 7)

Hackett's "seat" is, of course, a bench of some sort, but the word carries the trace of that other type of seat, the seat of some country gentleman. And the French for "seat" is, evocatively, "siège." Beckett's wordplay intensifies the charge that inevitably surrounds the issue of ownership in the Irish context, an issue that is especially loaded when raised in connection with a character whose distinctive signs (walking stick, painstaking politeness, Frenchified speech, connections to "the Glencullen Hacketts") link him to Anglo-Ireland. Mr. Hackett derives a sense of ownership from nothing more than his pleasure in what he "owns." Beckett hints playfully, here, at a radical critique of property.

The hinting and parodic play that characterize this scene typify Beckett's approach to the Anglo-Irish problematic. Here and elsewhere, Beckett's references to history and culture are intermittent, glancing, obscure, half-serious. He evokes Irish contexts in such a way as to raise questions about how meaningful he means them to be. This equivocation nicely complicates *Watt's* status as a Big House novel. It can seem as if Beckett drops teasing comparisons and provocative associations into the novel to *bait* us into reading it as a Big House novel. Allusions like those that identify Knott as Anglo-Irish are formulaic and pat, so impeccably stock-in-trade as to seem tongue-in-cheek. That Beckett's cultural references are rarely systematic or complete, that attempts to structure them into coherent political or historical allegories so often fail, augments our sense of their uncertain significance.

Furthermore, of course, *Watt*'s resonances extend beyond Ireland. Knott is not a full-bodied, realistically rendered social figure, like Bowen's Sir Naylor or Keane's Jasper Swift. He is a silhouette onto which we can project many faces, Anglo-Ireland being just one of them. And while extra-Irish readings may emerge from a novel like *The Last September* (which, as we have seen, one might read as a novel about the destabilization of certainty, meaning, and value), they are *de rigueur* in *Watt*. Indeed, such readings are more likely than localized ones, given how resolutely *Watt* ignores such concerns as the trauma of Anglo-Ireland's political and financial decline—the historical crisis that forms the core of so many novels in the Anglo-Irish tradition.

So Beckett dilutes cultural specificity, making it intermittent and only uncertainly meaningful. *Watt*'s apparently absent Anglo-Irish core, combined with its often ambiguous cultural allusions, give it an Anglo-Irish signature that is more wavering and faint than those of other novels in the tradition. This signature's impact on how we read the novel is crucial. Beckett did, we recall, insist that *Watt* was "only a game" (Harvey 1970, 222). The manner of Beckett's references to history and culture makes historical readings feel risky: at once grounded in the text and undermined by a nagging worry that Beckett might read them and grin. Beckett's allusions give a reader a troubling sense that to read *Watt* historically—to read it as a Big House novel—is to misread a trickster's clues and look for meanings that are not there.

Beckett is indeed up to tricks here, but the joke is on more than the reader. As Hugh Kenner has written, "Beckett invariably backs the mode he is practicing into its last corner, and is most satisfied if he can render further performance in that mode, by him, impossible. Every game is an endgame" (Kenner 1973b, 105). *Watt* backs the Big House novel into its last corner, invoking and then provisionalizing the genre, refusing to let Anglo-Ireland's paradigmatic literary form stand uncontested, stable, and whole.

This broad campaign has several discrete fronts. First, by writing an Anglo-Irish novel that raises the question of whether it should be read as one, Beckett takes a swipe at attitudes implicit in a body of fiction which, even when detailing Anglo-Irish decline and challenging cornerstones of Anglo-Irish culture, focuses on Anglo-Ireland in such a way as to imply its at least former precedence. The ambiguity of *Watt*'s status as a Big House novel, by contrast, demotes Anglo-Ireland. Second, by writing an Anglo-Irish novel that is immediately identifiable as such by means of stock references and images, Beckett associates the tradition so flatly evoked with lifeless literary habit. That Beckett would draw such an association is no surprise; it squares with his readings in both *Proust* and "Recent Irish Poetry." Finally, by writing an Anglo-Irish novel that cultivates an appearance of uncertain relation to culture and history, Beckett challenges assumptions that often remain unexamined when undertaking the project of writing and reading Anglo-Irish fiction as such: assumptions of an easy correspondence between text and culture. *Watt* emphasizes, instead, Beckett's famous "rupture of the lines of communication" (S. Beckett 1934b, 70). By repeatedly implying and then defying connections between the signifier (the Anglo-Irish novel) and the traditional signified (Anglo-Ireland), *Watt* unsettles our ability to take this "Anglo-Irish novel" as a cultural sign.

It is no small feat to have driven the term "Anglo-Irish novel" into provisionalizing quotation marks. It is a striking challenge to *and* a wry perpetuation of (compare "landed gentry," "English garrison," "Big House") the tradition out of which Beckett is working.

III

Keeping in mind that if it would be a mistake to take them dead seriously, it would also be a mistake to assume they do not tell, let us examine some of *Watt*'s other equivocal points of contact with the Anglo-Irish literary tradition.

Consider the novel's opening and closing scenes. The settings are not typical of Big House fiction: a Dublin street, a suburban train station. In their atypicality, these scenes relativize the Big House setting which so dominates other texts. But in atypical settings Beckett broaches stereotypical concerns. For example, these scenes launch the conventional assault on prescriptive bourgeois civility, an assault sustained in *Watt* (as in *Time After Time*) in an unflinching focus on the body. Here and elsewhere, Beckett deploys "language that refuses to be censored and maintains its right to explore every nook and cranny of human experience" (Knowlson 1996, 59). As we have seen, Elizabeth Bowen articulates Anglo-Ireland's conformist code of conduct this way: "Well, why not *be* polite—are not humane manners the crown of being human at all? Politeness is not constriction; it is a grace. . . . And are we to cut grace quite out of life? . . . In the interest of good manners and good behaviour people learned to subdue their own feelings. The result was an easy and unsuspicious intercourse" (Bowen 1940, 29). May Beckett may have agreed.

With an intensity new to Anglo-Irish fiction, Beckett satirizes "humane manners" and "unsuspicious intercourse." The genteel conversation that passes between Mr. Hackett and the Goffs is inanely, surreally civil: a ridiculous graciousness empty of content, a form as superannuated as the archaic poem Hackett reads (S. Beckett 1953, 11–12). Tetty Goff's unruffled hostessing of a dinner party during childbirth, and her equally unruffled account of that evening, reinforce Beckett's assault on genteel proprieties, echoing those surreal portraits of tennis and tea among ambushes that punctuate Bowen's *The Last September.*

In the railway station scene, Beckett takes aim at a graciousness not empty of content but filled with content running counter to gracious form. Mr. Gorman, the station-master, mimics Lady McCann's patronizing pleasantries to the men who work at the station: "Lady McCann will be upon us in ten minutes. . . . Hell roast her, said Mr Gorman. Good-morning, Mr Gorman, lovely morning, Mr Gorman. Lovely morning!" (S. Beckett 1953, 240). Juxtaposing her overbearing conviviality with Mr. Gorman's vivid hostility, Beckett unmasks Lady McCann's ostensibly good manners. When she arrives at the station to find there has been an accident—Watt was hit by the waiting-room door—she presides officiously over the scene. While the others ask questions about Watt, Lady McCann commands him to speak. And she asks, "Is it a white man?"—objectifying Watt and associating this scene's tense social matrix with social formations divided by race (244). Amid ample comedy and absurdity, then, this scene is rigid with class conflict that marshals sentiment against "polite" Anglo-Ireland. Clearly Lady McCann's nominal grace at once masks and expresses a repugnant class hierarchy, dramatizing that good manners need not equal good behavior, as some celebrations of civility would claim.

Beckett's representation of Knott's house constitutes another recognizable point of contact with Anglo-Irish culture and literary tradition, rehearsing as it does Anglo-Ireland's eternal return to its Big

House. Watt's experience of Knott's house echoes Bowen's of estates she visited: "When I visit other big houses I *am* struck by some quality that they all have—not so much isolation as mystery. Each house seems to live under its own spell, and that is the spell that falls on the visitor from the moment he passes in at the gates" (Bowen 1940, 25).[10] For Beckett as for Bowen, the house is more than a physical structure. It is a site of mystery that is, or seems, a sign: a place where meanings appear to reside and hanker to be pinned down. But Knott's house does not embody a lost social order or a noble European ideal. The estate that Bowen sometimes sees as a symbol of a valued culture is, in *Watt*, only uncertainly meaningful, and of what Watt is never sure. Beckett enjoys a self-conscious and ironic relation to the tradition that represents the Anglo-Irish estate as a site of meaning: he makes Watt's quest to comprehend this house the better part of his novel's "plot."

In another challenge to traditional representations of the Big House, Beckett summons some of its formulaic epithets: "this unfortunate house," "this wretched edifice," "this unhappy home." But the novel never fills these melodramatic labels with content, which makes them seem unearned and extreme. One might expect such labels to arouse one's curiosity, since they connote stories about the house that the novel never tells. But because the epithets are clichés, they stir less interest than indifference, reducing the story of Anglo-Irish decline to which they flippantly allude to an offhand cliché that is not worth narrating.

Further, Beckett extends the trope of the mysterious Big House by making it surreal. When Watt arrives, the house is dark, then inexplicably light. It is locked, then Watt finds himself inside. No transitions mark these changes; the house slides disconcertingly among being-states. In contrast to the specifically and lovingly substantiated houses of other Anglo-Irish texts, no detailed descriptions fix and preserve this one. It remains a slippery dream-product. And this house is no safe haven, no bulwark against threat, but a house of horrors that finally drives Watt mad. He longs to wrap up "safe in words the kitchen space, the extraordinary newel-lamp, the stairs that were never the same and of which even the number of steps seemed to vary, from day to day, and from night to morning, and many other things in the house, and the bushes without and other garden growths, that so often prevented Watt from taking the air, even on the finest day, so that he grew pale, and constipated" (S. Beckett

1953, 83). Beckett decisively darkens Ascendancy's sometime symbol of gracious culture, emphasizing its disturbing, disabling impact on Watt, evoking, perhaps, the psychological costs of Anglo-Irishness to Anglo-Irish writers and to others.

IV

The significance of Watt's encounter with Knott's house to the tradition of Anglo-Irish fiction cannot be overstated. The encounter constitutes a defining moment in Anglo-Irish literary culture. Watt is indeed, as I have indicated, a kind of Cartesian Everyman embarked on a quest for knowledge and meaning. But Watt's epistemological quest is not just any epistemological quest. It is precipitated and ultimately thwarted by his encounter with two icons of Anglo-Ireland: with Knott and Knott's house. And at Knott's, Watt seeks to understand just those topics that preoccupy the Anglo-Irish literary imagination: the Big House, its master, relations of master to servant, Protestant to Catholic. Watt's attempt to make "a pillow of old words" (S. Beckett 1953, 117) out of the sense data that barrages him at Knott's dramatizes the limits of hermeneutics in general but also the problematics of interpreting Anglo-Ireland in particular. In his Big House novel, Beckett makes the compulsion to narrate Anglo-Ireland *itself* the story. Casting his protagonist as a figure of the Anglo-Irish writer, Beckett turns the Big House novel self-reflexive, writing a fiction about, among other things, writing Big House fiction.[11]

"The danger," Beckett cautions in "Dante . . . Bruno . Vico . . Joyce," is in the "neatness of the identifications" (S. Beckett 1929, 9). Associating Watt with Anglo-Irishness, let alone calling him a figure of the Anglo-Irish writer, may seem a particularly dangerous identification given how broad his significance has been shown to be, how indeterminate his cultural identity appears, and how distant from the iconic figure of Anglo-Ireland—Knott himself—he remains. But Watt spends far less time in this novel serving Knott than he does serving the cultural imperative that drives Anglo-Irish writers: the imperative to account for Anglo-Ireland and its place in Irish history. Indeed, one might argue that serving this imperative requires or creates, for the Anglo-Irish writer, just the kind of distance from Anglo-Ireland that Watt, an outsider to Knott's house, maintains from Knott.

We can see glimmers of comparable literary self-consciousness in other novels in the tradition. Keane's parodies of purple Anglo-Irish prose, like Bowen's tongue-in-cheek section headings, bespeak both skepticism toward Anglo-Irish style and cognizance of Anglo-Irishness *as* style. But awareness of Anglo-Ireland's textuality pervades, indeed drives *Watt*—one of Beckett's most distinctive challenges and contributions to the tradition.

Though to a lesser extent than his employer, Watt is a compelling figure of the unknowable, as Mr. Hackett complains early on. When Mr. Goff insists he knows nothing of Watt, Mr. Hackett exclaims, "But you must know something. . . . One does not part with five shillings to a shadow. Nationality, family, birthplace, confession, occupation, means of existence, distinctive signs, you cannot be in ignorance of all this." Mr. Goff insists, "I tell you, nothing is known" (S. Beckett 1953, 21). Watt's ineffability stems in part from his contrast to other characters in the text, who often accrue associations that link them to distinctive Irish types: Mr. Knott the landowner; Mr. Graves the Catholic gardener; Mr. Nackybal the (ostensible) Gaeltacht Gael; Lady McCann; the university committee. Compared to these broadly drawn social types, Watt seems a blank. His capacity to thwart categorization stems also from the fact that those "distinctive signs" he does display contradict each other. If other characters appear pure breeds, Watt appears a mutt, with ties to a variety of social groups. He is a servant to land-owning Knott; he has needed to beg money of Mr. Goff for a boot. He is differentiated from the high and mighty Lady McCann not just in the railway scene but when he approaches her gate: "faithful to the spirit of her cavalier ascendants, she picked up a stone and threw it, with all her might, which, when she was roused, was not negligible, at Watt" (32). But Watt wears a gentleman's clothes: a vest and waistcoat; Mercier identifies him as a gentleman *manqué* (Mercier 1977, 54). He is confused several times in the course of the novel with both Knott and Hackett, apparent Anglo-Irishmen both (S. Beckett 1953, 115, 19). He probably attended university and is referred to as "the maddened prizeman" (248), "a punning reference to the Madden Prize, a scholarly award at Trinity College, Dublin" (Rabinovitz 1984, 164). Mr. Graves takes off his hat to him, as he always does "when in speech with his betters" (S. Beckett 1953, 144).

Watt is no Richard Naylor, no Jasper Swift; he is not a realistically drawn Anglo-Irishman. But as the details listed above suggest, he has much in common with that murky category named Anglo-Ireland.

His indeterminate placelessness and apparent blending of social strains in fact render him an evocative figure of that social formation described, as we have seen, as "neither English nor Irish, fish nor flesh" (Lyons 1979, 29). Like Anglo-Ireland, Watt is (as his name suggests) an unnamable ontological conundrum.

But it is the intellectual work Watt undertakes that links him most dramatically to the figure of the Anglo-Irish writer. Before Knott's and after Knott's, Watt does not need to know. It is his arrival there that precipitates his epistemological hunger and spawns his appetite for words. At Knott's, Watt

> desired words to be applied to his situation, to Mr Knott, to the house, to the grounds, to his duties, to the stairs, to his bedroom, to the kitchen, and in a general way to the conditions of being in which he found himself. For Watt now found himself in the midst of things which, if they consented to be named, did so with reluctance. And the state in which Watt found himself resisted formulation in a way no state had ever done, in which Watt had ever found himself, and Watt had found himself in a great many states, in his day. (S. Beckett 1953, 81)

The narrator is emphatic as to the recalcitrance of Mr. Knott's particular domain: "For there was no other place, but only there where Mr Knott was, whose mysteries, whose fixity, whose fixity of mystery, so thrust forth, with such a thrust. . . For there was no place, but only there where Mr Knott was, whose peculiar properties, having first thrust forth, with such a thrust, called back so soon, with such a call" (199).[12]

The episode of the Galls, "perhaps the principal incident of Watt's early days in Mr Knott's house," initiates Watt's quest to know and illuminates Beckett's conception of the Anglo-Irish writer's encounter with history and culture (S. Beckett 1953, 72). The Galls, a father and son, come to Knott's house to tune the piano. While there, they utter some cryptic comments about doom, and then leave. The episode troubles Watt because of "the vigour with which it developed a purely plastic content, and gradually lost, in the nice processes of its light, its sound, its impact and its rhythm, all meaning, even the most literal" (72—73). Beckett's narrator explains:

> This fragility of the outer meaning had a bad effect on Watt, for it caused him to seek for another, for some meaning of what had passed, in the image of how it had passed.

The most meagre, the least plausible, would have satisfied Watt, who had not seen a symbol, nor executed an interpretation, since the age of fourteen, or fifteen, and who had lived, miserably it is true, among face values all his adult life, face values at least for him. . . . [W]hatever it was Watt saw, with the first look, that was enough for Watt, that had always been enough for Watt, more than enough for Watt. And he had experienced literally nothing, since the age of fourteen, or fifteen, of which in retrospect he was not content to say, That is what happened then. . . . The incident of the Galls, on the contrary, ceased so rapidly to have even the paltry significance of two men, come to tune a piano, and tuning it, and exchanging a few words, as men will do, and going, that this seemed rather to belong to some story heard long before, an instant in the life of another, ill told, ill heard, and more than half forgotten. (S. Beckett 1953, 73–74)

Watt cannot experience the incident as vividly present or currently real. It has a vague, shadowy absence-presence, like family legend or cultural history, familiar and yet strange. The event pains Watt, causing him distress and intense anxiety. It is so pressing that it cannot, even by a man who has grown wise to the futility of interpretation, be left uninterpreted or accepted as "the simple games time plays with space" (75). It demands his immediate and conclusive attention.

Why does this episode so trouble Watt, and what leads me to read it as indicative of Beckett's conception of the Anglo-Irish writer's work? The episode is historically laden. As Harrington explains, "Gall" "has the local connotation of foreigner and colonist, as distinct from native and Gael . . . The whole matter of that distinction is as old as English colonization" (Harrington 1991, 127). Moreover, Beckett portrays the Galls' arrival at Knott's as a "fugitive penetration," an instance of a threshold being crossed by a stranger (S. Beckett 1953, 70). Their arrival at the isolated island of Knott's estate thus takes shape as a strange colonization, with the Galls figuring as the colonizers to Knott, the colonized. Beckett enacts the gesture that we see again and again in Anglo-Irish fiction: the attempt to challenge myths of essential difference between Ireland's historically opposed social formations by positing similarity rather than "clash of cultures" (Lyons 1979, v). In casting Knott's house as a penetrated island, the episode places Anglo-Ireland in Ireland's place, effectively blurring historical roles and upsetting cultural polarities. This blurring is reinforced by the name "Gall," for while "Gall" denotes "foreigner" and "colonist" it looks and sounds much like its ostensible opposite: "Gael."

But while this episode generates these discrete cultural readings, it is also a case study in Beckett's ambiguous handling of archetypal Anglo-Irish materials. These Galls seem colonizers in name only, coming, going, doing Knott no harm. The only harm they do is to poor Watt, who is compelled to try and figure them out. The parallels between Gall and colonist and Knott and colonized do not develop into a narrative of colonization that makes sense. The Galls gall Watt (and us) with a ghost of an ultimately uninterpretable narrative line. But this episode is, as such, revealing: in conjuring Irish history urgently *and* obliquely, this episode evokes the Anglo-Irish writer's experience of Irish history. Like writers wrestling with those pockets of history that compel them—Iris Murdoch with the Easter Rising, Molly Keane with interclass relations—Watt cannot shake his obsession with this incident. His mind pecks at it compulsively, in a futile struggle to utter the final word.

Beckett gives the notion of history's interpretability its most sustained exposition in his representation of Watt's tortured attempt to understand Knott. Knott is Watt's supreme obsession and the novel's central conundrum. Why aren't Knott's slops emptied on the first floor (S. Beckett 1953, 68)? Is there a pattern to Knott's getting up in the morning and going to bed at night (86)? What explains Erskine's trips up and down the stairs (119)? Watt's seemingly incidental questions have ontological and metaphysical dimensions; his effort to comprehend Knott mirrors human efforts to understand those we perceive as masters and gods. But Watt's inquiry has sociological and historical implications as well. Even his incidental questions add up (parodically, half seriously, always equivocally) to a question of central importance to the Anglo-Irish writer: how shall I account for the Anglo-Irish landowner and those charged historical facts—authority, ownership—for which he stands?

Knott elicits an array of responses from Watt. Knott is feared, loved, craved, resented. Watt muses, "[T]o many on the ground floor the nearness of Mr Knott must long be a horror, and long a horror to others on the first his farness" (S. Beckett 1953, 133). Watt quizzes himself futilely, "[W]hat conception have I of Mr Knott? None" (120). "[W]hat do I know of Mr Knott? Nothing" (119). Knott and his world ultimately prove "unspeakable" (85).

One tack Watt takes in trying to understand Knott is to conceive of him as a deity figure whose face he both wishes and fears to see (S. Beckett 1953, 146). Beckett's narrator tells us, "Watt had more and more the impression, as time passed, that nothing could be added to Mr Knott's establishment, and from it nothing taken away, but that as it was now, so it had been in the beginning, and so it would remain to the end, in all essential respects" (131). Like Watt's many attempts at understanding, this one proves inconclusive. Far from an unequivocal deity figure, Knott manifests traits at odds with those notions of pure and unchanging presence that Watt tries to impose on him. As the servant Arthur learns, Knott has a family; "Mr Knott too was serial, in a vermicular series" (253). And Knott is associated not just with eternal fixity but with flux. Watt's description of Knott's would-be completeness, quoted above, grows less biblically assertive as it goes on: so Knott's presence was now, as it was in the beginning, "and so it would remain to the end, in all essential respects, any significant presence, at any time, and here all presence was significant, even though it was impossible to say of what, proving that presence at all times, or an equivalent presence, and only the face changing, but perhaps the face ever changing, even as   perhaps even Mr Knott's face ever slowly changed" (131). Besides mirroring the writer's attempt to fathom Anglo-Ireland, this passage depicts Knott and the social formation he evokes as only apparently present and potent—a tenuous allusion to Anglo-Ireland's historical provisionality. Moreover, the passage portrays the myth of Ascendancy as myth: as a product of a subject's desire. Knott is he whom Watt longs to see as a god. And even this emphatically mythological myth of Ascendancy is not stable. Watt wants to call Knott divine, but the thought of Knott's being serial "would have pleased him" too (253). Watt's quest to call Knott a god is not just unsuccessful, it is ambivalent, not unlike the Anglo-Irish writer's competing urge to make and break Anglo-Irish icons.

Of course, Beckett's name for this iconic figure is provocatively iconoclastic. As "not," Knott is negation, void, absence, naught; he is essence, all right, but the essence of nothingness, the essence of lack of essence. And as "knot," Knott is the problem that cannot be solved. No master figure of order, or of a clear and distinct ideal of life, as Bowen would have it, he is the essence of disorder. As David Helsa concludes, "the domain of Knott [is] the domain of the absurd" (Helsa 1971, 84).

V

Other portions of Watt's quest to know Knott churn up more explosive issues. The equivocal announcement that opens the novel's second section carries an unambiguous cultural charge: "Mr Knott was a good master, in a way" (S. Beckett 1953, 68). Knott is master to two distinct groups in the novel—to his manservants and to the men and women who live nearby—and the novel spends ample energy mulling over his relations with both. Like other novelists' attempts to reckon with this topic, Beckett's investigation into the master-servant relation and the nature of service and work is shifting and inconclusive: alternately cool and hot, celebratory and condemning.

As Watt contemplates the origins, terms, and conclusions of Knott's relations with his house servants, he entertains competing theories of the master-servant relation. At times his analysis echoes Hegel's dialectical notion of lordship and bondage.[13] In Hegel's view, master and servant realize each other's existence; their relation paradoxically subordinates the master to the servant, insofar as the master's identity depends on the servant's acknowledgment and work. Thus, "just as lordship showed its essential nature to be the reverse of what it wants to be, so, too, bondage will, when completed, pass into the opposite of what it immediately is" (Hegel 1807, 237). Consistent with Hegel's analysis, Arsene, the servant who gives Watt a long introductory lecture on life at Knott's, posits the master-servant relation as one of mutual definition. The existence of the house and parlor maid, he muses, "is hardly conceivable" without the existence of a mistress or master, "whose existence also in a sense if you like depends on the existences of" the servants (S. Beckett 1953, 50–51).

But the novel's dominant conceit for the master-servant relation is love. Knott's servants, the experienced Arsene notes, move around him in "tireless love" (S. Beckett 1953, 62). Watt's own relation to Knott is one of unrequited love. Challenging the master-servant relation's look of stark, one-way hierarchy, Beckett suggests that the servant's love can resemble that of a guardian for a child or ward, as when Watt "did not care to leave Mr Knott all alone in the garden, though there was really no reason why he should not" (198); this idea is corroborated in the asylum scenes, where it is Watt, living in a "mansion," who has "attendants." But Beckett typically characterizes this love as that of an inferior for a superior, or one whom the inferior hopes will prove superior. The ostensibly godlike master is he whom the servant hopes will entail presence and be able to produce meaning and peace.

Confident that "the same things happen to us all, especially to men in our situation, whatever that is" (S. Beckett 1953, 45), Arsene gives an exposition of this deistic theory of service that seems positively lyrical. He describes the novice servant:

> He is well pleased. For he knows he is in the right place, at last. And he knows he is the right man, at last. . . . [H]e being what he has become, and the place being what it was made, the fit is perfect. . . . The sensations, the premonitions of harmony are irrefragable, of imminent harmony, when all outside him will be he, the flowers that he is among him, the sky the sky that he is above him, the earth trodden the earth treading, and all sound his echo. When in a word he will be in his midst at last, after so many tedious years clinging to the perimeter. These first impressions, so hardly won, are undoubtedly delicious. What a feeling of security! . . . All is repaid, amply repaid. For he has arrived. (S. Beckett 1953, 40–41)

In Arsene's view, service is a situation whose structure appears to solve the problem that plagues all Beckett protagonists: the humiliating coexistence of human will and desire on the one hand and meaninglessness and futility on the other. Service appears a solution not just because it places the servant in the presence of someone who seems presence incarnate, but because it prescribes behavior in relation to that presence, thereby creating what seems a closed system of self-reflexive meaning:

> For there is work to do. That is what is so exquisite. Having oscillated all his life between the torments of superficial loitering and the horrors of disinterested endeavour, he finds himself at last in a situation where to do nothing exclusively would be an act of the highest value and significance. And what happens? For the first time, since in anguish and disgust he relieved his mother of her milk, definite tasks of unquestionable utility are assigned to him. (S. Beckett 1953, 41)

Prohibiting choice, requiring the abdication of will, service seems bliss. Again Arsene echoes Hegel, who writes of labor: "this activity giving shape and form, is at the same time the individual existence, the pure self-existence of that consciousness, which now in the work it does is externalized and passes into the condition of permanence" (Hegel 1807, 238).

But like Watt when he tries to call Knott a god, the servant protests too much. Cracks splinter Arsene's beatific theory. "[T]o Mr Knott, and with Mr Knott, and from Mr Knott, were a coming and a being and a going exempt from languor, exempt from fever, for Mr Knott was harbour, Mr Knott was haven, calmly entered, freely ridden" but also "gladly left" (S. Beckett 1953, 135). Sitting in Knott's kitchen, Watt "removes his hat without misgiving, he unbuttons his coat and sits down, proffered all pure and open to the long joys of being himself, like a basin to vomit" (41). After describing the servant's pleasure at the prospect of performing useful tasks Arsene muses, "Is not that charming? But his regret, his indignation, are of short duration, disappearing as a rule at the end of the third or fourth month" (41).

These incoherent introductions of regret and indignation culminate, at the end of Arsene's long rumination, in a reversal more violent and conclusive. Arsene's by now clearly ironic perspective takes over. According to Arsene, in thinking well of service, the servant forces the issue:

> he comes to understand that he is working not merely for Mr Knott in person, and for Mr Knott's establishment, but also, and indeed chiefly, for himself, that he may abide, as he is, where he is, and where he is may abide about him, as it is. Unable to resist these intenerating considerations, his regrets, lively at first, melt at last, melt quite away and pass over, softly, into the celebrated conviction that all is well, or at least for the best. His indignation undergoes a similar reduction, and calm and glad at last he goes about his work, calm and glad he peels the potato and empties the nightstool, calm and glad he witnesses and is witnessed. For a time. For the day comes when he says, Am I not a little out of sorts, to-day? . . . But that is a terrible day (to look back on), the day when the horror of what has happened reduces him to the ignoble expedient of inspecting his tongue in a mirror. (S. Beckett 1953, 41–42)

The servant's happy definitions of service are revealed, as the passage proceeds, to be rationalizations aimed at keeping regret, indignation, and horror at bay. But Arsene's initial descriptions of service as blissful arrival, because they are initial and are cast as conclusive, have a staying power they would not if they were cast as rationalizations at the start. This narrative technique, combined with the fact that Beckett peppers Arsene's tribute with oblique challenges to it (as when Arsene calls the new servant's "premonitions of harmony" "first impressions"), communicates a blurred assessment of service. Arsene's soliloquy casts service as a jumble of bliss and horror.

Like Conrad, Beckett does not name the horror, but he does hint at what it entails, so that Arsene's jumbled assessment competes with a comparatively conclusive indictment of service, further muddying the issue. Beckett casts Knott's manservants as links in a volitionless chain of labor valued only for their ability to conform to Knott's alternating penchant for big and small men. In keeping with the market logic of capitalism, one may be exchanged for another. Knott's servants are shown to comprise just one in a series of series of things which Knott owns and exploits: Watt ponders "The possible relations between such series as these, the series of dogs, the series of men, the series of pictures, to mention only these series" (S. Beckett 1953, 136). Examination of Arsene's apparent paean to "tasks of unquestionable utility" reveals a Marxist conception of labor and value that further condemns the service Knott requires. That passage does not, as one might conclude on first reading, suggest that the servant derives worth from performing assigned work. In the midst of his apparently Hegelian tribute, Arsene voices a disruptive sense of service as "a situation where to do nothing exclusively would be an act of the highest value and significance." The structure of servitude is such, Arsene implies, that the servant experiences value in *not* working; since work derives from and belongs to the master, the servant must find identity in nonwork, nonentity. Servitude thus alienates the servant from a potential source of worth in the material world, as well as worth as perceived by self.

Beckett's most sustained explication of servitude's horror takes shape in the business of Watt and Knott's pot. Watt struggles to assign the word "pot" to one of Knott's pots—an example of Watt's broader struggle to understand his experience at Knott's. Insofar as naming is an act of appropriation, Watt's inability to name the pot marks his expropriation. Beckett suggests that Watt's difficulty is indeed a matter of dispossession as determined by servitude by emphasizing this pot is Knott's. "Looking at a pot, for example, or thinking of a pot, at one of Mr Knott's pots, of one of Mr Knott's pots, it was in vain that Watt said, Pot, pot" (S. Beckett 1953, 81).

This is no small problem for Watt. Like the episode of the Galls, it causes him deep pain, and the implications are dire:

Then, when he turned for reassurance to himself, who was not Mr
Knott's, in the sense that the pot was, who had come from without
and whom the without would take again, he made the distressing
discovery that of himself too he could no longer affirm anything that
did not seem as false as if he had affirmed it of a stone. Not that Watt
was in the habit of affirming things of himself, for he was not, but
he found it a help, from time to time, to be able to say, with some
appearance of reason, Watt is a man, all the same, Watt is a man,
or, Watt is in the street, with thousands of fellow-creatures within
call. And Watt was greatly troubled by this tiny little thing, more
troubled perhaps than he had ever been by anything. (S. Beckett
1953, 82)

Service and dispossession exact a terrible toll, here. They deprive the
servant of authority not just insofar as the servant must do the master's bidding; the deprivation goes deeper and the challenge to authority is more profound. Service alienates the servant from the surrounding world—from the products of his or her labor and from
experience itself, de-authorizing the ability to make sense of that experience. And dispossession extends to the self. Service de-autho-
rizes a sense of personhood. It constitutes an ontological affront.[14]

Vividly linking ontological, intellectual, and linguistic uncertainty
to the experience of service and dispossession, this much-analyzed
"pot" episode suggests a new way to read Beckett's long-standing preoccupation with those concerns. Perhaps Beckett's pervasive sense of
the tenuousness of self and of the distance between word and thing
have partial grounding in his experience of service and material dispossession as imagined here in *Watt*; perhaps Beckett's poststructuralist sense of language and postmodern conception of identity are
rooted not only in cosmopolitan intellectual movements such as Ex-
istentialism, but are nourished too by his imaginative engagement
with Irish culture.

As usual, a culturally informed reading requires qualification,
which has the effect of blunting the indictment of service *Watt* registers; the novel offers no conclusions on this topic. Beckett's treatment of servitude is not consistently serious. It does not refer literally
to Irish history, culture and politics. And the content of Watt's and
Arsene's ruminations on the master-servant relation is not all that interests Beckett. He is interested, too, in their manner; servants and
masters can seem just that much grist for the intellectual, linguistic
mill. Still, it is impossible to read that word "horror" or Arsene's com-

parison of a servant to a basin for vomit, and not have content register seriously. Such moments are among several in *Watt* when suddenly play seems to cease and tone to turn dead serious. Watt's anguish is terrible to witness, and Beckett seems to care. For all Beckett's self-reflexive literary play with Anglo-Ireland's symbolic Big House, these moments suggest that Anglo-Ireland and its iconographic estate are indeed sites of at least intermittent meaning for Beckett—not signs of inherently valuable culture but historical sites of the meeting of those parties who appear to make meaning (however indeterminant) in Ireland, or whose deeply flawed history sparks longing for meaning. For what such meetings mean, and whether they do mean, remains unclear in *Watt*. Service as bliss, service as an incoherent mix of bliss and horror, service as horror—*Watt* suggests all of the above, finally undecided on this topic, as on others.

VI

The story of the Lynches comprises the other focus of Watt's effort to evaluate Knott's and, by extension, Anglo-Ireland's exercise of authority. Watt may be unable to come to conclusions about Knott, but *Watt* comes within a hair's breadth of doing so here, the site of Beckett's least equivocal encounter with Anglo-Ireland.

A fragment in *Watt*'s Addenda evokes some of the issues and attitudes in question (S. Beckett 1953, 251–52). Walking in Knott's garden, Arthur comes upon "an old man, clothed in rags," who mistakes him for Knott. The ensuing scene, analogous to Lois's and Hugo's encounter with Michael Connor in *The Last September*, evokes an earlier social order. The man, who remains nameless, begs a penny from Arthur, whom he calls "your honour." He paints a romantic picture of their putatively shared past: "I remember you when I was a boy. . . . You was a fine lovely boy, said the old man, and I was another." He goes on, "Yer father was very good to me. . . . I helped to lay out this darling place." It is never clear whether the man's romanticization of the past is sincere or whether it is tactical. Like Bowen's Connor, he may be an only apparently affable peasant who is, in fact, coolly pursuing his own interests. His reminder, "You was always wetting yer trousers," is at best innocently hostile. Arthur certainly senses a charged undercurrent to the encounter. When the old man announces that he used to clean Knott's boots, Arthur replies defensively, "If it hadn't been you, it would have been another" (252). And the meeting agitates him. Having been mistaken for Knott "He did not know if he felt honoured or not" (251). As in the railway station scene, amid surrealism and farce Beckett sounds a chilling note of class tension.[15]

In the Lynch episode, Watt seeks to understand how it came to be that members of this prolific Catholic family living on the land around Knott's estate bring their dog around to eat Mr. Knott's left-over food. If we read Watt's attempt to understand the Galls as a fig-ure of the Anglo-Irish writer's attempt to comprehend Irish history, we might read this episode as a figure of the writer's attempt to wres-tle, more specifically, with the logic of interclass relations.

"Watt's instructions were formal: On those days on which food was left over, the food left over was to be given to the dog, without loss of time" (S. Beckett 1953, 93). Were "the dog" to reject the prof-fered food, these instructions would be violated; so an ample supply of dogs is kept hungry. Needless to say, this "venerable tradition, or institution" (116) casts Anglo-Irish custom as absurdly self-indul-gent. The grotesquely comic arrangement recalls Swift's "A Modest Proposal," but with some vicious and damning twists. Swift's narrator seeks to address the problem of Irish starvation by means of a hideous but, given the extremity of Ireland's destitution, perversely logical solution; Knott, by contrast, finds a perverse solution to an absurd non-problem by way of starvation.

That this episode's import extends beyond the Lynches in partic-ular and epistemological puzzles in general—that the issues at hand are deeply and specifically political—is made clear by Beckett's nu-merous allusions to the colonial situation. Beckett sets the episode in a landscape of unrelenting Irish poverty: "immense impoverished families abounded for miles around in every conceivable direction, and must have always done so"; there are and always were large num-bers of starving dogs in the neighborhood; any messenger a dog owner might have sent to retrieve Knott's leftovers might have eaten them himself, or sold them to some other needy party (S. Beckett 1953, 100, 91, 95). Beckett uses language that carries an explicit his-torical charge: the dogs are "exploited" by their owners; Knott main-tains "famished" dogs in a "famished" condition; he keeps "a kennel or colony of famished dogs" (99). Exploitation, famine, colony—the episode's historical analog could not be more clear.

Watt's speculations as to how Knott acquired the Lynches' coop-eration strengthen this evocation of ugly colonial relations. Maybe,

Watt thinks, Knott secured help "by fair words and occasional gifts of money and old clothes" (S. Beckett 1953, 99). Or maybe Knott thought it would be:

> better still that a suitable large needy local family of say the two parents and from ten to fifteen children and grand-children passionately attached to their birthplace should be sought out, and by a handsome small initial lump sum to be paid down and by a liberal annual pension of fifty pounds to be paid monthly and by occasional seasonable gifts of loose change and tight clothes and by untiring well-timed affectionate words of advice and encouragement and consolation, attached firmly for good and all in block, their children and their children's children, to Mr Knott's service. (S. Beckett 1953, 99)

The energy and bite of this passage is remarkable in a novel in which so much of the prose is desultory, mechanical and numb. The hot topic of historical cabin-castle relations calls Beckett out. All but unequivocally, Beckett condemns Knott *qua* Anglo-Ireland as an abusive colonial power.

Beckett writes close to the bone throughout the Lynch episode. The "cold eye" that he insisted had to be trained on personal experience before writing seems to have gone hot. He alludes to history less obliquely than he does in the episode of the Galls. He writes less abstractly than he does on the question of Knott, where the issue of epistemological futility remains focal. In the Lynch episode, abstraction is displaced by documentary-like specificity. Parody also abates. In his treatment of the Galls, even in his treatment of the master-servant relation, Beckett plays. Here, Beckett engages more earnestly, and reading historically is not risky but required. Beckett does distance the Lynches by making them stereotypically grotesque, evoking imperial representations of the Irish Other. And Watt's attempt to comprehend the Lynches' bond to Knott is yet another demonstration of intellectual and linguistic impotence. That the episode is followed by a long treatment of Watt's pointless attempt to understand what unites Erskine, Knott and the ringing bell casts the social commentary that precedes it as one in a series of pointless narratives. Even here, Beckett's narrative does not engage unequivocally with culture and history. But the ugliness and edginess of the Lynch episode make it more than a representation of some generic mental rut. Historical recollection and cultural critique bleed through comedy, absurdity, and literary play. In this episode, *Watt* verges close to losing self-consciousness, chronicling almost unequivocally this Anglo-Irish writer's distraught confrontation with Irish history.[16]

It is in the Lynch episode that Beckett describes Watt in terms that most clearly identify his kinship with Anglo-Irish writers. When Beckett's engagement with home culture is at its least veiled so too is the Anglo-Irish dimension of Watt's manifold identity. Both the manner and the matter of Watt's inquiry bind him to writers in the Anglo-Irish tradition:

> Not that for a moment Watt supposed that he had penetrated the forces at play, in this particular instance, or even perceived the forms that they upheaved, or obtained the least useful information concerning himself, or Mr Knott, for he did not. But he had turned, little by little, a disturbance into words, had made a pillow of old words, for a head. Little by little, and not without labour. Kate [the dog] eating from her dish, for example, . . . how he had laboured to know what that was, to know which the doer, and what the doer, and what the doing, and which the sufferer, and what the sufferer, and what the suffering, and what those shapes, that were not rooted to the ground, like veronica, but melted away, into the dark, after a while. (S. Beckett 1953, 117)

Laboring to know "which the doer, and what the doer," and "what the sufferer, and what the suffering"—that is the task that compels the bulk of Watt's narrative, and the bulk of Anglo-Irish fiction. Struggling to understand the relational identities of Ireland's historically opposed social groups, the Anglo-Irish writer turns a disturbance into words, makes a pillow for a head. Seeking to fathom the origins and outcomes of these groups' historical interactions, Anglo-Irish writers produce volume after volume of Big House fiction.

VII

In his representation of Watt's career at Knott's, then, Beckett offers a model of Anglo-Irish authorship radically different from the Yeatsian paradigm proposed some time ago by Seamus Deane (Deane 1985, 31–32). And *Watt* (the novel) corroborates the model that Watt (the character) provides. No apology for Anglo-Ireland or its literary tradition, *Watt* is a fluctuating and open-ended attempt to "penetrate the forces at play" in Irish history and culture, a narrative marked by traces of the strain of situating itself vis-à-vis its culture of origin.

As we have seen, *Watt* comprises a spectrum of responses to Anglo-Ireland. Though *Watt* contains damning indictments of Anglo-Ireland (as master to dehumanized servants, as lord to exploited serfs), it counters these indictments with competing interpretations (master as loved god, service as bliss). "Not rooted to the ground," *Watt's* representations of the compulsory Anglo-Irish topics shift and slip. The novel is riven, too, with generic and conceptual tensions: between absurd comedy and biting cultural critique, between fierce social commentary and the insistence that commentary is futile, between a vision of history as ineffable (as in the episode of the Galls) and a vision of history as crystal clear (as in the Lynch episode). Such tensions in the novel, like the ambiguity of its cultural references and their contrast to other clear and seemingly serious allusions, reveal *Watt* to be (among other things) a dynamic production of this writer's unstable relation to his home culture and his undecided conversation with himself over how to *account for* it.

Beckett's competing narrators also point back to this source (among others). This postmodern narrative gesture expresses an Anglo-Irish dilemma. I have argued that Watt may be seen as a figure of the Anglo-Irish writer. But it might also be said that Watt and Sam together constitute a figure of that writer. As we have seen, Watt tends to seek sunny interpretations of the things he is driven to name at Knott's. He is inclined to call Knott a god, the master-servant relation an egalitarian bond of love. But Watt's initial interpretations are faulty: they jibe neither with facts, nor with his own awareness of their tenuousness, nor with the gist of Sam's critical intelligence which intrudes to challenge them from time to time. Watt argues with himself over how to interpret Anglo-Ireland, but he also argues with Sam. Like the imaginary debate between himself and Watt that Arsene dramatizes in his meditation on service, Sam's and Watt's debate over the nature of Anglo-Ireland emblematizes the mind of this Anglo-Irish writer, and suggests a crucial source of the Anglo-Irish literary impulse. This debate is the spark that ignites Anglo-Irish fiction—novels in the process of inconclusive conversation with themselves and not, like Lady McCann's, rhetoric in an imperative mode.

I have speculated that Beckett's sense of the tenuousness of self and the distance between word and thing may have a root in his imaginative experience of dispossession and servitude as recorded in *Watt*. It is suggestive to consider other hallmarks of Beckett's later work in light of his "Anglo-Irish novel." That work has, in Hugh Kenner's words, "spiraled inward . . . to the center of the solitary world" (Kenner 1973b, 36). The past disappears; *The Unnamable* is "a book that is entirely 'present state'" (Abbott 1973, 110). The "action" of the late novels occurs out of time. While place remains burdensome, as Harrington shows, setting becomes less and less specifically Irish. Social realities like caste and class vanish. Like style, content itself all but disappears, in novels that approximate rhythm, pure structure, silence. The marked difference between Beckett's more socially realistic pre-*Watt* fiction and his more abstracted post-*Watt* work, along with the intermittently feverish pitch of *Watt*'s engagement with culture and history, provocatively mark *Watt* as a site of cultural struggle from which the "minimalization" of Beckett's work follows.[17]

It is difficult to imagine that Beckett's acquaintance with the quest to "utter and eff" Anglo-Ireland did not contribute to his conception of writing as failure and epistemology as futility. Watt's situation prefigures that of Beckett's late narrators. It is, as Kenner articulates it, "the situation of him who is helpless, cannot act, in the end cannot write, since he is obliged to write; the act of him who, helpless, unable to act, acts, in the end writes, since he is obliged to write" (Kenner 1973b, 201). It is precisely the situation of Sheridan Le Fanu's Reverend Jennings: the situation of the writer poised to narrate Anglo-Ireland. In *Watt*, Beckett chooses Anglo-Ireland as the site and Anglo-Irish themes as the vehicle for expressing epistemological crisis, the fall from omniscience, the beginning of the end of the novel. *Watt* suggests, then, that such cornerstones of Beckett's avant-garde vision may stem from more than a Continental conception of knowledge as generically problematic and language as generically flawed. Beckett's purportedly cosmopolitan ideas have some local roots in his conception of the compulsion to narrate Anglo-Ireland. *Watt* is not a novel in which early signs of later concerns make tentative appearances on mere Irish scaffolding, but fertile breeding ground revealing Anglo-Irish preconditions for the later work. Beckett's late narrators, his so-called "French heroes," have some Anglo-Irish blood in their veins.

Perhaps Beckett's wide array of unrelentingly isolated outcasts share this Anglo-Irish provenance. Beckett's late characters are, as

Kenner argues, "radically and metaphysically unassimilable . . . They will not fit into some vast social or fictional machine, as Joyce . . . fitted Leopold Bloom. Nor, in the late phase of the enterprise, will they fit into any known world. It is by program a fiction of outcasts" (Kenner 1973b, 33). The long line of Big House fiction is, of course, chock-full of marginalized misfits who express not just Anglo-Ireland's indeterminate placement between cultures, but the exile and "suffering of being" of the writer who examines home culture. Interestingly, the stories Beckett produced immediately after writing *Watt*—"The Expelled," "The Calmative," and "The End"—all center on characters who are expelled from home.

Other features of Beckett's work, likewise assumed to be standard Beckett fare or signs of his membership in avant-garde culture, might also be read as vestigially Anglo-Irish. Farce, surrealism, and black humor recur in more traditional Anglo-Irish novels, portraying a beleaguered culture's moribund social form as farce. They express a vision, as voiced by Standish O'Grady in 1900, of "this Protestant Anglo-Irish ascendancy which once owned all Ireland from the centre to the sea, . . . rotting from the land in the most dismal farce-tragedy of all time, without one brave deed, one brave word" (Lyons 1979, 73). They express, too, those bizarre juxtapositions—the dogged persistence of images of sanctity and loveliness in time of guerrilla war, financial decline and physical decay—that are characteristic of twentieth-century Anglo-Ireland. Perhaps such characters as Winnie, in Beckett's 1961 *Happy Days*, who works so hard at empty chit-chat and clings to her routine toilette while buried up to her waist in earth, like the compulsive characters of *Waiting for Godot*, extend the Anglo-Irish preoccupation with surreal entrapment in meaningless ritual and tragic-comic dependence on a superannuated ceremonial mode.[18] *Godot's* pervasive atmosphere of vague and futile waiting quite strikingly echoes the moods of novels like *The Last September, Time After Time*, and *Langrishe, Go Down*, which cast the end of Anglo-Ireland's story as pale anticlimax, to evoke the radically pointless situation of twentieth-century Anglo-Ireland in which "it seemed as though everybody were waiting" (Bowen 1942b, 30). Even Beckett's postmodern language critique might be read as a vestige of his Anglo-Irish heritage, extending as it does the intimations of a novel like Bowen's, where language turns brittle as polite chatter turns irrelevant and the beliefs it carries become obsolete. That Beckett's conception of language has some roots in cultural critique is borne out by those vivid scenes in *Watt* in which polite conversation likewise self-destructs.

It goes without saying that these features of Beckett's work link him to currents in world culture. As Kenner insists, Beckett's work bears the imprint of "contact with such notions as T. H. Huxley's view of man as an irrelevance whom day by day an indifferent universe engages in chess. We do not belong here, runs a strain of Western thought which became especially articulate in France after the War; we belong nowhere; we are all surds, ab-surd" (Kenner 1973b, 163). But these features of Beckett's art bear the imprint of contact with Anglo-Ireland, as well.

This fact has important implications not only for how we read Beckett but for how we understand the literary categories frequently invoked to describe and place him, helping to refine received ideas of literary modernism and postmodernism. Not self-evidently cosmopolitan and apolitical, not necessarily elite or avant-garde, "the modern" and "the postmodern" here echo local history and provincial culture. *Watt* requires that we supplement our conceptions of these cross-cultural twentieth-century trends with an acknowledgment of potentially heterogeneous local sources. Vividly implicated in the history and culture of the "backwater," *Watt* reveals that the ostensibly cosmopolitan is also the intensely provincial; the modern and the postmodern announce the absent presence of a traditional locality.

Placing *Watt* in the Anglo-Irish tradition opens new perspectives on Big House fiction as well. The Sam–Watt debate is one of many instances in *Watt* in which we see modernist and postmodernist intimations of other Anglo-Irish fiction played out and writ large. Beckett follows through on proclivities of more traditional Anglo-Irish novels—in this case, the phenomenon of the writer's internal debate—and takes them to textual extremes. Exploring the linguistic, ontological, and epistemological implications of the modern Anglo-Irish writer's situation, Beckett highlights that situation's modernist and postmodernist dimensions, illuminating how closely the Anglo-Irish predicament parallels the modernist crisis of meaning, knowledge, and value, and precipitates narrative in the interrogatory mode.

Beckett's "cosmopolitanization" of the Big House novel constitutes, perhaps, his most paradoxical contribution to the Anglo-Irish literary tradition. For it disperses the cultural claustrophobia against which Anglo-Irish writers often chafe. It disperses Anglo-Irish culture itself, the event that novels in this tradition tend to make their intermittently elegiac theme. But while it generates a novel that attests to the demise of a closed and coherent Anglo-Irish culture, it at the same time demonstrates Anglo-Ireland's relevance beyond the topical and local. *Watt* at once dilutes and expands the import of Beckett's culture of origin, relativizing but also revitalizing the Anglo-Irish novel. Composed, perhaps, at a greater remove from Anglo-Irish culture than any other novel in its tradition, *Watt* at once diminishes and extends the territory Anglo-Ireland can call its own.

6

Fiction Meets Ideology Critique: An Anglo-Irish Instance

Communities are to be distinguished not by their falsity/genuineness, but by the style in which they are imagined.
—Benedict Anderson, *Imagined Communities*

. . . the narrative tells itself.
—Roland Barthes, *S/Z*

THIS PROJECT BEGAN AS A STUDY OF THE RELATIONS BETWEEN twentieth-century Anglo-Irish fiction and what, early on, I called "Anglo-Irish ideology." After the manner of Fredric Jameson, Edward Said, Terry Eagleton, and others, I sought to explore how the modern Anglo-Irish literary imagination interacts with its ideological inheritance, which I defined loosely as that elusive network of conscious and unconscious beliefs, values, practices and feelings that invisibly structured the Anglo-Irish social order, encoding interests relevant to Anglo-Ireland's social power.

However, as I read and re-read the novels of Keane, Bowen, Beckett, and others, and as I sought to trace the workings of what I was calling "Anglo-Irish ideology" there, I found it increasingly difficult and finally impossible to compose a credible argument. These densely textured narratives made the practice of ideology critique feel something like painting by numbers—neglectful of nuance and shading. In practice, ideology theory provided an inadequate model of political consciousness as these novels represent it. The novels overran the theory, themselves providing a model of political consciousness that seemed more capacious and precise, though perhaps less conducive to the pursuit of social reform.

177

This final chapter examines some of the limits of ideology critique that I encountered while studying these texts, to suggest the limits of its relevance to these novels and to literary studies generally.[1] I will begin with a discussion of ideology theory itself. Taking Eagleton's *Ideology: An Introduction* as a case in point, I will extrapolate some of the basic assumptions underpinning ideology critique, and will reconstruct the problematic approach to these texts which those assumptions initially inspired. I will go on to sketch some tensions in ideology theory itself which are themselves suggestive of the theory's limited relevance to literary texts. I will conclude with a consideration of paradigmatic moments in Molly Keane's *Time After Time*, which proved resistant to ideology critique.

I

The basic framework of the theory and practice of ideology critique as it has operated in literary studies may be extrapolated from Eagleton's *Ideology: An Introduction* (1991).[2] Eagleton defines "ideology" as discourse interested in the outcome of power struggles central to a particular form of social life (Eagleton 1991, 8). "Ideology" alludes to "the way signs, meanings and values help to reproduce social power" (221). To apply this definition to twentieth-century Anglo-Ireland would require fine-tuning from the start. "Anglo-Irish ideology" might be said to refer to a system of signs, meanings, and values interested not in reproducing the Anglo-Irish social order (since it was, by the start of the twentieth century, beyond reproduction), but perhaps in justifying it, or longing for it.

In Eagleton's view, Freud teaches us much about the way ideologies work, one of his most fundamental lessons being that ideologies *do* work. Ideologies are "no mere inert by-products of social contradictions but resourceful strategies for containing, managing and imaginarily resolving them" (Eagleton 1991, 135): "what [Freud] points to as the fundamental mechanisms of the [unconscious] psychical life are the structural devices of ideology as well. Projection, displacement, sublimation, condensation, repression, idealization, substitution, rationalization, disavowal: all of these are at work in the text of ideology, as much as in dream and fantasy; and this is one of the richest legacies Freud has bequeathed to the critique of ideological consciousness" (185). Ideologies justify social behavior, rationalize self-interest, and naturalize such rationalizations by suppressing history and appealing to "common sense." Ideology, as such, proves a variant of what J. L. Austin calls "performative language," belonging "to that class of speech acts which get something done (cursing, persuading, celebrating and so on) rather than to the discourse of description" (19).

From this Freudian theory derives a literary critical practice that has much in common with psychoanalysis. Following Freud and Habermas, Eagleton explains that reading ideology "is not just a question of deciphering a language accidentally afflicted with slippages, ambiguities and non-meanings; it is rather a matter of explaining the forces at work of which these textual obscurities are a necessary effect." The critic reveals how a text's "lacunae, repetitions, elisions and equivocations are themselves significant," to bring to light "the concealed power interests by which these meanings are internally moulded" (Eagleton 1991, 133, 134).

Using Eagleton's basic assumptions as a frame, I sketched the following précis of "Anglo-Irish ideology." Anglo-Irish ideology, I hypothesized, would have certain characteristic preoccupations that would distinguish it from other ideologies. Crucial topics around which it would hover would include the land, the Other (most pressingly the Irish, but also the English), power, hierarchy, authority, and history; "Irishness" and "Anglo-Irishness" would also prove central concerns. As I have argued, Anglo-Irish fiction does indeed mull obsessively over these issues.

Anglo-Irish attitudes toward these topics, I speculated, would be colored by imperialist ideology, fostering oppositional notions of Irishness and Anglo-Irishness. The ideology would promote the clear and distinct difference of Irish and Anglo-Irish, Catholic and Protestant, tenant and landowner, cabin and castle, holding (or trying to hold) "Irishness" at bay as essentially Other. The fundamental opposition at work here would be of (Anglo-Irish) superiority and (Irish) inferiority, which, I expected to find, would be expressed and sustained in other familiar binarisms: culture versus nature, civilization versus barbarity, reason versus emotion, mind versus body, masculine versus feminine. This binary model would generate stereotypes of Irishness: quaint, passionate, drunk, romantic, timeless, childish, elemental, natural, bestial, unconceptual, superstitious—Arnold's idea of the Celt "as dreamer, imaginative, unblessed by the Greek sense of form, at home in the wild landscapes away from the metropolitan centres of highly organised social and political existence" (S. Deane 1979, 375).

But, I anticipated, Anglo-Irish ideology might invert this opposition as well, expressing an ambivalent relation to the Irish Other. In addition to casting Irishness as inferior, the ideology would idealize it as a brand of noble savageness, in terms of Irish innocence and freedom, for instance, in contrast to Anglo-Irish duty and responsibility. I imagined the ideology would project fantasies both "dark" and "light" onto the Irish Other, fostering and expressing attraction to and repulsion from that Other.

Yet Anglo-Irish ideology would be far from homologous with imperial English ideologies. For as James McElvoy has argued, "however important the Empire was as a formative factor in the Protestant experience in Ireland, it cannot have been the whole story, since it provided only a temporary framework, against which the perception of the uniqueness of their situation could be measured by Irish Protestants" (McElvoy 1983, 102). Indeed, novel after novel portrays the Anglo-Irish "gentry" in terms typically used to describe colonial *subjects* in Ireland and elsewhere: "always looking nervously over his shoulder, imitating the values and fashions of a distant metropolis" (Kiberd 1984, 14). And aspects of Anglo-Irish experience categorizable as neither "English" nor "Irish"—the most obvious being the uncertainty of Anglo-Ireland's geopolitical identity, announced by its hyphenated proper name—would further complicate this ideology. In comparison with "the cultural stridency and ethnic certitude that is perceived as emanating from the Catholic community," in Desmond Bell's view, "Protestant culture and ethnic identity is felt to lack coherence and confidence"; Anglo-Ireland suffers a "*no nation* view of Protestant identity and difference" (Bell 1985, 95, 92). Such peculiarities of Anglo-Irish experience would, I speculated, keep this ideology different from those others with which it has had such intimate and combative relations.

With this framework in mind, I went back to Anglo-Irish fiction.

II

Before describing the difficulties I encountered on that return, I would like to look more closely at Eagleton's theory of ideology, for it foretells those troubles. Eagleton's argument pursues two mutually exclusive agendas. On the one hand, *Ideology* comprises a rejoinder to "end-of-ideology" theorists who claim that too much has been made of ideology, or that it doesn't exist, or that it isn't distinguishable from any other form of discourse, or that it hasn't caused the harm the Marxists have claimed it has. As the heft and assurance of Eagleton's basic assumptions attest, *Ideology* is a monument to ideology's continued, pernicious existence, and an implicit argument for its overthrow.

On the other hand, *Ideology* also professes a staunch disbelief in "essentialism of ideology" (Eagleton 1991, 87). Heeding poststructuralism's lessons regarding the contingency of relations between art and culture, and the contingency of texts and their interpretations, *Ideology* attempts to rescue this "keyword" from reification and to inoculate ideology critique against criticism by Derrida and like-minded others.[3]

It is worth examining this argument in some detail, to draw out the refreshing complexity of Eagleton's anti-essentialist portrait of ideology, and to highlight its distance from the comparatively straightforward teleological assumptions about ideology outlined above. Placing these two strands of Eagleton's argument side by side reveals tensions in ideology theory which, in turn, hint at the problems that can emerge when one looks to deploy it as a tool for literary study.

Ideology is both phenomenologically diverse and internally complex, in Eagleton's view. To begin with, ideology is not simply a matter of conscious belief systems or articulable "world views." It involves unconscious beliefs and values as well. Eagleton invokes Raymond Williams's notion of a "structure of feeling" to capture the combination of conscious and unconscious content and form characteristic of ideologies. Ideologies are "elusive, impalpable forms of social consciousness which are at once as evanescent as 'feeling' suggests, but," Eagleton insists, "nevertheless display a significant configuration" (Eagleton 1991, 48).

Ideology also entails lived social practice. Following Althusser's materialist conception of ideology, Eagleton sees ideology as a function of "'lived relations' rather than theoretical cognition" (Eagleton 1991, 139). This function is crucial to ideology's propagation. Ideology does not come neatly after the fact of a subject, a by-product (an expression or reflection) of that subject's class subjectivity. Ideology is crucial in bringing that class subject into being.

The notion of ideology as "false consciousness"—as a mask or screen that disables subjects' vision—is one that Eagleton confronts head on. In an argument that does not quite square with his Freudian assumptions, he insists that ideology should not be understood simply as discourse that characterizes the world erroneously; rather, he argues, ideology involves a complex play of truth and falsehood. Much ideological discourse is "true at one level but not at another," Eagleton explains, "true in its empirical content but deceptive in its force, or true in its surface meaning but false in its underlying assumptions" (Eagleton 1991, 16–17). Eagleton extends his discussion of "false consciousness" beyond ideology's internal workings to consider its relation to social "context." He invokes Lukács: "Ideology for Lukács is . . . not exactly a discourse untrue to the way things are," Eagleton reasons, "but one true to them only in a limited, superficial way," a matter of "partial seeing" which "springs from specific historical causes" (99). Ideology is thus less "false consciousness" than "structurally constrained thought," "a kind of thought which finds itself baffled and thwarted by certain barriers in society rather than in the mind" (105).

If ideology bears a complex relation to the true and the false, it is, also, internally complex. It is fractured most obviously by those discontinuities rooted in its kinship with the unconscious. "No simple homology [between ideology and political interest] is at stake here," Eagleton argues: "[I]deological beliefs may signify certain interests, disavow, rationalize or dissemble them, run counter to them, and so on" (Eagleton 1991, 211–12). An ideology may also be divided into discrete "levels." Raymond Williams traces these levels to the "dominant," "residual," and "emergent" forms of consciousness that characterize complex social formations (47); V. N. Voloshinov identifies different ideological strata, the lowest of which are "made up of vague experiences, idle thoughts and random words which flash across the mind," and higher levels which "are more vital and substantial" and are "linked with ideological systems" (49). Eagleton adds that an ideology's internal dissonances may also be understood as a "conflict between 'practical' and 'official' forms of consciousness," "practical" consciousness entailing that derived from one's lived social experience, "official" consciousness approximating that inculcated by the "dominant" ideology (49).

An ideology's lack of unity and coherence stems, as well, from the nature of social groups. Eagleton rejects the notion (which he criticizes in the theories of Lukács and Lucien Goldmann, among others) of a class as a "collective subject" (Eagleton 1991, 111). He argues, "What we call a dominant ideology is typically that of a dominant social bloc, made up of classes and fractions whose interests are not always at one; and these compromises and divisions will be reflected in the ideology itself" (45).[4] He gives the example of nineteenth-century Britain, "where the economically determinant middle class largely 'delegated' its political power to the aristocracy. This is not a situation which any theory assuming a one-to-one relation between classes and ideologies can easily decipher, since the resultant ruling ideology will be typically a hybrid of elements drawn from the experience of *both* classes" (123).[5]

Eagleton goes on to make a case for ideology's relational ontology. Following Nicos Poulantzas and revising Althusser, he argues that "ideology, like social class itself, is an inherently *relational* phenomenon: it expresses less the way a class lives its conditions of existence, than the way it lives them *in relation to the lived experience of other classes*" (Eagleton 1991, 101, italics Eagleton's). "A dominant ideology has continually to renegotiate with the ideologies of its subordinates" (47)—and a subordinate ideology with those of its competitors and dominators, he might add. Thus each ideology is, in Eagleton's view, "constituted to the root by the ideology of its antagonist" (101), so that ideology "concerns less signification than conflicts within the field of signification" (11). Ideology is "the way power-struggles are fought out at the level of signification" (113). It is "the struggle of antagonistic social interests at the level of the sign" (195).

Not surprisingly, given such struggle, Eagleton calls ideology "a creative and open-ended affair" (Eagleton 1991, 50). If ideology is the pulling of signs this way and that in the battle for social power, ideology is not static, but fluid. It is, Eagleton might say, less a product than a process, or a phenomenon continually in process, in the process of trying to come to terms with its ideological neighbors and with itself.

Needless to say, we are a long way from the notion of ideology as an identifiable, pernicious social agent which also informs Eagleton's text. We have landed in the realm of Derrida's écriture, of Barthes's free-play of signifiers. Eagleton's finely wrought account does indeed thwart essentialist conceptions of ideology. Casting ideology as a conscious and unconscious phenomenon that encompasses thought, feeling, and action, a phenomenon that is internally discontinuous, and internally and externally dialogic, an entity with no identity in itself but only in its open-ended relations to competing ideologies—Eagleton's account portrays ideology as a phenomenon so elusive and complex as to reopen the question that Eagleton's book was to have answered: the question of what (and whether) ideology is. Eagleton's anti-essentialist definition of "ideology" undermines its usefulness as a category of analysis. At one point he goes so far in his argument against essentialism as to claim:

> The term "ideology" is just a convenient way of categorizing under a single heading a whole lot of different things we do with signs. The phrase "bourgeois ideology," for example, is simply shorthand for an immense range of discourses scattered in time and space. To call all of these languages "bourgeois" is of course to imply that they have something in common; but that common element need not be thought of as some invariable structure of categories. It is probably more useful here to think along the lines of Ludwig Wittgenstein's doctrine of "family resemblances"—of a network of overlapping features rather than some constant "essence." (Eagleton 1991, 193)

Such terms are decidedly looser than the precise, almost mechanistic terms of his theory's basic assumptions. Compare them, for instance, to this definition: ideology "must figure as an organizing social force which actively constitutes human subjects at the roots of their lived experience and seeks to equip them with forms of value and belief relevant to their specific social tasks and to the general reproduction of the social order" (222–23).

In addition to such poststructuralist qualifications, the study is replete with discrete moments that cast ideology as remarkably diffuse. Take, for example, this claim: "It may help to view ideology as less a particular *set* of discourses, than as a particular set of effects *within* discourses" (Eagleton 1991, 194). This description of ideology as a site of discursive struggle provides another vivid example: "Social classes do not manifest ideologies . . . : ideology is, rather, a complex, conflictive field of meaning. . . . Ideology is a realm of contestation and negotiation, in which there is a constant busy traffic: meanings and values are stolen, transformed, appropriated across the frontiers of different classes and groups, surrendered, repossessed, reinflected" (101). While this passage seems an accurate description of societies, like Ireland's, that are riven by struggles for power, it conflates "ideology" and "ideological field" in a way that undermines the notion of ideology as an identifiable, structured social agent which Eagleton forwards elsewhere. Likewise Eagleton's claim as to "the naivety of the belief that ideology always and everywhere involves fixed or 'transcendental' signifiers, imaginary unities, meta-physical grounds and teleological goals. . . 'Textuality,' ambiguity, indeterminacy lie often enough on the side of dominant ideological discourses themselves" (198). Here, Eagleton conflates "ideology" and "ideological discourse," as he conflates "ideology" and "ideolog-ical consciousness" elsewhere. Certainly in dismissing "transcenden-tal signifiers" and "teleological goals," he contradicts his founda-tional assumption that at the root of ideology, and perhaps of human consciousness itself, self-interest reigns.

Ideology contains silences that supplement these threats to ideol-ogy's ontological status. Most remarkably, it underplays the role of subjectivity. Obviously Eagleton acknowledges subjectivity in his cen-tral assumption that "the fundamental mechanisms of the psychical life are the structural devices of ideology as well" (Eagleton 1991, 185). But in his conclusion he insists, "though ideology is 'subject-centred', it is not *reducible* to the question of subjectivity" (223). This statement is an instance of a text-wide tendency to minimize the rel-evance of subjectivity to ideology's identities and operations. Throughout, at junctures when the logic of his argument would seem to impel him to comment on subjectivity's impact, Eagleton seems to evade it. He does not consider conceptions of the subject offered by psychoanalytic, poststructuralist, or feminist theory—in Teresa de Lauretis's words, "the concept of a multiple, shifting, and often self-contradictory identity, a subject that is not divided in, but rather at odds with language" (de Lauretis 1986b, 9). It is a curious tendency in a text so wedded to Freud.[6]

Like his minimization of subjectivity, Eagleton's conflations—of "ideology" with "ideological discourse" and "ideological conscious-ness"—are functions of a crux in ideology theory that he does not address. As he himself indicates, we never encounter disembodied ideology (Eagleton 1991, 45). Ideology always comes mediated: in signs, or action, or consciousness. Indeed, ideology seems insepara-ble from its media, which have, it appears, the power to disperse it into something other than "itself." Perhaps, then, we cannot talk meaningfully of the structures, forms, and operations of ideology *per se* but should limit our observations to the structures, forms, and operations of mediated ideology, or ideological media, as Eagleton does when "ideology" slips toward "ideological consciousness" and "ideological discourse" in his argument. In any case, what we talk about when we talk about ideology seems something other than the clear and distinct category Eagleton's argument sometimes claims we do.[7] Ideology *per se* has dire consequences in the real world. But ideology as a subject of analysis seems "itself" awfully difficult to spot.

In the end, Eagleton's *Ideology* indicates the uncertain ontology of the category it champions. Caught between the rock of his anti-essentialism and the hard place of his social agenda, Eagleton casts ideology as indeterminate and unlocatable on the one hand, and as definable and culpable on the other, to produce a portrait of ideology that bears more than a passing resemblance to the Anglo-Irish narratives considered here: shifting, undecided, open-ended, provisional. When push comes to shove, Eagleton turns his back on Derrida and tries to embrace Marx. The unequivocal definition quoted above, that declarative statement calling ideology an "organizing social force" equipping subjects "with forms of value and belief," appears in his penultimate pages. It seems a last-minute retreat from the implications of his text: from the possibility that ideology as "operated by" literature is a myth, a wish, an elusive object of Marxist desire. But even this closing statement alludes to those implications, in the interesting phrase, "must figure." Eagleton's "must" seems to protest too much that ideology *is* the concrete phenomenon he insists it is, and his "figure" raises the possibility that this late, positivist definition of ideology is perhaps no more than a trope.

III

These intimations of ideology theory's limits were borne out by problems that emerged as I tried to read novels from within Eagleton's theoretical frame. These texts, all of them, kept shaking that frame off. I will restrict this account to difficulties I encountered while reading Molly Keane's *Time After Time*. It was my early work with Keane's text that shaped my ultimate approach to this fiction, leading me to revise my relation to ideology theory and to conclude that, while as a social critic, Eagleton has much to say, as a literary critic, he has less.

Despite the poststructuralist qualifications that pervade Eagleton's theory, in practice ideology critique sends the reader in search of ideological perspectives, in textual moments when a predetermined ideology rears its ugly head. It launches the reader on what amounts to a hunt for authorial motive—self-interest, the need to mask guilt—which feels uncomfortably close to the discredited hunt for authorial intent.

As I sifted through texts seeking moments when they betrayed their ideological stripes, I kept coming up against these novels' interpretability, which posed serious obstacles to the quest for ideology. Sometimes these obstacles took the form of hard-to-locate point of view. Recall Keane's rendering of June Swift's daily walks along the Durraghglass drive:

> June walked the distance, back and forwards several times a day. She was familiar with its potholes and long, stony depths and she ignored the riot of briars and nettles on its once orderly verges. Close to the back of the house, a different and more precise archway from that of the farmyard led to the stableyard; a now derelict clock in the archway's face had once told the time. It still looked pretty. The stableyard was built round rather a grand semi-circle. Loose-boxes, weedy cobblestones to their doors, were empty—all but one. June's brown hens scratched about on the wide central circle of grass round which horses had been ridden and led and walked and jogged, or made to stand as they should, to be admired by afternoon luncheon guests on Sundays. (Keane 1983, 19–20)

As Bakhtin writes of the modern novel, "one often does not know where the direct authorial word ends and where a parodic or stylized playing with the characters' language begins" (Bakhtin 1981, 77). I feel comfortable asserting that this passage communicates a combination of contemporary affection for the decaying estate and nostalgia for its good old days, when horses stood still in the yard as they should. I feel uncomfortable deciding what center of consciousness generates it. Does the passage transcribe June's frame of mind? Or is the passage authorial? A sure answer to the question must precede judgment of the passage's relation to ideology, for without that answer, we cannot be sure whether Keane here holds an anachronistic attachment to Anglo-Ireland up for critique, or whether she enacts it, perhaps unaware, herself. As ideology critic, I tried and failed to charge Keane with the latter. As if attachment to homeplace is self-evidently culpable; as if it is a tendency that one as a matter of course ought to outgrow—two of numerous untenable assumptions upon which ideology critique rests.[8]

Keane's description of May's kitchen garden provides a comparable case of indeterminate point of view:

> Ivy might cloak and drag at its walls, docks and nettles invade its distances, but those parts maintained by her vigilance were May's thrust into a conceit of happiness. Every foot of the walled wilderness that could be kept under cultivation was of vital importance to May. It was her province. She fought for its maintenance with all the strength of her immense will. The rotations of peas, beans, spinach; the triumphant hatchings in battered frames of new potatoes for Easter; the continual supplies of parsley, chives, mints (in choice varieties), thymes, oregano and basil were the successes May brought to birth, properly in their seasons or their perpetuities. (Keane 1983, 120)

As I have argued, May's willful conquest of this "territory" (121) evokes the conquest of Irish land. But like Beckett, Keane here evokes history in imagery sufficiently grotesque and absurd as to make us wonder whether she wants us to take that evocation seriously. Add to that ambiguity the passage's indeterminate point of view—is its jubilant tone May's? is it Keane's?—and it becomes impossible to say what relation the passage bears to ideology. Is Keane satirizing conquest, or is she relishing it?

More debilitating to my attempt at ideology critique: sometimes portions of text could be read any number of competing ways, not due to unsettled point of view but to a more intrinsic interpretability. Like Beckett's and Bowen's, Keane's novel contains many moments that can be seen to uphold Anglo-Irish culture or to condemn it, depending on how one wants to read them. Keane's portrait of the Swifts' hired Irish man, Christy Lucey, is rife with such ambiguities. Does Keane's representation of this evasive Irishman validate imperial stereotypes? Or does it demystify them, revealing their foundations in Anglo-Ireland's unjust claims on his labor? Is Keane unmasking colonialist attitudes, or is she enacting them? Though the text leaves both possibilities open, the reader in search of ideology is driven to select one defining moment of truth, one prevailing point of view, where the text finally settles down and means.[9]

I say the text leaves "both" possibilities open. The text allows other possibilities as well. This account of my reading experience is taking on the binary rhythm of ideology critique, just as my account of Anglo-Irish fiction began to. Eagleton's poststructuralist qualifications notwithstanding, ideology critique predisposes a reader to discern one of two options: a literary text "moves now with, now athwart the ideology of its text" (Eagleton 1976a, 68). But in its representation of Christy, as elsewhere, Keane's text bears relations to ideology that are much less stable and clear than black or white, "with" or "athwart." *Time After Time* announces relations so nuanced, multiple, and shifting that critical prose has difficulty capturing them. As Roland Barthes has claimed, "the narrative tells itself" (Barthes 1974, 213).

Indeed, some textual moments may be deemed at once "ideological" and "anti-ideological." I often found rejection and acceptance of stereotypical Anglo-Irish attitudes inextricably intertwined in Keane's text. Her ill-mannered assault on bourgeois proprieties provides a memorable example. Keane's audacious focus on the body calls to mind an adolescent's willful campaign for autonomy from authority which is at the same time a plea for its reinstatement and a vivid acknowledgment of its reign. Does Keane here subvert Anglo-Irish ideology? Comply with it? The text does not sanction a decision. Heed interpretability, *Time After Time* shows, and ideology critique comes to seem an exercise in willful over-reading.

In addition to encountering an abundance of textual recalcitrance, I found myself stopped short by burgeoning misgivings of my own. Ideology critique, I realized, was requiring me to adopt an attitude toward texts that was inconsistent with my previous critical practice. And my way of reading Keane's text was proving inconsistent with the way I encourage my students to read. In practice, ideology critique rests upon a methodology very similar to the one of which we try to break novice readers: the habit of setting out to explore a text knowing in advance what one will find. This habit is accompanied by the assumption that discrete *a priori* truths (as students articulate them they tend to be truisms like "hard work pays off" or "be satisfied with what you have") exist somewhere outside the text, to which the text bears clear witness. Since my aim as a teacher is to encourage students to see how often novels, stories, plays, and poems *fail* to corroborate preconceived ideas, writing ideology critique while teaching proved a fruitfully discordant task.

In describing ideology critique as "a matter of explaining the forces at work of which . . . textual obscurities are a necessary effect" (1991, 133), Eagleton commits the paradigmatic student error. Setting the critic up as a center of omniscience capable of discerning "necessary" truth, he hunts for "concealed power interests," rationalizations of oppression, and so on. This approach presumes that literary texts are definitively and essentially constituted by an unending pattern of attempted rejection and inevitable reinscription of ideology. As Eugene Goodheart has written, "ideology critics imply in their very activity that they possess not only an objective knowledge of self-interest and power, but also a superior moral grasp of the cultural and historical situation in which they find themselves" or of which they write (Goodheart 1997, 16). The approach assumes that readers cannot learn *from* novels, merely *about* them.[10]

This additional reductive assumption underpins ideology critique: the assumption that "human nature" is always already, at rock bottom, a matter of self-interest; that when we unveil interest we locate the authentic and the real. Even when a novel seems to reject a given ideology, ideology theory reads that rejection as a ruse, a ploy to win expiation, just another mask. Presuming that material conditions create the self and that struggle between those who dominate and those who are dominated (whether across lines of gender, class, race, or ethnicity) is the defining human relation, ideology critique totalizes human consciousness, refusing the possibility of such dispositions as partial innocence, sometime generosity, intermittent sincerity and goodwill. It discredits the possibility that a human subject might act against self-interest or the interest of his or her nominal identity group. And it bears, as a result, a necessarily negative relation to the text. It proceeds in a scolding tone, with the critic shaking a finger at writers for not having written different (read "truer," "purer," "less bourgeois," "less imperialist") novels, for not having been wise or brave enough to eschew unenlightened ideas.[11]

Which is not an irrelevant thing to say about a text, perhaps. But it does not seem the most telling thing, particularly in light of ideology's uncertain ontology, its indeterminate relation to literary texts, these novels' competing ideological and anti-ideological tendencies, and all their subtle stances in between. Like Eagleton, I am interested in how writers try and fail to escape cultural binds. I have written here of novelists' ambivalences toward their culture of origin, a focus that shares the same topical territory as ideology critique. And certainly human subjects' intellectual autonomy has its limits. But these novels have taught me that writers can respond to tight spots like Anglo-Ireland's in ways that are infinitely more rich, complex and credible than ideology critique allows. These novels chart intricacies of attitude—variations upon and combinations of acceptance and rejection of "ideological perspectives"—that the binary logic of ideology critique excludes. Its Manichean worldview jars with the complexity and subtlety of human consciousness dramatized in these novels.

Ideology critique similarly oversimplifies the "author's" relations to his or her text and the text's relations to its readers. The author's politics (if they are identifiable) like the author's cultural identity (if it is definable) do not in fact equal the author's text. Nor do they determine readers' reproductions of that text. Readers may read what they will there.

Moreover, ideology critique abrogates novels' affective power. These narratives' disjunctions and reversals connote intellectual, psychological, and moral struggles that must have been painful. I remain struck by how compelling these novels show ideological struggle to be. I remain struck by their power to build sympathy for a social group with a deeply flawed and far from sympathetic role in Ireland's history. These are responses for which ideology critique does not allow. Prohibiting a reader's empathic engagement with a text, dismissing it on its face as bourgeois, naive, and false, ideology critique cancels these novels' capacity to build bridges across age-old cultural divides by affecting readerships other than their own.

For these reasons, ideology critique and these novels have not mixed. Approaching these texts with ideology in hand felt, in the end, beside the point. Ideology theory may tell part of these novels' story but it fails to illuminate what seems to me most interesting about them. Of course, as Barthes reminds us, no single critical perspective can. Perhaps a critic's relations to ideology theory and to literature are, at bottom, a matter of temperament and circumstance. Like Gayatri Spivak, "I would rather think of the text as my accomplice than my patient or my analysand" (Spivak 1989, 289). I have acquired a taste for novels' play of significances, their surplus of meanings, though I would not champion the novel as an inherently democratic form, as Bakhtin and Barthes do. Irving Howe's 1957 meditation on politics and the novel continues to strike a chord:

> The political novel . . . is peculiarly a work of internal tensions . . . [t]he novel . . . tries, above all, to capture the quality of concrete experience. Ideology, however, is abstract, as it must be, and therefore likely to be recalcitrant whenever an attempt is made to incorporate it into the novel's stream of sensuous impression. The conflict is inescapable: the novel tries to confront experience in its immediacy and closeness, while ideology is by its nature general and inclusive.

Yet it is precisely from this conflict that the political novel gains its interest and takes on the aura of high drama. (Howe 1957, 20, 22)

I retain many questions about ideology and its relation to literature. But I would hazard this: neither literature nor criticism is reducible to ideology, and neither may definitively transcend it. Literature never claimed it could.

Notes

Chapter 1. Some Contexts for Reading . . .

1. I will explore some of the limitations of the terms "Anglo-Ireland" and "Ascendancy Ireland" in the following chapter. As Gerald Dawe and Edna Longley point out: "Protestant Ireland now means 'Ulster Protestant,' not 'Anglo-Irish'" (iv). The distinction between Northern Irish Presbyterianism and southern Anglicanism should not be underestimated. "The Church of Ireland constituency—Anglican, Anglo, Anglo-Irish—has always worn its Unionism or Nationalism more lightly than has the Ulster Scots dissenting tradition" (v). Northerner John Hewitt warns: "'Call an Ulster Scot an Anglo-Irishman and see what happens'" (vi).

2. For a discussion of the relation of Big House fiction to English country house poetry, see Vera Kreilkamp's *The Anglo-Irish Novel and the Big House* (1998, 17–20).

3. For a relatively recent instance of this kind of identity-politics-driven misreading, see Anthony Coleman's "The Big House, Yeats, and the Irish Context" (1992). Richard Kearney, by contrast, argues that "if Yeats's desire to obviate the divisive ruptures of Ireland's colonial history found refuge in the mythic timelessness of the *Anima Mundi*, it was no more than provisional—a refuge repeatedly harassed by the intrusions of history. . . Yeats's entire work may be viewed in this wise as an endless vacillation between the rival claims of myth and history, that is, between the ideal of a timeless unifying tradition and the reality of a divisive and fragmenting modernity" (1988, 20). Edward Said calls Yeats a "poet of decolonization," crediting him with "adumbrating the liberationist and utopian revolutionism in his poetry that had been belied, and to some extent canceled out, by his late reactionary politics" (1990, 84, 89).

4. As W. J. McCormack reports, "Deane has modified his earlier acceptance of an eighteenth-century ascendancy class. He has also drawn attention to a striking metamorphosis in the sub-genre of 'Big House fiction' in that it now addresses itself to touristic, rather than residential, forms of imperception" (1992, 35). For some additional perspectives on the work of Higgins and Banville see: "Reinventing a Form: the Big House in Aidan Higgins's *Langrishe, Go Down*" (Kreilkamp 1992); *The Anglo-Irish Novel and the Big House* (Kreilkamp 1998); and "'This Lawless House'—John Banville's Post-Modernist Treatment of the Big-House Motif in *Birchwood* and *The Newton Letter*" (Burgstaller 1992).

5. For comparable readings, see: "The Big House in the Recent Novel" (Donnelly 1975); "Reflecting Absent Interiors: The Big-House Novels of Charles Lever" (Morash 1992); "Shadows of Destruction: The Big House in Contemporary Irish Fiction" (Parkin 1988); "The Big House and Irish History" (Rauchbauer 1992b); *Elizabeth Bowen: An Estimation* (Lee 1981); and W. J. McCormack (1985, 1992, 1993). Morash's essay is particularly incisive. He reads Lever's post-1854 fiction as "a sustained interrogation of the role of the Big House, both as a social institution and as a subject of fictional representation," calling it a "reflection on (and of) an absent social institution for which fiction became the necessary (but superfluous) supplement" (67, 74).

6. Kreilkamp's first chapter, "Fiction and History," provides an especially rich introduction to the study of Anglo-Irish fiction (1998, 1–25). Needless to say, her work has provided rewarding intellectual company.

7. For essays in Bhabha's collection that expand on the notion of nation as narration, see especially Timothy Brennan's "The national longing for form," Doris Sommer's "Irresistible romance: the foundational fictions of Latin America," Sneja Gunew's "Denaturalizing cultural nationalisms: multicultural readings of Australia," and James Snead's "European pedigrees/African contagions: nationality, narrative, and communality in Tutuola, Achebe, and Reed."

8. John Harrington has written in similar terms of the relation of Samuel Beckett's work to Ireland: "Beckett's work offers Ireland as predicament, as 'troublesome complexities,' and without partisanship" (1991, 190).

9. For a sketch of cultural studies approaches to modernism (including citations), see Scott Heller's "New Life for Modernism" (1999a) and "Beyond the Usual Suspects: Scholars Expand the Modernist Canon" (1999b).

10. For more on the relation between modernism and postmodernism, one might begin with Fredric Jameson, *Postmodernism; or, The Cultural Logic of Late Capitalism* (1991) and Linda Hutcheon, *A Poetics of Postmodernism: History, Theory, Fiction* (1988).

11. Besides Beckett, Bowen is the writer addressed here whose relation to modernism and postmodernism has been studied most closely. See John Coates, "Elizabeth Bowen's *The Last September:* The Loss of the Past and Modern Consciousness" (1990); Sandra Kemp, "'But how describe a world without a self?' Feminism, fiction and modernism" (1990); W. J. McCormack, *Dissolute Characters: Irish literary history through Balzac, Sheridan Le Fanu, Yeats and Bowen* (1993); Robert Caserio, "The Heat of the Day: Modernism and Narrative in Paul de Man and Elizabeth Bowen" (1993); Andrew Bennett and Nicholas Royle, *Elizabeth Bowen and the Dissolution of the Novel* (1995).

12. Like Fekete, I use the term "problematic" to refer to a "social, ideological, or theoretical framework within which complexes of problems are structured and single problems acquire density, meaning and significance" (217–18).

13. See Julian Moynahan, *Anglo-Irish: The Literary Imagination in a Hyphenated Culture* for a relevant discussion of Le Fanu and "the politics of Anglo-Irish gothic" (1995, 108–14 and 127–35).

14. See also McCormack's "Setting and Ideology: with Reference to the Fiction of Maria Edgeworth" (1992) and Maurice Colgan's "After Rackrent: Ascendancy Nationalism in Maria Edgeworth's Later Irish Novels" (1982).

CHAPTER 2. "THE PARADOX OF THESE BIG HOUSES"

1. These attempts to describe and define Anglo-Ireland include: F. S. L. Lyons, *Culture and Anarchy in Ireland: 1890–1939* (1979, 18–26); Julian Moynahan, *Anglo-Irish* (1995, 3–11); Otto Rauchbauer, "The Big House and Irish History: An Introductory Sketch" (1992b); L. P. Curtis, Jr., "The Anglo-Irish Predicament" (1970, 37–62); Desmond Bell, "Contemporary Cultural Studies in Ireland and the 'Problem' of Protestant Ideology" (1985, 91–95); Declan Kiberd, "Anglo-Irish Attitudes" (1986, 13–16). W. J. McCormack works to distinguish the mythological Ascendancy from the historical Anglo-Ireland(s) throughout his *Ascendancy and Tradition* (1985). Ascendancy is one of many myths R. F. Foster examines in *Modern Ireland 1600–1972* (1989), part of his effort to revise the misrepresentations generated by the Anglocentric point of view that once dominated the study of Irish history. "[O]ne must emphasize," he insists throughout, "the contradictions within the general picture," including "the ambivalent complexity of relationships" among Ireland's "varieties of peoples" (54, 45, 3). For his consideration of Anglo-Ireland, see especially Chapter 8, "The Ascendancy Mind" (167–94).

2. Katharine Tynan offers another provocative definition of Anglo-Ireland; its reversals tell worlds about the problematics of Anglo-Irish identity that I am tracing: "[T]he Anglo-Irishman, although he achieves great things at times, is, in the rank and file of him, somewhat harsh. He has the John Bullish attitude towards sentimentality without the real sentiment which John Bull is unaware of possessing, although it jumps to the eye of everyone else. He has somewhat of the Celt's irritability and jealousy; in fact, these things grafted upon him make for an intolerance which is far from being Celtic" (Tynan 1913, 142; quoted in Taylor 1969, 38). Likewise the self-definition proffered by Hugo Montmorency in Bowen's *The Last September*, used as epigraph to this chapter.

3. Andrew Parker, Mary Russo, Doris Sommer, and Patricia Yaeger (1992a, 5). They are quoting, first, Perry Anderson, "Nation-States and National Identity" (1991, 3) and, second, John Breuilly, *Nationalism and the State* (1982, 380).

4. See McCormack, "Edmund Burke and the Imagination of History," for a detailed discussion of the rise of another important term by which Anglo-Ireland has been known: "Ascendancy" (1985, 43–96). See also Foster, *Modern Ireland* (1989, 170).

5. Gates offers this pithy anecdote about the operations of "race" in the Irish context: "In 1973 I was amazed to hear a member of the House of Lords describe the differences between Irish Protestants and Catholics in terms of their 'distinct and clearly definable differences of race.' 'You mean to say that you can tell them apart?' I asked incredulously. 'Of course,' responded the lord. 'Any Englishman can.'" See "Writing 'Race' and the Difference It Makes" (5).

6. We must read all of J. C. Beckett's claims in light of his desire to show that "Ireland without [the Anglo-Irish] would be not only a different but a poorer country" (11). Still, his explanation of Anglo-Ireland's early conviction of legitimacy has real force: "In an age when property and power went hand in hand, when notions of universal franchise and majority rule had not yet gained currency, when the romantic nationalism of race and language that was to dominate the succeeding age had hardly come to birth, their claim was not so absurd as it seems to us" (53).

7. The history of Anglo-Ireland is more involved and interpretable than any introductory sketch can suggest. See R. F. Foster, *Modern Ireland 1600–1972* (1989); F. S. L. Lyons, *Culture and Anarchy in Ireland* (1979, 18–26); F. S. L. Lyons, *Ireland since the Famine* (1973); W. E. H. Lecky, *A History of Ireland in the Eighteenth Century* (1892); Terence Brown, *Ireland: A Social and Cultural History, 1922 to the Present* (1985, 80–106); Jack White, *Minority Report: The Protestant Community in the Irish Republic* (1975); J. C. Beckett, *The Anglo-Irish Tradition* (1976); Otto Rauchbauer, "The Big House and Irish History: An Introductory Sketch" (1992b). I have relied heavily on these sources.

8. Moynahan's *Anglo-Irish* offers a comparable narrative of Anglo-Ireland's "downward curve" (1995, 11).

9. For more on such differences, see Klaus Lubbers, "Continuity and Change in Irish Fiction: The Case of the Big-House Novel" (1992); Andrew Parkin, "Shadows of Destruction: The Big House in Contemporary Irish Fiction" (1988).

Chapter 3. To Tell and Not to Tell

1. As Mary Breen observes, "Keane tended to present herself as a philistine" in "deprecating self-parody" (203)—perhaps to mitigate her critique of home culture, perhaps to mirror that stereotypically anti-intellectual culture.

2. Gielgud also played Jasper Swift in a television adaptation of *Time After Time*.

3. When asked why she resumed writing she said: "The children were gone and married, and I was on my own. And also, money was pretty bad, and the children both needed some. And I said: 'Well, I've been frightfully idle,' you know" (Keane 1991a, 26). This and Keane's subsequent books appeared under her own name.

4. These reviews included: William Boyd's "Revenge of the Innocent," *Times Literary Supplement* (1981), Mary Holland's "Codes," *New Statesman* (1981), and Rachel Billington's "Fictions of Class," *The New York Times Book Review* (1981). Margot Jefferson reviewed *Good Behaviour* with *Time After Time* in *The Village Voice* ("Every Other Inch a Lady," 1984), as did V. S. Pritchett in *The New York Review of Books* ("The Solace of Intrigue," 1984).

Aosdàna is a government-sponsored organization supporting Irish artists. Keane explains: "*Aosdàna* (meaning 'Ireland's treasures') was a term that encompassed all the travelling musicians, poets and storytellers who found hospitality, feastings, and an audience at the scattered courts of the continually warring Gaelic and Celtic chieftains" (Keane 1993, x).

5. For discussions of Keane and gender, see Vera Kreilkamp, "Social and Sexual Politics in the Big House: Edith Somerville and Molly Keane" (1988) and "The Persistence of Illusion in Molly Keane's Fiction" in *The Anglo-Irish Novel and the Big House* (1998), especially 184–86; Ann Owens Weekes, *Irish Women Writers* (1990); Rudiger Imhof, "Molly Keane, *Good Behaviour, Time After Time* and *Loving and Giving* (1992a); Rachel Jane Lynch, "The Crumbling Fortress: Molly Keane's Comedies of Anglo-Irish Manners" (1996); Mary Breen, "Piggies and Spoilers of Girls: The Representation of Sexuality in the Novels of Molly Keane" (1997).

6. V. S. Pritchett's comparative assessment of the two novels is atypical. Reviewing *Good Behaviour* and *Time After Time*, he named the latter "Molly Keane's

real novel." "It is rich, and remarkable for the intertwining of portraits and events. It is spirited, without tears. The ingenious narrative is always on the move" (7, 8).

7. The emphasis of Kreilkamp's *The Anglo-Irish Novel and the Big House* (1998), from which the observations I have just quoted are drawn, differs from that of her early essays. Though the essays document Big House novels' critiques of home culture, they emphasize their ambiguity. In "Social and Sexual Politics in the Big House," for instance, Kreilkamp labels them "ambivalent novels," arguing: "Ironically qualified nostalgia for this arrogant and decadent culture, which exists always as a memory of power rather than as a real ascendancy, is implicit in most novels in the tradition. The great achievement of Big House novelists lies in their ability simultaneously to evoke and to judge the prodigal glamor of a society in which they themselves are implicated" (1988, 75). In "The Persistent Pattern: Molly Keane's Recent Big House Fiction," she draws important distinctions between *Good Behaviour* and *Time After Time*, asserting, for example, that in *Time After Time* "Keane faces the decline of her culture and the accompanying aging of her childless characters with a wry admiration which is missing from the darker and more brutal vision of the Anglo-Ireland she presents in *Good Behaviour*" (1987, 460).

8. Keane provides this account of her first encounter with Bowen, which took place at a London literary party to which (she insists) she did not want to go: "There was an old man there who had been fishing on the river at home, and . . . he introduced me to Elizabeth Bowen, who was *so* nice to me. I thought nothing of her, this literary lady with rather a bad stammer. . . . Later, I got to know Elizabeth, in Ireland, and she became a great friend" (Kierstead 1986, 104). On a visit to Bowen's Court, Keane recalls, "The plan was that we would both write in the morning. For the entire two weeks, I sat and listened to the ceaseless clacking of Elizabeth's typewriter and couldn't think of a *thing* to write about. Not a scribble. It was *awful*, but such a lovely idea" (112).

9. As Ellen O'Brien observes, the Swifts' disabilities suggest "a genetic decay hiding in the Anglo-Irish line," and constitute one component of the novel's "general state of abjection" (46). Elizabeth Bowen invokes disability as a defining trope in her essay, "The Big House": "The big house people were handicapped, shadowed and to an extent queered—by their pride, by their indignation at their decline and by their divorce from the countryside in whose heart their struggle was carried on" (1940, 27). Representations of disability in Anglo-Irish fiction merit further study.

10. See Mary Russo, "Female Grotesques: Carnival and Theory" for a provocative discussion of the feminist implications of the "reintroduction of the body and categories of the body (in the case of carnival, the 'grotesque body') into the realm of the political" (214).

11. Henry McDowell provides this background: "Some time in the 1970s agricultural wages increased and so did National Insurance for domestic workers. The cost of running a Big House with a cook who depended on an endless supply of produce from a large walled garden, and cream and butter from the dairy, was taken into account. 'One can buy a lot of vegetables for twelve-hundred pounds' concluded a Big-House owner about to save that amount in wages by closing the garden door. . . . Where an old butler retired or died there was no replacement because there was no footman trained to take his place. If there were no servants

then why eat in the dining-room? In County Tipperary, an elderly couple in their ancestral home were to be found cooking, eating, and sitting in one room, before the place was sold up to become a hotel" (288–89).

12. For a classic discussion of the literary production of the rural ideal, see Raymond Williams's analysis of representations and misrepresentations of "the facts of labour" in *The Country and the City* (1973, 94).

13. The jacket of the 1985 Obelisk edition of the novel nicely echoes this tonal instability. The front cover is pure caricature: a cartoonlike drawing of the Swifts posed before a mantle in a mock family portrait. But on the back cover we find a photograph of Keane. Her face looks like May's as pictured on the front; she is roughly dressed, like Baby June; she holds what looks like April's little dog, dressed in a coat. Is this text satire or is it autobiography?

To the extent that it is black comedy, it announces Keane's ties to both Bowen and Beckett. In *The Last September*, Bowen hints at black comedy; Beckett, of course, writes it full blown. Bowen's Anglo-Irish characters are at once laughable and sad; Beckett's clowns, unlike Keane's, can barely be called characters.

14. This effect derives in part from the fact (as Breen puts it) that there is no "central ground of moral rightness" in Keane's fiction (207). "Without the moral guidance of the narrator, it is the implied reader who judges" (209). Thus, Breen argues, Keane's representations of Ireland and England in *Devoted Ladies* (1934) make it "extremely difficult to decide which place the novel approves of" (216). Likewise in *Taking Chances* (1929): "We are left oscillating between many different moral perspectives, several of which seem to be irreconcilable" (219).

15. Paul Deane goes so far as to say that "despite their genteel poverty, seeming futility, even ridiculousness, these members of the gentry actually work and contribute to life," and that by novel's end "the lives of the apparently futile aristocracy have turned around." In his view, Keane "decided that their virtue was not lost at all, but only sleeping, waiting for the opportunity to waken from the ineffectuality of a dream life into productive life again" (41, 43).

16. Providing the kind of *intertextual* disjunctions that characterize the work of many Anglo-Irish writers, Elizabeth Bowen in particular, Keane's essays and interviews contain passages in which she appears to do *ubi sunt* straight. Consider this description, taken from the introduction to an anthology she compiled with her daughter, in which she records what could be called the Platonic Form of the Big House: "Sometimes the remnants of a stable-yard, a half-circle of elegant Georgian architecture, heartbreakingly unspoilt, fanlights over every loose-box door, will cling to the ruin of a house. Wild birds fly in and out through the windowless and doorless spaces to circle the linked drawing-rooms and morning-rooms where, less than a hundred years ago, aunts mended sheets with darns finer than *petit point*, unaware in their elderly innocence of the merry tales such sheets could tell. Grey tweed skirts from Donegal fell to their ankles, long and undisturbed as fluted pillars" (1993, ix). Of course, one can't help wondering if the passage constitutes a self-aware *performance* of Anglo-Irishness, introducing, as it does, an anthology that may well have been compiled to capitalize on Keane's late literary and financial successes.

17. In her introduction to *Molly Keane's Ireland* Keane elaborates: "language helped to maintain a class difference down the years. The settled ascendancy spoke English between themselves. . . . Only the beautiful languages of fox hunt-

ing, racing, shooting and fishing were shared and broke the silence between the classes in that great union of sport that is careless of politics and innocent of terrorism" (Keane 1993, xv–xvi).

18. Ellen O'Brien comments: "The lower body strata must remain unspecified," beyond language (43).

19. In current usage the term "tinkers" is considered derogatory. In *The Irish Tinkers*, anthropologist George Gmelch clarifies: "'Tinkers' is the term used by the settled Irish and the name by which most foreigners know the group. 'Travellers' and 'Travelling People' are the terms the people themselves use, and 'itinerants' is the government designation and the term used by the news media" (4). See also *Irish Travellers, Culture and Ethnicity*, eds. May McCann, Séamas Ó Síocháin, and Joseph Ruane (1996, vii).

20. Kreilkamp, by contrast, asserts that in "her last three novels, Keane sloughs off the affectionately condescending tone toward the native Irish that controls her early works and recalls the class-bound vision of Catholic Ireland found in earlier Big House fiction" (Kreilkamp 1998, 190). Writing from within the frame of an erroneous "developmental history" (Lloyd 1999, 2), Kreilkamp concludes that the late fiction entails progress from the early work; her desire to rescue Big House novels from the nationalists may lead her to overstate their subversive energies.

21. The following recollection of summer vacations with her aunts may shed light on Keane's (and other Anglo-Irish writers') representations of Irishness: "The aunts, both rabid Protestants, forbade us to speak to the nuns [who passed the house after early mass], being genuinely alarmed with the idea of our early seduction by the gamy rituals of the Roman Catholic church. . . . We might be coaxed into lighting candles for the health and benefit of absent kittens and faraway ponies. How were the aunts to tell what was to follow on that first childish step toward Rome?" (Keane 1991b, 144–45).

22. Thus Ellen O'Brien's claims regarding Keane's inversion of stereotypical patterns of abjectification, in which "the refined Anglo-Irish body requires its abject opposite," may require fine-tuning (57).

23. Ann Hulbert also notes this similarity: "Keane depends on curiosity to spin out her old-fashioned fiction. So does cousin Leda to ensnare the Swifts. In fact, Keane seems to mirror in Leda the manipulative imagination that is at work in her own art" (40).

24. Leda's name, which evokes many, many readings, may be relevant here. Raped by Zeus, Leda gave birth to Helen, and Clytemnestra, and the catastrophic disruptions that they in turn helped author. Also, Keane was well aware of the legendary power of the ancient Irish poets: "Courts and kings dared not refuse them hospitality, although they were sometimes boisterous and troublesome, because their satire was much feared" (1993, xi). The connotations of Leda's name, like Keane's documented knowledge of the poet's power, may corroborate these suggestions of Keane's anxiety of authorship.

CHAPTER 4. ELIZABETH BOWEN'S *THE LAST SEPTEMBER*

1. Bowen's representations of Anglo-Ireland have garnered more critical attention than either Beckett's or Keane's. Richard Gill claimed that "among con-

temporary writers in Ireland who lived through the 'broken world' of the Troubles and their aftermath, it is Elizabeth Bowen who has the most memorably identified herself with the Big House" (178). In 1974, Gary Davenport maintained "In the most important sense, she was an Irish writer"; "the culture of the Anglo-Irish 'big house' . . . became a major thematic center for her art" (27, 28). Hermione Lee refined his observation, calling Bowen "an 'Anglo-Irish' writer" with a "kind of double vision which the Anglo-Irish writer seems obliged, by history and temperament, to possess" (1981, 19, 18). For other readings of the cultural contexts and attitudinal complexities of Bowen's fiction, see McCormack, *Dissolute Characters* (1993); Julia McElhattan Williams, "'Fiction with the Texture of History': Elizabeth Bowen's *The Last September*" (1995); Phyllis Lassner, *Elizabeth Bowen: A Study of the Short Fiction* (1991). Vera Kreilkamp maintains that "Of all Irish novelists, Elizabeth Bowen is most complexly associated with the waning ascendancy culture" (1998, 141), and her detailed discussion of Bowen's oeuvre suggests the extent to which Bowen's loyalties remained divided to the end. Her reading of *The Last September*, however, is emphatic: "this early novel is subversive of ancestral pieties" (151–52).

2. In *Dissolute Characters*, W. J. McCormack takes not *The Last September* but *The Heat of the Day* as Bowen's important "Anglo-Irish" novel, arguing that it "is a far more complex inquiry into the foundations of the relationship between Britain and Ireland than the Chekhovian *Last September* [sic]" (1993, 210). "[T]he unique contribution of *The Heat of the Day*, not to Irish or Anglo-Irish literature (for such classifications are presumptuous and coercive), but to literary history," in McCormack's view, is that "it interrogates what 'a country' might be. . . . The radical refusal to see 'a country' as one particular country states in other terms the radical refusal to see one character as not an other" (240). McCormack goes on to make this acute observation: "Bowen's disaffection with 1930s England is a statement, necessarily and essentially negative, of her relation towards Ireland. Yet no positive assertion of an Irish identity is possible or desirable, for such a declaration would lack complexity of even the most elementary kind. Internally . . . , her attitude can be compared to the Nietzschean *ressentiment* of Robert Kelway. But in relation to Irish literary history, it stands in contrast to the politics of W. B. Yeats" (236). Compare Robert Caserio's observation: "Narrative is the necessary third term standing among and beyond oppositional constructions" in Bowen's work (275).

3. Andrew Bennett and Nicholas Royle offer a comparable reading of Bowen's entire oeuvre, in which they "[map] the transformations of the twentieth-century novel in general" (x). They "focus on the novels of Elizabeth Bowen," they explain, "precisely *because* . . . they supposedly represent a tradition of the realist novel untouched by the vagaries of modernist or postmodernist experimentalism" (xiv). Phyllis Lassner offers this kindred claim: "In her comedies of manners [Bowen] not only questions the morals of country and city life, but those literary traditions which reflect, express and prefigure them: romance elements and domestic realism are never taken at face value" (1991, 143). Patricia Coughlin analyzes the disorienting power of Bowen's equivocal tone in *Friends and Relations* (1931) this way: Bowen's "dry irony seems rather equivocal . . . because the ironic narrative voice—which Bowen must have learned very largely from Jane Austen and which announces a correct set of judgements on manners and morals—is

predicated upon the existence of a set of incontrovertible social norms which attract the consent of a coherent social world, whereas such a consensus is no longer in being in the twentieth century" (120).

4. See Phyllis Lassner, *Elizabeth Bowen: A Study of the Short Fiction* for a discussion of Bowen's approach to "rituals of gentility" (1991, 76). Lassner's discussion shows how decisive the impact of Bowen's "Anglo-Irish" experience may have been on her presumably "non-Irish" novels and stories.

5. See Raymond William's *The Country and the City* (1973) for a formative analysis of such repressions, particularly in English country house poems.

6. R. B. Kershner might explain Danielstown's absent presence by way of psychology rather than history: "From the beginning of Bowen's imaginative life, houses are essential, but never *given*. Bowen's Court is the overwhelming, central reality of her childhood. And yet she does not *live* there" (409). Working from Bachelard's notion that "the original site of our dreaming, indeed its embodiment, is our original house" (407), Kershner suggests that "what Bowen projects in [many] stories is the sense of the house as primal, belonging to the realm of dream, reverie, and the uncharted territory of unconscious being" (410). The implications for both *The Last September* and Beckett's *Watt* are suggestive. For other discussions of Bowen's representations of house and setting, see: Barbara Seward, "Elizabeth Bowen's World of Impoverished Love" (1956); Sister M. Corona Sharp, "The House as Setting and Symbol in Three Novels by Elizabeth Bowen" (1963); Walter Sullivan, "A Sense of Place: Elizabeth Bowen and the Landscape of the Heart" (1976); Toni O'Brien Johnson, "Light and Enlightenment in Bowen's Irish Novels" (1987).

7. Robert Caserio discusses the indeterminacy and moral ambiguity of character in Bowen's work from a different angle. He calls *The Heat of the Day* a novel of moral choice which "exhibits the choosing as a process at once free and constrained, active and passive, because choices are determined by historical and cultural contexts and contingencies"; "Bowen implies that it is impossible either to participate in or to know the narrative called history if we do not recognize that it somehow deprives us of free agency. History and choice express both volition and ethical and political constraint. As Paul Ricoeur says (following Marx), 'We are only the agents of history inasmuch as we also suffer it'" (276–78). Caserio's argument has significant implications for our understandings of both Anglo-Irish fiction and ideology theory.

8. Coates argues: "One of the most obvious features of *The Last September* is its unusually symmetrical structure, the three parts of almost equal length, drawing attention to a design. These divisions and their titles . . . unavoidably suggest a pattern . . . Clearly [Bowen] thought the interplay important. The encounters and conversations of the novel, above all the choice of just that particular 'cast' of characters and of the particular way in which they interact, are meant to be significant" (205–6). Lassner also discusses Bowen's "use of opposition as a technique" (1991, 160–61).

9. For a compelling discussion of Bowen's "representations of woman-to-woman attachment," see Patricia Coughlin's "Women and Desire in the Work of Elizabeth Bowen" (1997). Regarding Lois's relation to Marda Coughlin writes: "It is quite plain, even comically so, that Gerald's death is mostly a relief to Lois,

whereas her attachment to Marda is what we might call emotionally in earnest" (124). She adds: "One might also consider Marda as Lois's ego-ideal, in the Freudian vocabulary: one whom Lois can admire and look up to as a perfected version of oneself, a self *in potentia*" (134). See Lassner's *Elizabeth Bowen* for a broad discussion of Bowen's interest "in testing the formation of female character against the literary and social traditions which had been responsible for its development" (1991, 15); Lassner argues that "More than any of her fiction, [*Friends and Relations*] treats domestic ideology at both surface and depth" (17).

10. W. J. McCormack notes the notion of "the Big House novel"—which "merges the work and the author in an undiscriminating way"—"is exceptionally offensive when the author (as woman) is debarred or legally circumscribed in relation to property ownership, and it might be revealing to consider the use of domestic setting by Irish women writers as a preemptive strike against continued male monopoly in the ownership of landed estate" (1992, 36).

11. See also Patricia Parker, "Rhetorics of Property: Exploration, Inventory, Blazon" (1987).

12. See the Introduction to *Nationalisms and Sexualities* (A. Parker et al. 1992a, 3–4). This quotation draws on Judith Butler, *Gender Trouble: Feminism and the Subversion of Identity* (1, 13).

13. In explaining her choice of texts in *Irish Women Writers* Weekes admits, "Given the goal of seeking a cross-cultural tradition, an equal number of Anglo- and Gaelic-Irish novelists is desirable, but nineteenth-century Gaelic-Irish women, uneducated and impoverished, have left few written records" (1990, 17). Other studies of contemporary Irish women writers, like Tamsin Hargreaves's of Edna O'Brien, Julia O'Faolain, Molly Keane, and Jennifer Johnston, are less problematic on this count than Weekes's, as the situations of women writers from different Irish traditions are more fairly comparable in the late twentieth century (1988). Even here, though, one wonders how differences among these writers might be illuminated by a consideration of historical and cultural differences.

14. Toni O'Brien Johnson's and David Cairns's *Gender in Irish Writing*, which aims to combine "three of the most significant of contemporary analytical approaches: gender, colonialism and post-modernism" (2), contains one essay (out of eight) that is devoted to the work of an Anglo-Irish woman: Christine St. Peter's "Jennifer Johnston's Troubles: A materialist-feminist reading" (112–27).

15. Weekes refers to Miller's "Emphasis Added: Plots and Plausibilities in Women's Fiction" (1981).

16. Of all the Anglo-Irish writers considered here, Somerville and Ross appear the least ambivalent regarding stereotypical notions of Anglo-Ireland's relation to Ireland. For discussions of Somerville and Ross's attitudes toward the Anglo-Irish problematic, see Wayne Hall, *Shadowy Heroes* (1980, 64–75); Ann Owens Weekes, "Somerville and Ross: Ignoble Tragedy" (1990, 60–82); Ann Power, "The Big House of Somerville and Ross" (1964); Maureen Waters, *The Comic Irishman* (1984, 19–21).

17. James M. Cahalan offers an unconvincing reading of gender in *The Irish R.M.*, arguing that the stories carry "a subversively gendered portrait of strong, vital women" (90). He rests his case chiefly on the fact that "the Big Houses were really run by women" (99).

18. Keane's earlier novels—such as *Young Entry* (1928), *Full House* (1935), and *Two Days in Aragon* (1941)—tend likewise to sideline questions of gender, in provocative and sometimes frustrating narratives about the status of Anglo-Irish women. *Young Entry*'s Prudence and Peter are much less resistant to the myth of femininity than Bowen's Lois is; their text resolves itself in apparent (though unconvincing) feminine fulfillment in marriage. *Full House* gives us a Charlotte Mullen figure in Miss Parker the governess, a personification of the plight of the unattractive, unmoneyed woman. *Two Days in Aragon* seems on the whole content to accept women's conventional roles; it rejects "drawing room values" (Keane 1941, 150) not for their gender bias but, like Beckett, for their surrealism.

19. Coincidentally, *The Last September* and *A Room of One's Own* were published in the same year. Though Bowen's writing was influenced by Woolf's from the start, the two didn't meet until 1932, and did not become "more intimate and relaxed" friends until 1935, when Bowen moved to London (Lee 1997, 619, 641). Woolf visited Bowen's Court in 1934, and offered this well-known account of the house: "Elizabeths [sic] home was merely a great stone box, but full of Italian masterpieces and decayed 18th century furniture, and carpets all in holes—however they insisted upon keeping up a ramshackle kind of state, dressing for dinner and so on" (quoted in Lee 1997, 641).

20. Coughlin, also reading *The Last September* as an interrogation of "prescribed narratives of femininity," argues that "[t]he interrogation centres on Marda" (123).

21. Bowen's letters and essays are full of accounts of inequities she suffered as a "lady" in a patriarchal culture. Like Lois, she received a scattershot education: "I had not gone to a university; I formed part of no intellectual group or aesthetic coterie. I read widely, but wildly" (1949c, 119–20). Like Lois, she found herself at frighteningly loose ends. At having become a writer, Bowen crows, "I myself was no longer a tennis girl but a writer; aimlessness was gone" (1952a, 124). She imagines her servant's reaction to the sight of her writing: "She was used to seeing a gentleman at his desk—my grandfather at his accounts, my father over his legal documents—but she might well have considered a typewriter inhuman company for a woman (1944, 262).

22. Chessman argues: "Women, in Bowen's vision, are inherently outsiders to discourse, unless they turn traitor and defect to the other side"; she examines how Bowen's "profound ambivalence toward her own powers of authorship" plays itself out in pairs of women characters in her novels, one remaining an object of narrative, the other an author (70). In the semi-autobiographical *The Last September*, one might argue, this pair is Lois and Bowen herself.

23. The contrast between the conclusion of *The Last September* and that of Jennifer Johnston's *The Old Jest* (1979) is instructive. As Tamsin Hargreaves describes it, "In *The Old Jest* eighteen year old Nancy, on the verge of self-discovery, attempts first—in the well-worn, traditional manner—to find out who she is by finding out who her father was. But at the end of the novel . . . she feels that, quite irrespective of who her parents are, she will be able to find the courage to take the psychological leap into her own adult independent existence, to find herself, to find her voice in her own expression and writing" (300).

24. In highlighting its many points of connection to literary modernism, Coates minimizes *The Last September*'s provincial roots, arguing that "the book is essentially

an exploration of the individual's search for meaning and order at a time of cultural fracture. . . . The focal point of *The Last September* is not a political crisis or a social upheaval but one of those moments when it becomes obvious that, in Thomas Mann's well-known phrase, 'the wisdom of the past has become nontransferable,' or in D. H. Lawrence's remark in *Kangaroo*: 'It was in 1915 the old world ended'" (206).

25. Harriet Blodgett writes of Lois's "inwardness, emotional fastidiousness," her "fear of psychic death" (39, 44). Lassner points to Lois's "fear of the 'actual,'" her "fear of being absorbed, by sex or by home" (1986, 48). Paul Parrish reads Lois as a romantic idealist who "suffers because she has required of her relationship with Gerald a perfectibility it cannot attain" (93). See also Barbara Seward's "Elizabeth Bowen's World of Impoverished Love" (1956).

26. Lady Naylor is the only woman character in the text who does not seem diminished by marriage. But Bowen emphasizes how very limited her range is. After marriage as before, Lady Naylor occupies a narrow social channel and, as Hermione Lee maintains, that channel narrows over time. Lee calls Lady Naylor "a diminished version of those powerful matriarchs of *Bowen's Court*. Her scope is reduced; her field of activity is now limited to preventing the marriage of Lois and Gerald, a piece of plotting which events render supremely redundant" (1981, 52). The novel's closing image of Lady Naylor standing before her burning house provides a vivid climax to Bowen's critique of "being a woman." For the house is not just a symbol of the Anglo-Irish order and its codes but of the domestic order as well. The married couple stands and watches the destruction of hearth and home, the domestic space for which the woman marries and over which she exerts what power she has. In the end, even for Myra Naylor, there is no domestic space over which to reign.

27. Andrew Murphy argues that unlike England's other colonial subjects, the Irish were perceived as "imperfect" or "proximate" others (1999). See also Ann Rosalind Jones and Peter Stallybrass, "Dismantling Irena: The Sexualizing of Ireland in Early Modern England" (1992).

28. See Spivak, "Three Women's Texts and a Critique of Imperialism" (1985).

29. For other studies of gender and imperialism, see Suvendrini Perera, *Reaches of Empire: The English Novel from Edgeworth to Dickens* (1988); Firdous Azim, *The Colonial Rise of the Novel* (1993); Jenny Sharpe, *Allegories of Empire: The Figure of Woman in the Colonial Text* (1993); Sara Suleri, *The Rhetoric of English India* (1992); Moira Ferguson, *Colonialism and Gender Relations from Mary Wollstonecraft to Jamaica Kincaid: Caribbean Connections* (1993); Laura Donaldson, *Decolonizing Feminisms: Race, Gender, and Empire-Building* (1992).

30. This articulation of this concept is Meyer's; she writes, "*Wuthering Heights* becomes so interested in the dark character's position in and of itself, rather than in its figurative capacity" that Heathcliff's character "increasingly escapes the bounds of metaphor" (107).

31. Cronin claims "the dilemma of Lois Farquar is made representative of the isolation and doom of her whole tribe," arguing that "[t]he link between the two is stressed and Lois's failure to connect her destiny either to the past, as represented by Hugo, or to the future, embodied in Gerald, bespeaks the failure of the Anglo-Irish to relate themselves fruitfully to either side of their nominal hyphen"

(121). See also Julia McElhattan Williams, "'Fiction with the Texture of History': Elizabeth Bowen's *The Last September*" (1995).

32. For a very different argument regarding Bowen's representation of gender, see Caserio's discussion of *The Heat of the Day* (278–82).

CHAPTER 5. WATT . . . KNOTT . .

1. For views on more expressly political dimensions of Beckett's work, see Claudia Clausius, "Bad Habits While Waiting for Godot: The Demythification of Ritual" (1987); Stephen Watt, "Beckett by Way of Baudrillard: Toward a Political Reading of Samuel Beckett's Drama" (1987); W. J. McCormack, "Seeing darkly: notes on T. W. Adorno and Samuel Beckett" (1986b); David Lloyd, "Writing in the Shit: Beckett, Nationalism, and the Colonial Subject" (1989); Sean Golden, "Familiars in a Ruinstrewn Land: *Endgame* as Political Allegory" (1981); Darko Suvin, "Preparing for Godot—or the Purgatory of Individualism" (1967); Thomas Cousineau, "*Waiting for Godot* and Politics" (1984); Tony Pinkney, "Nationalism and the Politics of Style: Julien Benda and Samuel Beckett" (1988); M. R. Axelrod, *The Politics of Style in the Fiction of Balzac, Beckett and Cortazar* (1992); Geoff Wade, "Marxism and Modernist Aesthetics: Reading Kafka and Beckett" (1992); James Knowlson, "Catastrophe: ¿Ensayo teatral o profecía política?" (1990); Henry Sussman and Christopher Devenney, eds., *Engagement and Indifference: Beckett and the Political* (2001); David Weisberg, *Samuel Beckett and the Cultural Politics of the Modern Novel* (2000).

2. On Beckett and Ireland, see also John P. Harrington, "Beckett, Joyce, and Irish Writing" (1992); Vivian Mercier, *The Irish Comic Tradition* (1962); James Atlas, "The Prose of Samuel Beckett: Notes from the Terminal Ward" (1975); Marilyn Gaddis Rose, "The Irish Memories of Beckett's Voice" (1971); Mary Power, "Samuel Beckett's 'Fingal' and the Irish Tradition" (1981–82); J. C. C. Mays, "Mythologised Presences: *Murphy* in Its Time" (1977); Sighle Kennedy, "Spirals of Need: Irish Prototypes in Samuel Beckett's Fiction" (1974); Gregory A. Schirmer, "The Irish Connection: Ambiguity of Language in *All That Fall*" (1981); John Fletcher, "Joyce, Beckett, and the Short Story in Ireland" (1992); Francis Doherty, "*Watt* in an Irish Frame" (1991); Bernard Hibon, "Samuel Beckett: Irish Traditions and Irish Creation" (1972); Bernard O'Donoghue, "Irish Humor and Verbal Logic" (1982); Patrick Rafroidi, "Pas de Shamrocks pour Sam Beckett: La Dimension irlandaise de *Murphy*" (1982); Stan Smith, "Historians and Magicians: Ireland Between Fantasy and History" (1982); Francis Warner, "The Absence of Nationalism in the Work of Samuel Beckett" (1971); Mary Junker, *Beckett: The Irish Dimension* (1995).

3. I have found no evidence that Beckett read novels in the Anglo-Irish tradition. Beckett's early essay, "Recent Irish Poetry," demonstrates his acquaintance with Irish letters generally and a fair number of Anglo-Irish writers in particular, especially those he calls "the antiquarians" or "twilighters," "the poets of the Revival" (1934b, 70, 71); he mentions Sir Samuel Ferguson, Yeats, Synge, AE, F. R. Higgins, and Monk Gibbon. Of his acquaintance with Anglo-Irish drama we know more. Harrington reports that "Synge, Yeats, and O'Casey are the names most prominent in Beckett's memories of the Abbey Theatre. . . . [T]he Irish dramas

most vivid in his memory were 'several' of O'Casey's plays; Yeats's plays . . . ; 'most' productions by Synge in the late 1920s; and two plays by Lennox Robinson" (1991, 175). Knowlson reports: "Beckett could remember very clearly seeing premieres of Sean O'Casey's *Juno and the Paycock* and *The Plough and the Stars* at the Abbey. But he also went to Lennox Robinson's *The White Blackbird*, T. C. Murray's *Autumn Fire*, and Brinsley Macnamara's *Look at the Heffernans!*" When Knowlson asked Beckett "who he himself felt had influenced his own theater most of all, he suggested only the name of Synge" (1996, 70–71). Regarding Yeats, Knowlson observes: "[Beckett] always loved and admired much of Yeats's poetry, while finding certain (though not all) of his plays dull as ditchwater" (181).

4. Gordon Armstrong reports this 1985 conversation with Beckett on the subject of autobiography (the translations are Armstrong's): "Question: Are you ever going to write your autobiography? Beckett: There are two answers to your question, one from Francis Bacon: '*De nobis ipsis silemus*' ['Let us be silent about ourselves'] and one from René Descartes: '*Bene qui latuit bene vivit*' ['He lived well who hid well']" (249). Yet, as Knowlson shows, Beckett's work is laced with traces of biography, most of them "far from straightforward" (1996, 574). Insofar as *Watt* is autobiographical, of course, it derives in part from Beckett's experience of the Second World War. *Watt* is Beckett's "souvenir of the Occupation" (Kenner 1973b, 24), a representation of "the experience of the refugee tramping wearily along the roads of France, doing manual labor in the service of others in order to survive, living with a heightened sense of exile" (Harvey 1970, 349).

Regarding Beckett's relation to Ireland and Irish politics: Beckett's was "a fervently loyalist and royalist family" (Knowlson 1996, 99). Partition, Knowlson notes, occurred while Beckett was at Portora; "And although he himself felt that the event scarcely impinged on him at the time, passing across the border at the beginning and end of each term, seeing British troops stationed nearby, and then returning to the capital of a new country that was in the process of forming itself must have had some impact on his developing political awareness" (53–54). Knowlson speculates that the friendship of the "vehemently anti-British" Tom MacGreevy "probably led [him] . . . to identify more fully with his own Irishness" (99). Bair offers this anecdote. When asked "how a small country like Ireland could have produced so many great writers," Beckett reportedly responded, "It's the priests and the British. They have buggered us into existence. After all, when you are in the last bloody ditch, there is nothing left but to sing" (282).

Beyond Ireland, Beckett had long-standing and wide-ranging political involvements: his commitment to human rights, his opposition to apartheid and racism, his support for Amnesty International and Oxfam, and for political freedom in Eastern Europe (Knowlson 1996, 21).

5. For discussions of Beckett and Anglo-Irishness, see James Knowlson, *Damned to Fame: The Life of Samuel Beckett* (1996, 386–87); Terence Brown, "Some young doom: Beckett and the child," (1986) and "Louis MacNeice's Ireland" (1989); Declan Kiberd, "Samuel Beckett and the Protestant Ethic" (1985); Michael Allen, "A Note on Sex in Beckett" (1985); Richard Kearney, "The Demythologizing Intellect" (1985b); J. C. C. Mays, "Young Beckett's Irish Roots" (1984); D. E. S. Maxwell, "J. M. Synge and Samuel Beckett" (1985); Vivian Mercier, *Beckett/Beckett* (1977), especially "Ireland/The World"; Mary Junker, *Beckett: The*

Irish Dimension (1995, 21–24); Thomas Kilroy, "The Anglo-Irish Theatrical Imagination" (1997–98, 8–9). None of these studies addresses *Watt* in any detail.

6. The Becketts' former parlor maid told Knowlson she "had to wear a white apron and a cotton frock in the morning and a white cap and in the afternoon I had a black frock with rubber cuffs and rubber collar and a small little cap with black velvet just across the front. And you couldn't go to the door in the afternoon without being dressed. If somebody came with a letter you had a silver tray and they put it on the tray" (1996, 39). Her account recalls both the absurd matter and the blank manner of many passages in *Watt*.

7. Later, of course, Beckett would memorably condemn Church of Ireland Protestantism as having "no more depth than an old school tie" (Bair 1978, 18).

8. As Gordon Armstrong has pointed out, the bare bones of Beckett's biography resemble point for point that of Synge, "the quintessential Anglo-Irishman" (Lyons 1979, 66). Both were born near Dublin to upper middle class parents, both attended Trinity, both studied in Germany and Paris, both broke with bourgeois propriety in becoming artists (Armstrong 1990, 175). There, of course, the broad similarities end. Where Synge chose impatriation, Beckett chose exile.

9. Beckett's Anglo-Irish heritage may shed light on a passage in *More Pricks Than Kicks*'s "Dante and the Lobster" over which Ruby Cohn puzzles (S. Beckett 1934a, 11–12). She calls the image of Cain in the moon "a curious and sudden introduction of relative seriousness" in an otherwise comic story (1962, 31). "Cain is treated with compassion. It is interesting, too, that this was almost the only unrevised paragraph in the story. Dante's image of Cain in the moon recurs to haunt Beckett in *Malone Dies*, but neither here nor later is it evoked in parody. Although the abrupt tonal shift may add to the comic, this paragraph seems to be a relatively sober anomaly in the volume" (32). Cain is, in the passage, the object of both pity and curse. The passage's divided assessment of Cain, along with its unrevised somberness, make sense in an Anglo-Irish context. The figure of Cain might carry a terrific charge for an Anglo-Irish writer who, given Irish history, might feel kinship with the branded brother killer and who, given Irish history, might also feel cursed.

10. Harrington also notes this similarity (Harrington 1991, 126).

11. Angela Moorjani also sees Watt as an artist figure: as one of Beckett's "pseudo-self-portraits" deep in the process of writing endlessly self-reproducing discourse (60). Lawrence Harvey argues that Watt becomes an artist at Knott's: "in search of the form of meaninglessness" (380), Watt "abandons reason . . . and gives up the attempt to know for the attempt to make. He becomes a storyteller" (373). Harrington places Watt directly in the Anglo-Irish literary tradition. But Harrington sees Watt as Anglo-Irish in that, like the Big House novel, he is "passive, nostalgic, and traditionalist," a "revivalist" who generates "conventional, traditional, comforting fictions" (1991, 115, 121–22). Harrington attributes the disruption of these comforting fictions to the narrator Sam: "Watt yearns for a satisfactorily ordered retrospect, and Sam dismantles the hypotheses of such a construction" (131). Watt does long for "the old words, the old credentials" (S. Beckett 1953, 85), and he and Sam do have a crucial debate. But Watt is too aware of the insufficiency of "the old words" to be a revivalist. He sadly acknowledges his epistemological failures, often dismantling his narratives himself. And

far from complacent or "[satisfied] with fabricated meanings" (126), Watt is tortured by their inadequacy. In polarizing Sam and Watt into representatives of antithetical "local historical hypotheses" (1991, 148), Harrington overstates Watt's revivalist yearning and neglects his modernist skepticism. Watt, himself, is polarized.

12. Leslie Hill also points to Watt's arrival at Knott's as the catalyst of his "amnesic confusion" (27). In a compelling reading, Hill argues that "the figure of Knott has the effect on Watt of demolishing the already fragile structure of his identity as a subject of filiation. Knott, as it were, usurps and cancels out the memory of Watt's dead father." Knott is, Hill concludes, a figure of "paternal engulfment" (27). He is also a figure of cultural engulfment, of threatened absorption by home culture.

13. Victor Carrabino finds this dialectic central to *Waiting for Godot* and *Endgame*. See "Beckett and Hegel: The Dialectic of Lordship and Bondage" (1985).

14. *Watt* thus suggests a conception of hierarchy and power very different from that which Steven Connor finds in Beckett's late plays. Connor offers a Foucauldian reading of an "alternating structure of power" in which characters are "merely positions in a circulation of power and control, in which each participant plays the role of torturer and victim, master and servant" (181).

15. *Watt* sounds a similar note in the episode of Mr. Nackybal, the ostensible west-of-Ireland peasant. As Harrington argues, this episode "satirizes idealization of the peasantry as a matter of pragmatics by TCD academics with limited enthusiasm or comprehension of their job"; it satirizes, too, "the literary idealization of a mostly fictional 'Kiltartan' peasantry by, in particular, Yeats, Lady Gregory, and Synge" (1991, 132–33). But this episode also carries more expressly political themes. Mr. Fitzwein of the university examining committee protests to Mr. Louit: "you would not have us believe that this man's mental existence is exhausted by the bare knowledge . . . of what is necessary for his survival" (S. Beckett 1953, 174). Beckett here chides the inclination to minimize the plight of the poor and disenfranchised, whose struggle to survive may indeed be all-encompassing. Ann Beer reports that Beckett's manuscript records anagrams, "including Caliban-Canibal-Nacibal" (72). The trace of "Caliban" in "Nackybal" reinforces the scene's historical and political significance.

16. Harrington, by contrast, reads the Lynch episode as a satire of "Gaelicism and the anticolonialist ideology," "an elaborate construction less concerned with poverty than with obsessive detail," in which "Beckett neutralizes suggestions of abject misery and class poverty with the irony of footnotes" (1991, 129–31). In my view, history's emotional charge outweighs and outlasts ironic undercutting here. Watt may enjoy "a comparative peace of mind" (Harrington 1991, 117) after grasping the arrangement that puzzled him, but the reader does not. The scene and the pressing issues it evokes remain etched in memory. Compare this reading of *Worstward Ho*: "In spite of its almost manic use of wordplay, the text is far too tortured and tormented to be judged a mere linguistic exercise. And there *is* a human subtext after all, in spite of the narrator's tactics of reducing, shedding, and omitting" (Knowlson 1996, 595).

17. Ann Beer also sees *Watt* as a transitional text: linguistically mixed, neither English nor French, marking Beckett's relinquishment of his mother-tongue. See

"Watt, Knott and Beckett's Bilingualism" (1985). The transition that Beer charts might be read as a component of the broader interrogation of home culture that I am tracing.

18. Mercier (rather too literally) identifies Winnie as "a daughter of the Anglo-Irish gentry who has spent the approved number of years at a good Church of Ireland boarding-school" (1977, 218). Naming Beckett "the last of the Anglo-Irish playwrights," Thomas Kilroy (too unequivocally) calls *Happy Days* an elegy "for the codes of civility, however banal, of polite Anglo-Irish society, its codes of literacy, . . . its codes of eccentricity" (1997–1998, 8, 9). Knowlson offers this nice bit of history regarding a National Théâtre production of the play in 1974: After listening to Beckett read the script in what director Peter Hall described as a "gentle Anglo-Irish brogue," Dame Peggy Ashcroft, who was to play Winnie, insisted "that the role was crying out to be played in an Anglo-Irish accent. With Hall's and (more reluctantly) Beckett's agreement, she adopted a brogue modeled on that of her good friend the poet laureate, Cecil Day-Lewis" (1996, 534).

Chapter 6. Fiction Meets Ideology . . .

1. Ideology theory does not appear integral to Vera Kreilkamp's wide-ranging study of Anglo-Irish fiction, though she briefly describes the novels' relation to ideology this way: they "all emerge from ideologies, from systems of belief and representations of experience that have served to define and account for history in particular ways and that for Eagleton signify 'the way in which men live out their roles in class society'" (1998, 16).

2. See Raymond Williams, *Keywords: A Vocabulary of Culture and Society*, for a concise history of "ideology" (1985, 153–57). For other instances of ideology critique in theory and practice see, among others: Edward Said, *Culture and Imperialism* (1994); Fredric Jameson, *Postmodernism or, The Cultural Logic of Late Capitalism* (1991); John B. Thompson, *Studies in the Theory of Ideology* (1984); Rob Nixon, *London Calling: V. S. Naipaul, Postcolonial Mandarin* (1992). For critiques of this practice see, among others: Robert Alter, *The Pleasures of Reading in an Ideological Age* (1989); Eugene Goodheart, *The Skeptic Disposition: Deconstruction, Ideology, and Other Matters* (1991) and *The Reign of Ideology*, especially "From Culture to Ideology" (1997, 13–43); Kenneth Burke, *Permanence and Change* (1984).

3. Eagleton is clearly backtracking from the positivism of *Criticism and Ideology: A Study in Marxist Literary Theory*, where he claims that the task of criticism is "to show the text as it cannot know itself, to manifest those conditions of its making . . . about which it is necessarily silent. . . To achieve such a showing, criticism must break with its ideological prehistory, situating itself outside the space of the text on the alternative terrain of scientific knowledge" (1976a, 43). Such positivism seems persistent but masked in *Ideology*.

4. This is essentially the same point as that made by Judith Lowder Newton in "Feminism and the New Historicism," though, as we have seen in connection with *The Last September*, Newton emphasizes gender as a source of fissures in a class ideology. As Newton argues, a class ideology will be "multiply fractured by contradictions and tensions," since subjects are positioned differently in the social formation (163).

5. Moreover, Eagleton argues, "A dominant class may 'live its experience' in part through the ideology of a previous dominant one: think of the aristocratic colouring of the English *haute bourgeoisie*. Or it may fashion its ideology partly in terms of the beliefs of a subordinated class—as in the case of fascism" (1991, 101).

6. Nor does Eagleton consider the possibility that a subject's relations to ideology will be structured not just by factors in the "public" social formation as governed by class struggle, but by forces in the "private" realm as well. As Judith Lowder Newton argues, "Family life, . . . the dynamics of mother/father/child relations (in the modern nuclear family) should be part of our construction of 'material conditions'" (164). Of course, heeding family dynamics, like heeding gender, might make it difficult to identify ideological formations, by fragmenting them into collections of diversely formed subjectivities among which family resemblances might prove difficult to discern.

7. If Eagleton skims over the question of mediation in *Ideology*, he implicitly puts it center stage in *Criticism and Ideology* (1976a). Interestingly, there Eagleton suggests it is the action of the literary text and the fact of ideology's being carried (Eagleton might say "operated") by a text that accounts for much if not all ideological discontinuity.

8. Recall this recollection by Keane, which may well be an autobiographical analog to this passage: "Ballyrankin stood on the banks of the River Slaney. It was really awfully pretty. You reached it through a very long avenue, with a gate lodge at each end. And there were large, sort of parklike fields around us, with beautiful trees in them—really good trees—and a lovely stableyard, in that way people had then, built in a big oval adjoining the vast kitchen premises of the house" (Kierstead 1986, 99). But, echoes notwithstanding, this account does not clarify, for the reader in search of ideology, where authorial word ends and characterization begins in the comparable passage in *Time After Time*.

9. Yet Kreilkamp concludes: "With the detached, even chilling, vision of her own class that dominates her last three novels, Keane sloughs off the affectionately condescending tone toward the native Irish that controls her early works and recalls the class-bound vision of Catholic Ireland found in earlier Big House fiction" (1998, 190).

10. I owe this articulation of this idea to John Burt.

11. See Margaret Scanlan's "Rumors of War: Elizabeth Bowen's *Last September* and J. G. Farrell's *Troubles*" for a relatively raw instance of this kind of argument: "[T]here is certainly much that [Bowen] omits. She has not avoided . . . the *Gone with the Wind* syndrome that haunts so many novels of the American South. Her Irish Catholic characters have as little depth as Butterfly McQueen's Prissy; the injustices on which Bowen herself saw Anglo-Irish life to have been founded are not a subject over which her Protestant characters brood at second-hand, as Jack Burden or Quentin Compson brood over slavery. To read, for example, Frank O'Connor's autobiographies in tandem with *Last September* [sic] is to experience a sense of shock at the discovery, for example, that throughout his childhood O'Connor's mother earned one-shilling-and-sixpence for a twelve-hour day as a cleaning woman. Aware of such poverty, can a reader seriously be expected to grieve over the death of a house or feel sympathetic with the collapse of a set of values that it

symbolizes?" (78–79). Though his essay on *The Last September* drifts from time to time toward a problematic essentialism ("Like others of her kind, [Bowen] lived at a certain remove from her own emotions"), Declan Kiberd counters: "it was scarcely her fault if she had found such knowledge unavailable"; "in her early years, she had been so sheltered that she had no idea that Protestants did not make up the majority religion in Ireland" (136–37).

References

Abbott, H. Porter. 1973. *The Fiction of Samuel Beckett: Form and Effect.* Berkeley: University of California Press.

Adams, Alice. 1991. Coming Apart at the Seams: *Good Behaviour* as an Anti-comedy. *Journal of Irish Literature* 20, no. 3: 27–35.

Ahmad, Aijaz. 1992. *In Theory: Nations, Classes, Literatures.* New York: Verso.

Allen, Michael. 1985. A Note on Sex in Beckett. In *Across a Roaring Hill: The Protestant Imagination in Modern Ireland.* Edited by Gerald Dawe and Edna Longley, 39–47. Dover, N.H.: Blackstaff.

Allum, Percy. 1980. The Irish Question. *The Crane Bag* 4, no. 2: 643–51.

Alter, Robert. 1989. *The Pleasures of Reading in an Ideological Age.* New York: Simon and Schuster.

Althusser, Louis. 1971. *Lenin and Philosophy.* New York: Monthly Review Press.

Anderson, Benedict. 1991. *Imagined Communities: Reflections on the Origin and Spread of Nationalism.* New York: Verso.

Anderson, Perry. 1991. Nation-States and National Identity. *London Review of Books,* 9 May, 3.

Arendt, Hannah. 1968. *Illuminations.* Translated by Harry Zohn. London: Fontana/Collins, 1992.

Armstrong, Gordon. 1990. *Samuel Beckett, W. B. Yeats, and Jack Yeats: Images and Words.* Lewisburg, Pa.: Bucknell University Press.

Arnold, Matthew. 1855. Stanzas from the Grand Chartreuse. In *Victorian Poetry and Poetics.* Edited by Walter E. Houghton and G. Robert Stange, 476–78. Boston: Houghton Mifflin, 1968.

———. 1868. Culture and Anarchy. In *English Prose of the Victorian Era.* Edited by Charles Frederick Harrold and William D. Templeman, 1117–88. New York: Oxford University Press, 1956.

Atlas, James. 1975. The Prose of Samuel Beckett: Notes from the Terminal Ward. In *Two Decades of Irish Writing: A Critical Survey.* Edited by Douglas Dunn, 186–96. Chester Springs, Pa.: Dufour.

Austen, Jane. 1813. *Pride and Prejudice.* New York: Signet, 1980.

Austin, J. L. 1962. *How To Do Things With Words.* London: Oxford University Press.

Axelrod, M. R. 1992. *The Politics of Style in the Fiction of Balzac, Beckett and Cortazar.* London: Macmillan.

Azim, Firdous. 1993. *The Colonial Rise of the Novel.* New York: Routledge.

Bachelard, Gaston. 1969. *The Poetics of Space.* Boston: Beacon Press.

Bair, Deirdre. 1978. *Samuel Beckett: A Biography.* New York: Harcourt.

Baker, Houston. 1987. *Modernism and the Harlem Renaissance.* Chicago: University of Chicago Press.

Bakhtin, M. M. 1981. *The Dialogic Imagination: Four Essays.* Edited by Michael Holquist. Translated by Caryl Emerson and Michael Holquist. Austin: University of Texas Press.

———. 1984. *Rabelais and His World.* Translated by Hélène Iswolsky. Bloomington: Indiana University Press.

Banville, John. 1973. *Birchwood.* London: Panther, 1984.

Barthes, Roland. 1972. *Mythologies.* Translated by Annette Lavers. New York: Hill and Wang.

———. 1974. *S/Z.* Translated by Richard Miller. New York: Hill and Wang.

———. 1975. *The Pleasure of the Text.* Translated by Richard Miller. New York: Hill and Wang.

Beckett, J. C. 1976. *The Anglo-Irish Tradition.* Ithaca: Cornell University Press.

Beckett, Samuel. 1929. Dante . . . Bruno . Vico . . Joyce. In *Disjectica: Miscellaneous Writings and a Dramatic Fragment,* 19–34. New York: Grove, 1984.

———. 1934a. *More Pricks Than Kicks.* London: Calder and Boyars, 1970.

———. 1934b. Recent Irish Poetry. In *Disjectica: Miscellaneous Writings and a Dramatic Fragment,* 70–76. New York: Grove, 1984.

———. 1938. *Murphy.* New York: Grove, 1957.

———. 1953. *Watt.* New York: Grove.

———. 1954. *Waiting for Godot.* New York: Grove.

———. 1959. *Three Novels by Samuel Beckett: Molloy, Malone Dies, The Unnamable.* New York: Grove, 1965.

———. 1964. *Happy Days.* New York: Grove.

———. 1984. *Disjectica: Miscellaneous Writings and a Dramatic Fragment.* Edited by Ruby Cohn. New York: Grove.

Beer, Ann. 1985. Watt, Knott and Beckett's Bilingualism. *Journal of Beckett Studies* 10: 37–75.

Bell, Desmond. 1985. Contemporary Cultural Studies in Ireland and the "Problem" of Protestant Ideology. *The Crane Bag* 9, no. 2: 91–95.

Bennett, Andrew, and Nicholas Royle. 1995. *Elizabeth Bowen and the Dissolution of the Novel.* New York: St. Martin's Press.

Beverley, John. 1993. *Against Literature.* Minneapolis: University of Minnesota Press.

Bhabha, Homi. 1990a. Introduction: narrating the nation. In *Nation and Narration,* 1–15. New York: Routledge.

———, ed. 1990b. *Nation and Narration.* New York: Routledge.

Billington, Rachel. 1981. Fictions of Class. Review of *Good Behaviour*, by Molly Keane. *New York Times Book Review*, 9 August, 13, 34.

Blodgett, Harriet. 1975. *Patterns of Reality: Elizabeth Bowen's Novels*. Paris: Mouton.

Bowen, Elizabeth. 1929a. *The Last September*. New York: Penguin, 1987.

———. 1929b. Preface to *The Last September*. New York: Avon, 1979.

———. 1931. *Friends and Relations*. London: Constable.

———. 1934. The Mulberry Tree. In *The Mulberry Tree: Writings of Elizabeth Bowen*. Edited by Hermione Lee, 13–20. New York: Harcourt Brace Jovanovich, 1986.

———. 1940. The Big House. In *The Mulberry Tree: Writings of Elizabeth Bowen*. Edited by Hermione Lee, 25–30. New York: Harcourt Brace Jovanovich, 1986.

———. 1942a. *Bowen's Court*. New York: Ecco, 1979.

———. 1942b. *Seven Winters: Memories of a Dublin Childhood*. Dublin: Cuala Press.

———. 1944. The Most Unforgettable Character I've Met. In *The Mulberry Tree: Writings of Elizabeth Bowen*. Edited by Hermione Lee, 254–64. New York: Harcourt Brace Jovanovich, 1986.

———. 1949a. The Art of Virginia Woolf. In *Collected Impressions*. New York: Knopf.

———. 1949b. *The Heat of the Day*. New York: Knopf.

———. 1949c. Preface to *Encounters*. In *The Mulberry Tree: Writings of Elizabeth Bowen*. Edited by Hermione Lee, 118–21. New York: Harcourt Brace Jovanovich, 1986.

———. 1950. The Bend Back. In *The Mulberry Tree: Writings of Elizabeth Bowen*. Edited by Hermione Lee, 54–59. New York: Harcourt Brace Jovanovich, 1986.

———. 1952a. Preface to *The Last September* (second U.S. edition). In *The Mulberry Tree: Writings of Elizabeth Bowen*. Edited by Hermione Lee, 122–26. New York: Harcourt Brace Jovanovich, 1986.

———. 1952b. Review of *The Anglo-Irish*, by Brian Fitzgerald. In *The Mulberry Tree: Writings of Elizabeth Bowen*. Edited by Hermione Lee, 174–76. New York: Harcourt Brace Jovanovich, 1986.

———. 1975. *Pictures and Conversations*. New York: Knopf.

———. 1986. *The Mulberry Tree: Writings of Elizabeth Bowen*. Edited by Hermione Lee. New York: Harcourt Brace Jovanovich.

Boyd, William. 1981. Revenge of the Innocent. Review of *Good Behaviour*, by Molly Keane. *Times Literary Supplement*, 9 October, 1154.

Boylan, Clare. 1993. Sex, Snobbery and the Strategies of Molly Keane. In *Contemporary British Women Writers: Narrative Strategies*. Edited by Robert E. Hosmer, Jr., 151–60. New York: St. Martin's Press.

Breen, Mary. 1997. Piggies and Spoilers of Girls: The Representation of Sexuality in the Novels of Molly Keane. In *Sex, Nation, and Dissent in Irish Writing*. Edited by Éibhear Walshe, 202–20. New York: St. Martin's Press.

Brennan, Timothy. 1990. The national longing for form. In *Nation and Narration*. Edited by Homi Bhabha, 44–70. New York: Routledge.

Breuilly, John. 1982. *Nationalism and the State*. Chicago: University of Chicago Press.

Brienza, Susan D. 1987. *Samuel Beckett's New Worlds: Style in Metafiction*. Norman: University of Oklahoma Press.

Brothers, Barbara. 1978. Pattern and Void: Bowen's Irish Landscapes and *The Heat of the Day*. *Mosaic* 12: 129–38.

Brown, Terence. 1985. *Ireland: A Social and Cultural History, 1922 to the Present*. Ithaca: Cornell University Press.

———. 1986. Some young doom: Beckett and the child. *Hermathena* 141: 56–61.

———. 1989. Louis MacNeice's Ireland. In *Tradition and Influence in Anglo-Irish Poetry*. Edited by Terence Brown and Nicholas Grene, 79–96. Totowa, N. J.: Barnes and Noble.

Burgstaller, Susanne. 1992. "This Lawless House"—John Banville's Post-Modernist Treatment of the Big-House Motif in *Birchwood* and *The Newton Letter*. In *Ancestral Voices: The Big House in Anglo-Irish Literature*. Edited by Otto Rachbauer, 239–56. Dublin: Lilliput Press.

Burke, Kenneth. 1984. *Permanence and Change*. Berkeley: University of California Press.

Burkman, Katherine, ed. 1987. *Myth and Ritual in the Plays of Samuel Beckett*. Rutherford, N. J.: Fairleigh Dickinson University Press.

Butler, Herbert. 1985. The Country House After the Union. In *Escape from the Anthill*, 45–56. Mullingar, Ireland: Lilliput Press.

Butler, Judith. 1989. *Gender Trouble: Feminism and the Subversion of Identity*. New York: Routledge.

Butler, Marilyn. 1972. *Maria Edgeworth: A Literary Biography*. Oxford: Clarendon Press.

Buttner, Gottfried. 1984. *Samuel Beckett's Novel "Watt."* Translated by Joseph P. Dolan. Philadelphia: University of Pennsylvania Press.

Cahalan, James M. 1993. "Humor with a Gender": Somerville and Ross and *The Irish R. M. Éire-Ireland* 28: 87–102.

Carey, Phyllis and Ed Jewinski, eds. 1992. *Re: Joyce'n Beckett*. New York: Fordham University Press.

Carrabino, Victor. 1985. Beckett and Hegel: The Dialectic of Lordship and Bondage. *Neophilologus* 65: 32–41.

Caserio, Robert L. 1993. The Heat of the Day: Modernism and Narrative in Paul de Man and Elizabeth Bowen. *Modern Language Quarterly* 54: 263–84.

Chessman, Harriet S. 1983. Women and Language in the Fiction of Elizabeth Bowen. *Twentieth Century Literature* 29: 69–85.

Chodorow, Nancy. 1974. Family Structure and Feminine Personality. In *Woman, Culture and Society*. Edited by Michelle Zimbalist Rosaldo and Louise Lamphere, 43–66. Stanford, Calif.: Stanford University Press.

———. 1978. *The Reproduction of Mothering*. Berkeley: University of California Press.

Clausius, Claudia. 1987. Bad Habits While Waiting for Godot: The Demythification of Ritual. In *Myth and Ritual in the Plays of Samuel Beckett*. Edited by Katherine Burkman, 124–43. Rutherford, N. J.: Fairleigh Dickinson University Press.

Coates, John. 1990. Elizabeth Bowen's *The Last September*: The Loss of the Past and the Modern Consciousness. *Durham University Journal* 51: 205–16.

Cohn, Ruby. 1962. *Samuel Beckett: The Comic Gamut*. New Brunswick, N. J.: Rutgers University Press.

———. 1973. *Back to Beckett.* Princeton: Princeton University Press.

Coleman, Anthony. 1992. The Big House, Yeats, and the Irish Context. In *Ancestral Voices: The Big House in Anglo-Irish Literature.* Edited by Otto Rauchbauer, 123–45. Dublin: Lilliput Press.

Colgan, Maurice. 1982. After Rackrent: Ascendancy Nationalism in Maria Edgeworth's Later Irish Novels. In *Studies in Anglo-Irish Literature.* Edited by Heinz Kosok, 37–42. Bonn: Bouvier.

Connor, Steven. 1988. *Samuel Beckett: Repetition, Theory and Text.* New York: Basil Blackwell.

Contemporary Authors 114: 263–66. 1985. S.v. Keane, Molly Nesta.

Corkery, Daniel. 1931. *Synge and Anglo-Irish Literature: A Study.* New York: Russell and Russell, 1965.

Coughlin, Patricia. 1997. Women and Desire in the Work of Elizabeth Bowen. In *Sex, Nation, and Dissent in Irish Writing.* Edited by Éibhear Walshe, 103–34. New York: St. Martin's Press.

Cousineau, Thomas. 1984. *Waiting for Godot* and Politics. In *Coriolan: Théâtre et politique.* Edited by Jean-Paul Debax and Yves Peyre, 161–67. Toulouse: Service des Publications, Université de Toulouse-Le Mirail.

Cronin, Anthony. 1990. *The Anglo-Irish Novel,* Vol. 2: 1900–1940. Savage, Md.: Barnes and Noble.

Curtis, L. P., Jr. 1970. The Anglo-Irish Predicament. *Twentieth Century Studies* 4: 37–62.

Davenport, Gary T. 1974. Elizabeth Bowen and the Big House. *Southern Humanities Review* 9: 27–34.

Dawe, Gerald, and Edna Longley, eds. 1985. *Across a Roaring Hill: The Protestant Imagination in Modern Ireland.* Dover, N.H.: Blackstaff.

Deane, Paul. 1991. The Big House Revisited: Molly Keane's *Time After Time. Notes on Modern Irish Literature* 3: 37–44.

Deane, Seamus. 1979. An Example of Tradition. *The Crane Bag* 3, no. 1: 373–79.

———. 1985. The Literary Myths of the Revival. In *Celtic Revivals,* 28–37. Boston: Faber and Faber.

———. 1986. Heroic Styles: The Tradition of an Idea. In *Ireland's Field Day* 6–8. Notre Dame, Ind.: University of Notre Dame Press.

de Lauretis, Teresa, ed. 1986a. *Feminist Studies/Critical Studies.* Bloomington: Indiana University Press.

———. 1986b. Feminist Studies/Critical Studies: Issues, Terms, and Contexts. In *Feminist Studies/Critical Studies,* 1–19. Bloomington: Indiana University Press.

Derrida, Jacques. 1976. *Of Grammatology.* Translated by Gayatri Chakravorty Spivak. Baltimore: Johns Hopkins University Press.

———. 1979. *Spurs: Nietzsche's Styles.* Translated by Barbara Harlow. Chicago: University of Chicago Press.

Doherty, Francis. 1991. *Watt* in an Irish Frame. *Irish University Review: A Journal of Irish Studies* 21: 187–203.

Donaldson, Laura. 1992. *Decolonizing Feminisms: Race, Gender, and Empire-Building.* Chapel Hill: University of North Carolina Press.

Donnelly, Brian. 1975. The Big House in the Recent Novel. *Studies* 64: 133–42.

Donoghue, Denis. 1986. Bair's Beckett. In *We Irish: Essays on Irish Literature and Society*, 253–57. New York: Knopf.

Eagleton, Terry. 1976a. *Criticism and Ideology: A Study in Marxist Literary Theory*. New York: Verso.

———. 1976b. *Marxism and Literary Criticism*. London: Methuen.

———. 1991. *Ideology: An Introduction*. New York: Verso.

———. Fredric Jameson, and Edward Said. 1990. *Nationalism, Colonialism and Literature*. Minneapolis: University of Minnesota Press.

Edgeworth, Maria. 1800. *Castle Rackrent*. New York: Oxford University Press, 1980.

Fanon, F. 1965. *The Wretched of the Earth: The Pitfalls of Nationalist Consciousness*. New York: Grove.

Faulkner, William. 1936. *Absalom, Absalom!* New York: Modern Library, 1964.

Federman, Raymond. 1965. *Journey to Chaos: Samuel Beckett's Early Fiction*. Berkeley: University of California Press.

Fekete, John. 1977. *The Critical Twilight*. London: Routledge and Kegan Paul.

Ferguson, Moira. 1993. *Colonialism and Gender Relations from Mary Wollstonecraft to Jamaica Kincaid: Caribbean Connections*. New York: Columbia University Press.

Flanagan, Thomas. 1966. The Big House of Ross-Drishane. *Kenyon Review* 28: 54–78.

Fletcher, John. 1992. Joyce, Beckett, and the Short Story in Ireland. In *Re: Joyce 'n Beckett*. Edited by Phyllis Carey and Ed Jewinsky, 20–30. New York: Fordham University Press.

Foster, R. F. 1989. *Modern Ireland 1600–1972*. New York: Penguin.

Foucault, Michel. 1979. *The History of Sexuality*, Vol. 1: *An Introduction*. Translated by Robert Huxley. London: Allen Lane.

———. 1980. *Power/Knowledge: Selected Interviews and Other Writings 1972–1977*. Edited by Colin Gordon. Translated by Colin Gordon, Leo Marshall, John Mapham, and Kate Soper. New York: Pantheon.

Friel, Brian. 1984. *Translations*. London: Faber and Faber.

Gates, Henry Louis, Jr. 1985. Writing "Race" and the Difference It Makes. *Critical Inquiry* 12: 1–19.

Geertz, Clifford. 1973. *The Interpretation of Cultures*. New York: Basic Books.

Gellner, Ernest. 1983. *Nations and Nationalism*. Ithaca: Cornell University Press.

Gibbon, Monk. 1977. Am I Irish? *The Crane Bag* 1, no. 2: 113–14.

Gilbert, Sandra and Susan Gubar. 1979. *The Madwoman in the Attic: The Woman Writer and the Nineteenth-Century Literary Imagination*. New Haven: Yale University Press.

———. 1988. *No Man's Land: The Place of the Woman Writer in the Twentieth Century*, Vol. 1: *The War of the Words*. New Haven: Yale University Press.

Gill, Richard. 1972. *Happy Rural Seat: The English Country House and the Literary Imagination*. New Haven: Yale University Press.

Glendinning, Victoria. 1977. *Elizabeth Bowen: Portrait of a Writer*. London: Weidenfeld and Nicolson.

Gluck, Barbara Reich. 1979. *Beckett and Joyce.* Lewisburg, Pa.: Bucknell University Press.

Gmelch, George. 1985. *The Irish Tinkers: The Urbanization of an Itinerant People.* Prospect Heights, Ill.: Waveland Press.

Goetsch, Paul. 1992. The Country House in George Moore's *A Drama in Muslin.* In *Ancestral Voices: The Big House in Anglo-Irish Literature.* Edited by Otto Rauchbauer, 79–92. Dublin: Lilliput Press.

Golden, Sean. 1981. Familiars in a Ruinstrewn Land: *Endgame* as Political Allegory. *Contemporary Literature* 22: 425–55.

Gontarski, S. E. 1985. *The Intent of Undoing in Samuel Beckett's Dramatic Texts.* Bloomington: Indiana University Press.

Goodheart, Eugene. 1991. *The Skeptic Disposition: Deconstruction, Ideology, and Other Matters.* Princeton: Princeton University Press.

———. 1997. *The Reign of Ideology.* New York: Columbia University Press.

Gunew, Sneja. 1990. Denaturalizing cultural nationalisms: multicultural readings of Australia. In *Nation and Narration.* Edited by Homi Bhabha, 99–120. New York: Routledge.

Hall, Wayne. 1980. *Shadowy Heroes: Irish Literature of the 1890s.* Syracuse, N.Y.: Syracuse University Press.

Hardwick, Elizabeth. 1949. Elizabeth Bowen's Fiction. *Partisan Review* 16: 1114–21.

Hargreaves, Tamsin. 1988. Women's Consciousness and Identity in Four Irish Women Novelists. In *Cultural Contexts and Literary Idioms in Contemporary Irish Literature.* Edited by Michael Kenneally, 290–305. Totowa, N.J.: Barnes and Noble.

Harrington, John P. 1991. *The Irish Beckett.* Syracuse, N.Y.: Syracuse University Press.

———. 1992. Beckett, Joyce, and Irish Writing: The Example of Beckett's "Dubliners" Story. In *Re: Joyce 'n Beckett.* Edited by Phyllis Carey and Ed Jewinsky, 31–42. New York: Fordham University Press.

Harvey, Lawrence. 1970. *Samuel Beckett: Poet and Critic.* Princeton: Princeton University Press.

Hassan, Ihab. 1967. *The Literature of Silence: Henry Miller and Samuel Beckett.* New York: Knopf.

Hegel, G. W. F. 1807. *The Phenomenology of Mind.* New York: Harper Torchbook, 1967.

Heller, Scott. 1999a. Beyond the Usual Suspects: Scholars Expand the Modernist Canon. *The Chronicle of Higher Education,* 5 November, A23.

———. 1999b. New Life for Modernism. *The Chronicle of Higher Education,* 5 November, A21–A22.

Helsa, David. 1971. *The Shape of Chaos.* Minneapolis: University of Minnesota Press.

Hibon, Bernard. 1972. Samuel Beckett: Irish Traditions and Irish Creation. In *Aspects of the Irish Theater.* Edited by Patrick Rafroidi, Ramonde Popot, and William Parker, 225–41. Lille: Publications de l'Université de Lille.

Higgins, Aidan. 1966. *Langrishe, Go Down.* London: Calder and Boyars, 1972.

———. 1977. *Scenes from a Receding Past.* London: Calder.

Hill, Leslie. 1990. *Beckett's Fiction: In Different Words.* Cambridge: Cambridge University Press.

Holland, Mary. 1981. Codes. Review of *Good Behaviour* by Molly Keane. *New Statesman,* 13 November, 26.

Howe, Irving. 1957. *Politics and the Novel.* New York: Horizon Press.

Hulbert, Ann. 1984. Visitations. Review of *Time After Time* by Molly Keane and *Stones for Ibarra* by Harriet Doerr. *The New Republic,* 30 January, 40–41.

Hutcheon, Linda. 1988. *A Poetics of Postmodernism: History, Theory, Fiction.* New York: Routledge.

Imhof, Rudiger. 1992a. Molly Keane, *Good Behaviour, Time After Time* and *Loving and Giving.* In *Ancestral Voices: The Big House in Anglo-Irish Literature.* Edited by Otto Rauchbauer, 195–203. Dublin: Lilliput Press.

———. 1992b. Somerville and Ross: *The Real Charlotte* and *The Big House of Inver.* In *Ancestral Voices: The Big House in Anglo-Irish Literature.* Edited by Otto Rauchbauer, 95–107. Dublin: Lilliput Press.

Inglis, Brian. 1962. *West Briton.* London: Faber and Faber.

Ireland's Field Day. 1986. Notre Dame, Ind.: University of Notre Dame Press.

Iser, Wolfgang. 1973. *The Implied Reader.* Baltimore: Johns Hopkins University Press.

Jameson, Fredric. 1981. *The Political Unconscious: Narrative as a Socially Symbolic Act.* Ithaca: Cornell University Press.

———. 1991. *Postmodernism; or, The Cultural Logic of Late Capitalism.* Durham, N.C.: Duke University Press.

Jeffares, A. Norman. 1986. Foreword. *Beckett at 80.* Edited by Terence Brown and Nicholas Grene. *Hermathena: A Trinity College Dublin Review* 141: 7–9.

Jefferson, Margot. 1984. Every Other Inch a Lady. Review of *Good Behaviour* and *Time After Time* by Molly Keane. *The Village Voice,* 17 April, 42.

Johnson, Toni O'Brien. 1987. Light and Enlightenment in Bowen's Irish Novels. *ARIEL: A Review of International English Literature* 18: 47–62.

Johnson, Toni O'Brien, and David Cairns, eds. 1991. *Gender in Irish Writing.* Philadelphia: Open University Press.

Johnston, Jennifer. 1976. *How Many Miles to Babylon?* New York: Penguin, 1988.

———. 1979. *The Old Jest.* Garden City, N.Y.: Doubleday, 1980.

Jones, Ann Rosalind, and Peter Stallybrass. 1992. Dismantling Irena: The Sexualizing of Ireland in Early Modern England. In *Nationalisms and Sexuality.* Edited by Andrew Parker et al., 157–71. New York: Routledge.

Jordan, Heather Bryant. 1992. *How Will the Heart Endure: Elizabeth Bowen and the Landscape of War.* Ann Arbor: University of Michigan Press.

Junker, Mary. 1995. *Beckett: The Irish Dimension.* Dublin: Wolfhound Press.

Keane, Molly. [M. J. Farrell]. 1928. *Young Entry.* London: Virago, 1989.

———. 1929. *Taking Chances.* New York: Virago, 1987.

———. 1934. *Devoted Ladies.* New York: Virago, 1984.

———. 1935. *Full House.* New York: Penguin, 1987.

———. 1941. *Two Days in Aragon.* New York: Penguin, 1986.

————. 1981. *Good Behaviour.* New York: Dutton, 1983.

————. 1983. *Time After Time.* New York: Dutton, 1985.

————. 1989. *Queen Lear.* New York: Penguin.

————. 1991a. Interview. Molly Keane: Something Old, Something New. In *In the Vernacular: Interviews at Yale with Sculptors of Culture.* Edited by Melissa E. Biggs, 22–27. Jefferson, N.C.: McFarland and Company.

————. 1991b. Memoirs of an Anglo-Irish Childhood. *Gourmet,* February, 80ff.

————. 1993. Introduction. *Molly Keane's Ireland: An Anthology.* Edited by Molly Keane and Sally Phipps, ix–xvii. London: HarperCollins.

Kearney, Richard. 1977. Interview with Herbert Marcuse. *The Crane Bag* 1, no. 1: 81–89.

————. 1984. Faith and Fatherland. *The Crane Bag* 8, no. 1: 55–66.

————. 1985a. Between Conflict and Consensus. *The Crane Bag* 9, no. 1: 87–89.

————. 1985b. The Demythologizing Intellect. In *The Irish Mind: Exploring Intellectual Traditions.* Edited by Richard Kearney, 267–93. Dublin: Wolfhound Press.

————. 1988. *Transitions: Narratives in Modern Irish Culture.* New York: St. Martin's Press.

Kemp, Sandra. 1990. "But how describe a world seen without a self?" Feminism, fiction and modernism. *Critical Quarterly* 32: 99–118.

Kenneally, Michael, ed. 1988. *Cultural Contexts and Literary Idioms in Contemporary Irish Literature.* Totowa, N.J.: Barnes and Noble.

Kennedy, Sighle. 1974. Spirals of Need: Irish Prototypes in Samuel Beckett's Fiction. In *Yeats, Joyce, and Beckett: New Light on Three Modern Irish Writers.* Edited by Kathleen McGrory and John Unterecker, 153–66. Lewisburg, Pa.: Bucknell University Press.

Kenner, Hugh. 1973a. *A Reader's Guide to Samuel Beckett.* New York: Farrar, Straus and Giroux.

————. 1973b. *Samuel Beckett: A Critical Study.* Berkeley: University of California Press.

————. 1983. *A Colder Eye.* New York: Penguin.

Kenney, Edwin J., Jr. 1975. *Elizabeth Bowen.* Lewisburg, Pa.: Bucknell University Press.

Kershner, R. B. 1986. Bowen's Oneiric *House in Paris. Texas Studies in Literature and Language* 28: 407–23.

Kiberd, Declan. 1984. Inventing Irelands. *The Crane Bag* 8, no. 1: 11–23.

————. 1985. Samuel Beckett and the Protestant Ethic. In *The Genius of Irish Prose.* Edited by Martin Augustine, 121–30. Dublin: Mercier.

————. 1986. Anglo-Irish Attitudes. In *Ireland's Field Day,* 13–16. Notre Dame, Ind.: University of Notre Dame Press.

————. 1997. Elizabeth Bowen: The Dandy in Revolt. In *Sex, Nation, and Dissent in Irish Writing.* Edited by Éibhear Walshe, 135–49. New York: St. Martin's Press.

Kierstead, Mary D. 1986. A Great Old Breakerawayer. *The New Yorker,* 13 October, 97–107.

Kilroy, Thomas. 1971. *The Big Chapel.* London: Faber and Faber.

———. 1997–1998. The Anglo–Irish Theatrical Imagination. *Bullán: An Irish Studies Journal* 3, no. 2: 5–12.

Knowlson, James. 1990. Catastrofe: ¿Ensayo teatral o profecía política? *Primer Acto: Cuadernos de Investigación Teatral* 233: 38–41.

———. 1996. *Damned to Fame: The Life of Samuel Beckett.* New York: Simon and Schuster.

Koenig, Rhoda. 1984. The Blind Side of the Heart: two Irish novels of seduction and betrayal. Review of *Time After Time,* by Molly Keane, and *Foggage,* by Patrick McGinley. *Harper's,* January, 74–76.

Kosok, Heinz, ed. 1982. *Studies in Anglo–Irish Literature.* Bonn: Bouvier.

Kreilkamp, Vera. 1987. The Persistent Pattern: Molly Keane's Recent Big House Fiction. *The Massachusetts Review* 28: 453–60.

———. 1988. Social and Sexual Politics in the Big House: Edith Somerville and Molly Keane. *Éire–Ireland* 23: 74–87.

———. 1992. Reinventing a Form: The Big House in Aidan Higgins's *Langrishe, Go Down.* In *Ancestral Voices: The Big House in Anglo–Irish Literature.* Edited by Otto Rauchbauer, 207–20. Dublin: Lilliput Press.

———. 1998. *The Anglo–Irish Novel and the Big House.* Syracuse, N.Y.: Syracuse University Press.

Kristeva, Julia. 1974. *La Révolution du langage poetique.* Paris: Seuil.

———. 1982. *The Powers of Horror: An Essay on Abjection.* Translated by Leon Roudiez. New York: Columbia University Press.

Lafferty, James J. 1982. Perceptions of Roots: The Historical Dichotomy of Ireland as Reflected in Richard Murphy's *The Battle of Aughrim* and John Montague's *The Rough Field.* In *Studies in Anglo–Irish Literature.* Edited by Heinz Kosok, 399–410. Bonn: Bouvier.

Laigle, Deirdre. 1984. Images of the Big House in Elizabeth Bowen: *The Last September. Cahiers du Centre d'Etudes Irlandais* 9: 61–80.

Lasdun, James. 1984. Life's Victims: Recent Fiction. Review of *The Life and Times of Michael K.,* by J. M. Coetzee, *Marcovaldo,* by Italo Calvino, *The Philosopher's Pupil,* by Iris Murdoch, *Shame,* by Salman Rushdie, and *Time after Time,* by Molly Keane. *Encounter* 62: 69–73.

Lassner, Phyllis. 1986. The Past Is a Burning Pattern: Elizabeth Bowen's *The Last September. Éire–Ireland* 21: 40–54.

———. 1990. *Elizabeth Bowen.* Savage, Md.: Barnes and Noble.

———. 1991. *Elizabeth Bowen: A Study of the Short Fiction.* New York: Twayne.

Lawrence, D. H. 1920. *Women in Love.* New York: Penguin, 1976.

Layoun, Mary N. 1990. *Travels of a Genre: The Modern Novel and Ideology.* Princeton: Princeton University Press.

Lecky, W. E. H. 1892. *A History of Ireland in the Eighteenth Century.* London: William Collins Sons.

Lee, Hermione. 1981. *Elizabeth Bowen: An Estimation.* Totowa, N.J.: Barnes and Noble.

———. 1997. *Virginia Woolf.* New York: Knopf.

Le Fanu, Joseph Sheridan. 1864. *Uncle Silas: A Tale of Bartram–Haugh.* New York: Dover Publications, 1966.

———. 1869. Green Tea. In *The Oxford Book of Irish Short Stories.* Edited by William Trevor, 78–108. New York: Oxford University Press, 1991.

Lloyd, David. 1989. Writing in the Shit: Beckett, Nationalism, and the Colonial Subject. *Modern Fiction Studies* 35: 71–86.

———. 1999. *Ireland After History.* Notre Dame, Ind.: University of Notre Dame Press.

Longley, Edna. 1985. Poetry and Politics in Northern Ireland. *The Crane Bag* 9, no. 1: 26–40.

Lubbers, Klaus. 1992. Continuity and Change in Irish Fiction: The Case of the Big–House Novel. In *Ancestral Voices: The Big House in Anglo–Irish Literature.* Edited by Otto Rauchbauer, 17–29. Dublin: Lilliput Press.

Lukács, Georg. 1963. *The Meaning of Contemporary Realism.* Translated by John Mander and Necke Mander. London: Merlin.

———. 1971. *History and Class Consciousness: Studies in Marxist Dialectics.* Cambridge: MIT Press.

Lynch, Rachel Jane. 1996. The Crumbling Fortress: Molly Keane's Comedies of Anglo–Irish Manners. In *The Comic Tradition of Irish Women Writers.* Edited by Theresa O'Connor, 73–98. Gainesville: University Press of Florida.

Lyons, F. S. L. 1973. *Ireland since the Famine.* London: Wiedenfeld and Nicolson.

———. 1975. A Question of Identity: A Protestant View. *Irish Times,* 9 January.

———. 1979. *Culture and Anarchy in Ireland: 1890–1939.* Oxford: Clarendon.

Malcomson, A. P. W. 1978. *John Foster: The Politics of the Anglo–Irish Ascendancy.* Oxford: Oxford University Press.

Mariante, Ben. 1985. Social Movements into Ideology in Ireland. *The Crane Bag* 9, no. 2: 8–11.

Mays, J. C. C. 1977. Mythologised Presences: *Murphy* in Its Time. In *Myth and Reality in Irish Literature.* Edited by Joseph Ronsley, 197–218. Toronto: Wilfred Laurier.

———. 1984. Young Beckett's Irish Roots. *Irish University Review* 14: 18–33.

Maxwell, D. E. S. 1985. J. M. Synge and Samuel Beckett. In *Across a Roaring Hill: The Protestant Imagination in Modern Ireland.* Edited by Gerald Dawe and Edna Longley, 25–38. Dover, N.H.: Blackstaff.

McCann, May, Séamas Ó Síocháin, and Joseph Ruane, eds. 1996. *Irish Travellers, Culture and Ethnicity.* Belfast: The Institute of Irish Studies, The Queen's University of Belfast for the Anthropological Association of Ireland.

McCormack, W. J. 1985. *Ascendancy and Tradition in Anglo–Irish Literary History from 1789 to 1939.* Oxford: Clarendon.

———. 1986a. *The Battle of the Books: Two Decades of Irish Cultural Debate.* Mullingar, Ireland: Lilliput.

———. 1986b. Seeing darkly: notes on T. W. Adorno and Samuel Beckett. *Hermathena* 141: 22–44.

———. 1992. Setting and Ideology: With Reference to the Fiction of Maria Edge-worth. In *Ancestral Voices: The Big House in Anglo–Irish Literature*. Edited by Otto Rauchbauer, 34–60. Dublin: Lilliput Press.

———. 1993. *Dissolute Characters: Irish literary history through Balzac, Sheridan Le Fanu, Yeats and Bowen.* New York: Manchester University Press.

McDowell, Henry. 1992. The Big House: A Geneologist's Perspective. In *Ancestral Voices: The Big House in Anglo–Irish Literature*. Edited by Otto Rauchbauer, 279–92. Dublin: Lilliput Press.

McElvoy, James. 1983. Catholic Hopes and Protestant Fears. *The Crane Bag* 7, no. 2: 90–105.

McMahon, Sean. 1968. John Bull's other Ireland: A Consideration of *The Real Charlotte* by Somerville and Ross. *Éire–Ireland* 3: 119–35.

Meisel, Perry. 1987. *The Myth of the Modern: A Study in British Literature and Criticism after 1850*. New Haven: Yale University Press.

Mercier, Vivian. 1955. Beckett and the Search for Self. *The New Republic*, 19 September, 133.

———. 1962. *The Irish Comic Tradition*. Oxford: Clarendon.

———. 1977. *Beckett/Beckett*. New York: Oxford University Press.

Meyer, Susan. 1996. *Imperialism at Home: Race and Victorian Women's Fiction*. Ithaca: Cornell University Press.

Miller, David. 1978. *Queen's Rebels, Ulster Loyalism in Historical Perspective*. Dublin: Gill and Macmillan.

Miller, Nancy. 1981. Emphasis Added: Plots and Plausibilities in Women's Fiction. *PMLA* 96: 36–48.

Moers, Ellen. 1976. *Literary Women*. New York: Doubleday.

Moore, George. 1886. *A Drama in Muslin: A Realistic Novel*. Gerrards Cross: Colin Smythe, 1981.

Moorjani, Angela. 1982. *Abysmal Games in the Novels of Samuel Beckett*. Chapel Hill, N.C.: Department of Romance Languages, University of North Carolina.

Moran, D. P. 1905. *The Philosophy of Irish Ireland*. Dublin: James Duffy, M. H. Gill and Son.

Morash, Christopher. 1992. Reflecting Absent Interiors: The Big–House Novels of Charles Lever. In *Ancestral Voices: The Big House in Anglo–Irish Literature*. Edited by Otto Rauchbauer, 61–76. Dublin: Lilliput Press.

Moynahan, Julian. 1982. The Politics of Anglo–Irish Gothic: Maturin, Le Fanu and "The Return of the Repressed." In *Studies in Anglo–Irish Literature*. Edited by Heinz Kosok, 43–53. Bonn: Bouvier.

———. 1995. *Anglo–Irish: The Literary Imagination of a Hyphenated Culture*. Princeton: Princeton University Press.

Mullin, Molly. 1991. Representations of History, Irish Feminism, and the Politics of Difference. *Feminist Studies* 17: 29–50.

Murdoch, Iris. 1965. *The Red and the Green*. New York: Penguin, 1967.

Murphy, Andrew. 1999. *But the Irish Sea Betwixt Us: Ireland, Colonialism, and Renais-sance Literature*. Lexington: University Press of Kentucky.

Murphy, John A. 1975. *Ireland in the Twentieth Century*. Dublin: Gill and Macmillan.

Murray, Christopher. 1992. Lennox Robinson, *The Big House, Killycreggs in Twilight* and "The Vestigia of Generations." In *Ancestral Voices: The Big House in Anglo–Irish Literature*. Edited by Otto Rauchbauer, 109–19. Dublin: Lilliput Press.

Newton, Judith Lowder. 1989. History as Usual? Feminism and the "New Historicism." In *The New Historicism*. Edited by H. Aram Veeser, 152–67. New York: Routledge.

Ní Dhomhnaill, Nuala. 1996. What Foremothers? In *The Comic Tradition in Irish Women Writers*. Edited by Theresa O'Connor, 8–20. Gainesville: University Press of Florida.

Nixon, Rob. 1992. *London Calling: V. S. Naipaul, Postcolonial Mandarin*. New York: Oxford University Press.

O'Brien, Conor Cruise, and Maire O'Brien. 1972. *The Story of Ireland*. New York: Viking.

O'Brien, Ellen. 1999. Anglo–Irish Abjection in the "Very Nasty" Big House Novels of Molly Keane. *Literature, Interpretation, Theory* 10: 35–62.

O'Brien, Eoin. 1986. *The Beckett Country: Samuel Beckett's Ireland*. London: Faber and Faber.

O'Donoghue, Bernard. 1982. Irish Humor and Verbal Logic. *Critical Quarterly* 24: 33–40.

O'Faolain, Sean. 1949. *The Irish*. New York: Devin–Adair.

Parker, Andrew, Mary Russo, Doris Sommer, and Patricia Yaeger. 1992a. Introduction. In *Nationalisms and Sexualities*, 1–18. New York: Routledge.

———, eds. 1992b. *Nationalisms and Sexualities*. New York: Routledge.

Parker, Patricia. 1987. Rhetorics of Property: Exploration, Inventory, Blazon. In *Literary Fat Ladies: Rhetoric, Gender, Property*. New York: Methuen.

Parkin, Andrew. 1988. Shadows of Destruction: The Big House in Contemporary Irish Fiction. In *Cultural Contexts and Literary Idioms in Contemporary Irish Literature*. Edited by Michael Kenneally, 306–54. Totowa, N.J.: Barnes and Noble.

Parrish, Paul. 1973. The Loss of Eden: Four Novels of Elizabeth Bowen. *Critique: Studies in Modern Fiction* 15: 86–100.

Perera, Suvendrini. 1988. *Reaches of Empire: The English Novel from Edgeworth to Dickens*. New York: Columbia University Press.

Pilling, John. 1976. *Samuel Beckett*. London: Routledge and Kegan Paul.

Pinkney, Tony. 1988. Nationalism and the Politics of Style: Julien Benda and Samuel Beckett. *Literature and History* 14: 181–93.

Poovey, Mary. 1988. *Uneven Developments: The Ideological Work of Gender in Mid–Victorian England*. Chicago: University of Chicago Press.

Poulantzas, Nicos. 1973. *Political Power and Social Classes*. Translated by Timothy O'Hagan. London: Sheed and Ward.

Power, Ann. 1964. The Big House of Somerville and Ross. *The Dubliner* 3: 43–53.

Power, Mary. 1981–1982. Samuel Beckett's "Fingal" and the Irish Tradition. *Journal of Modern Literature* 9: 151–56.

Pritchett, V. S. 1984. The Solace of Intrigue. Review of *Good Behaviour* and *Time After Time*, by Molly Keane. *The New York Review of Books*, 12 April, 7–8.

Pullen, Charles. 1987. Samuel Beckett and the Cultural Memory: How to Read Samuel Beckett. *Queen's Quarterly* 94: 288–99.

Rabinovitz, Rubin. 1984. *The Development of Samuel Beckett's Fiction*. Urbana: University of Illinois Press.

Rafroidi, Patrick. 1982. Pas de Shamrocks pour Sam Beckett: La Dimension irlandaise de *Murphy*. *Etudes Irlandais* 7: 71–81.

Rauchbauer, Otto, ed. 1992a. *Ancestral Voices: The Big House in Anglo–Irish Literature*. Dublin: Lilliput Press.

———. 1992b. The Big House and Irish History: An Introductory Sketch. In *Ancestral Voices: The Big House in Anglo–Irish Literature*, 1–15. Dublin: Lilliput Press.

———. 1992c. The Big House in the Irish Short Story after 1918: A Critical Survey. In *Ancestral Voices: The Big House in Anglo–Irish Literature*, 159–93. Dublin: Lilliput Press.

Ricoeur, Paul. 1988. *Time and Narrative*. Vol. 3. Chicago: University of Chicago Press.

Rimmer, Alison. 1989. Molly Keane. In *British Women Writers: A Critical Reference Guide*, 379–80. New York: Continuum.

Robinson, Hilary. 1980. *Somerville and Ross: A Critical Appreciation*. New York: St. Martin's Press.

Robinson, Lennox, Tom Robinson, and Norma Dorman. 1938. *Three Homes*. London: M. Joseph Ltd.

Rose, Marilyn Gaddis. 1971. The Irish Memories of Beckett's Voice. *Journal of Modern Literature* 2: 127–32.

Rosenberg, Carroll Smith. 1986. Writing History: Language, Class, and Gender. In *Feminist Studies/Critical Studies*. Edited by Teresa de Lauretis, 31–54. Bloomington: Indiana University Press.

Russo, Mary. 1986. Female Grotesques: Carnival and Theory. In *Feminist Studies/Critical Studies*. Edited by Teresa De Lauretis, 213–29. Bloomington: Indiana University Press.

Said, Edward. 1978. *Orientalism*. London: Pantheon.

———. 1983. *The World, the Text, and the Critic*. Cambridge: Harvard University Press.

———. 1990. Yeats and Decolonization. In *Nationalism, Colonialism and Literature*. Edited by Terry Eagleton et al., 69–95. Minneapolis: University of Minnesota Press.

———. 1994. *Culture and Imperialism*. New York: Random House.

Scanlan, Margaret. 1985. Rumors of War: Elizabeth Bowen's *Last September* [*sic*] and J. G. Farrell's *Troubles*. *Éire–Ireland* 20: 70–89.

Schirmer, Gregory A. 1981. The Irish Connection: Ambiguity of Language in *All That Fall*. *College Literature* 8: 283–91.

Seward, Barbara. 1956. Elizabeth Bowen's World of Impoverished Love. *College English* 18: 30–37.

Sharp, Sister M. Corona. 1963. The House as Setting and Symbol in Three Novels by Elizabeth Bowen. *Xavier University Studies* 2: 93–103.

Sharpe, Jenny. 1993. *Allegories of Empire: The Figure of Woman in the Colonial Text.* Minneapolis: University of Minnesota Press.

Shenker, Israel. 1956. Moody Man of Letters. *The New York Times*, 6 May, sec. 2, 1, 3.

Smith, Stan. 1982. Historians and Magicians: Ireland Between Fantasy and History. In *Literature and the Changing Ireland.* Edited by Peter Connolly, 133–56. Buckinghamshire, England: Smythe.

Snead, James. 1990. European pedigrees/African contagions: nationality, narrative, and communality in Tutuola, Achebe, and Reed. In *Nation and Narration.* Edited by Homi Bhabha, 231–49. New York: Routledge.

Somerville, E. Œ. and Martin Ross. 1894. *The Real Charlotte.* Edited and with an introduction by Virginia Beards. New Brunswick, N.J.: Rutgers University Press, 1986.

———. 1899. *The Irish R. M.* New York: Penguin, 1984.

———. 1917. *Irish Memories.* London: Longmans and Green.

———. 1925. *The Big House of Inver.* London: Zodiac Press, 1973.

Sommer, Doris. 1990. Irresistible romance: the foundational fictions of Latin America. In *Nation and Narration.* Edited by Homi Bhabha, 71–98. New York: Routledge.

Spivak, Gayatri. 1985. Three Women's Texts and a Critique of Imperialism. *Critical Inquiry* 12: 243–61.

———. 1989. Political Commitment and the Postmodern Critic. In *The New Historicism.* Edited by H. Aram Veeser, 277–92. New York: Routledge.

Suleri, Sara. 1992. *The Rhetoric of English India.* Chicago: University of Chicago Press.

Sullivan, Walter. 1976. A Sense of Place: Elizabeth Bowen and the Landscape of the Heart. *Sewanee Review* 84: 142–49.

Sussman, Henry, and Christopher Devenney, eds. 2001. *Engagement and Indifference: Beckett and the Political.* Albany: State University of New York Press.

Suvin, Darko. 1967. Preparing for Godot—or the Purgatory of Individualism. *Tulane Drama Review* 11: 23–36.

Taylor, Estella Ruth. 1969. *The Modern Irish Writers: Cross Currents of Criticism.* New York: Greenwood.

Thompson, John B. 1984. *Studies in the Theory of Ideology.* Berkeley: University of California Press.

Tompkins, Jane P., ed. 1980. *Reader–Response Criticism: From Formalism to Post–Structuralism.* Baltimore: Johns Hopkins University Press.

Torchiana, Donald. 1966. *W. B. Yeats and Georgian Ireland.* Evanston, Ill.: Northwestern University Press.

Tynan, Katherine. 1913. *Twenty-five Years.* London: Smith, Elder and Co.

Veeser, H. Aram, ed. 1989. *The New Historicism.* New York: Routledge.

Voloshinov, V. N. 1986. *Marxism and the Philosophy of Language.* Cambridge: Harvard University Press.

Wade, Geoff. 1992. Marxism and Modernist Aesthetics: Reading Kafka and Beckett. In *The Politics of Pleasure: Aesthetics and Cultural Theory.* Edited by Stephen Regan, 109–32. Philadelphia: Open University Press.

Walshe, Éibhear, ed. 1997. *Sex, Nation, and Dissent in Irish Writing.* New York: St. Martin's Press.

Warner, Francis. 1971. The Absence of Nationalism in the Work of Samuel Beckett. In *Theatre and Nationalism in Twentieth–Century Ireland.* Edited by Robert O'-Driscoll, 179–204. Toronto: Toronto University Press.

Waters, Maureen. 1984. *The Comic Irishman.* Albany: State University of New York Press.

Watson, George J. 1979. *Irish Identity and the Literary Revival: Synge, Yeats, Joyce and O'Casey.* New York: Barnes and Noble.

Watt, Stephen. 1987. Beckett by Way of Baudrillard: Toward a Political Reading of Samuel Beckett's Drama. In *Myth and Ritual in the Plays of Samuel Beckett.* Edited by Katherine Burkman, 103–23. Rutherford, N.J.: Fairleigh Dickinson University Press.

Weekes, Ann Owens. 1990. *Irish Women Writers: An Uncharted Tradition.* Lexington: University Press of Kentucky.

———. 1997. Molly Keane. In *Modern Irish Writers: A Bio–Critical Sourcebook.* Edited by Alexander G. Gonzalez, 149–52. Westport, Conn.: Greenwood Press.

Weisburg, David. 2000. *Samuel Beckett and the Cultural Politics of the Modern Novel.* Albany: State University of New York Press.

Wheatley, Christopher J. 1999. *Beneath Iërne's Banners: Irish Protestant Drama of the Restoration and Eighteenth Century.* Notre Dame, Ind.: Notre Dame University Press.

White, Jack. 1975. *Minority Report: The Protestant Community in the Irish Republic.* Dublin: Gill and Macmillan.

Williams, Julia McElhattan. 1995. "Fiction with the Texture of History": Elizabeth Bowen's *The Last September. Modern Fiction Studies* 41: 219–42.

Williams, Raymond. 1973. *The Country and the City.* New York: Oxford University Press.

———. 1977. *Marxism and Literature.* New York: Oxford University Press.

———. 1985. *Keywords: A Vocabulary of Culture and Society.* New York: Oxford University Press.

Woolf, Virginia. 1929a. Geraldine and Jane. In *Collected Essays* IV. Edited by Leonard Woolf, 27–39. London: Chatto & Windus, 1966–1967.

———. 1929b. *A Room of One's Own.* New York: Penguin, 1993.

———. 1938. *Three Guineas.* New York: Harcourt Brace Jovanovich, 1966.

Yeats, W. B. 1925. *The Senate Speeches of W. B. Yeats.* Edited by Donald R. Pearce. London: Faber and Faber. 1961.

———. 1989. *The Poems.* Edited by Richard Finneran. London: Macmillan.

Žižek, Slavoj. 1989. *The Sublime Object of Ideology.* London: Verso.

Index

Abbott, H. Porter, 151, 173
abject, the, 59–60, 85, 197 n. 9, 199 nn. 18 and 22. *See also* the body
AE. *See* Russell, George William
Allen, Michael, 206 n. 5
Alter, Robert, 209 n. 2
Althusser, Louis, 181, 183
Anderson, Benedict, 19
Anderson, Perry, 195 n. 3
Anglicanism, 37–38, 207 n. 7. *See also* Church of Ireland
Anglo-Ireland: as absent presence, 31, 34, 47, 162; and class, 37, 42–43, 113, 115, 150–51, 155; definitions of, 14–15, 30–39, 195 nn. 1 and 2; and England, 24, 31–32, 35, 39–45, 47, 48, 50, 96–97, 103, 105–7, 113, 131, 134, 179–80; and femininity, 60, 123, 125, 128–30, 149, 203 n. 20; and gender, 112–44; heterogeneity of, 104–5, 115–16, 124–33, 140–41, 148–50, 158–59; and Ireland, 31–34, 70–72, 75–85, 100–103, 107–13, 125, 142–43, 151–52, 155, 160–61, 179–80, 202 n. 16; and masculinity, 124–33; naming of, 31–34, 43–44, 48–49, 193 n. 1, 195 nn. 1 and 4; paradoxical nature of, 30–34; and patriarchy, 116, 118–22; and political power, 20, 25, 35, 40–42, 44–49; representations of, 13–20, 30–34, 67–75, 125, 158–59, 199–200 n. 1. *See also* Anglo-Irishness; Protestant Ascendancy

Anglo-Irish fiction: affective power of, 191; and English country house poetry, 15, 193 n. 2; and genre, 62, 92–93, 105, 130, 152–54, 172, 198 n. 13; and identity politics, 15, 19, 103–4, 193 n. 3; and ideology theory/critique, 17, 25, 28–29, 177–92, 201 n. 7; indeterminate point of view in, 66–67, 69, 71–72, 107–8, 187–88, 210 n. 8; interpretability of, 62, 75–85, 103, 107–10, 142–44, 187–89; and modernism/postmodernism, 20–28, 35, 50, 91–93, 130, 146–47, 167–68, 172–76, 193 n. 4, 194 nn. 9–11, 200–201 n. 3, 203–4 n. 24; and postcolonial studies, 13–20, 194 n. 7; and poststructuralism, 17–18, 167–68; reader-response and, 62–63, 105, 191, 198 n. 14; relevance of, 19–20; self-consciousness in, 157–58; styles of, 19, 23–29, 55, 92, 158
Anglo-Irish problematic, 23, 55, 62–67, 146–47, 152, 157, 179, 194 n. 12; Anglo-Irish women's relation to, 114; in Somerville and Ross, 202 n. 16
Anglo-Irish women: and the Anglo-Irish problematic, 114; in relation to Ireland, 114, 116–17, 129, 136–44; and subjectivity, 126, 135
Anglo-Irish writers: and authority, 23, 26, 85–87, 171–73; contradictory inclinations of, 24–27, 31–32, 90, 158,

229

DATE DUE

GAYLORD			PRINTED IN U.S.A.